girls will be girls

Leslea Newman

selected titles by lesléa newman

NOVELS
Good Enough to Eat
In Every Laugh a Tear
Fat Chance (for young adults)

SHORT STORY COLLECTIONS
A Letter to Harvey Milk
Every Woman's Dream
Secrets

POETRY
Love Me Like You Mean It
Still Life with Buddy
Sweet Dark Places

NONFICTION
SomeBODY To Love: A Guide to Loving the Body You Have
Writing from the Heart: Inspiration & Exercises for Women Who Want to Write

HUMOR
Out of the Closet and Nothing to Wear
The Little Butch Book

ANTHOLOGIES
My Lover is a Woman: Contemporary Lesbian Love Poems
Pillow Talk: Lesbian Stories Between the Covers
Pillow Talk II: More Lesbian Stories Between the Covers
The Femme Mystique

CHILDREN'S BOOKS
Heather Has Two Mommies
Matzo Ball Moon
Remember That
Saturday Is Pattyday
Too Far Away to Touch

girls will be girls

A NOVELLA AND SHORT STORIES

lesléa newman

 alyson books
los angeles | new york

© 2000 BY LESLÉA NEWMAN. ALL RIGHTS RESERVED.

MANUFACTURED IN THE UNITED STATES OF AMERICA.
COVER DESIGN BY CHRISTOPHER HARRITY.

THIS TRADE PAPERBACK ORIGINAL IS PUBLISHED BY
ALYSON PUBLICATIONS,
P.O. BOX 4371, LOS ANGELES, CALIFORNIA 90078-4371.
DISTRIBUTION IN THE UNITED KINGDOM BY
TURNAROUND PUBLISHER SERVICES LTD.,
UNIT 3 OLYMPIA TRADING ESTATE, COBURG ROAD, WOOD GREEN,
LONDON N22 6TZ ENGLAND.

FIRST EDITION: JANUARY 2000

00 01 02 03 04 **a** 10 9 8 7 6 5 4 3 2 1

ISBN 1-55583-537-6

LIBRARY OF CONGRESS CATALOGING-IN-PUBLICATION DATA
  NEWMAN, LESLÉA.
    GIRLS WILL BE GIRLS : A NOVELLA AND SHORT STORIES / LESLÉA
NEWMAN. – 1ST ED.
      ISBN 1-55583-537-6
      1. UNITED STATES–SOCIAL LIFE AND CUSTOMS–20TH CENTURY FIC-
TION. 2. LESBIANS–FICTION. I. TITLE.
    PS3564.E91628G57 2000
    813'.54–DC21   99-29477 CIP

CREDITS
"SUPPER" FIRST APPEARED IN *AM I BLUE: COMING OUT FROM THE
  SILENCE,* EDITED BY MARION DANE BAUER. HARPERCOLLINS, 1994.
"A RELIGIOUS EXPERIENCE" FIRST APPEARED IN *FRIDAY THE RABBI
  WORE LACE,* EDITED BY KAREN X. TULCHINSKY. CLEIS PRESS, 1998.
"THE *BABKA* SISTERS" FIRST APPEARED IN *THE OY OF SEX,* EDITED BY
  MARCY SHEINER. CLEIS PRESS, 1999.
"WHATEVER HAPPENED TO BABY FANE?" FIRST APPEARED IN *BLITHE
  HOUSE QUARTERLY,* WINTER EDITION, 1999.
COVER PHOTOGRAPH OF FLOWERS BY PHOTODISC. PHOTOGRAPH OF
  NAILS BY IMAGE CLUB.

for Mary Vazquez,
my one and only

contents

Acknowledgments

For professional guidance and expertise I thank Scott Brassart, Angela Brown, and Greg Constante of Alyson Publications, and the writers Robin Bernstein, Melinda Blau, Meryl Cohn, Bill Mann, Gerry Gomez Pearlberg, Lawrence Schimel, Sarah Schulman, Marcy Sheiner, and Jess Wells. For friendship and support that goes above and beyond the call of duty, I thank Jane Covell, Janet Feld, Roger Grodsky, Jon Hirsch, Pamela Kimmel, Deborah King, Judy O'Brien, Lynne Roberts, Laurie Sandman, Marilyn Silberglied-Stewart, Bibi Stein, Susanna Stein, Reya Stevens, and Faye and Bucky Wilson. Finally, I am grateful beyond words to my dearest friend, Tzivia Gover, for her generous spirit, and my beloved companion, Mary Vazquez, for her soft, generous heart.

Family Is Family

No, no, no, I don't want no coffee, no cake, thank you very much, I don't want to sit down, I don't want to take my coat off. Frankly, I don't even want to be here, but a promise is a promise, and I promised my daughter I'd come, though believe me I'd rather be home in front of the TV with my feet up, tonight is what, Wednesday, I think *The Nanny* is on. I'm welcome to stay anyway? Thank you very much, Mrs. Hostess With The Mostess. Don't take things so personally, you'll never get through life that way, if you want a little advice. What? Instead of telling everyone what I don't want, why don't I tell everyone what I do want? What do you think I want, Mrs. Busybody? I want what everybody wants and what is obviously too much to ask for: a grandchild or two or three, God forbid. What would have been so terrible, would the world really have come to an end if Eleanor Hershberger had a little munchkin to bounce around her lap, if she could feel his tiny bootied feet stamping up and down her more than

---

Note: A Yiddish and Hebrew glossary appears at the end of the book.

ample thigh, if she could hear the word *Bubbe* fly out of his sweet little mouth, *Bubbe*, or Grandma or even Nana? At this point I wouldn't care what he called me as long as he was healthy and happy, and—my daughter the liberal would kill me for saying this—Jewish or if not Jewish at least a hundred percent white. All right, I know what you're thinking, beggars can't be choosers at this stage of the game, and, believe me, I would beg, I would gladly get down on my knees, swollen with arthritis as they are, and crawl all the way to Boca and back if I thought it would do any good, which it wouldn't. My daughter's not an imbecile, she went to a very expensive school, Hampshire College, which is where all the trouble started in my opinion. What kind of college is that, coed dorms they live in—with coed saunas yet, have you ever heard of such a thing? The kids major in frisbee-throwing, and the teachers aren't much better. Grades they don't even give out, you get evaluations instead. For my money I want a real report card, but never mind. The point is she don't need a Ph.D., my daughter, to know exactly what it is her father and I both want.

How I of all people raised such a selfish, self-centered, self-absorbed, self-obsessed child is way beyond me. Didn't we give her everything? A roof over her head, food on her plate, clothes on her back, ballet lessons, tap lessons, piano lessons, violin lessons, a hundred Barbie dolls, a thousand stuffed animals. Nothing was too good for her, our darling daughter, whatever she wanted she got, including her father, him she had wrapped around her little finger from the minute she was born. Me she didn't want to know from. After all, who was I, just some dumb *shmuck* up there on the table with her legs spread wide for all the world to see; I was nobody, just some *nudnick* who practically died up there with her feet in the stirrups so her royal highness could take her first breath and come into this world safe and sound with all ten fingers and all ten toes perfectly intact. So long we waited for this miracle, this bundle of joy. Two miscarriages I had already and on top of that I'd buried my father too. So young he was, a heart attack, my mother came home from the store, and there he was, dead at the kitchen table, the soup she had served him for lunch, ice cold. She was never the same after that, my mother. I had to take care of her on top of everything else I had to do—the cooking, the cleaning, the shopping. The point is, and thank you for asking, that heartache was no stranger to my family, and with all that was going on, it was a miracle I got pregnant again in the first place, and then I had trouble holding on to the baby, flat on my back I had to stay for the last two months, but did I complain? No, not a word, not one word because when I finally gave birth, when I finally put my brand-new, perfect baby daughter into my mother's arms, my mother cried, and then she laughed, and that was the first time I saw my mother laugh in two whole years. Not a smile, I'm telling you, since the day my father died, that's how much she loved her husband, that's how much I love my Irving—what's that? Is he here? What are you, crazy? Tell our troubles to a roomful of strangers, Irving would rather stick needles in his eyes. He don't even know that I'm here, why should I bother him with our crazy daughter's problems? See, that's how much I love my Irving, and that's how much I wanted my daughter to love her husband and her children—the same way you love your own family, the same way they're supposed to love you.

She's my one and only, my daughter. Such a hard time I had, the doctor said I shouldn't have no more, and then he shoved the papers at me to sign, and so groggy I was with the drugs and with the pain, I signed on the dotted line. Then my tubes they cut, and of course I regret that now, but it's too late already anyway, what can I do, I'm not crazy like that *meshugeneh* in her 60s who just gave birth. I read about her in the *Times*. Just you wait, lady, some day your precious offspring who you sacrificed everything for will come home with green hair and pierced eyebrows and tattooed cheeks, and you'll think, *This is the thanks I get?* Not a grandson or even a granddaughter, though I always hoped my daughter would have a boy, girls can be so difficult, and believe me I should know. No, not a grandchild at all, just two cats, Mulvah and Delores, have you ever heard such names? The kids, she calls them, to add insult to injury, to rub salt into my old wounds like they don't hurt me enough. "I took the kids to the clinic," she says to me on the phone. Once in a while we talk, every couple of months or so, have you ever heard of such a thing? Like strangers we are, *nu*, my bank teller, the kid who brings the paper, the auto mechanic I talk to more than I talk to my own flesh and blood. And when we do talk, that's what she tells me: "The kids needed allergy shots," like they're her children. She did it on purpose, my *tochter*, she knew once there was a cat in the house, Irving and I would never visit, I hate cats, always have. I was very concerned when she got them. "What's gonna be when you have a baby?" I asked. "A long time cats can live, and they can be very jealous." I didn't go on and tell her cats have been known to smother babies in their sleep; they wait until you go to bed, and they don't have to wait long, so exhausted from a newborn you are, you sleep the sleep of the dead, so as soon as they hear you snoring, the cats, they climb up into the crib and lean against the baby's mouth and nose with their big furry backs, and they cut off the air supply, and that's the end of it. But I kept my mouth shut because I didn't want to hear her say, "Eleanor," in that exasperated tone she always uses, like her mother is so stupid, such a moron she is, she still thinks the world is flat.

Eleanor she calls me, *nu*, have you ever heard of such a thing? One day when she was 12 years old she woke up and decided Mommy or Mom or even Ma was too good for her mouth. From then on it was Eleanor or sometimes Ellie, which is what Irving calls me, or when she's in a mood, just El, like she don't have time to say all those syllables, she has much more important things to do than talk to her own mother who only wants the best for her, who gave up the best years of her own life to clothe her and feed her and *shlep* her to the doctor, the dentist, and later, when she was older, to the movies, the mall. We thought maybe she was meeting a boy, Irving and I, but what did we care? After all, it's normal. I didn't mind as long as she was careful. I was young once too, you know, hard to believe, you're just meeting me today for the first time, what do you know, but it's true: a thousand years ago, around the Ice Age it was, I wasn't bad looking, I had a fella or two on my arm. Not that my mother didn't watch me like a hawk, but all right, she was from the old country, she had seen plenty of things in her time, she had a right to be a little afraid, a little cautious. But she had nothing to worry

about, my mother, I would never do anything to embarrass
her or the rest of the family and drag our name down into the
mud, like certain people who shall remain nameless, though
she's broadcast her name loud and clear from coast to coast
for all the world to hear.

What is her name? I haven't said it yet? Well, there's a reason for that, which I'll get to in a minute, Mrs. Buttinsky.
What's your big hurry, you got a plane to catch? For your information, my daughter is famous. She's a performance artist,
which, in case you don't know, is someone who actually gets
paid to be completely obsessed with herself. You may have
heard of her, Virginia Dentata? What the hell is wrong with
Susan Hershberger is what Irving and I want to know. I suppose it could have been worse, right, she could have named
herself New Jersey. But Virginia Dentata, it's a joke, you know
what it means? Dentata means teeth, you know like dentures,
dentist, Dentyne. And Virginia, well, one day when she was
about six years old, Susan comes home from kindergarten, and
she says right there at the dinner table, "Mommy, why do ladies
have Virginias?" Straight out of a Woody Allen movie, when
Woody Allen was still Woody Allen, before he took up with his
girlfriend's adopted daughter, have you ever heard of such a
thing? All right, *nu*, what can I tell you, everybody's got problems, even Woody Allen. But listen, never mind Woody Allen
already, Irving and I thought it was so funny, Virginias, we got
a good laugh out of it, like I said I was a bit of a looker back
then. Those were the days Irving and I still had a good time
once in a while, hard to believe now or even remember, but I
can still hear him after supper, when I was doing the dishes,
he'd sneak up right behind me and whisper, "Want to take a

ride to Virginia later?" his voice soft and sweet in my ear.

So, Virginia Dentata, get it? I'll give you a another hint: Her show is called *Virginia is for Lovers*, like the bumper sticker, ha ha, very funny, where she got such a sense of humor from, God only knows, certainly not from my side of the family. It's a sex show, for God's sake, I went once. No, of course she didn't know, it's not like she's ever invited Irving and me; I read about it in the paper. I pick up the *Village Voice* once in a while, I know what goes on in this world. So there was her name, Virginia Dentata, and I'm thinking, Susan's in a show, why didn't she tell us? Why wouldn't she want her own parents to come? We went to all her plays in high school, *Guys and Dolls*, they did, *How to Succeed in Business*, you know the shows. She's always been a performer, my daughter, she likes to be the center of attention, all right, who doesn't? But anyway, why wouldn't she invite Irving and me unless she was doing something that made her feel ashamed? So one night when Irving was working late—some dinner meeting he had, you know he works like a dog, my Irving—I took my life in my hands and went into the city, down to Avenue A. That's some neighborhood she works in, my daughter, she lives there too. So hard we worked, like slaves, to get our kids out of the city, they should only know what a tree looks like, a flower, a blade of grass. They should only know what peace and quiet feels like, not to have a stranger on top of you every five minutes. I remember the first apartment Irving and I had was in Brooklyn, in the basement it was, I would look out the window, and all I'd see was shoes. But all these suburban kids had it too easy, they ran back to the city the first chance they could get. For them it's a lark to live in the bad neighborhoods, it's a thrill to trip over a bum lying in the gutter, it's exciting to see a family in the subway who ain't got what to eat. Take it from me, it wouldn't be so exciting if Daddy wasn't waiting in the office, Susan's calls he always takes, and if she needs a couple hundred to make the rent, he whips out his checkbook and puts in a little extra, too, his daughter should buy herself a little present, another ring to put in the side of her nose, like an animal. I tell him, Irving, if she can't pay the rent, let her come home, her room is still here just like she left it, but he says, leave her alone, it's just until she gets on her feet. Ha, Irving knows as well as I do that those feet are almost 40 years old. It's time for her to get her head together, never mind her feet.

What was her show about? Don't ask. She gets up on stage, and believe me I use the term loosely, there was no stage, just a curtain stretched across the floor. She gets up there, and in front of everybody she takes off her trench coat, and a good coat it is, too, a London Fog, I remember when we bought it for her, and underneath she's wearing nothing but a...a...I don't know what to call it, a G-string, a loin cloth, whatever, and attached to this tiny piece of fabric that's barely covering her *pupik*, she's got a wind-up toy, you know, it's a mouth, and when you wind it up the teeth clatter. I remember the dentist used to give them out to all the kids after he cleaned their teeth. So very funny, right? It's supposed to be man's greatest fear, but, believe it or not, Irving had a few other things to worry about when Susan was growing up, besides if I was growing teeth somewhere they didn't belong, like how he was going to pay the mortgage, the car payments, the orthodontist—his lovely daughter should have lovely teeth—the eye doctor—his lovely daughter should have lovely contact lenses, guys seldom make passes at girls who wear glasses. Not that we had anything to worry about in that department, but who knew that yet? I'm telling you, our daughter was perfectly normal in every way, and not only that, she was planned for, she was longed for, she came out all in one piece, perfect, with ten fingers and ten toes and with such a head of long, black, curly hair, the nurses all took turns combing it, the day we left the hospital, they tied it up in a ponytail with a pink ribbon, and everybody cried, such a *simcha* it was. You know what that means, a *simcha*, such a happiness, it almost makes you bust. I'm telling you, who knew that gorgeous, sweet-cheeked baby girl would grow up to cut off all her beautiful curls, tattoo a woman with wings on her left cheek, pierce her nose, her eyebrows, her chin, her tongue, and God only knows where else, and if God does know, I prefer He keep it to Himself. And if that wasn't bad enough, our precious baby girl who I stayed up all night with, the littlest sneeze, the tiniest cough I was there, our darling first and only born, named for her Great Uncle Shmuel—he never even made it to this country, what happened to him you don't want to know, don't even ask—who knew our very own Susan would grow up to take off all her clothes in front of perfect strangers, and worse than that, set up housekeeping in the East Village with a woman named Max who walks like a man and talks like a man and dresses like a man and probably smells like a man, though I'm in no hurry to get that close, but isn't a man, unless Susan's not telling me something I don't even want to know. Sure, anything's possible—don't you watch *Oprah*? She's got men on there who used to be women, and women

who used to be men.… In fact, the other day, and this is what
I really want to talk to you about, the other day she had on
this woman, JoAnn Loulan her name was—see, I wrote it
down—this woman says she's a lesbian, but she has a
boyfriend, so isn't it possible that Susan can keep being a lesbian but have a boyfriend, too? And maybe then a baby, God
forbid, what would be so terrible? She never had a boyfriend,
not one boy did she ever bring to the house, so how can she
be so sure she wouldn't like it? So stubborn she is, my Susan,
I remember when she was a little girl she knew exactly what
she would eat and what she wouldn't eat, and once she made
up her mind, forget about it. Like rigatoni. For some reason,
she took one look at it and decided it wasn't for her. It's just
like spaghetti, I told her, it's just a different shape. Just take
a bite, just try it, and if you don't like it, you don't have to eat
it. But she wouldn't budge. She shut her mouth tight as a
drum and that was that. You know why she wouldn't eat it?
Because her mother asked her to. If I make a suggestion, right
away Susan thinks it's a bad idea, so I keep my mouth shut,
if I say something she don't want to hear, that's it, it's all over,
it'll be another six months before she picks up the phone to
see if Irving and I are still alive.

And what's gonna be, I want to ask her. Sure, she don't
want to hear this, but her mother and her father with his big,
fat checkbook are both getting old, we ain't gonna be around
forever, and then what? Then she'll be all alone in this world
without a family, and family is family—that's the most important thing. Who else is gonna be there for you through thick
and thin, who else can you turn to when you have nowhere
else to go? Where would my mother be if she didn't have Irv-

ing and me, wearing diapers and eating mashed carrots and peas in a nursing home, God forbid? Listen, you and I both know that Max ain't gonna stick around forever. She's somebody's daughter too, maybe she'll come to her senses yet, maybe she'll get married someday. All right, good-looking she ain't, but still, she could fix herself up nice—some lipstick she could put on, a dress she could wear. She got a nice figure, Max, and besides, there's someone out there for everyone, believe me, I see plenty of homely girls on the street with bellies out to here and a wedding ring on. I'm telling you, everybody needs a family. That's why God made things the way they are, a boy and a girl and a couple of kids. Six billion people can't be wrong, right? Only my Susan knows better than the whole human race, a husband and a baby ain't good enough for her, only another woman she wants.

What? Of course I know she's not the only one. Yes, I've heard of *Ellen*. No, I never watched it; I don't need to be reminded of my troubles at night, at night I try to relax. Anyway, thank God they took it off the air, it's bad enough the woman lives like that—she's got to go on national TV and tell the whole world, too? *Oy*, her poor mother. What's that, her mother's part of this group? Really? Is she here? No? Well that's too bad. What kind of group is this anyway? PFLAG? No, I never heard of it. What does it stand for? Parents and Friends of Lesbians and Gays. What does that mean? You all have children like my Susan? *Oy*, I'm so sorry, but misery loves company, right? What do you mean, you're not miserable, there's nothing to be sorry about, you're proud that your children are funny? Go on, you don't mean it, I never heard of such a thing. You do mean it? Really? Then you're all as *meshugeh* as your kids are. Of course I should have known Susan would send me somewhere crazy, what does she know from normal people, people who aren't sick in the head, people who know what's what. No, she didn't tell me nothing, she just sent me a piece of paper with a date, a time, an address. She said it was a place I could get help. I thought she meant help for her, not help for me—do I look like a person who needs help? She's very clever, my Susan, she struck a deal with me. She said if I went she would come home for *Rosh Hashanah*, she hasn't been to *shul* with us in years, since she was in college she hasn't been home for the holiday. And everybody's dying to see her, so of course I said I'd come.

All right, I came, I saw, can I take this little brochure here, so I can show Susan I kept my word? They're free, very nice, such a bargain, thank you very much. OK, I've said all I have to say then, good-bye and good luck to all of you, and may God look down upon you with pity, upon you and me both and send a miracle down our way, it could happen, after all, anything is possible. Like Cynthia and Sol Greenblatt, you remember what happened to them? It was in all the papers; you must have read about it. I happen to know them very well, they live right next door. Their son Matthew had that terrible accident, remember? Skiing he was, I'm telling you, that boy had no business up on top of a mountain, if God wanted us to slide down icy hills, He would have put wings on our feet. Anyway, it was terrible, they said he'd never walk again. But P.S., last year he ran the New York marathon, on plastic legs he ran it, but never mind, he made it to the finish line, all 26 miles he ran. Such a sweet boy he was, such a good boy, years ago we thought maybe Matthew and Susan, you know, such beautiful children they would have made, but now of course it's out of the question. But the point is, if God made a miracle for the Greenblatts, maybe he could make a miracle for the Hershbergers too? We're not such terrible people, all of you look like very nice people too, despite your children, no offense, all I'm saying is as long as we're all alive, anything is possible. One must never give up hope. Even in the camps they never gave up hope, so maybe someday, God willing, Susan will wake up and become a person, and I won't have to be ashamed.

All right, that's it, that's all I have to say, this time I'm really going. You know what a Jewish good-bye is? There's an old joke: WASPS leave and never say good-bye, Jews say good-bye and never leave. It's true, no? So laugh a little, we've all got problems, right? After all, we're not here tonight on account of our good looks, or because we got nothing better to do. Yes, yes, it was very nice meeting all of you too. Thank you very much for listening, I'm sorry to have taken up so much of your time. I don't know if I'll be back—thank you for asking—but I'll tell you what, maybe I'll strike a bargain with Susan, she thinks she's the only one who knows how to play *Let's Make a Deal*? Maybe if I come back here, she'll come home for Irving's birthday, a surprise we'll make for him, he'll be 75 in June, it would give him such pleasure if Susan came home. I won't even *hock* her to wear a dress or take the hardware out of her face or put a little makeup on. You see, I'm not such a terrible person, I know how to compromise. You gotta give a little, take a little, just like the song goes. You can't be selfish, you can't always have everything your way, you have to think about the other person every once in while. Maybe someday Susan will understand that's what family is all about.

The Kiss

The kiss was expected. The kiss was demanded. No one else was aware of the command. It was given with a slight tilt of the head, a presentation of the cheek. Lisa would rather press her mouth against dead horse meat than her own mother's flesh, but she steeled herself and placed her lips against the sagging skin. It was the only way to get what she wanted—and to avoid getting what she didn't want.

The kiss came every year in August when Mrs. Weiss took Lisa shopping for back-to-school clothes. They always went to the Dress Depot, and by now the salesgirls knew better than to ask if they needed any help. It was obvious they needed a lot more help than girls with tight sweaters, teased hair, and seven gold loops running up each ear could give them.

Maybe this year won't be so bad, Mrs. Weiss thought as she pulled the car into a parking space. She turned the engine off and looked over at her daughter, but all she could see was the dark curtain of hair Lisa had pulled shut between them a long time ago. "Ready?" she sang out with false bravado and cheer. Lisa's reply was to hurl herself out of the car and slam the door shut without a word. Her mother leaned across the front seat to lock Lisa's door before she grasped her handbag firmly, got out of the car, and headed for the store. Lisa followed with all the enthusiasm of a death-row inmate walking toward her execution. Mrs. Weiss pulled open the door with grim determination and was momentarily soothed by the sound of a bell tinkling softly over their heads like the unexpected song of a bird as they stepped inside.

Before the door even had a chance to slam shut behind them, Mrs. Weiss hurried toward a row of clothes like they were her long-lost friends and started sliding dress after dress down a rack. Her fingers fondled the fabric of each one eagerly, as if she were searching for a message stamped in a secret code like braille, a message that would explain the mystery of her own daughter who stood a few feet away, scowling, her arms folded tightly across her chest. When Lisa was a baby, Mrs. Weiss imagined these shopping trips: the two of them, so alike you'd think they were sisters—even their hands don't give them away!—oohing and aahing over prom dresses and then having a nice lunch at the mall, giggling like schoolgirls over books and boys, and then sharing a naughty dessert they knew they shouldn't be eating, but oh, why not, just this once....

Mrs. Weiss sighed and selected an outfit from the rack. "How about this?" she asked, holding up a brown and gold tweed skirt and matching jacket.

Lisa lifted her eyes from the floor with great effort and looked over at her mother as though she were an alien: initially interesting but ultimately too disgusting for words. "I wouldn't be caught dead in it," she pronounced before looking down at the floor again. Mrs. Weiss returned the outfit to the rack and chose another: a green-and-red-plaid wool jumper with a pleated skirt. She held the garment up to her shoulders and let it drape down her body, kicking her right foot out to check the length. "This is cute."

"It looks like Christmas paper."

"It comes in black and white too."

"Forget it."

"It's cute. And the dropped waist is slenderizing."

"Then you wear it."

"Fine. You pick something out." Mrs. Weiss put the jumper back and folded her arms. Lisa stepped forward, and her mother stepped back, like two dancers who despised each other, doing a do-si-do.

Lisa fingered each garment on the rack with disgust, as if she were picking through a garbage can of rotten meat oozing maggots and worms. Finally she chose something: a black sleeveless minidress with a plunging neckline, a slit up the back, and lace filled cutouts on either side. "How's this?"

Mrs. Weiss studied the dress while choosing her words carefully. "Don't you think it's a little old for you?"

Lisa looked at her mother like she was the most pathetic person on the planet. "As if I'd even look good in something like this," she muttered to herself. Then louder, "It was a joke, Mother." Lisa had been calling Mrs. Weiss nothing but "Mother" since she was 12 years old, but still, every time she said it, the stiff, formal word stung the air like a slap.

"I'm going over to the sales rack," Mrs. Weiss announced, trying not to sound eager to put some space between herself and her own flesh and blood. Lisa didn't respond.

Soon the bargaining would begin. Mrs. Weiss would return to Lisa with half a dozen dresses slung over her arm, their hangers clanging, and define her terms: If Lisa picked out three outfits, she'd let her go to the mall by herself and give her money for two new pairs of jeans. Jeans and a leather vest, Lisa would argue. Mrs. Weiss would promise the vest in exchange for a pair of shoes for the holidays. Lisa would agree to the shoes if she could also get a pair of boots. Mrs. Weiss would give in to the boots only if Lisa wound up with five outfits, one for every day of the week.

Lisa wouldn't argue further. She really didn't care anyway since she never wore these outfits to school. Oh, she left the house in them all right, but then she headed straight for the garage, where she changed into black jeans and a black sweater or T-shirt, depending on the weather. Then she changed again when she got home from school. "My mother is so stupid," Lisa often bragged to her friends, as if Mrs. Weiss didn't know her daughter went to school in the same filthy clothes all week. She had found one of Lisa's outfits neatly folded and stashed behind some old winter coats one day when she went into the garage looking for an extra plant hanger. She had picked up the garment tenderly, as though it were something hurt and alive, and stroked the smooth purple wool, soothing it, in the same way she was now stroking a soft velour pullover. She added it to the pile over her arm and headed back to Lisa.

"Let's go try these on."

Let's not and say we did, Lisa thought as she silently followed her mother across the store. She took the clothes and pulled the curtain of the dressing room shut before her mother could even think about coming inside. "I'll wait out here," Mrs. Weiss called, as if it were her idea. Lisa undressed slowly, avoiding her own reflection, which was no small feat as there were mirrors everywhere, designed to expose her body from every imaginable angle. Lisa knew exactly what she looked like and had no need to be reminded of her imperfections: the sagging boobs, flabby stomach, lumpy thighs. She stood there in her bra, panties, and knee socks, rattling the hangers around so her mother would think she was trying something on. Sure enough, Mrs. Weiss called out, "Can I see?" with an edge of hope in her voice that made Lisa sick. *What does she think, I'm going to pull open the curtain—ta da!—and there, standing before her very eyes will be the pretty, smiling, well-dressed, cheerful daughter she's always wanted?* "Can I come in?" Mrs. Weiss called again.

"No." Lisa said, spitting out the word. She let a little more time go by and then selected a few outfits. "These'll do." Lisa thrust several hangers through the slit in the curtain, and Mrs. Weiss accepted the clothes from her daughter's disembodied arm. "I'll meet you at the cash register," she said, walking away.

Lisa got dressed quickly and then sat down on the little pink dressing room stool for a few minutes. She knew that no matter how long she took, her mother wouldn't pay until Lisa was out there beside her. She'd stall by pretending to look at scarves, earrings, and belts, but she wouldn't approach the cash register until she knew Lisa was there to witness what a good mother she was to spend all this money on her daughter. *You're very lucky, Lisa. Not every girl has such a wonderful mother. Some girls don't even have enough to eat, let alone new outfits every year.*

Lisa got up from the stool like she was a hundred years old and dragged herself out into the store. Sure enough, as if on cue, her mother was just dumping her load onto the counter. Mrs. Weiss watched the salesgirl, who was just a few years older than Lisa, snip off price tags. "This is so cute," Mrs. Weiss said, fingering a black-and-white tweed jacket. "I'm so glad this one fit."

"It's adorable." The salesgirl held the jacket at arm's length to admire it before folding it carefully, sleeve to sleeve, shoulder to shoulder.

Encouraged, Mrs. Weiss went on. "They're wearing skirts a bit longer this year, aren't they?" Lisa couldn't care less whether or not they were wearing skirts at all.

"Just above the knee," the salesgirl said, smoothing the jacket into a bed of orange tissue paper. "Oh, I *love* this." She held up a maroon wrap-around skirt with gold buttons going up the side.

"Isn't it lovely?" Mrs. Weiss basked in the glow of attention from someone who so clearly shared her own good taste. Lisa watched her mother and the salesgirl from a short distance, feeling like she was going to puke. She imagined herself spewing green bile over racks and racks of clothing. *Wouldn't that be lovely? Wouldn't that be adorable?* Lisa watched the salesgirl through narrow, slitted eyes. She had what looked like a miniature red, curly telephone cord wrapped around her forearm with some keys attached. Lisa wanted to strangle her with it—her and her mother, who was now making quite a show of searching through her wallet for her charge card.

Finally they were done. The salesgirl lifted two enormous

shopping bags over the counter, and to Lisa's amazement, actually said, "Have a nice day." This was Lisa's cue. She stepped forward and took the bags while Mrs. Weiss fussed with her things, returning her charge card to her wallet and her wallet to her purse, searching for her sunglasses, her keys, all the while her head at that slight, beckoning angle, the same tilt of head their dog Polly used when you asked her a question: "Want to go out, Polly? Want to go out?"

Lisa knew her mother was waiting for the kiss, knew she would wait all day if she had to, knew just how long she herself had before her mother's patience turned into embarrassment and then rage, which would turn into Lisa's own misfortune when the two of them got home. Lisa waited a little longer each year, just to see what her mother would do. They couldn't stand there forever. The store would close eventually. Lisa knew she was pushing it, knew her mother was just as stubborn as she was, knew her mother did not want to look foolish in front of that idiot salesgirl, whom she wished was her own adorable daughter.

"What do you say, Lisa?" Mrs. Weiss hissed through clenched teeth while the salesgirl looked down, pretending to busy herself with a tangle of hangers.

I hate your guts, Mother, raced through Lisa's mind, but Mrs. Weiss knew that already. What Lisa really wanted was to take a bite out of her mother's cheek. She imagined her mother's face would crunch like an apple and then taste sour, rotten, like something that had to be spit out at once. Or maybe sickeningly sweet. Yes, that was it. Lisa leaned toward her mother until her lips were up against her face and whispered with all the saccharin she could muster, "Thank you,

Mommy." Mrs. Weiss grabbed the counter, almost swooning from the feel of her daughter's breath against her cheek. As Lisa pressed her lips against her mother's flesh, Mrs. Weiss shut her eyes, pretending just for an instant that she had given birth to the daughter she had always wanted. Then she let the counter go and opened up her eyes.

Supper

We are all sitting at the kitchen table: my father, my brother, my grandmother, and me. My grandmother looks little, like a child almost, waiting to be served. My mother stands at the stove with her back to us, spooning something onto white china plates. Pot roast. She hands my father his plate first, of course, then my brother, then my grandmother, and last of all me.

My mother sits down with her own plate. She is on Weight Watchers and measures everything she eats on a little white postage scale she keeps next to the toaster. I have only carrots and potatoes on my plate. I am a vegetarian, so I have rinsed the pot roast's gravy off the vegetables. Everyone is pouring themselves something to drink: my father, Mott's apple juice; my brother, orange soda; my mother, diet Pepsi; me, Poland Springs. Often my mother remarks, "What am I running here, a restaurant? I've never seen anything like it. Everyone has to have their own private drink." Tonight, though, she simply looks at my grandmother and asks, "What do you want to drink, Ma?"

"I don't care, some soda," my grandmother replies.

My mother lifts the heavy bottle of orange soda my brother has just put down. My grandmother says, "What's that, orange? Don't give me that, give me something diet, I got too fat already." My mother puts down the orange soda with a sigh and pours my grandmother her drink.

We eat in silence. Forks and knives clink against plates, ice cubes rattle in glasses, my father chews loudly across the table from me as he sops up his gravy with Wonderbread. The refrigerator clicks on and begins to hum, and outside through the screen door I can hear the bells of Mr. Softee fading down the street.

My grandmother is not eating. Instead she studies each of us in turn, as if she is trying to make up her mind. Her gaze falls upon me.

"Jocelyn, here, take some of mine, I don't need so much. You're too skinny, here, take a piece of meat." Her plate is up in the air, hovering above mine, fork poised to scrape.

"No, Grandma, I don't want any. You know I don't eat meat."

"You don't eat no meat? What's the matter with you? Who don't eat meat? Everybody eats meat." She looks around for support of her argument but, finding none, tries a different track. "*Oy,*" she says in a gentle voice, "what my mother wouldn't have given, when I was your age, to have a piece of meat to put in my mouth, I shouldn't go hungry. Here, *mameleh,* take a piece of meat, it wouldn't kill you." She stabs a piece of pot roast, which waves off the end of her fork like a flag.

"Grandma, I don't want it."

"Here, Jeffrey," she says to my brother, who knowing he was next has been busily shoveling food into his mouth, hoping to be excused. "Take some from my plate. I can't eat all this."

"No, Grandma. There's more in the pot if I want more. You eat it." My brother's voice is tired, as if he's said this a thousand times before, which in fact he has.

"I can't eat all this," my grandmother says to no one in particular or perhaps to God.

"Ma, it's enough already," my mother says. She has finished eating and rises to put her plate in the sink. My grandmother slowly puts a piece of carrot into her mouth. My father and brother finish eating and leave the table: my father heading for the den to watch TV, read the newspaper, and fall asleep on the couch; my brother grabbing his baseball cap to run outside and play stickball with his friends.

I push my food around my plate as my mother clears the table. A cool breeze tickles the back of my neck as she opens the refrigerator to put away the half-empty bottles of soda.

"Jocelyn, I'm going upstairs to lie down. Will you finish cleaning up?" I don't bother answering, since I'm the one who cleans up every night.

I bring my plate over to the sink, and as I return to gather the dirty napkins, my grandmother pushes her plate away. "*Oy*, I'm so full, I'm busting already," she says to me. She pushes her chair back with another *oy*, stands up, and brings her plate to the sink.

"I'll do the dishes. You don't have to." I take the plate from her hand.

"All right," my grandmother says with a shrug. "You want

some applesauce maybe, a piece of sponge cake?"

"No, Grandma, I'm not hungry. And you know I never eat dessert."

"Not hungry, no dessert, listen to her, she don't eat enough to keep a bird alive—a piece of carrot and half a potato." I can feel my grandmother studying my back as I run the water. It takes a while for it to get hot. "What's the matter with you, you don't eat no meat, you don't want no cake.…" She pauses, trying to figure me out. "Jocelyn, darling, the boys ain't gonna like it if you get too skinny. Believe me, I know."

I turn to see her smiling and wagging her finger at me, the nail shiny and red. I blush in spite of myself but not for the reason she thinks.

My grandmother thinks I have a boyfriend, but I don't. I don't even like boys. I don't know why. Maybe it's the same reason I don't like meat and I don't like dessert. I told my best friend Karen about it. I told her right after I'd gone for a walk with this guy Mark from my social studies class. He kissed me over by the handball courts, and I almost lost my lunch.

Karen said we should practice, maybe then I would like it more. She says she didn't like it at first so much either, but you kind of get used to it. We were up in my room studying—or pretending to study, really—with our books scattered all over my bed just in case my mother walked in, which wasn't too likely because a bunch of her friends were over playing bridge, and my brother and I have been instructed in no uncertain terms that unless one of us is having a heart attack, *nothing* is to interrupt my mother's bridge games. Anyway, Karen pushed aside our books and told me to lie down on the bed. "This is what Bruce does," she said, and then she climbed on top of me and put one of her legs between mine. Bruce is Karen's boyfriend, and he's a senior, so I guess he knows what he's doing.

Then she kissed me. Her mouth was soft, not like Mark's at all. She showed me what you do with your lips and your tongue and even your teeth. I started feeling funny between my legs, where her thigh was pressing, like I had to go to the bathroom or something.

"Then if you really like the guy, you can let him touch your boobs," she said. "Want me to show you?"

"Sure."

She lifted my shirt and pulled my bra down, so my breast popped out of the cup. Then she put her mouth on my right nipple, like a baby. "You stroke my hair," she said, so I did. It felt nice. I felt all warm and soft inside, and I wet my pants for sure, but I didn't even care. Karen showed me on my other breast too, and then we stopped. She said that after I go out with Mark again, if I still don't like kissing him, we can practice some more. I didn't tell her I wouldn't go out with Mark again if my life depended on it. Maybe we can practice some more anyway. I just don't like boys. But I would never tell Karen that. And I definitely would never tell my grandmother. She already thinks there's something wrong with me, and I guess maybe there is.

I put my hand under the faucet. The water, like my face, is finally hot. "Why don't you go inside and watch TV with Daddy?" I say to my grandmother, who is still watching me.

"All right," she says with a shrug. "I'm an old lady. What do I know? Nothing." She shuffles off to the den, and as soon as I hear her footsteps fade down the hall, I run the water full blast and pick up her plate. But instead of scraping the pot roast into the brown paper bag from Waldbaum's we keep in the middle of the floor for garbage, I pick up the pieces of meat and put them into my mouth, one by one by one.

The *Babka* Sisters

S it down, *shah*, you ready? You got your tin can going there, you want to make a test, make sure my voice is good, everything is working all right? OK, so now I'm gonna tell you a story, a story I never told nobody. Why I'm telling you, a stranger, I don't even know, but all right, *eppes*, it's time.

Once upon a time, a long, long time ago, around the Stone Age it was, *takeh*, I was a young *maidl*, and quite a looker I was too. I know what you're thinking, you look at me now and what do you see? A fat old lady wrinkled like a prune danish with hair like cotton candy. But, *nu*, I had quite a shape in those days, my hair I wore in a braid down my back thick as a man's arm, my skin was smooth as a baby's *tuchus*. You don't believe me, but you wait, *mamela*. Gravity ain't got no favorites; it catches up to everyone, *eppes*, someday even you.

So my childhood ain't nothing to talk about. An ordinary girl I was, I went to school, I came home, I helped my mother with the housework. Sure, five children she had, four boys and me, so who else is gonna help her? I had friends, too, boys and girls, no one special, there was a group of us that stuck together, to the movies we went, and to get a *nosh* at the diner, dancing once in a while, you know we did all the things young people do.

And then, when I was 16, a new girl moved into the neighborhood, and that girl, I had such a feeling for, I just couldn't take my eyes from her. You know the expression "love at first sight," sure, who doesn't, well of course that's what it was, but what did I know, we was two girls; girls don't fall in love with girls, who ever heard of such a thing? I just knew I wanted to be her friend, help her out, you know, show her around. It could be overwhelming, such a place, to a person who first walks in and don't know from it, *eppes*, it takes a while to get used to, it was a very big school.

Look, here's a picture of her, my Evie. You see, here we are both in the last row. That's our class picture from 11th grade, we was both tall girls; now I'm all stooped over like an old turtle, but back then my spine was straight as a *Shabbos* candle, from my posture my mother was always proud. Ain't she gorgeous, my Evie? Look at that dark curly hair, black as midnight it was, Medusa, I used to call her, *eppes*, it was that hair that started the whole thing. Dark curly hair and blue eyes, very unusual for a Jew, but I'm telling you, her eyes were as blue as mine are brown, you can see, under the cataracts my eyes are dark like coffee you drink when there's no milk in the house. And could she fill out a gym suit, my Evie! Listen, years ago, no girl wanted to be skinny, like sticks, all you girls are now. What do they call them, the supermodels there, *feh*, one puff of wind could knock them right down. We used to laugh at girls like that, girls with no hips, no *tuchus*. We used to feel sorry for them, the poor things.

So where was I? Oh, Evie, of course, Evie. The first day I saw her, she was in the lunchroom sitting all by herself, *takeh*, and I was ashamed, a whole school, maybe 500 boys and girls, maybe a thousand, and not one person held out a hand. Nobody said, you must be lonely, here, I'll sit with you, I'll talk to you, I'll show you where to take your tray. And blind they all was, they couldn't see this was no ordinary girl, this girl was something special, a gift from God she was, and nobody could see what was sitting there right before their very eyes?

So I got my sandwich, egg salad I got, and a carton of milk, and I took my *tuchus* over and put it down on the seat right next to her. "How do you do? I'm Ruthie," I said, and that's when I knew I was lost, when I looked for the first time into those eyes. Like diamonds they twinkled, like stars, like the sun dancing on the ocean in a million pieces, all that and more was shining in my Evie's eyes.

"I'm Evie," she said. "How do you do?" and I couldn't even answer her, my voice was gone, on a trip it went, a vacation all of a sudden it took, I couldn't find it, so I went to take a drink of milk, but I was so nervous, can you believe it, I started to choke. And to make things worse, Evie clapped me on the back, and when I felt her hand touch me, even through my sweater and blouse, I felt a charge, like a jolt, like I just put instead of the plug my finger in the socket, God forbid, but I swear, sure as I'm sitting here, it's true. And Evie was so concerned, she looked at me, so serious. "Are you all right?" she asked, and all I could see was those two eyes above me, blue as the sky, like God finished making the heavens, and he had a little fabric left over and decided the only thing left to

do was make those little bits of heaven into Evie's eyes. Finally I got hold of myself, and we ate our lunch and had a
conversation, about what I couldn't tell you, whatever young
girls talk about, school and families, this and that. Whatever
she said, I don't think I heard a word. I was too busy drowning in those blue, blue eyes.

Evie and I became fast friends after that. Every day we ate
lunch together, every day together we walked home from
school. Evie lived around the corner from me, how lucky
could I get, I began to think maybe I did shine a little bit in
God's eyes. Sometimes we'd study at Evie's house, sometimes
we'd study at mine. We became like a part of each other's
families; I would eat supper by her, she would eat supper by
me. The "*babka* sisters," my mother used to call us, you know
what *babka* is, darling? A dessert so sweet, with cinnamon
they make it sometimes, sometimes with chocolate. Evie and
I loved it, we ate it all the time, so my mother gave us like a
nickname, you know like a joke. "Look who's here, the *babka*
sisters," she'd say after school when we rang the bell.

Sometimes we'd have sleepover dates too. It was nothing
unusual, all the girls did in those days. Evie would sleep over
at my house, I had my own room, not that we was so rich, but
because it ain't nice: A girl can't sleep with her brothers, so
what could my mother do? Evie had a sister—Shirley her
name was—and they shared one room, two beds they had, two
dressers, two desks, everything matching, you know, except
the two girls, they didn't match so good. They was different as
day and night, they used to fight like cats and dogs, so over to
our house Evie came, every chance she could.

So where was the boys, I bet you're thinking. Two teenage

girls, gorgeous like we was, and neither of us had a fella? Me, the boys was never interested in, I was too much of a tomboy for them. My mother used to wring her hands, "Ruthie, take little steps, why do you have to walk like a truck?" And Evie, I think the boys were afraid of her, so beautiful she was, and so smart, she beat them by a mile, and then they'd have to get past me, of course, to get near her, we was always together, and I wouldn't let them so easily by.

Sometimes when Evie and I were up in my room studying, I'd watch her out of the corner of my eye. So gorgeous she looked studying or writing or just chewing her pencil. If she glanced up, I'd look away quickly, but once in a while I'd meet her gaze. And sometimes I caught her staring at me too. "What?" I'd say, feeling kind of nervous, though I didn't know why. "Nothing," Evie would answer with a shrug and a smile.

One night Evie was sleeping over, it was *Shabbos*, I remember, my mother had made such a beautiful supper: her *matzo* ball soup that she was famous for all up and down the avenue, and fresh *challah* from the bakery, and a roasted chicken, we was so full we was busting after, such a feast it was. Evie and I helped my mother with the supper dishes, and then we first had coffee and *babka*—no matter how stuffed we was we always had room for *babka*—and then we went up to my room. Evie had been a little quiet that night, and a few times I caught her staring at me across the supper table, but I didn't ask no questions. I figured if she had something to tell me, she'd tell. She looked a little moony that night, and I was only afraid she shouldn't tell me she had a crush on a fella, she couldn't spend so much time with me now, on dates she was gonna go, and believe me if that's what Evie was going to say, I wasn't in a big hurry to find out.

Evie went into the bathroom to get undressed like she always did, and I got undressed as well. We both wore long, white nightgowns—cotton they were, everybody did back then. I turned off the light, lifted back the covers, and got into bed. It was dark, but not so you couldn't see; the moon shone right in my window, I still remember—it was full that night. Like a spotlight it was, shining down on Evie when she came back to my room. Like a movie star she looked, I remember, there was something different about her, and then I realized what it was: Instead of in a braid, all her hair, all those thick black waves were loose and hanging down.

"Ruthie, will you brush my hair?" Evie asked, her voice slow and thick and dreamy, and when I climbed out of bed and went to her, my movements were slow and dreamy too. I took the brush from Evie's hand and stood behind her in the moonlight, brushing her hair from the crown of her head all the way down to her tiny, tiny waist. Up and down my hands went, brushing her hair for hours it seemed, days maybe, long after the last knot was untangled, long after her hair shone like a wet, black stone. Hypnotized I was, like a spell I was under, I couldn't move a muscle except for my arms that couldn't stop brushing, brushing. I only wanted that moment to never end: me, Evie, the hairbrush, the moonlight. If I died right then and there I wouldn't be sorry, because I had already tasted a bit of heaven. But thank God my time wasn't up, for what happened after that I wouldn't have missed for anything: Evie turned around, the hairbrush clattered down from my hand, and before I even knew what was happening, there she was, my girl in my arms.

"Ruth," she whispered, and her mouth was so close to mine, I could feel her sweet breath on my skin, and I breathed it in, wanting every part of her. "Ruth," she said again, not Ruthie, but Ruth, like my name was holy, a prayer that could only be answered with her name, "Evelyn," like the song of the nightingale it was, so sweet on my lips. "Evelyn," I said again, "Evelyn." "Ruth," she answered, and then she put her mouth on top of mine, and then we didn't say no more.

Her lips, how can I describe her lips? Sweeter than *challah*, they were, sweeter than *babka*, and soft, so soft, I was almost afraid if I licked them they would dissolve on my tongue, they would melt away like water. When Evie kissed me, the world as I had always known it came forever to an end, and a new world, a world so sweet, so fine, so holy and precious, took its place instead.

It was Evie who broke that kiss and led me to the bed, the same bed we had slept in together for so many nights, but like *Pesach*, I knew this night would be different than all other nights, I knew there would be no nightgowns that evening to separate flesh from flesh. Evie was so confident, so unashamed, so proud, *takeh*, of her feelings for me, that I wasn't even afraid. She took my hands and put them on her breasts, and I gasped at their softness, their firmness, their ripeness, so smooth and white her breasts were, her nipples so hard and rubbery and sweet, I swooned to take them under my tongue.

What, so surprised you are that an old woman like me should talk so? All you young girls with your blue hair and pierced eyebrows, up there at the university in your women's history class—you think there was no such girls in my time, you think you're the first, you think maybe you invented it? Well, I've got news for you: There's more to tell, so either turn your tin can off, and I'll keep quiet, or put your eyes back in your head, sit still, and listen.

Now then, I'll never forget that night as long as I live. So gentle Evie was, but so fierce too, like a *Vildeh Chayah*, you know what that means, like a wild little beast. "Here," she said, putting my hand where it never went before. "Harder," she said, "lower. Like this." And she'd put her hand on top of mine and show me what to do. Where she learned such things I didn't know, I didn't want to know. What did I care? All I wanted was to hear her breath coming hard and fast against my ear, her little cries of "*Oy, oy, oy*," and then "Ruthie, my Ruthie," and then just "yes, yes, yes." Oh, how she crooned as my hands went up and down, in and out, all over her, my Evie who trembled, and shook, and yelped so loud—I was only afraid my mother shouldn't come in—and then finally fell back against the pillow and was still.

And if that wasn't enough, *dayenu*, then Evie decided it was my turn. And when she put her hands on me, when she put her mouth on me, when she set my body on fire, I melted into the bed, *takeh*, like a puddle of *shmaltz* I was, all ooze and no bone. And then, hours later, when the moon had moved halfway across the sky and the stars were almost gone, we fell asleep, close, Evie's sweet little hand in mine.

The next morning we got up late, so quiet the house was, I knew it was empty except for that devilish look in Evie's eye. We picked up where we left off the night before, and so

caught up in each other we was, we didn't hear my mother's
foot on the step, we didn't hear her hand on the knob, my
poor mother, so innocent she was, what did she know, she
threw open the door, and said, "So, *nu, babka* sisters, it's almost noon, ain't you getting up?" But of course we was up
already, Evie was up on top of me, in fact, stark naked she
was, her hips going up and down like a horse on a merry-
go-round, her arms reaching for the sky.

"*Gottenyu, vey iss mir*, my God!" My mother shrieked, Evie
rushed to cover herself, the door slammed, I started to cry.

"Don't," Evie whispered, licking my tears like a puppy.
"It's all my fault. I couldn't stop myself."

"What'll we do?" I wailed, but before Evie could answer,
my mother came upstairs again. This time she knew enough
to knock. "Ruthie, I think your friend better go home now,"
she said—"my friend," she couldn't even say her name—and
then one-two-three, Evie was gone.

Oy, was I in trouble, was my goose cooked, I'm telling
you. My mother wouldn't even look on me, so ashamed she
was. And my father didn't know what to do, he knew something was wrong, but he didn't know what. My mother
wouldn't speak of such things to him, but with one look she
told him and my brothers I was in trouble but good. So no
one talked to me at home, but never mind, I had bigger
problems to worry about. On Monday when I went back to
school, Evie was absent. I couldn't remember her ever being
absent before, and I was worried sick. What happened to
her? Did she hurt herself, did her parents know? Were they
punishing her, did she maybe run away? I only wanted to
run to her house, but I didn't dare, so much trouble I was in

already, if I didn't come straight home from school, my
mother would kill me for sure. And I wanted to be right by
the phone when Evie called—surely she would at least call?
But call she didn't; instead a letter came. All typed up it was,
all formal, like a business letter it was, *eppes*, and this is what
it said:

> *Dear Ruthie:*
>
> *I don't want to see you anymore. What we did was wrong,
> we should be ashamed of ourselves. It's a blessing your moth-
> er came in when she did. We're still young, we still have a
> chance to live the life God wants us to, with a husband and
> children and grandchildren, God willing. I am getting help
> from the rabbi, and I hope you will do the same.*

And she signed it "Evie," and that was all.

Turn off the tape recorder, will you, darling? I need a
minute to catch my breath here, maybe a drink of water you
could get me, there's a cup there, over by the sink. It still
feels like a punch in the stomach, I remember reading that
letter over and over, a thousand times I read it, and all the
while I could barely breathe. I called her, of course, right
away I called her, but her mother wouldn't let her come to
the phone. She never even came back to school again,
eppes, a few months later the whole family moved away, and
Evie, my sweet, sweet Evie, was gone.

So what can I tell you? The years went by, life went on, it
don't wait for nobody, *eppes*, I graduated from school, I got
married, two children I had, a boy and a girl. I never really
had feelings for my husband, but he was a good man, kind,

a good provider. And my children, may they live and be well and call me once in a while, my children I loved, of course, after all they are my own flesh and blood. With my husband, I did my duty, when he wanted me to come to him, I came, he deserved that much after all, and I tried not to let him know for me it was nothing, a waste of my time, but, *eppes*, such a thing is hard to hide, I think, *takeh*, he knew. I tried not to think about Evie, too painful it was, like a thousand knives going right through my heart, but every once in a while I couldn't help myself. I'd see someone who looked like her on the street, and I'd wonder, where is she now, is she married, is she happy, is she all right, but of course I never knew.

And then one day, years later it was, the children were already married, I think my little granddaughter was already born, my little Madeline—ooh, you should have seen her, darling, so smart, so cute, like a little pumpernickel she was. Anyway, one day out of nowhere, Evie's face came to me like a dream, like a vision, I just couldn't get her out of my mind. By this time my husband was gone already, he died young, a heart attack it was. Did he love to eat, my Harry. I always told him to lighten up on the butter, go easy on the eggs, but did he listen to me? No, so, *nu*, here I was, a widow at 53, that ain't so old, but already I was going a little crazy—every time I turned around, Evie's face I saw, on the bus, on the TV, late at night when I closed my eyes. Five days it's like this, and then all of a sudden, as suddenly as she came, just as suddenly, she's gone. And then four days after that, a letter I got, it fell into my hands from nowhere, straight out of the sky:

Dear Ruthie:

Maybe you don't remember me, so many years it's been, and who knows, maybe it's best to let sleeping dogs lie. But I was in the hospital last week, five days I was there, a stroke they thought I had, an aneurysm maybe. They're still not sure, but I'm telling you, I almost died. A person changes from an experience like that, you know, I got home, everything looked different. I started thinking long and hard about my life—such a close call it was, but God in his wisdom took pity on me and gave me a second chance. So, nu, I started thinking about you, Ruthie. I know you never wanted to see me again, you said so in the letter, I still have it, after all these years I could never throw it away, and maybe you still don't want to know from me, but I thought what could it hurt, so much time has passed, I'm going to write to you, and maybe you could write back to me and let me know you're still alive. Are you OK, Ruthie? Are you happy? Have you had a good life? If you don't want to answer, I'll understand, but I want you to know I never forgot you, and I ain't mad on you for what happened.

Your old friend,
Evie

My heart started pounding so, I was only afraid I shouldn't have a heart attack. I sat down on the kitchen chair and read the letter again, once I read it, twice, a thousand times. I couldn't believe Evie had found me again after all these years. *Nu*, I'm still in the old neighborhood, I only moved a few blocks away, *eppes*, but still, I had a different last name. Maybe she'd hired a detective, I didn't know, I was too excited, I only found out later she knew someone who knew someone who knew someone.... You know it was a miracle from God that brought us back together, plain and simple, that's what it was. And finally after all these years, I knew what had happened, I put two and two together, I realized my mother wrote Evie a letter, the same letter Evie's mother wrote to me, and neither one could be further from the truth. I told Evie so, I sat down right then and there and wrote her a letter, my hand trembling so, I didn't know if she would be able to make out the words, so shaky they were on the page. I told her I loved her then and I loved her now. I told her how I couldn't stop thinking about her the five days she was in the hospital, like a vision she was, her face pale as a ghost. Two days later I picked up the phone and heard her voice, three days after that I picked her up at the airport and held her in my arms.

This time there was no one to hide from, no one to come up the stairs and disturb us. Now we had all the time in the world to frolic in each other's arms. For days we stayed in bed, days and days and days, until I said, "Evie, *mamela*, we have to eat, *eppes*," and we stopped what we was doing to order in Chinese food and then got back in bed to feed each other with chopsticks, with our fingers, licking chow mein off each other, laughing all the while. At first I was shy with Evie, a blushing bride I wasn't no more, the flesh and the ground was having a meeting, you know what I'm saying, I wasn't no spring chicken, but Evie told me, *shah*, "You're beautiful, Ruthie, just like I remembered." And I remembered too. My hand remembered her breast, my mouth remembered her thigh. Two widows we were, two grown-up ladies with grown-up children yet, it's hard for you to imagine, but, oh, such a time we had, Evie and me, such noises that came out from

our throats, our bodies bucking up and down so, I was only
afraid we wouldn't break the bed, and they'd find us there all
in a tangle, two old ladies who couldn't *utz* themselves up
from the floor. You, you're young yet, you think you know
from sex, but just wait, and, boy, did I wait, for over 30 years
I waited to put my hands on her, my Evie, to lick her breasts,
her belly, to drown once more in her smile, her eyes. Did we
rock, did we roll, did we shriek, I'm surprised the house did-
n't burn down, so hot for each other we was. It's a well-kept
secret, darling, but you should know, old ladies do know from
such pleasures, believe me, you'll see. You think you got it
good now, just you wait. You know, like they say, the best is
yet to come.

I don't even regret the years we spent apart, Evie and I.
God has his reasons, after all, and I'm not even mad no more
on my mother, may she rest in peace. She only did what she
thought was best, she and Evie's mother, too. Evie and I had
14 good years together until God looked down one day and
said why should Ruthie Epstein have it so good, such a gorgeous *maideleh* she has, it's enough already, and God put up
his hand and said to Evie, "Come," and so she did, so sweet
she was, so good, God took a look and decided He wanted her
all for Himself. All right, Evie and me, we've been separated
before, God wants me down here and her up there, *eppes*,
who am I to complain? Fourteen years we had, and, boy, did
we make up for lost time, believe me, I'm telling you.

So that's all there is, there ain't no more. You can turn off
your robot there, I told you enough, a secret I keep close to
my heart that I never told nobody before. Even my own children didn't know, why should I tell them? They thought it

was so nice, a roommate I had, I shouldn't be lonely, and
when they came to visit, Evie slept somewhere else, the house
was big, we had plenty room. I'll tell you something, even
when the children wasn't visiting, sometimes she slept in another room; when you're old sometimes you want to spread
out, you got a little gas maybe, you need a night to yourself.

All right, I'm tired now, so much talking, talking, talking,
but I hope you got what you wanted. I hope you get an A in
your women's history class. All right, history, herstory, whatever, this is my story, it's a mystery, *eppes*, why I was so lucky,
so blessed, you should only be so lucky, may God shine such
good fortune down on you. Believe me, God has his ways,
eppes, you think it's a coincidence that out of all the old ladies
in this nursing home here, you picked me to interview, into
my room you came waltzing in? You and me, we've got something in common. We're cut from the same cloth, darling, *nu*,
I can tell. And listen, *mamela*, it's nothing to be ashamed of.
Maybe your mother don't like it, your father, whoever, give
them time, it's a different world today, they'll come around.
You're young, you're a beautiful girl even with the purple eyebrows, *eppes*, you should only live and be well and find your
own Evie, God willing, and may she live and be well and have
a long happy life together with you.

A Religious Experience

My girlfriend, Melissa, also known as the *shayneh maidel* from Manhattan, has skin the color of a perfectly toasted bagel, lips like lox, and teeth white as cream cheese. Her eyes are two dark poppy seeds, and her hair is luscious as chocolate *babka*. Ooh, I could just eat her up, my little *Vildeh Chaya* with her *shiksa*-straight nose and *Gone With the Wind* waist—the only woman in the world who makes Vanessa Williams look like chopped liver. But I can't. Not today anyway, because today is *Yom Kippur*, the one day of the year that my fetching femme won't let me lay a finger on her. And nothing makes a butch hornier than a slap on the wrist followed by those four little words: "Hands off the merchandise."

For those of you who have strayed from the fold as I have, let me fill you in. *Yom Kippur* (pronounced "Yum Kip-PAH" by us Noo Yawkers and "Yome Kip-POUR" by the rest of the world) is the most important Jewish holiday of the year. To celebrate it, we Jews refrain from eating, drinking, talking on the phone, riding in a car, working, watching TV, and making love. Some holiday. It's also the day that God (spelled "G-d" by the true chosen people) opens His little black book and decides who gets to stick around for another year and who gets to kick the bucket. So all of us Yid kids put on our Sunday best (only in our case it's our Saturday best) and *shlep* ourselves to *shul* to atone for our sins. Except for yours truly, of course, who hasn't set foot in a synagogue since 1979, the year I got caught in the coat room, nibbling on the neck of the rabbi's daughter, because I thought it was a sin for such a drop-dead gorgeous *girlchik* to be sweet 16 and never been kissed.

So much for religion. I don't really believe in God and all that, but Melissa does. She almost didn't even date me because she thought I was a *goy*. "Laurie Dellacora," she mulled my name over. "What kind of Jewish name is that?"

"My mother's maiden name is Lipshitz," I told her. "Thank God my parents didn't decide to hyphenate." Then I explained further that my mother's side of the family is Russian Jewish and my father's side is Italian Catholic, which didn't please Melissa too much because as she said, she had her heart set on a purebred. But what could she do? Jewish butches are awfully hard to find. Plus the fact that I am quite handsome and charming, if I do say so myself, especially when I want to be. And I definitely wanted to be, the day I met Melissa. Lucky for me the Jews believe that everything is passed down through the motherline, and any rabbi worth his weight in Manishevitz would proclaim I was one of the tribe (as would Hitler, by the way). My parents didn't care all that much about either religion, to tell you the truth, except during the month of December when we had both a *menorah* and a Christmas tree in the living room, which was fine with me because it meant I got lots of presents. But other than that, I never really cared about religion one way or the other.

Until I met Melissa. Let's just put it this way: If my being a Jew makes her happy, then it makes me happy too. Melissa likes to celebrate the Sabbath by lighting candles and eating *challah*, which is A-OK by me. She also likes to get down and dirty on Friday nights (and Saturday mornings too) because the Jews believe it's a *mitzvah* to make love on the *Shabbos*. Now there's a tradition I can certainly get behind (and on top of) on a regular basis. We have a lovely little thing going on Friday nights, my Melissa and I. After work we have a nice dinner, and then while I'm doing the dishes, my Sabbath bride whips up an out-of-this-world noodle *kugel* that she pops into the oven. It takes about an hour to bake, which is just about how long it takes for us to get cooking too. And somehow, even though we usually have a pretty big supper, an hour later we're simply starving.

But that's about as far as it goes when it comes to tradition, no matter how magnificently Zero Mostel sings about it on Melissa's tape of *Fiddler on the Roof*. I mean, I'll be the first to admit Melissa has me wrapped around her little pink-tipped pinkie, but the one thing she cannot do, no matter how hard she tries, is convince me to go to *shul*.

"Are you sure you don't want to come?" she asks this morning, sitting on the edge of our bed, pulling a sheer silk stocking over her shapely thigh.

"I never said I didn't want to *come*," I reply, sitting down next to her, but as soon as our auras touch, she moves away.

"On *Yom Kippur*, Laurie? You should be ashamed of yourself," Melissa says, but to tell you the truth, I'm not. In fact, I'm kind of proud that even after all this time, four years, seven months, and 14 days to be exact, my beautiful babe can still drive me delirious with desire. And don't think she doesn't work it. After she's got both her stockings on, Melissa stands to slide her slip over her hips and then bends over to pour her bodacious bosom into her bra. Then she steps into her dress and turns around. "Will you zip me?" she asks, lifting a yard of hair to show off the back of her neck. Even though we're not really into S/M, I could swear Melissa is getting quite a thrill out of torturing me like this. But if she thinks her little act is going to convince me to go to synagogue and sit stone still on a cold folding chair for hours, listening to some old guy chant in a language I don't understand while my stomach gurgles in harmony (I'm fasting along with Melissa as a sign of solidarity), she's got another thing coming.

"I'm going now," Melissa says, putting on a coat since the autumn air's a little crisp. "Last call for services."

"I'll pass," I say, coming over to kiss her good-bye, but as soon as I come near her, Melissa backs away.

"Unh-unh-unh," she says, wagging her finger at me. Then she flounces down the steps, and knowing I'm watching her, moons me when she reaches the bottom. Since Melissa has nothing on underneath her holiday frock except a garter belt, I have to hang onto the banister to keep from falling down the stairs. She laughs, straightens up, and leaves, locking the door behind her.

So now what? There's nothing to do but go back to bed, since Melissa didn't have to work too hard to convince me to take the day off. "*Yom Kippur* is supposed to be a complete

Sabbath," she said. So, fine. Just because I don't observe the religion doesn't mean I shouldn't enjoy the perks. I doze off for a while and then sit up and watch a little TV. But it's no use. All I can think about is my Melissa. Those dark, dark eyes. Those pouty, pink lips. Those big, beautiful breasts. That amazing ass.

Well, why not? Here I am in bed, and I can't think of one good reason not to let my fingers do the walking. I mean, what the hell, I've got all day. And here's something I don't understand: If, as Melissa says, *Yom Kippur* is a complete *Shabbos*, the holiest day of the year, the Grand Poobah of Sabbaths, and ordinarily it's a *mitzvah* to make love on the Sabbath, then why wouldn't it be a blessing to spend all day in bed with your beloved? Like, let's be consistent here, you know what I mean?

I take off my T-shirt and boxer shorts and start by running my hands lightly up and down my body. I'm strong and in pretty good shape, if I do say so myself. I'm not doing too badly in the flab department either, except for some recent developments around my stomach area, but, still, I'll be damned before I start drinking Miller Lite. I don't care if I gain a pound or two as long as I stay in shape, mostly so I can sling my *zaftig* sweetie over my shoulder and bundle her off to bed the way she likes. And the way I'd like to, right now.

But, like it or not, this is a solo performance. I rub my palms around my nipples in small circles and wait for them to get hard. It takes a while because, frankly, I don't have the kind of body I'm attracted to. I'm pretty flat, unlike Melissa, who's a 38D, which I always tell her stands for "Delicious." Melissa can come just from having me lick and suck her breasts, which amazes me. I, of course, can come just from making her come, which amazes Melissa, but, hey, what can I say? It's a butch thing, I guess.

I'm not exactly getting turned on here, so I shut my eyes and pretend my hands are touching the body of my beloved, which means I have to leave the breast department and travel south. I move my hands down my body and start stroking the insides of my thighs, which, like Melissa's, are as smooth and silky as puppy ears. Then I start petting my pubic hair and pulling on it gently, the way that drives Melissa wild—I mean when I do it to her, of course; I would never touch myself in front of my girlfriend, although I like it when she touches herself in front of me. The first time I asked her if she'd ever do that, she just smiled and took her top off. In fact, she kind of got off on it. It's a femme thing, I guess.

I actually start to get a little worked up, so I use my left hand to make small circles around my clit. Ah, instant relief, like an itch that's dying to be scratched. And then my right hand gets a little bored, I guess, because there's no other way to explain what happens next. All of a sudden, my middle finger sneaks in where no one has gone before. My snatch, the final frontier.

Wow, I'm surprised at how hot and wet and soft I am inside. *Well, what were you expecting*, I ask myself, *sandpaper?* I've never penetrated myself before, or let Melissa, even though she tries sometimes and pouts when I say she can't. But, I don't know, it seems too much of a femme thing, to let someone in like that. I almost can't stand doing it to myself—if you want to know the truth—so I make sure my eyes are shut tight and continue to pretend I'm touching my lady.

I keep the finger that's inside still, the way Melissa likes, and I keep rubbing my clit back and forth with my other hand. I'm breathing pretty heavy now, and before I even think about it, I slide another finger inside. Whoa, I guess there's room at the inn, because before I even know what I'm doing, finger number three joins the rest of the crowd. Dare I go for four? No, I have a better idea. When my girl's really hot and open for me, she likes my thumb inside, all the way up to the fleshy part that joins it to my hand, and my middle finger up her butt. I go for it, and before I can even say, "Come for me, baby," my hips are moving, my legs are shaking, and I'm practically drooling all over myself, but I don't care. Thank God there's no one around to see me like this. No, wait a minute. I wish there were someone around to witness me losing total control. But not just any someone. A certain someone named Melissa. I know how much I love her when I see her giving me everything she's got. I wonder if she would feel the same way. Or would she laugh at me and demand I turn in my butch card?

"Melissa, Melissa," I yell as I come and come and come. It takes a few minutes for me to stop shaking and a few more after that for me to catch my breath. When I'm finally my usual calm, cool, collected self, I remove my fingers and thumb from my various orifices and reach for Melissa, but of course she's not here. That's the thing about masturbation: Afterward there's no one to hold and squeeze and say I love you to while you look deep into her eyes. There's no one to stroke and pet and whisper sweet nothings to while she rests her head on your shoulder. There's no one to even say, "Wow, I never knew you could come like that," so I get out of bed and say it to myself in the bathroom mirror. "Wow, I never knew you could come like that."

"There's a lot of things about me you don't know," I say to my reflection as I wash my hands. I mean, I've always been the one who got off on pleasing my lover, and I've never gotten any complaints. But I know Melissa wishes she could do some of the things to me that I just did to myself. I swore long ago I'd never flip. But now that I've flipped myself, who knows? After all, it is a new year. Maybe it's time for a change.

So, is Melissa going to stay in *shul* all day or what? It's only a little after one o'clock, which means I have five hours to go until the holiday is over. Officially, *Yom Kippur* ends at sunset, but since we stopped eating at five-thirty yesterday, I convinced Melissa we could break the fast at five-thirty today. I wonder if that means we can fuck at five-thirty too. I certainly hope so. You'd think I'd have had enough for one day, but for some reason I'm hornier than ever. In fact, I can hardly wait to get my hands on that girl.

I take a shower, get dressed, make the bed, listen to some music, and wait for Melissa to get home. When she finally walks in around four-thirty, I go to scoop her up in my arms, but she's too excited to sit still.

"Laurie, you won't even believe what happened to me in temple today," she says, fluttering all over the room. Maybe the poor girl is delirious from lack of food—I know I am—not to mention lack of caffeine. "So, I'm sitting there, right, just minding my own business, reading along with the prayer book and everything," Melissa says, "and then like halfway through the service, the rabbi stands and the ark is open, so the whole congregation stands too. And then this new cantor goes up to the *bima,* and she starts to sing, and she has the most amazing voice, I swear, it's like an angel is in the room. I was wishing you were there to hear her, Laurie, and then it was almost like you were there, right next to me. I could, like, *feel* your presence or something. And I was swaying to the cantor's voice, and then my whole body started to shake and shudder, and I had to sit down even though the ark was still open, because I really thought I was going to faint. My heart was beating really fast, I could barely catch my breath, and my face was all red, almost like when, almost like, well, you know." Melissa looks down demurely.

"Wait a minute, was this cantor a butch or a femme?" I fold my arms in a huff. Maybe I should have gone to synagogue with Melissa after all.

"She was a femme, silly. Anyway, that's not the point. The point is, these, like, waves started rippling through my body, and all I could think about was you, like I could practically hear your voice, like you were calling me or something, and then I sat back down, and I swear my whole chest was all flushed, like it is after we make love. It was totally amazing, like some sort of religious experience or something."

Am I good or what? I think, my heart starting to beat fast too. "So, um, like what time was this?" I ask, trying to sound nonchalant.

"What time?" Melissa looks up at the clock. "I don't know. Why?"

"Just curious."

"I don't know, let me think." Melissa tilts her head. "It must have been around one o'clock because then the rabbi started his sermon, and he always does his sermons around then."

"I see," I say, more to myself than to her.

"So, what did you do today?" Melissa asks, coming to sit down next to me on the couch, but not too close since the sun has yet to set.

"Oh, not much. Just hung around. Thought about you," I say putting my arm across her shoulder.

"Lau-*rie.*" Melissa rolls her eyes, but she isn't really annoyed because she doesn't pull away. "God, I'm starving, aren't you?"

"You betcha. What are you in the mood for?"

"Well, I bought a bagel-and-lox spread to break the fast with, but what I really feel like eating is a huge piece of noodle *kugel.* What about you?"

"I'd kill for a *kugel* right now," I say.

"I know," Melissa jumps up. "I'll put one in the oven, and by the time it's ready, we'll be able to eat." She bustles around the kitchen, putting up water to boil for the noodles, beating eggs, melting butter, and before I can even offer to help the *Shvitzing* Gourmet, our dinner's sizzling in the oven.

"Will you help me do the dishes?" Melissa asks, wiping her hands on a kitchen towel.

"I have a better idea," I say, coming up behind her and putting my arms around her waist. "Let's get into bed while it's baking."

"Lau-*rie,*" Melissa says again, but I can tell she's weakening. Her eyes are all big like they are when she wants me.

"C'mon, love," I whisper in her ear, letting my tongue linger. "I've got a surprise for you."

"Ooh, what is it?" Melissa squeals. Melissa loves surprises.

"You'll see," I say, taking her by the hand.

"Is it something to eat?" she asks, her stomach rumbling.
"Not really," I answer, "but it's finger-licking good."
And it is.

Boy Crazy

"Well, I guess my days of traveling light are over." Brenda hefted an enormous canvas bag onto Deidre's and Gloria's counter. "Look at all this stuff. Snacks for Timmy, toys for Timmy…"

"Ooh, let me see that little lamb." Deidre licked a drip of mayonnaise off her pinkie and picked up the small stuffed animal. "Look how cute it is. Jimmy would just love this. Where'd you get it?"

"You'll have to ask Lilly. She picked it up one night after work. I think she got it at Bradlee's." Brenda opened Deidre's refrigerator and pushed back a bowl of homemade cole slaw to make room for Timmy's lunch.

"I think I'll get one for Jimmy. Do you mind?"

"Mind? Why would I mind?" Brenda opened a can of beer and helped herself to a frosted mug from the freezer. "Hell, take that one." She motioned toward it with her glass. "Timmy won't even miss it."

"Brenda, shame on you." Deidre went back to her potato salad, which needed a bit more paprika. "That's probably his favorite toy."

"Trust me, he'll never even know it's gone. Not with all the toys he has. Lilly spoils him rotten."

"Hi, girls." Mimi came in the kitchen door and tossed her car keys on the counter.

"Ah, remember that? The life of the unencumbered." Brenda stared at the counter, where Mimi's keys lay sprawled next to her oversize bag. "That's like a before and after picture of my life."

"Oh, you poor, poor thing." Mimi was all sympathy. "Where are the little beasts—I mean darlings—anyway?"

"Aren't they playing out front?" Deidre asked, ready to panic.

"I didn't see them." Mimi poured herself a Coke.

"Relax, they're out back with the butches." Brenda pointed out the window. "Look how cute they are."

"The butches?" Mimi smacked her lips. "They're adorable. Especially the one in the hot chili peppers baseball cap," she added loud enough for the women out back to hear. Mimi's girlfriend Tina, upon hearing the compliment, turned and tipped her hat to the ladies.

"I wasn't talking about the butches." Brenda rapped on the window pane with her knuckles. "Hey, Timothy and Jimothy, you play nice now. No fighting over that ball. You know how to share."

Neither Jimmy or Timmy even bothered looking up at Brenda, but Gloria smiled and waved.

"How are the coals doing, honey?" Deidre called through the window.

"They're almost ready." Gloria poked at the grill with a stick.

"Don't let them play too close to the barbecue." Brenda sighed. "I better go out there."

"My God," Mimi shook her head. "The only thing worse than a Jewish mother is a lesbian mother. What?" She raised both her hands palm up to the ceiling as everyone looked at her. "I can say it, I have a Jewish mother. And anyway, it's true."

"That grill is very hot. If it ever got knocked over…"

"Take a chill pill, Brenda. The butches can handle it. Hey, Deidre, want me to do something?"

"Why don't you cut up some strawberries and melon for the fruit salad?" Deidre pointed with her chin. "Everything's over there by the toaster oven."

"Here, I'll wash, you chop." Brenda opened a cabinet and took out a colander.

"Where's Lilly anyway?" Mimi asked, rummaging through several drawers in search of a sharp knife.

Brenda shrugged. "Tardy as usual. That girl will be late to her own funeral."

"Maybe that's her now." Deidre cocked her ear as a car door slammed. "Nope. That's Valerie, Nora, and Sammy."

"Hello, ladies." Valerie plopped her bag, which was even bigger than Brenda's, down on the counter.

"Hi. Where's Nora and Sammy?"

"They went out back. Got any iced tea? It's going to be a scorcher."

"In the fridge." Deidre covered the bowl of potato salad with plastic wrap and looked out the window again. "My God, look how big Sammy's gotten. I just saw him a few weeks ago."

"Isn't it amazing?" Valerie came over to the window sill. "I wish he would un-Velcro himself from Nora's side, though. He's such a mama's boy. He sticks to her like glue."

"He plays with Jimmy sometimes, when it's just the two of them," Deidre said. "But when Timmy's around…"

"Do you have something to say about my Timmy?" Brenda put her hand on her hip in mock indignation.

"Of course not." Deidre feigned indignation as well. "It's just that when Timmy's around, Jimmy doesn't have eyes for anyone else."

"Who can blame him?" Brenda dumped a pile of rinsed strawberries into Mimi's chopping bowl. "Timmy feels the same way. You know how he is about the car."

"Still?" Valerie rolled her eyes.

"Still." Brenda sighed. "The only way I can get him in without a fight is to say, 'Want to go play with Jimmy?' And when we turn your corner," Brenda addressed Deidre, "he gets so excited. He can be sound asleep, but the minute we hit Magnolia Lane, he's wide awake and ready to go."

"Hello, everyone," Lilly came in the door and gave Brenda a big kiss. "Where's my boy?"

"Where do you think?"

"Playing with Jimmy out back."

"Bingo."

"Doesn't he want this?" Lilly picked up Timmy's lamb. Deidre shot Brenda a look.

"I brought it in so it wouldn't get dirty," Brenda said, all innocence.

"Is he behaving himself?" Lilly asked, riffling through Brenda's bag.

"Are we having behavior problems?" Deidre asked.

"Not a big deal. Just a little biting incident last week."

"Jimmy went through a biting stage. They all do."

"Not all of them," Valerie said proudly. "Sammy never did."

"Hey, how was his appointment with Dr. Lerner?"

"Fine. He's right on schedule with height, weight—"

"Does Dr. Lerner call you 'Mommy'?" Deidre interrupted her. "I've told him my name a dozen times, but he insists on calling me that."

"Oh, he does it to everyone," Brenda cut in. "I don't mind. As long as he doesn't call Lilly 'Daddy.'"

Everyone laughed. Everyone but Mimi, that is. "Can we please talk about something else?" She let out a huge yawn to show her friends the extent of her boredom. "Remember the good old days when we used to talk about art, politics, sex...."

"I'm going to go see if the boys want a drink. It's hot out there." Lilly headed out back just as Gloria came inside, then returned to ask, "By the way, did Timmy have a BM today?"

"Oh, for God's sake." Mimi pretended to gag and then popped a strawberry into her mouth.

"I'm ready for those hamburgers." Gloria opened the refrigerator and took out the meat. "We'll eat in about 20 minutes, OK?"

"Aye, aye, Captain." Deidre saluted Gloria who stole a kiss off her bare shoulder before leaving the kitchen just as Tina came inside.

"Hey, Mimi, did we bring any sunscreen?"

"It's in the car. I'll get it." Mimi headed out.

Soon everyone was coming and going, carrying salads,

hamburger rolls, plastic silverware, cold drinks, and bug repellent. Deidre, who loved to entertain, often joked that she should put in a revolving door to make life easier for her and her guests. When the hamburgers were ready, Gloria slid them onto a serving platter and joined her friends at the picnic table, who were all busy piling their plates high with food.

"Jimmy, come get something to eat." Deidre cut up half a hamburger on a small plate and motioned to him. Jimmy, who was clearly more interested in playing than eating at the moment, ignored her.

"Jimmy." Deidre crossed the lawn and came scurrying back two seconds later. "Brenda, where's Timmy?"

"What do you mean, where's Timmy? Isn't he over there playing with Jimmy?"

"No."

"No? What do you mean, no?"

"Oh, my God." Nora put her arm around Sammy, who was sitting right next to her on a lounge chair.

"Don't panic," Tina said. "We'll find him."

"He was there one second ago, I swear it." Lilly knew that Brenda would blame her if anything ever happened to Timmy.

"Timmy! Timmy!" Gloria took off for the front yard while Valerie combed the back. Tina ran down the driveway and out to the road, which, thank God, was empty of blood and bone. Nora stayed put with Sammy, and Deidre sat with her, Jimmy held tightly on her lap. Brenda and Lilly worked together as a frantic unit, their cries of "Timmy! Timmy!" getting shriller and shriller by the minute as they combed the neighborhood.

"Where do you think he could be?" Nora asked Deidre.

"He couldn't have gone too far." Deidre sounded more re-assuring than she actually felt. She could see Brenda and Lilly knocking on her neighbor's door, and she knew she would totally fall apart if Jimmy ever disappeared like that.

"Nobody's seen him." Brenda and Lilly came back to where Deidre and Nora were sitting just as Tina, Gloria, and Valerie returned. "What are we going to do?"

"Hey, where's Mimi?" Tina asked.

"Yoo-hoo!" Just as her name was spoken, Mimi appeared in the yard, a wet and muddy Timmy held tightly to her chest.

"Timmy! Oh, my God! Where did you find him?" Brenda and Lilly flew across the grass and took Timmy in their arms, much to Mimi's relief.

"Do I hear a 'thank you'? Do I hear a 'we'll pay the dry-cleaning bill'?" Mimi brushed off her top to no avail. "He was happy as a clam, playing in a mud puddle two doors down."

"You naughty, naughty boy," Brenda said, fussing over Timmy's dirty wet feet. "Don't you ever run away like that again."

"Say it like you mean it," Lilly reminded Brenda, "or he won't learn. He won't take you seriously."

"Come inside with Mommy, so I can clean you off." Brenda ignored Lilly, who followed her into the house.

"We're coming too." Nora got up, and, of course, Sammy trailed her like a shadow as she and Valerie headed for the kitchen.

"Wait, I'll get you some towels." Deidre, still holding Jimmy, scurried after her guests. Gloria shrugged and went inside as well.

Mimi and Tina were left to themselves. They picked up their plates and sat down to eat, reveling in the peace and quiet around them. Neither of them said anything, but when Mimi picked a bit of wet fur off her T-shirt, and Tina fished a soggy rawhide chew out from under her seat cushion, each knew exactly what the other was thinking: *Thank God we found each other, the only two lesbians left on the planet who have yet to go to the dogs.*

Laddy Come Home

"Matthew, shut up. Just turn around right now, sit down, and don't let me hear another word."

Oh, boy. It's going to be a long wait while they try to decide whether our plane can take off in the middle of these thunderstorms. Especially sitting next to these two. And wouldn't you know it: Of all the names in the world, the kid has to be named Matthew. Just like my son. My former son. My ex-son? I don't know what Matthew is to me anymore—a memory, a wish, a dream? No, Matthew is real; I have his photo right here in my wallet to prove it to myself. Sometimes I look at it ten times a day, and sometimes I let weeks go by before I take my heart in my throat and gaze at his big blue eyes, his toothless smile, his dimpled cheeks. When I look at Matthew's face, I feel such pain—it's actually a physical pain—like my chest is being ripped open and someone very strong is tearing my heart in two. This happens without fail, every time I look at a photo of Matthew. It's happening right now, in fact, but I don't mind. It's actually kind of comforting. And it's the only thing I have left.

How does a mother lose her son? Well, first of all, I'm not Matthew's mother. We were always clear about that. I was (am?) Matthew's parent. Molly is his mom. Long before Matthew was born or even conceived, Molly told me she didn't believe in all that *"Heather Has Two Mommies* crap."

"A child knows exactly who his mother is," she said. We were in the bedroom folding laundry, and she fished my favorite pair of Levi's from the mound of clothes on the bed.

"Fine with me," I plucked a pair of her lace panties from the pile. "I always thought I was more daddy material anyway." To prove my point, I brought her undies up to my face and pretended to sniff them.

"Tory, that's disgusting." Molly snatched her lingerie away.

"C'mon." I snatched Molly, and together we tumbled on top of our clothes. "Let's make a baby right now."

"Oh, you." Molly hit my back with a clean knee sock, but her protest wasn't even half hearted.

"Call me Daddy," I whispered, as my hands found their way underneath her sweater.

"You're not my daddy," she whispered back.

"Not yours, silly," I said, unhooking her bra. "The kid's," I reminded her as my palms made small circles over her hardening nipples. "I'm the kid's daddy. His lesbian daddy."

"His laddy." Molly sighed with pleasure as I lapped at her breasts. So even though Matthew wasn't conceived that night (though believe me, if two lesbians could make a baby, he would have been), I was conceived—Laddy—and the word was music to my ears. Finally, a name for me, the butch parent. Not a mommy or a co-mother or a godmother or a special friend or an aunt. A lesbian daddy. Laddy. It fit like a glove, like the latex glove on my hand that fit snugly into Molly's vagina, the same vagina that Matthew would zoom through on his way into the world that would welcome him with four loving, female arms.

Molly always knew we'd have a boy. And not because statistically it's more probable, especially if you use frozen sperm, which we did. That was another discussion. Molly couldn't decide if we should use a known donor or not, but I was dead set against it. "Just like he can't have two mommies, he can't have a Daddy and a Laddy," I argued as we pored over the donor books we'd gotten from the clinic in California.

Molly slammed the book she was looking through shut. "But don't you think it's unfair that he'll never know who his daddy is?"

"He won't have a daddy. He'll have a laddy. And a donor. Giving sperm does not a daddy make." I was studying the portfolio of Potential Sperm Donor Number 47903. Brown hair, blue eyes, med student, tall, athletic… "You know half the people on this planet don't know who their daddy is. They ask their mother, and she says, 'Oh, I don't know. I was young, I was drunk, I met him in a bar one night, I think his name was Joe.…' Our kid's going to have two parents who are crazy about him. He doesn't need a third party to gum up the works."

"I guess." Molly shrugged, still not convinced, so we compromised: We settled on an "open donor" policy, which means that when Matthew turns 18, he can search for him if he wants to. I hope he doesn't want to find his donor, though. I hope he wants to find me.

Anyway, like I said, Molly always knew she was going to have a boy. "Mother's intuition," she would say, already smug in her maternal role. We never said things like, "This is the baby's room. This is his or her crib, these are his or her toys...." We just used that good old masculine pronoun from day one. Actually from before day one, when Matthew was just a concept, a twinkle in Molly's eye. "You need to know I'm going to have a baby," she said to me on our very first date. "A son."

"You're pregnant?" I looked down at her belly, which I hate to admit was much flatter than mine.

"No. I mean, not yet." She corrected herself. "But someday I will be."

"Someday your prince will come," I sang and then bowed with a flourish. "Did I ever tell you I'm the lesbian formally known as Prince?"

She laughed and kissed me, and that was it. I was smitten from day one, brought the U-Haul over on day two, just like the old lesbian joke. But now the joke's on me because who knew back then, when I was looking deep into Molly's love-filled eyes and squirting a turkey baster full of sperm up into her waiting womb, that those same blue eyes would one day flash lightning bolts of pure hatred clear across the room while she screamed, "You're nothing to Matthew, and you're nothing to me. Can't you get that through that thick skull of yours, Tory? Now get the hell out of here, and leave us alone."

Who knew, who knew? As I sit here in this overheated, airless terminal, I stare at the faces around me, wondering where everyone is going. Who's rushing off to meet a lover, who's about to have her heart broken, who's going to be met at the other end of this journey by someone filled with anger and rage, whose world is about to crumble as they look on helplessly, unable to understand?

The day Matthew was born, I had such an intense feeling in my chest, it was like my heart had swelled up to ten times its normal size to hold inside all the love I felt for my precious, new family. I was absolutely in awe of Molly and what she had gone through in the last 24 hours. "You're a Goddess," I whispered, smoothing a blonde curl off her sweaty forehead. "An absolute Goddess."

She smiled the smile of a woman who knew she had just completed a job well done. The nurse had taken Matthew away to clean him up, so we were alone for a few minutes. Molly closed her eyes, and I thought perhaps she had fallen asleep. "You OK, Mommy?" I whispered, even though we'd both sworn we would never fall into that obnoxious habit so many straight couples have of calling each other Mommy and Daddy. Amazing what flies out the window once you're a parent.

"Never been better, Laddy," Molly whispered back, weakly squeezing my hand. Then the nurse appeared in the doorway with Matthew, and as soon as she stepped into the room, Molly was wide awake and sitting up, reaching for the baby as he moved toward her, like metal shavings to a magnet. She took him to her breast, and, I tell you, being in that room with my lover and our child on the first day of his life was the closest I've ever come to being in paradise.

Matthew was a good baby, not too colicky, though it was over a year before he slept through the night. Molly had to get up most of the time because she was breast-feeding, and I think that's when the resentment started. But what could I do? I couldn't nurse. Though one night when Molly was just too tired to go to him, I picked him up from his crib and put him to my breast. I had tried everything: singing to him, walking him, rocking him. I was desperate for him to quiet down, so I thought, *Why not?* And it seemed to work. For a minute anyway. He stopped crying immediately as his mouth found my nipple. He sucked and then sucked harder, and then he sucked harder until *I* almost started to cry. I never knew a baby's jaw could be so strong. But Matthew was no dummy. He soon figured out that the well was dry, and then he really started bawling his little head off. I had no choice but to take him into our bedroom where Molly was sitting up and waiting, the milk from her breasts already letting down.

"Just give him to me," she said, clearly irritated that I couldn't handle the situation, but it was clear she was pleased too: pleased that Matthew wanted her, only her, no one but Mommy would do, no one but Mommy could satisfy his little baby needs.

What can I say? I did the best I could. We got through the sleepless nights, the teething, the toilet training.… I supported my family financially so Molly could stay home with Matthew. Funny how day care—like nonmonogamy—works a whole lot better in theory than in practice. "I don't want to miss the best years of his life," Molly said, even though our original plan was for her to go back to work, at least part-time, before Matthew was two. "I don't want some stranger taking care of my son."

How those words have come back to haunt me. When I think about them now, when I hear Molly's voice echoing in my mind, I feel like such a goddamn idiot I could puke. You know, it's like when your lover is having an affair, and everyone in the entire town knows about it—everyone but you, that is—and you feel like such a fucking imbecile. Molly always referred to Matthew as "my son." I never once heard her use the pronoun "our." Of course, now that I think about it, it's obvious, but back then I guess I just didn't notice. I was too busy busting my ass, working two jobs and racing back to the apartment in-between just so I could hear Molly sing out to Matthew, "Who's ho-o-ome?" and hear Matthew answer, "Laddy!" as he came tearing into the front hallway as fast as his chubby little legs could carry him, to fling himself into my open arms for a big hug and a kiss before I had to turn around and go back to the old salt mines again.

I mean, it seemed we were a family. We looked like a family, we sounded like a family, we smelled like a family…sometimes even a happy family. Of course, now I feel incredibly stupid for not taking steps to legally protect myself, but who knew, who knew? Besides, I couldn't have adopted Matthew even if Molly had allowed me to, because we didn't live in some hippie, groovy, liberal state like Massachusetts or New York. We lived in Oregon. Need I say more? The world around Molly saw her as a single mother, and despite Matthew's and my relationship, that's how she began to see herself too. She became very territorial around Matthew, and I began to feel like a third wheel—not a parent, not a spouse, merely the breadwinner. Our "marriage," which of course wasn't legal either, was in name only. I could hardly remember the last time we had made love. When Molly was pregnant, we'd go at it like bunnies, she was so goddamn sexy with her belly and boobs all soft and round, her skin all lit up with that "pregnant glow." But after Matthew was born, the shop was closed. First of all, Molly insisted on Matthew's crib being in our bedroom, and I certainly wasn't about to go to town in front of our son. I begged her to let him sleep in his own room; why did we spend a fortune cleaning it and painting it and decorating it, if he wasn't even going to use it? But Molly had to be as close to him as possible. "You don't understand, Tory," she said. "It's a biological thing. I just have to be near him. It's an ache, a physical pain right here," she pointed to her chest, "when we're that far apart." I hated when she pulled biological rank, and she knew I hated it, but there was just no arguing with her. (How ironic now, that same ache only she could feel is as familiar to me as my own flesh and blood.) Anyway, Molly said she was too sore from giving birth to take part in any extracurricular activities, and then when she was nursing, she didn't want me anywhere near her breasts. "Please," she'd say, smacking my hands away, "it's bad enough he's at me every other minute." But she didn't really mean it, about Matthew anyway. Molly loved nursing him. When he was feeding, a look of sheer bliss came over her face, a look I had never, ever seen. Yes, I'll admit I was jealous. Yes, it's undeniable that a mother and child have a special bond no one else can share. I knew that. That's why I wasn't mommy number two. I was Laddy. At least I thought I was.

One Saturday afternoon when Molly had taken Matthew to the park, I was poking through some papers in the desk in the hallway, looking for something—I can't remember what—when I found a letter to Molly from her parents. This was a bit strange, since Molly wasn't very close to her parents; as far as I knew, the only mail they ever sent each other was a card during the holidays. Molly's parents were pretty lukewarm about her being a lesbian, and they were even less thrilled when she told them she was pregnant. At first they wanted nothing to do with us or their grandson—they took the party line: "It's one thing if you want to live like that, you're both adults. But how can you possibly inflict that kind of lifestyle onto a child?"—but Molly convinced them to visit shortly after Matthew was born, and, of course, her parents fell in love with him right away, as soon as they laid eyes on him. Me, they hardly spoke to, but I didn't really care. I was just glad they were there, for Molly's sake; it meant so much to her that I didn't let it get to me. After all, I was hardly the son-in-law of their dreams, and I was sure they'd come around eventually. And even if they didn't, so what? They lived clear across the country, down south in Atlanta where Molly grew up, so it wasn't like we'd be spending oodles of time with them.

My parents, well, that's a whole other story. They don't even know they have a grandchild. I haven't spoken to them in many, many years, ever since I came out to them at the tender age of 20. I knew they wouldn't be thrilled that their daughter was a dyke, but then again, they'd never been thrilled with anything I'd done. From day one they hated the clothes I wore, the music I listened to, the friends I made. I always felt like an alien in my family; I was so different from my parents and my sister, who was so close to my mother and father, she still lived at home with them, even at the ripe old age of 27. But, still, I loved them, and they loved me. Or so I thought. Anyway, I wanted them to know I had found someone and that

I was happy. And besides, what could they do to me? I was 3,000 miles away, which wasn't an accident. I knew I had to pick a school as far away as possible in order to live my life the way I wanted. So I moved out here to go to the University of Oregon, and during my senior year I fell in L-O-V-E love. I really wanted them to know. Everyone else knew; Roberta and I were hardly shy when it came to public displays of affection. Plus, call me crazy, but I began to feel guilty about living off their money when I was keeping such a big secret from them, a secret I doubted they would meet with approval.

Back in those days, my parents called every Sunday morning, my mother on the kitchen phone, my father on the upstairs extension. The conversations were always the same: "How are you?" "Fine." "How's school?" "Good." "What's new?" "Nothing." But this Sunday would be different.

"How are you?" My mother asked.

"Fine," I answered.

"How's school?" asked my father.

"Good."

"What's new?" My mother was right on cue.

I took a deep breath. "I have big news," I broke the script. "I met someone. I'm in love."

"That's wonderful," my mother said, after a pause.

"What does he do?" asked my father.

"Uh...student," I said, not wanting to break the news with a pronoun.

"What's his name?" my mother piped in.

I took another deep breath. "Mom, Dad, I'm really glad you're happy for me." I glanced down at a piece of paper covered with notes I had scribbled for the occasion. "I know you love me and want me to be happy, and I know you want to share in my happiness." I realized I was sounding stiff and sort of like an idiot, but somehow I needed to stall for a minute or two. Somehow this was much harder than I had expected.

They waited while I rambled on a bit, my lover's name stuck in my throat like a bit of food that had gone down the wrong pipe and would choke me to death unless I found a way to remove it. Finally I spit it out: "Mom, Dad, her name is Roberta. She's really, really great. I know you're just going to love her...."

Silence. I couldn't even hear if they were still breathing or not. Then my father's voice: "We'll call you back tomorrow with our decision."

"Your decision? About what?"

No answer but a click.

"Mom?"

Another click. Then a dial tone. I stared at the phone stupidly until that recording came on: "Please hang up. There appears to be a receiver off the hook. Please check your main telephone...." I did what the recording told me and sat staring at the phone for a long, long time. Finally I dragged myself to bed, but I couldn't sleep at all that night, wondering what on earth their decision would be. What in the world were they even deciding about? My fate? What could they do, lock me up? I was over 18, and besides, it was the '80s, they didn't do stuff like that anymore. Or did they? Roberta was away for the weekend, so I sweated through the longest Sunday night of my life alone. The phone rang at exactly nine o'clock the next morning, and I jumped to answer it, only to hear my father utter two short sentences:

"We're moving. Don't try to find us."

"What?" I couldn't believe what I had just heard. "Dad, you don't have to move. I won't come home. Wait a minute. Let me talk to Mom. Hello?" But the line was dead, and there was no answer when I called back, even though I let the phone ring over a hundred times. I tried to call them on and off all day and the day after as well. On Wednesday their phone rang once, and then I heard a click. "Mom? Dad?"

"The number you have reached, 555-6247, has been disconnected. No further information is available for the number 555-6247. If you need assistance, please hang up and dial zero-zero for an operator. The number you have reached, 555-6247..."

I couldn't believe it. I must have listened to that recording for more than an hour, until my ear was numb against the receiver and my heart was numb in my chest. My parents were gone, and I had no idea where to search for them. I grew up in Pennsylvania, which is a pretty big state. Besides, they could have gone anywhere, and more importantly, they didn't *want* me to find them. I couldn't believe even my sister was going along with this, but she was always a wuss, Daddy's little girl, Mother's little helper. I was the one who didn't fit in, and now they were done putting up with me.

As you can imagine, I was a wreck that last semester in college. Somehow I managed to graduate and find myself a job and an apartment. I never planned on staying in Oregon, but where was I going to go? Home? I didn't even know where that was anymore. Roberta moved on to graduate school in

Colorado, and we gave the long-distance thing a shot, but after a while our relationship petered out. I dated some, was in and out of lots of short-term relationships (What do lesbians eat for breakfast? Cereal monogamy.), but no one felt right until I met Molly. And even though I was terrified to make a commitment, I gritted my teeth and took the plunge. After all, I was already 35, and she was 37. We weren't spring chickens any longer. We both knew what we wanted. We wanted each other. And a baby. A family. Once I had a new family, I reasoned, I could let go of the old one. I could stop looking at every 60-year-old woman on the street, wondering, *Is she my mother?* I hear that's what kids who were adopted do: They search for their mothers their whole lives, always on the lookout because you never know, she could be right there, right around the next corner. I looked for years, and then one day I just stopped. You know why? Because out of the blue, on an ordinary Tuesday morning, I got a phone call from my sister consisting of two words: "Mom's dead," followed by a click. I even dialed star 69 to try and trace the call, but my sister's smart—she made it from a pay phone. How I sobbed that night, how I howled, how I let it all out: 14 years of grief. And Molly was terrific; I have to give her that. She stayed right with me, holding me, rocking me, wiping my tears, pressing tissues up to my nose and telling me to blow. She knew the depths of my pain, so I ask you: How could she take Matthew away from me? Molly knew what I went through looking for my mother; she knew I'd spend the rest of my life looking at boys of a certain age with brown hair and blue eyes, silently asking, *Are you my son?* Yes, Molly and Matthew disappeared from my life as suddenly and completely as my parents had, and it all started the day I found that letter.

I know it's wrong to read other people's mail—in fact, it's a federal offense—but I also know what you don't know can kill you. And that letter practically was the death of me. I'll spare you the opening pleasantries and family gossip and just get to the point: Molly's parents were absolutely ecstatic that Molly and the baby were thinking of moving back home, and of course they could stay in her old room until they found a place of their own or as long as they wanted. *We've already bought a crib and a high chair and a car seat, and we're just counting the days until you arrive.* By the time I got to that sentence, my breath was coming in short little gasps, and I had to sit down because I felt weak in the knees. My heart pounded in my chest, little beads of sweat covered my face, and I swear I saw spots before my eyes.

I took a few deep breaths, got myself some water, and tried to calm down and remain rational, but it was no use. When Molly and Matthew came home from the park, I just exploded. "What the hell is this?" I barked, waving the letter at her. "When did you decide to move back to Georgia? And when were you planning to tell me?"

"Tory, calm down, you're scaring Matthew." Molly was squatting down in front of him, unsnapping his blue corduroy jacket with the red racing stripes going up the side—a jacket that, by the way, my hard-earned money had paid for. "Let's go get some juice." She took Matthew by the hand and headed for the kitchen, tossing me some words over her shoulder, "We'll talk about it later."

"We'll talk about it right now," I yelled, charging after

them. "I want Matthew to see this and hear this, so he'll know if he winds up living with your homophobic parents, it wasn't my choice and it wasn't my fault."

"Will you calm down?" Molly was sitting at the kitchen table with Matthew in her lap, and they both stared at me with identical blue eyes, like I was totally insane, which I was. "I'm just thinking about it as an option, Tory, and even if I decide to go, it won't be for a long time...."

"We're counting the days?" I waved the letter in her face again.

Molly kissed the top of Matthew's head and opened her arms. "Why don't you go into the living room, sweetheart? Laddy and Mommy have to talk about something. I'll put *101 Dalmatians* on for you."

I sighed. Another promise to ourselves we'd failed to keep: We weren't going to be the kind of parents who would use the boob tube as an instant baby-sitter. But I could hardly worry about that now.

Molly came back, and I could tell by the way she stood against the doorway and folded her arms that everything had already been decided. "I've been thinking," she began.

"About what?" I spat.

"Tory, this isn't easy for me either, you know. Things haven't been good between us for a while now—"

"No shit, Sherlock."

Molly ignored me. "—and I was thinking maybe you should stay with some friends or something while I sort things out."

"It looks like you've already sorted things out." I couldn't let go of the goddamn letter, and I waved it in her face again. "Unless this is some type of joke, Molly, and if it is, I don't find it the least bit funny."

"It's not a joke, Tory." Molly's voice had an air of finality to it. "I'm thinking of going home."

"Home? Molly, you're almost 40 years old. You can't move back in with your parents."

"Why not? Just because your parents would never help you out doesn't mean I should say no if my parents are willing to help me."

I couldn't even respond, what she had just said was so unbelievably cruel. But Molly was relentless. Obviously she had been thinking about this for a long time.

"Tory, Matthew has only one set of grandparents...."

"That's not my fault."

"I'm not saying it's your fault. All I'm saying is, they *are* his next of kin, and he should know who they are."

"And what am I, chopped liver?" I was more than furious at Molly. I was scared. Sure, I knew things between us hadn't been going well, but we could work it out. All the parenting books I'd read said couples went through a lot of stress the first couple of years of a child's life. We just had to hang in there. We could work it out, as long as we both wanted to work it out. But that was the problem: I could tell Molly didn't want to. "Tory," she spoke to me like I was the child instead of Matthew. "What's the longest you've ever been in a relationship?"

She knew the answer as well as I did. Before Molly, my record had been less than a year.

"So," she took my silence as some kind of tacit agreement. "How do you expect to work this out?"

I didn't bother answering. *Fine,* I thought. *Break up with me. See if I care.* Molly, I could live without, no problem, especially after tonight. But Matthew, that was another story.

"What about Matthew?" I asked, my voice an angry bark.

"You can see him once a week, and some weekends. I have a schedule all written out. When you're feeling calmer, I'll show it to you."

"But what happens if you move back to Georgia?" I asked, my voice barely a whisper. I couldn't believe this was happening to me.

"No one said I was moving, Tory. I only said I was thinking about moving."

"But how can you even think about doing such a thing?"

"Tory, let's not future-trip, OK? If I do move, we'll cross that bridge when we come to it. We'll work it out."

"Like hell we will," I screamed, releasing all the fury I held inside.

"Tory, can we talk about this when you're feeling calmer? You know how I hate it when you yell like that."

"When I yell? You think this is yelling? I haven't even begun to yell, Molly." I yanked open the door and stormed out of the house before I really lost it. The rain was coming down in sheets, just like it is right now, but I didn't care. I walked the streets for hours. What did it matter if I caught a cold or the flu or walking pneumonia? My life was already over. *When you're feeling calmer...* God, I hated when Molly talked like that. It was always the same: The more agitated I got, the calmer she got. Like she was so goddamn superior: *She* never got angry; *she* never got upset. It was always crazy Tory who was out of control, crazy Tory with her fucked up temper....

Finally I walked off the tip of my anger enough to go home.
I was soaked to the skin, and I had nowhere else to go. The
house was dark—not that I had expected Molly to wait up for
me—and I already felt like an intruder as I quietly took off my
soggy clothes and crept down the hallway to Matthew's room
(at this point he was finally sleeping in his own room, not that
it mattered anymore). He was sound asleep on his side wearing his Dalmatian pajamas, a stuffed Pongo guarding his pillow. God, how I wanted to snatch him up and get the hell out
of there. But I knew I could never do such a thing. Take
Matthew away from his Mommy? It was inconceivable. As inconceivable as taking him away from his Laddy.

So I talked to him. I told him how much I loved him and
what a special little boy he was and that no matter what, he'd
always be my precious son, and I'd always be his Laddy. I told
him parents do crazy things sometimes, and sometimes they
even have to go away, but still, your parents are always your
parents, they always love you, no matter where they are. And
then I got all choked up, and the tears started streaming down
my face as steady as the rain outside Matthew's bedroom window, as steady as the rain that's now coming down in buckets
on the runway. I didn't know if I was talking to Matthew about
me and Molly or talking to myself about my own parents—my
poor mother, dead and gone, and my father, who as far as I
knew was still alive and kicking, though I didn't know where.
All I know is I said what I had to say, kissed the top of his
sweet-smelling head, and dragged my weary ass into the living room to try and catch some shut-eye on our poor excuse
for a couch.

Over the next few days I pleaded with Molly to let me stay

and try to work things out. I begged, I bargained, I offered to
go to couples counseling. I even said I would move to Georgia with her if she wanted me to. But it was no use. So I found
myself a little apartment on the other side of town and set it
up with half the living room as Matthew's space, with a tiny
foam sofa that unfolded into a pint-size bed.

"Isn't this fun?" I asked him the first day he came to visit.
We were having an afternoon snack of peanut butter and
crackers in front of the TV, a regular pair of bachelors, watching the ball game on a Saturday afternoon.

"Where's Mommy?" Matthew asked.

"She'll be here later, sport. Want to draw a picture?" I laid
out some magic markers, and we whiled away the afternoon.
When Molly came to pick him up at six o'clock, I couldn't
even look at her, but Matthew leapt into her arms, just as he
had a million years ago when we were a family, when I'd
walked in the front door, living for those three words: "Who's
ho-o-ome?" "Laddy!"

True to her word, Molly had a schedule all worked out. She
put Matthew in day care a few days a week so she could go
back to work, and I got to pick him up on Thursdays. Plus he
slept at my apartment one weekend every month. Of course,
I didn't get to see him as much as I wanted, but there were
phone calls in-between, and once in a while a scribbly picture
that Matthew had made especially for me at school would arrive in the mailbox. His teachers all knew who I was since I
picked him up on Thursdays, though I think I puzzled them:
Why was this family "friend" so interested in Matthew's
progress? I grilled them incessantly: Did he know his colors?
Did he know his numbers? Did he know his ABCs? At home

we'd practice: "What's this letter for?" I'd ask, pointing to an
M. "Matthew and Mommy," he'd yell, pleased they were on the
same team. "And what's this letter for?" I asked, drawing a big
L. "Laddy!" Matthew would shriek, with just as much enthusiasm. I lived to hear that word leap from his mouth, relieved
that Matthew still knew exactly who I was, even though Molly
pretended not to. At least her plans to move back to Georgia
seemed to be on hold. She liked her job, she liked Matthew's
school, and she had even started dating someone, a big, bad
butch named Lenore. Sure, I was jealous, but I was somewhat
relieved too. As long as Molly was in love, she'd want to stay
here, which is all I really cared about. *This arrangement really isn't so bad,* I'd try to convince myself whenever I was feeling down, which was like every other minute. *I can deal with
seeing Matthew once a week and one weekend a month until
he turns 18.* I could, but Molly couldn't. One day out of the
blue, Molly called and told me she had decided once and for
all: They were definitely moving to Georgia.

"What?" I had to sit down, my legs were shaking so. I tell
you, I hate the goddamn telephone. "You can't do that to me,
Molly. You can't do that to Matthew."

"I'm doing this *for* Matthew," Molly said. "He needs to
know his roots. He needs to know his grandparents, and they
need to know him. They don't even know what his favorite
color is; they've never even seen him ride a bike. He's their
only child's only child, Tory. And they're his only grandparents. He's never even tasted his grandma's grits. He's never
even had one sip of his grandma's sweet tea."

Oh, spare me. I couldn't believe I hadn't seen this coming.
Didn't we know enough lesbians who got into the whole god-

damn roots thing once they had a kid? Like our friends, Mindy and Shoshanna, who hadn't set foot in a temple in more than a decade. All of a sudden, they were card-carrying synagogue members, and their kids were going to Sunday school. Sometimes I thought that was the whole reason lesbians even had children, to get back in their parents' favor. Though who was I to talk? Maybe even I would have gone that far, if I thought my efforts would be met with success. Maybe. But I didn't have that chance.

"What about your job, Molly? I thought you liked it."

"I do like it, but it's no big deal. A job's a job."

"What about Lenore?" I asked, grasping at straws.

"That's none of your business, Tory." Molly's voice was sharp. "Let's keep this between you and me...and Matthew. I'm very concerned about him."

"Concerned? Is he having problems at school? What do you mean, concerned?"

"I've been reading these parenting books, you know? And they all say if Matthew's going to separate from you, it's best to do it as early in his life as possible. It'll be less damaging to him that way."

What about me? I wanted to scream. *What about how damaging this will be to me?* But all I could do was repeat Molly's words. "Separate? What do you mean, separate?"

"Tory, I've been very generous with you, but what did you think, we could go on like this forever? Eventually I'm going to get seriously involved with someone else, and you're going to get involved with someone else. I don't want to have to take all these other people into consideration when I make major decisions about my life, and I don't want my son's life to be that complicated either. Like, I read this article in *The Advocate* about a kid who has a mother and a co-mother and a godmother and a stepmother. It's ridiculous. Even that kid in Matthew's class who has a mother and a stepfather and a father and a stepmother—I mean, he has like eight grandparents and all these uncles and aunts. It's too much for a child to have all these adults laying claim on him. I think it's best for everyone if we just make a clean break right now."

Suddenly I remembered something else about Molly: her disdain for the way lesbians take years to break up with each other and how sometimes we keep living together for a while, how often we remain in each other's lives, as friends, even best friends. "That is so sick," she'd say, after hearing about yet another lesbian couple who'd broken up but decided to keep running their business together. "It's never going to work, and then they're going to have to break up as business partners all over again," she said. "You know what that's like? That's like cutting off a dog's tail an inch at a time. You just torture the poor thing and prolong its agony. I say give it one good whap," she karate-chopped the edge of the table with the side of her hand, "and that's that. Sure, it hurts like hell, but then it's over, and you can get on with your life."

My head was spinning, and my voice was all choked up inside my throat. "Can I at least come over and say good-bye?" I whispered hoarsely.

"Oh, sure." Now Molly was all warmth and generosity. "Come over whenever you feel like it. We're not leaving for at least a month. And I want to keep our schedule intact until we go. It's better if things are consistent for Matthew. I don't want to upset him."

Is she nuts? I asked myself as Molly prattled on and on. She doesn't want to upset him? Then why is she moving him 3,000 miles away from one of his parents?

"You know how he likes his little routine to be the same every day—he's such a creature of habit." Molly laughed. "He's already been out of sorts because I've started doing a little packing. We're having a huge tag sale, Tory. You should really come over. There's some stuff here you might want. I've got so much to do."

Including showing up in court, I told her silently. Sure, I was losing my son, but not before I put up one hell of a fight. But again it was useless. Each lawyer I called was worse than the other. "You're the kid's mother? His mother's lover? His mother's former lover? So, what is it you think I can do for you?" Fucking Oregon. One lawyer even had the nerve to suggest I call Oprah. "This sounds right up her alley," he said with a chuckle.

Finally, I admitted defeat. What made me think I could convince a judge to acknowledge my place at the table when I couldn't even find myself a lawyer? I decided I'd just enjoy the days I had left with Matthew and rearrange my life so I could spend all my vacation time in Georgia. I got three weeks a year. Maybe I could come for a week at Christmas and spend two weeks there in the summer. August in Atlanta wasn't exactly my idea of a good time, but I'd put up with it to see Matthew. Or maybe Molly would let him come spend a few weeks with me. She said we'd work it out, didn't she? She said we'd cross that bridge when we came to it. Well, now here we were, and I wasn't going to let them leave until we at least had some sort of game plan as to the next time I was going to see my son.

To this day, I don't know how it happened. Chalk it up to living in a small town, where, I swear, some days it feels like everyone I see on the street knows the color of my underwear. Somehow Molly must have heard I was calling law offices. I know one of the attorneys I spoke to had a dyke we knew working part-time in his office. And a woman whose kid was in Matthew's class was a paralegal for one of the other lawyers who wouldn't take my case. Both women said the same thing when I confronted them: "Everything that happens in the office is strictly confidential," but I don't trust many people nowadays; I don't know who to believe anymore. All I know is someone must have spilled the beans because nothing else could explain why Molly did what she did the horrible way she did it.

It happened on a Thursday, my day to pick up Matthew from day care. I arrived right on time, as I always did, but his teacher said Matthew wasn't there. "He didn't come to school today," she said, and then turned to deal with someone else's son. I was a bit puzzled but not too worried. Maybe Matthew had a cold, or maybe Molly took a day off from work and just wanted him home with her. Once in a while she called in sick and gave herself and Matthew a holiday. *She probably just forgot to call and tell me,* I thought as I went to the office to use the phone. I called Molly's number, but she didn't answer. Instead I heard a very familiar recording: "The number you have reached, 555-1232, has been disconnected. No further information is available...." This time I didn't wait until the end of the recording. I jumped in my car and drove across town to their apartment as fast as I could. But it was too late. They were already gone.

It's a wonder I didn't kill myself that night. A heart can only take so much. To lose one family overnight almost destroyed me, but to lose another... And Molly knew exactly what she was doing to me. She more than anyone else knew how this would devastate me. What harm would there be in letting me come over and say good-bye? What was going on in her head? Was she afraid I would try to kidnap Matthew? I could never be that cruel—unlike some people.

You know, recently I was reading a copy of *People* magazine, and I came across a story about a couple who adopted a little girl and then lost her when the kid's biological parents came knocking at the door. After a few months, they went on with their lives, took a chance, and adopted another kid. So why don't I do the same? I'll tell you why. You can't replace a kid like a dog or a cat that's died, or a sweater that's been shrunk in the wash. Those things are replaceable; people aren't—though I wouldn't be surprised if Molly's already replaced me. It's been a year to the day since I've seen Matthew, and I never thought it would go this far. I thought for sure they'd call me after a week, a month, certainly a year. But no, not a peep. So this morning when I woke up, I knew what I had to do: call the airlines and jump on a goddamn plane. I couldn't take it anymore. I have such a longing for him, such a yearning, such an ache, such a bottomless *howl*. And I have so many questions: Does Matthew even remember me? What has Molly told him about his deadbeat lesbian dad? Does he think I don't love him anymore? What else can he possibly think? Why else would I disappear out of his life like that? He's still too little now, but eventually he'll convince himself he must have done something terribly, terribly wrong for me to abandon him. Believe me, I know.

The thunderstorms have passed now and Matthew, the Matthew in the seat next to me, is sound asleep on his mother's lap. Soon we'll be boarding, and you'd think I'd be excited, but to tell the truth I wouldn't mind if the plane was delayed another hour or so. I'm not in an awfully big hurry. What's a few more hours after all this time? I doubt I'll even be able to find Molly and Matthew—Molly's parents changed their phone number too—and even if I do, I'm sure Molly won't let me anywhere near him. She probably has a restraining order against me. But it doesn't matter. All I want is to have my feet on the same ground as his for a few days; I want my head under the same sky. I want to be in the same time zone as Matthew. I want to know that if the wind is at my back, the wind is at his back; if the sun is in my eyes, the sun is in his eyes. It's not much, but it's all I have. For today, anyway. For today, this is as close as I can get to my boy, my Matthew, my son.

Homo Alone

The phone rang just as Deborah deposited a half dollar–size plop of creme rinse on top of her head. "Oh, shit." She stepped out of the shower without bothering to turn off the water and padded into the kitchen on sopping wet feet. "Hello?"

"Is Emily Tannenbaum there?"

"No, she isn't."

"Is Mr. Tannenbaum there?"

"There is no Mr. Tannenbaum," Deborah snapped. "Who is this?"

"This is Gretchen, calling from Sears about the vacuum cleaner."

"You can talk to me about the vacuum cleaner."

"Oh, are you Emily's mother?"

Deborah snorted. "No, I'm her lover."

The woman from Sears paused. "Excuse me?"

"I said I'm her lover. I know all about the vacuum cleaner."

The woman paused again. "I'm afraid I don't understand.

Is Emily Tannenbaum a man or a woman?"

This time Deborah let a few seconds go by before she responded. *"Emily* Tannenbaum? Lady, what do you think?"

"I think I'll call back another time."

"Fine." Deborah slammed down the phone and returned to the shower. *Stupid bitch*, she thought as she worked the creme rinse through her hair. The last person she wanted to think about this morning was Emily—Emily, who was her lover, the key word here being *was*. Was, as in past tense. As in was not any longer. As in what was wrong with Emily anyway? Deborah couldn't believe that one day out of nowhere, two weeks before graduation, Emily had decided she was bisexual and needed to "explore her options." *Give me a break,* Deborah thought, scrubbing her scalp a little more vigorously than necessary. "That's what you get for dating a Smithie," she chastised herself. When she had started going out with Emily, Deborah had never even heard the term LUG: Lesbian Until Graduation. And she wished she had never heard of it now. *Christ, instead of diplomas, Smith College should just give out diaphragms,* she thought, bowing her head to give her hair one last good rinse. And of all people, Emily, the Big Dyke on Campus. If a solicitor called and asked Emily if Mr. Tannenbaum was home, she would say, "Sure, but you can't speak to him."

"Why not?" Gretchen from Sears would ask.

"Because we chopped him up into teeny, tiny pieces and put him in the freezer," Emily would answer before hanging up the phone.

Those were exactly the kind of girls you had to watch out for, Deborah reminded herself. The ones that went from one extreme to the other. First they shaved their heads, pierced their nipples, and changed their names to Glenda Goddess-Worshipper or Diana Diesel-Dyke. Then they turned around and married a nice Jewish doctor, had 2.5 kids, and bought a station wagon. Which was exactly what Emily was doing. Deborah had been absolutely furious when she found out. *She* had proposed to Emily long before Allen was even in the picture. "That's very sweet," Emily had said when Deborah got down on one knee. "But I'm way too young to make a commitment." *Emily must have aged very quickly in the last six months,* Deborah thought as she slipped on her robe and went back into the kitchen for a second cup of coffee. Either that or she'd gotten herself knocked up, a possibility Deborah didn't even want to consider, as that would prove beyond a shadow of a doubt that the woman who wouldn't let Deborah penetrate her with fingers, tongue, or sex toy ("That's so patriarchal.") had let Allen Plotnick pulverize her pussy with his penis. And chances were high that Emily was preggo, because Deborah's ex didn't even know Allen for three months before a big old *schlocky*-looking diamond ring appeared on her finger. She and Deborah, on the other hand, had gone out for over two years. "Two years I wasted on that *hasbian*," Deborah told the Xena poster on the wall. "And she wouldn't even move in with me." Deborah had begged Emily to give up her tiny dorm room and move into her two-bedroom apartment, but Emily wouldn't budge, afraid her parents would find out. "You know what Daddy says," Emily told Deborah. "No permission, no tuition." And she had giggled, even though Deborah didn't find it the least bit funny.

The closest Emily had come to making a commitment was

buying Deborah the vacuum cleaner. "If we're still together when I graduate, I'll move in," she'd said. "Meanwhile, you'll have Esther to keep you company." Yes, Emily had named the vacuum cleaner Esther and bought Deborah one of those stupid coverings to go over the vacuum that made it look like a three-foot doll standing in the corner. Deborah thought it was the ugliest thing she had ever seen. It had a mop of orange yarn hair tied in two pigtails, buttons for eyes, a red stitched smile, and a blue gingham dress. Of course, Emily had doctored Esther up a little by draping a T-shirt over her that said I'D RATHER BE MUFF DIVING and hanging a three-inch labyris around her neck, the same labyris Emily had worn, once upon a time when she was busy smashing the patriarchy instead of fucking it. Deborah stared at Esther ruefully, wondering what Gretchen the Sears lady would think about that.

Deborah put half an English muffin in the toaster oven and sighed. She knew it was going to be a bad day: She hadn't even been awake an hour and already she had spent way too much time thinking about Emily. But Deborah didn't know just how bad the day was going to be until the phone rang again and she picked it up.

"Hi, Debbie."

There were only a handful of people on the planet who still insisted on calling her that, none of whom she wanted to speak to at the moment.

"Hi, Ma. How are you?"

"Fine, fine. Listen, Debbie, I need to know if you're coming for Thanksgiving or not."

Oh, God, Thanksgiving. Deborah had forgotten all about it.

"Can I let you know next week?"

"No, I need to know now so I can plan."

"What's there to plan?" Deborah was stalling for time. "It's not like I eat a lot, and I can bring my own folding chair."

"Debbie." Deborah could practically hear her mother frown. "Do you have other plans?"

"No, but…"

"Great, we'll see you around four o'clock. Come earlier if you want, and be careful how you drive. There'll be lots of traffic."

"I know how to drive, Ma." Deborah tried to remind her mother that, believe it or not, she actually was an adult, as opposed to a four-year-old who had somehow managed to get her driver's license. But Mrs. Lewis had already hung up.

"Oh, great." Deborah heard the bell on the toaster oven ring, but she had completely lost her appetite. "I don't want to go home for the holidays, Lucy." Again Deborah addressed the poster on the wall. Deborah had been doing a lot of mother work in therapy lately, and when her therapist asked her who her ideal mother would be, she hadn't hesitated. "Lucy Lawless."

"As Xena or herself?" her therapist had asked.

"Both," Deborah answered. And after the session she ran out and bought herself the poster, which she talked to more frequently than she thought healthy, but what the hell. "So, what do you think, Xena? Should I go home for the holidays or what?"

Xena of course didn't reply, but Deborah remembered what Emily had to say when she asked her the same question last spring after Mrs. Lewis invited Deborah home for Passover. Emily stood up from the table, her mouth full of

French toast, and put her hands on the back of Deborah's shoulders. "March," she said, steering her across the apartment.

"What do you see in here?" she asked, making Deborah halt in the bedroom.

Deborah looked around. "My bed, my dresser, a picture of you and me at Gay Pride, my laundry basket…"

"And what do you see in here?" Emily turned Deborah around so she was facing the living room.

"My TV, my couch, your leather jacket, your Birkenstocks, your book bag…"

"And what about in here?" Emily dragged Deborah back into the kitchen. "The point is," Emily said, after they had toured the entire apartment. *"This* is your home. I just can't stand it when dykes start in with this 'home for the holidays' crap, like the homes we've created for ourselves don't really count. Now, if you want to talk about going to your *parents' house* for the holidays, I'd be happy to discuss it with you."

"What about going homo for the holidays?" Deborah suggested.

"Don't we go homo every day?" Emily asked, then answered her own question by giving Deborah a kiss that tasted like maple syrup and lasted the rest of the afternoon.

They had gone to Deborah's parents' house for Passover, and it was quite the experience. Deborah's brother, David, had been there with his wife and two children. He had also brought along their nanny, and Deborah could tell her parents were proud of themselves for being liberal enough to actually allow a person of color to sit beside them in their own dining room. Deborah's father had made a great showing of introducing her to everybody: "This is Vonda," he said, putting his hand on her shoulder and leading her around. During the *seder,* he had addressed all his explanations to her. "We call this *matzo,* Vonda," he said, breaking a piece in two and offering her the bigger half. "When we had to flee the evil Pharaoh in Egypt, there wasn't time to wait for the bread to rise." Mr. Lewis spoke as if he had actually been there himself. "So, we baked the dough—"

"Daniel." Vonda spoke sharply. "Leave your brother alone."

"He started it." The two little boys were wrestling over a Game Boy that wasn't supposed to be at the table.

"Michael, give me that." Vonda held out her hand, and Michael pushed his chair back. But before he could climb down from it, Daniel shoved him, and he lost his balance, hitting his head on a corner of the table.

"Ow! Ow!" Michael wailed into Vonda's arms.

"It's OK, Michael," David soothed him from across the table. "You're OK. Nothing happened, big boy. You're fine. That didn't hurt."

"Sure," Deborah whispered to Emily. "Tell the kid how he feels. Deny his reality. Teach him big boys don't cry. Way to go, brother."

When everything had calmed down, they continued the *seder,* reading responsively from the ancient Maxwell House *Haggadah* Deborah's father still insisted upon using. Deborah wasn't sure whether she believed in God, but if She did exist, She sure had an ironic sense of humor, because who got to read aloud the part about slavery? Why, Vonda, of course.

"Once we were slaves," Vonda looked around the room fixing each family member with her eyes, "but now we are free."

Deborah didn't dare look at Emily, who was kicking her under the table, afraid she would burst out laughing, which would not have gone over well at all. Since Emily was sitting next to Vonda, she read next, and when she changed the word *forefathers* to *ancestors,* all hell broke loose.

No wonder Deborah's mother hadn't asked if Emily was coming to this year's *seder,* even though Deborah had yet to tell her Emily was no longer part of her life. Oh, Mrs. Lewis would have tried to sound sympathetic upon hearing the news all right. Deborah could just hear her mother say, "Oh, honey, I'm so sorry," in a tone of voice that made it clear she wasn't sorry at all. Then she'd add something philosophical like, "Don't worry, Debbie. There are plenty of fish in the sea." And again, without saying a word, Deborah would know her mother meant she hoped Deborah would try some fish of the male persuasion. Going home alone while being homo alone was not a great idea, but what could Deborah do, dial Rent-a-Dyke? *Maybe I'll fall in love between now and November 24th,* Deborah thought, finally retrieving her ice-cold breakfast from the toaster oven. *Yeah, right. And maybe Esther the vacuum cleaner will get up and dance.*

Thanksgiving Day was bright and sunny, one of those cold, crisp, snappy days that makes you glad to be alive. Deborah—who had been hoping for a tornado, hurricane, freak snowstorm, or any kind of disaster that would make driving impossible—was out of luck. She alternated blasting the Spice Girls with the Rude Girls on her tape deck as she drove two

hours east to the Boston suburb her parents called home.
C'mon now, she said to herself as she turned the corner of her
old block. *It won't be so bad. They're your parents. They love
you. It might even be kind of fun.* "Oh, sure, easy for you to
say," Deborah had barked at her therapist who uttered those
same words to her a few weeks ago. Her therapist had tried to
get her to think positively, but she had reminded the woman
that her name was Deborah, not Pollyanna. Then her therapist changed tactics and asked her what she could bring along
with her so she would be able to hold onto herself and not
feel so invisible out there all alone in Heterosexual Land. Did
she have a something special she could keep in her pocket
like a crystal, a gem stone, a rock?

"How about my Xena poster?" Deborah mused aloud.
"With a six-foot Amazon plastered on my mother's kitchen
wall, I'd feel a hundred times better." Her therapist hadn't
said anything, but, bless her heart, she had found Deborah a
miniature chakram, the embroidery hoop-shaped weapon
Xena used to fight the enemy wherever she encountered it.
Deborah had been very moved by this present and attached it
to her key ring, which she now attached to her belt loop as
she got out of the car.

"Well, here goes nothing." Deborah started up the driveway, but before she could take a deep breath to steady herself, the front door flew open.

"Debbie's here," her mother called into the bowels of the
house. "Come in, sweetheart, I was getting worried about you.
I bet there was lots of traffic."

"Ma, it's only ten after four."

"Maybe you should stay over, Debbie. Why should you

drive home in the dark? Give me your coat. What did you do to your hair? I thought you said you were growing it out. You came by yourself this year?" Mrs. Lewis wasn't even remotely successful at hiding the delight in her voice. "Everyone, Debbie's here," she announced again as her daughter unsnapped her leather jacket.

Deborah drifted into the kitchen behind her mother, ambivalent as always about the strict gender division of the party: girls in the kitchen preparing the food, boys in the living room watching the game. On one hand, she could almost get into bonding with the female contingent of her family; on the other hand, she hated that the women had no qualms about serving their menfolk hand and foot. In fact, right on cue, Mrs. Lewis handed Deborah a tray of Ritz crackers covered with Velveeta cheese. "Why don't you take these inside, dear, and say hello to your father?"

"Debbie!" Mr. Lewis half rose out of his chair to greet his daughter but then got distracted by some movement on the wide-screen TV. "C'mon you idiot, run with the ball. Run! Ach, bunch of losers." He took the tray from Deborah and set it down on the coffee table. "How are you, sweetheart? Wait a minute, he dropped the ball? He *dropped* it?" Deborah's father dropped himself back down into his seat, shaking his head in disbelief.

"I'm fine, Dad," Deborah answered her father, even though she knew he couldn't hear her. No one in the room acknowledged her presence—not her brother David, not her nephews Michael and Daniel, not her uncle Marvin, and not her cousin Peter. Deborah went back into the kitchen because she didn't know what else to do. Her mother handed her a potato peeler and a bag of lettuce to wash.

"Debbie will make the salad. She always makes such good salads. She has a knack for it." Mrs. Lewis started emptying the contents of the refrigerator's vegetable bin onto the kitchen counter. "Aren't these tomatoes gorgeous? And look at the size of this green pepper—isn't that something? Don't forget to peel the cucumbers, Debbie. You know your father hates the rind."

"How are you, darling?" Deborah's Aunt Rona looked up from the Stove Top stuffing mix she was pouring into a microwaveable casserole dish. "What are you doing with yourself these days?"

"Well, I just started a new project at work that's really interesting. I'm in charge of—"

"Oh, my God, the rolls!" Aunt Rona grabbed a pair of pot holders and yanked open the oven door. A dark cloud of smoke billowed out. "Quick, quick, get me something to put these on. And somebody open the door before the smoke alarm goes off."

"I'll do it." Sharon, Deborah's sister-in-law, opened the back door and started fanning the smoke in her direction.

"Where's Vonda?" Deborah asked her, instead of saying hello.

"Vonda? Oh, we got rid of her months ago. I never liked that girl's attitude. We've had the worst luck finding someone who isn't afraid of a little hard work. Can you believe we've been through three or four since the summer and a new one starts Monday? I hope to God she works out. I can't take this anymore. Can I close the door yet?" Sharon yelled into the room.

"Close it, close it. I'm freezing already." Deborah's mother spooned some lumpy gravy over the turkey, which was sitting in a bathtub-size aluminum foil roasting pan on top of the stove. "Debbie, I'll finish the salad. Why don't you go inside and set the table? Everything's over there." She pointed with her chin just in case Deborah happened to miss the piles of plates, cups, saucers, and salad bowls stacked two feet high on the kitchen table. Deborah grabbed some dishes, glad for the chance to escape into the dining room and have a minute or two alone. But to her amazement when she stepped into the dining room, she found she wasn't alone at all.

"Aunt Sadie?" Deborah gasped. She dropped the plates on the table and went over to a woman sitting by the window in a wheelchair. "Aunt Sadie, how are you?" Deborah knelt down and stared into her great-aunt's eyes, which were as empty as the brand new gravy boat Sharon had just placed on the dining-room table. Deborah stayed where she was for a minute before she straightened up and went back into the kitchen. "Ma," she tried to keep her voice steady. "Why is Aunt Sadie sitting in the dining room all by herself?"

"Why? You want to know why?" Mrs. Lewis sighed. "The nursing home called and begged me to take her, so what could I do? She was the only one on her floor who had no place to go, and the nurses there, they deserve a day off once in a while. They have families too."

"Why is she sitting all by herself in the dining room?" Deborah repeated her question, then moved out of the way so Aunt Rona could get a stick of butter out of the refrigerator. "Why don't you bring her in here with us?"

"Debbie, it's too crowded in here. She'd only be in the way. We're tripping over each other as it is. Besides, she likes sitting by the window. She always has, ever since I was a little girl."

"But Ma—"

"Debbie, please, we'll all be in there before you know it, as soon as the game is over." Mrs. Lewis looked toward the living room, and as if on cue, a rousing cheer erupted from that direction. "Sharon, honey, can you taste this and tell me if it needs more salt?"

Deborah knew she had been dismissed, so she returned to the dining room, but instead of setting the table, she knelt down in front of her great-aunt Sadie again and took her hand.

"I'm really, really happy to see you, Aunt Sadie. I'm sorry it's been such a long time." How long had it been? Deborah couldn't remember the last time she had visited the nursing home. *Oh, great,* she thought. *Not only am I lousy daughter, I'm a lousy great-niece too.* "I had no idea your health had gotten so bad," she said in a shaky voice. Out of nowhere tears filled her eyes. "You must be really lonely. Does my mother or Aunt Rona ever come visit you?" Aunt Sadie continued to stare out the window with dull, lifeless eyes.

"Listen, Aunt Sadie, everyone's going to be in here soon, and it's going to be a total zoo. So do you mind if I just sit a minute with you?" Deborah straightened up and pulled a dining room chair next to her great-aunt. They sat in silence for a few minutes, and Deborah felt a tentative peacefulness, tinged with unbearable sadness. "You know, we never really got a chance to know each other," Deborah said to her great aunt. "I wish you could tell me what your childhood was like, what my grandparents were like, what my mother and Aunt

Rona were like when they were little girls." Aunt Sadie didn't move or even blink. "Well, I can tell you about me, Aunt Sadie, even if you can't tell me about you. OK?" Since Aunt Sadie didn't nod, Deborah nodded for her and began.

"First of all," Deborah gripped the chakran hanging from her belt loop and took the plunge. "First of all, I'm a lesbian, Aunt Sadie. Did anyone ever tell you that? Your very own great-niece is a big old boot-stomping, lavender-wearing, rainbow flag-carrying diesel dyke." Just saying the words out loud in her parents' house was terrifying, yet having said them, Deborah found herself sitting up straighter in her chair. "See these hands, Aunt Sadie?" She lifted her palms and flexed her fingers. "These hands have given *mucho* pleasure to a lot of women. Don't be shocked. I don't mean hundreds or anything. Let's just say more than a few." She lowered her hands and placed them on Aunt Sadie's arm. Her great-aunt didn't flinch or pull away. "I was really in love with this one woman, Aunt Sadie. Her name is Emily. I'm sorry you never got to meet her. We're not together anymore. She's getting married, to a man, and I think she's even having a baby. Can you believe it? I can't believe it. I really, really miss her." The tears that had been simmering in Deborah's eyes spilled onto her cheeks. She brushed them away with the side of her hand, sighed, and sat back in her chair.

"Debbie, is the table done? We're almost ready." Mrs. Lewis came into the dining room and started dispensing plates and glasses to each place setting. "Turn her around, would you?" She opened the top drawer of the sideboard with a yank and started counting out silverware. "You'll sit over there next to her, OK, Debbie? She needs help cutting her food."

"They lost, the bums." Mr. Lewis came into the dining room the minute the table was set. "Need any help in here, Harriet?"

"Your father." Deborah's mother shook her head, smiling. "His timing has always been perfect."

"Like everything else about me, right baby?" He put his arm around his wife's ample waist. "When do we eat?"

Soon they were all sitting around the table: David and Sharon at one end with Michael and Daniel between them; cousin Peter across from David, flanked by his parents, Aunt Rona and Uncle Marvin; Deborah with Aunt Sadie on one side of her father; Deborah's mother across from her; and of course the head of the table was claimed by Mr. Lewis, who stood over the turkey, a huge carving knife in his hand.

"All righty," Mr. Lewis sang out, lifting the knife like he was a conductor and it was a baton. "Who wants what?"

"I'll take a wing," David spoke first.

"Dark meat for me," said Peter.

"We want light meat, right, Debbie?" Mrs. Lewis winked at her daughter. "We don't want to lose our girlish figures."

"What about giving thanks?" Deborah tried to inject the original meaning of the feast into the holiday. "Shouldn't we say grace?"

"Oh, right, grace. Hey, Grace," Mr. Lewis called over his shoulder. "Let's eat."

Soon the conversation consisted entirely of "Please pass the this" and "I'd like some more of that," punctuated by the clanking of serving spoons against platters. "Everything is so delicious," Aunt Rona mumbled with her mouth full, "if I do say so myself."

"Michael, watch it," Sharon pointed to her son's soda glass. "Daniel, move that away from the edge of the table, please."

"I'll do it," Michael shouted, knocking the glass over in his enthusiasm.

"I didn't do it," Daniel announced, reaching over the spill for more mashed potatoes.

"Finish what's on your plate first. I told you he wasn't big enough for a glass," David scowled at Sharon. "Where's his plastic cup?"

"I am so big enough," Michael yelled.

"You are not." Daniel yelled back.

"Boys." Sharon got up from the table to get paper towels.

"Sit, sit. I'll take care of it." Mrs. Lewis sprang up, as did Aunt Rona. "Harriet," she said, "you sit. You've been working like a dog all day. Debbie, darling, get up and get your mother some paper towels. They're in the kitchen."

Why can't David go? Deborah wanted to whine. *It was his kid who spilled the soda, not mine.* But she knew if she said the words out loud, she'd sound as immature as Michael and Daniel, who were only three and four years old.

Soon everyone was stuffed, and a lull descended upon the room. The men sat back and loosened their belts while the women bustled about, clearing off the table: all the women except Aunt Sadie, who sat with a gob of yam on her chin, and Deborah, who refused to lift another finger until one of her male relatives got up to help.

"Who wants coffee?" Mrs. Lewis asked, her index finger poised to count.

"How about some pumpkin pie?" Aunt Rona placed a pie on the table and started cutting slices.

"Small ones for the boys," Sharon said, setting out a pitcher of milk and a box of Sweet 'n' Low.

"I want a big piece, Aunt Rona," Michael yelled.

"Me, too." Daniel chimed in. "Make mine bigger than Michael's."

"Boys." Deborah could see Sharon was ready to crack. "Let's take your pie inside. I'll put Raffi on the stereo for you."

"Yay!" Michael and Daniel raced out after their mother. Soon the sounds of "The Wheels on the Bus" and "Baa Baa Black Sheep" could be heard faintly over the rumbling dishwasher.

"Ah, peace and quiet," David sighed.

"They're such good boys," Mrs. Lewis said.

"Angels, absolute angels," Aunt Rona threw her own son a look. "What I wouldn't give to have two gorgeous grandsons like that." She cut a sliver of pie and popped it into her mouth. "If you eat it with your fingers, it doesn't count, right, Debbie?" Deborah didn't bother to reply.

Despite the coffee, everyone sank into the traditional post-turkey stupor. Even Deborah's mother and aunt let the dessert dishes linger on the table as the men talked about cars and computers and the women picked at the food. Sharon came back in and snuck a bite of pie from David's plate before sinking into her chair. No sooner had she sat down than the boys came tearing into the room again.

"Daddy, can I sit on your lap?" Michael started to climb up David's legs without waiting for an answer.

"No, I want to sit on your lap." Daniel tried to push him off.

"What happened to Raffi?" David asked. "Don't you want

to listen anymore?"

"We can hear it from here," Daniel said, as the dishwasher switched to a quieter cycle and the words to "Row Row Row Your Boat" filled the room.

Aunt Rona clapped her hands and started singing along. "C'mon boys. Row, row, row your boat…"

Deborah rolled her eyes, wondering if it was too early to excuse herself and head home. Just as she was about to rise, something off to the left caught her eye. It was Aunt Sadie, who had suddenly come to life, clapping her hands, bobbing her head, and bouncing her body to the music.

"Aunt Sadie?" Deborah was mesmerized, watching her great-aunt sway to the song. Her movements started out small but then grew larger and larger until she was half out of her chair.

"Aunt Sadie, calm down. What are you doing? You're going to hurt yourself." Mrs. Lewis was at Aunt Sadie's side in an instant, her hand steadying the back of her wheelchair. "Rona, give me a hand here. Is it time for her medicine? She's not supposed to get excited."

"You're the one who's getting excited, Ma," Deborah pointed out. "Leave Aunt Sadie alone. She's not hurting anybody. If she wants to dance, let her dance." Of course, no one listened to Deborah.

"Aunt Sadie, sit down." Rona joined Mrs. Lewis, and together they tried to subdue their aunt, but it was no use. Deborah could tell Aunt Sadie was very strong. Finally, they gave up, and then, as if it were all her idea, Deborah's mother gave a wave of her hand. "*Nu,* so dance, Aunt Sadie. C'mon, we'll all dance. What are you doing, the samba, the rumba, the lindy hop?" She tried to make a joke.

Aunt Sadie, who hadn't uttered a word in years, at least not that anyone present could remember, opened her mouth and spoke loud and clear. "I'm doing the lesbian, Harriet. You know the lesbian. Deborah taught me. Anyone can do it."

Deborah couldn't believe her ears. She didn't know which was more amusing, what Aunt Sadie had just said or the expression of sheer horror that had come over her mother's face. Time stood still as Deborah glanced about the room, noticing the same shocked look had etched itself onto the face of everyone else as well. Even Michael and Daniel, sensing something important was happening, kept absolutely still. In fact, everyone stayed frozen as they watched Aunt Sadie shaking her booty to the beat, a huge smile plastered across her face, as Raffi sang, "This old man, he played one, he played knick knack on my thumb...." Deborah didn't know whether to laugh or cry until Aunt Sadie raised both her arms and turned in Deborah's direction. Then Deborah knew there was absolutely nothing she could do. Nothing except scrape back her chair, stand up, go to her great-aunt, and dance.

Whatever Happened to Baby Fane?

Times are getting tough for a loud, proud, Jewish fag hag like *moi*. My friends are dropping like fruit flies, as Fane used to say. Yes, used to say, for my beloved Fane has left us all in the dust for that Great Back Room in the sky.

Fane. I first met him a year before his untimely demise at an open poetry reading held at Queers-R-Us, our local coffee shop/hangout/pick-up joint. Ours is a small community where everyone knows everyone (and more than likely has slept with everyone), so I noticed him right away. His hair fell to his shoulders in thick black ringlets not unlike my own (later we found out we'd both gone through a "Jew-fro" stage at the exact same time). He was wearing perfectly pressed black jeans (which he admitted, when asked, were dry-cleaned), cowboy boots, and a black T-shirt that said I SURVIVED THE BRONX. Being a born and bred Brooklyn girl who has never been short on *chutzpa*, I promptly introduced myself.

"I'm Missy," I said, extending my hand.

"Fane," he replied shaking it, which inspired me to slide the top of my jersey off my shoulder in a *Flashdance* sort of way and burst into song: "Fane! You're gonna live forever. You're gonna learn how to fly." Fane laughed, a deep, scratchy, throaty, big-enough-to-live-in laugh, and I was, as they say, smitten from day one.

"Sit, sit, *tateleh*. I'll buy you a *cawfee*," I said in my best Brooklynese, but Fane had other plans. One of the poets, a tall, dark handsome lad built like Michaelangelo's David, was the sole reason Fane had just sat through three hours of Allen Ginsberg wannabes, so if anyone was going to have the pleasure of his company for the rest of the evening, it certainly wasn't going to be me.

"I'll *cawl* you," Fane promised, matching my New Yawk accent vowel for vowel. He wrote my number on a napkin, stuffed it into his back pocket, and went off to pursue the stud of his dreams. I didn't really mind, though. I was sure Fane would call, and he did, the very next day. "I'll take that cup of coffee now," he said in a weary voice that let me know he'd been up the better part of the night and could really use it.

"C'mon over," I said, putting some water up to boil. Fane arrived in a T-shirt that said START YOUR DAY WITH ME and asked for a grand tour of the house. I showed him my meager digs: a small living room, kitchen, and tiny bedroom.

"Is this the closet?" he asked, opening the door without waiting for my reply. He took a step inside and started moving my clothes down their rack like a housewife at Macy's Close-Out, looking for the ultimate sale. "Nope, nope, uh-uh, no…" He moved my blouses, pants, and the occasional skirt aside until his eyes lit up. "Now, this is perfect," he said, lifting up a silver lamé minidress I bought on a whim and hardly ever wore.

"Wait, it has matching mules." I dug through my Imelda Marcos—size shoe collection until I found the three-inch heels.

"Excellent." Fane oohed and aahed over the shoes, holding them up to the light for closer inspection. "Are they comfortable?"

"I've never worn them," I paused dramatically, "standing up anyway."

Fane took a step back as his hand flew up to his heart. "My dear," he said in a false British accent, "you absolutely shock me."

I rolled my eyes. "Oh, c'mon, Fane. You know how those butches are."

"I know no such thing. Anyway, I didn't peg you for such a femme."

"I didn't say I was a femme."

Fane studied me. "Well, you're certainly not what I'd call a butch."

"I'm what's known as a hard-top convertible," I said, which made Fane laugh out loud. He balanced one silver shoe on the flat of his hand and asked, "Can you walk in these?"

"Sure, why? You want to borrow them?"

Again Fane feigned shock. "*I* don't want to wear them, Missy. I want *you* to wear them"—this time Fane paused dramatically—"to my funeral." And that's how I found out Fane had AIDS. He had left New York City for our small seaside town because he was looking for a quiet place to live. And a quiet place to die.

Fane and I became fast friends or—you should pardon the expression—buddies. It was one of those friendships where you meet someone and immediately feel you've known them forever. Or maybe our friendship fast-forwarded so quickly and deeply because Fane knew he didn't have a lot of time left (hence his favorite T-shirt, I'M LOOKING FOR MR. RIGHT AWAY). In any event, Fane and I started hanging out on a daily basis. I had recently joined the ranks of the gainfully unemployed, and Fane had taken early retirement. So what do two queers do with so much time on their hands? They rent movies, of course. Fane and I were both total film buffs. In fact, when asked, I told people I was using my unemployment to write a screenplay, thus our daily screenings could be written off as research.

Perhaps Fane and I bonded so well because we had each spent most of our respective childhoods in darkened movie theaters eating stale popcorn and lusting after the stars we saw in front of us on the silver screen. We both agreed *Dr. Zhivago* was our all-time favorite movie. Fane had a major crush on Omar Sharif, while I had it bad for Julie Christie. We'd both had our first sexual encounters while watching a movie: Fane had gotten beat off by someone his father's age while watching *The Man Who Knew Too Much*, and I, believe it or not, had actually fallen for the popcorn trick while watching *Love Story*. For those of you who don't know about the popcorn trick (Fane didn't), it's when a guy cuts a hole in the bottom of his popcorn bucket and sticks his penis inside. Then when his date reaches in for a handful of corn, she comes up instead with a handful of dick.

"I'll have to try it sometime," Fane said after I explained it to him.

"Just don't try it with me," I said, like Fane ever would. We were sitting on his leather couch as we did every morning, having already downed an entire pot of coffee Fane had brewed with cinnamon sprinkled over the grounds. Today's film was *Hush...Hush, Sweet Charlotte*. Fane opened the bag of chocolates that lay between us—and was usually devoured before the opening credits stopped rolling—and started happily munching away. Fane made no apologies for his bad habits: He smoked like a chimney, ate chocolate by the pound ("I like it like I like my men: dark, hard, and bittersweet"), and drank Jack Daniels with dinner every night, not enough to get drunk, just enough to take the edge off and help him fall asleep.

After the movie, we took our usual walk into town for a leisurely lunch and stroll by the water. Fane led the way to the breakwater and climbed carefully over the rocks. "Have I told you this is where I want my ashes scattered?" he asked, one hand held up to shield his eyes from the sun glinting off the sea.

"Only a million times, Fane."

"And have I told you I want you to sing 'Where Have All the Faggots Gone?' at my memorial?"

"Yes, dear."

"And have I told you—"

"What a control queen I am?" I cut in to finish his sentence.

"And damn proud of it." Fane chuckled until his laugh turned into a cough, which turned into a wheeze, which turned into a gasp, which finally, after a scary moment, turned into steady, shallow breathing once again. After Fane caught his breath, we slowly made our way back to his place so he could nap and I could read a book or just watch him sleep. I loved being in Fane's house; he was an art collector, and the walls of his apartment were covered with paintings and drawings, all beautifully framed. My favorite piece of his didn't hang on the wall, though. It sat on Fane's mantle: a shiny green, ceramic high-heeled shoe that had once belonged to his grandmother and was now used as a candy dish. "It's so I always remember the little Jewish princess inside me," Fane said, waiting to see if I'd take offense.

"It takes one to know one," was my politically incorrect reply.

I asked Fane about his grandmother, and he told me she was the only one in his family who had truly loved him, but she was long gone, as was his mother, both victims of breast cancer. And his father? "The old geezer isn't exactly proud of his *faygeleh* son," Fane said, lighting up a cigarette. "I haven't even seen him since my mother's funeral, and that was more than 15 years ago. My father's new wife, the Wicked Bitch of the Bronx," Fane exhaled with a vengeance, "is much younger than my old man, and she doesn't want her two sons to know about their fairy stepbrother. And my father, the world's most hen-pecked husband, can't stand up to her. Ach, the hell with them. It's their loss, right?" Fane stabbed his cigarette out in a Mr. Peanut ashtray, even though he hadn't even smoked half of it.

Clearly, Fane was done with the conversation, but I wasn't. "Does your father know you're sick?"

"He doesn't even know I'm alive." Fane snorted, and then started choking on some phlegm. I didn't want to upset him further, so I dropped the subject and didn't bring it up again.

Besides being tired and having that awful cough, for a long time Fane showed no overt signs of having AIDS. We didn't talk about his illness much, but it was always with us. I remember one day in particular when we were having Sunday brunch with a trick of his named James and a friend of mine named Hal. James was all stuffed up with allergies, Hal had a splitting headache, and I was doubled over with menstrual cramps.

"And how are you?" someone finally thought to ask Fane.

He waved his hand as if to brush away the question. "Besides having a fatal disease," he shrugged, "I'm fine."

"AIDS is not a fatal disease," James reminded Fane between sneezes.

"Tell it to my T cells," Fane said. "All three of them."

"What about the new cocktails?" Hal asked.

"Cocktails, *shmocktails*. I tried them, remember?" We all did remember, because it would be hard to forget how sick Fane had gotten on the new drugs, which seemed to work for almost every other person on the planet. Practically every day as we sauntered through town, Fane and I would see someone who had been at death's door the month, the week, the day before, and now not only were they fine, they looked better than they had even before they'd gotten sick. Fane, on the other hand, was the exception who proved the rule. He had been much, much sicker on the drugs than off them, with stomachaches, cramps, and worst of all, nonstop diarrhea. His doctors made him try several different combinations, but nothing worked except going off meds completely. As soon as the drugs were out of Fane's system, he felt 100 percent better— but only for a little while. Then his downhill slide began.

A few months before he died, Fane started giving away his clothes. Always on the thin side, he now made Kate Moss look fat as Divine. "Here, take this." He handed me a gorgeous cashmere cardigan the color of cranberry juice right after we'd finished watching Susan Hayward in (and I kid you not) *I Want to Live!*

"Too big?" I asked, holding the sweater up to my shoulders.

"No," Fane answered. "It clashes with my lesions."

And so it began. First Fane went blind (very *Wait Until Dark*), and then he went bald (very *King and I*). Despite all the outward signs, I was taking a Scarlett O'Hara approach to the whole thing. "I'll think about it tomorrow," I told my reflection in the bathroom mirror every morning before I went off to Fane's. I was still holding onto my denial, even when Fane's ex-lover Rudy moved from New Jersey to live with him so he wouldn't have to go to a hospice. I was hurt that Fane hadn't asked me to be his roommate, and when I told him so, he just smiled and started singing that old Dinah Shore hit, "It's So Nice to Have a Man Around the House."

"But Fane," I broke in mid chorus, "I'm unemployed. How can Rudy take that much time off work?"

Fane's reply shocked me. "Missy, dear," he said, "It's not going to be that much time."

Still, I ignored the writing on the wall and held my chins and my hopes up, but both were dashed one afternoon when out of the blue, Fane uttered three little words: "Call my father."

"Your father?" I couldn't have been more surprised if Fane had asked me to call the man on the moon.

"I want to see him—well, not *see* him," he said, reminding us both he was blind. "It would be nice if he came before I died."

"OK." I picked up the receiver and dialed. Fane immediately closed his eyes and fell asleep, or pretended to. Either way, I was on my own.

"Mr. Oppenheimer?" I asked, even though I knew it was Fane's father. It had to be; his voice sounded just like his son's. "I'm a friend of Fane's, and I'm calling because..."

"Who is it, Harold?" I could hear Mr. Oppenheimer's wife yelling in the background. "Just hang up if it's a solicitor. Don't tell them anything."

"Who is this?" Fane's father asked.

"My name is Missy, and Fane asked me to call you because he's sick."

"How sick?" Mr. Oppenheimer's voice dropped to a whisper, like a kid who didn't want his mother to know he was on the phone.

"Sick enough for him to ask me to call you," I said, not knowing any other way to make my point. "He'd like you to come."

"When?"

"As soon as you can."

"I'm really busy at the office right now," Mr. Oppenheimer said a little too quickly. "Maybe I'll make it out there in a few weeks."

"He may not have a few weeks," I said, choking on the words I had resisted saying for so long. "Look, here's the number: 555-0542. Why don't you call when you can fit your only offspring into your busy schedule?" Without waiting for an answer, I hung up.

Fane immediately opened his eyes. "Is he coming?"

I relayed our conversation.

"Pussy-whipped prick," he muttered before closing his eyes again.

Mr. Oppenheimer didn't call back that week, and I was afraid we were running out of time. Everyone else came to visit: Fane's friends from New York, the dean of the college where he had taught, even his ex-wife, Prudence. Rudy and I didn't let anyone stay too long, as even a half-hour visit tired Fane out. Ever the gracious host, he would never admit his guests were a drain. He just held court from the hospital bed we had dragged into the living room, barking orders to whomever was closest at hand. "Get Martin a pillow for his chair; he has a bad back. Bring Bethany a Pepsi; she likes it straight up, no ice." Fane needed to show all of us he was still in command, and I, for one, needed to believe it was so, for as long as I possibly could.

Fane was getting weaker by the day, so I called his father again. "Look, he's your son," I said to Mr. Oppenheimer, as if I were telling him something he didn't already know. "Can't you honor your own son's dying wish by coming to see him?" I even played the Jewish trump card: guilt. "Mr. Oppenheimer," I said, "how are you going to feel if you never see Fane again? Are you really going to be able to live with that?"

"He's the one who should have thought of that a long time ago," Fane's father said, "before he started living a ho-mo-sex-u-al lifestyle." Mr. Oppenheimer stretched out the word to make sure I knew what it meant. "This is all Fane's fault. He made his bed, and now he's lying in it."

No, Daddy dearest, I wanted to say. *I made his bed, and now he's dying in it.* But I doubted Mr. Oppenheimer would appreciate gallows humor at this point, so I just hung up and went in to tell Fane what had happened. But when I saw, despite everything, the look of hope on his face, I just couldn't do it. "I got a busy signal," I lied, not having the heart or perhaps the guts to tell Fane what his father had said. "I'll try again later," I added, but I doubt Fane believed my ruse.

It didn't much matter anyway, because the next day Fane took a turn for the worse, and the end really began. First he stopped eating, except for the bits of chocolate I'd hold up to his mouth for him to lick like a lollipop. Then he stopped smoking, which was really distressing to me. Fane and I had fought bitterly about his cigarettes. I never let him smoke in my house, so even when he was well enough to go out, he hardly ever came over. When he first became bedridden, I had to hide his matches so he wouldn't fall asleep with a lit cigarette and burn down the house. Now he was too weak to smoke, yet his lips pursed and his cheeks sucked in as if he were inhaling, even in his sleep. And half the time it was hard to tell whether Fane was asleep or awake because mostly what he did was lie motionless in bed with his eyes closed. Once, when I was sitting by his side, he asked me if I was waiting for the D train, and I knew he wasn't asleep or awake. He was in another world, waiting for the subway in the Bronx. I tried not to show him how panicked I was. "Fane," I said calmly, "you're not in New York. You're on the Cape in your apartment." But he didn't believe me, and besides, I realized that wherever he thought he was had to be a whole lot better than where he actually was, so I joined him there. "God, Fane," I said, "do you think this train will ever come?"

"Whenever it'll come, it'll come. I'm not in such a big hurry to get where I'm going," was his somber, startling reply.

Sometimes, just for old times' sake, I'd put a movie into the VCR so Fane could at least listen to the sound track, but he wasn't really interested anymore. Nor was he much for conversation, so mostly I just sat with him and massaged his dry skin with almond-scented moisture cream. "You have such soft hands," I said to Fane after rubbing them awhile.

"You have such a soft heart," he replied. It was the last thing he ever said to me, because the next morning he lost the ability to speak.

Rudy and I became very protective of Fane after that. We decided his days of entertaining were over. People still dropped by constantly, bringing bags of food Fane could no longer eat, and though they would never admit it, some of Fane's friends seemed relieved when I told them he no longer had the strength for company. They stayed around anyway, and soon Fane's kitchen became the hottest hangout in town.

"Did Fane ever tell you about the time he baked a batch of pot brownies for the faculty Christmas party?" one of his colleagues asked the crowd sitting around Fane's kitchen table.

"I think that was the year he dressed up as a nun," a former boyfriend added.

"What was his name, Our Mother of the Perpetual Hard-on?" a recent trick asked.

"He was always the life of the party," another colleague remarked.

"Was?" I hissed through clenched teeth. "*Was*? He isn't dead yet, you know."

"Sheesh, what's with her?" Everybody looked at me as if I had gone mad, which I had.

"I think all of you better clear out," I said, and I sure didn't have to ask them twice. And if they thought I was nothing but a big party pooper, who cared? I just couldn't stand sitting around Fane's kitchen table, telling stories about him and laughing, when he lay upstairs in the living room dying, so near and yet so very far.

The last night of Fane's life, Rudy and I were downstairs in the kitchen eating a late supper of cold Kentucky Fried Chicken someone had dropped off earlier. It was a crisp August night, with just the right amount of chill in the air, and the sky was covered with stars.

"Listen to the wind." Rudy looked up from the drumstick he was gnawing on and cocked his head to the side. "It just came up out of nowhere. Weird. It sounds like a ghost."

"It's spooky," I agreed, mid chomp. Then we looked at each other in horror, realizing at the same time it wasn't the wind at all. It was Fane. We dashed up to the living room, and there was Fane, sitting up in bed for the first time in over a month. His eyes were wide with terror, and sounds were coming out of his mouth I had never heard from a human being before.

"Fane, it's Rudy. I'm here, baby. Lie down." Rudy tried to lower Fane back onto the bed, but he was too agitated to relax.

"I'll call the nurse." I ran for the phone and speed-dialed hospice. After I explained to the nurse what was going on, she explained to me what was going on. "Fane's body and spirit are battling it out now," she said in a voice filled with kindness. "There's nothing you can do but witness his struggle."

"Isn't there anything to make him more comfortable?" I asked.

"You have morphine there, right? Give him eight drops under the tongue now and eight more in half an hour. That should calm him down."

I told Rudy what to do, and together we got the drugs into Fane, but they didn't do any good. He continued to moan and groan and pant and sweat like he was about to give birth or come or both. *Well, what did you expect?* I asked myself as I ran to get a cold washcloth to soothe his sweaty head. *Did you really think Fane would look at you, take one last breath, and fade away like Margaret O'Brien playing Beth in* Little Women? Fane was not ready to die and did not want to die. And though we didn't want him to go either, we made ourselves tell him it was time to let go.

"C'mon, Fane," Rudy said. "You don't have to put up a fight anymore. We know how brave you are. You can go."

"It's OK, Fane." I tried to sound like I believed it. "We'll be all right without you. Just relax and give in to it. Let go."

"No!" Fane roared once between gasps for breath. Rudy and I could barely look at each other; we were so ashamed of betraying Fane like that. But what else could we do? Nothing except wait for Rudy's watch to beep, telling us it was time to give Fane morphine again. I filled the eyedropper, and Rudy brought it up to Fane's mouth. Another 15 minutes went by before Fane's breathing slowed and he lay back down. I thought he had stopped breathing altogether, but after about half a minute, he drew in another raspy breath: the death rattle. Rudy and I kept talking to Fane, since we had both been told that hearing was the last sense to go. Another 20 minutes went by, and then Fane took in one final breath, exhaled noisily through his open mouth, and was still.

"He's gone," Rudy said. "Bye, Fane."

"Bye, Fane," I echoed, and then out of nowhere I began to chant ancient Hebrew words I thought I had forgotten long ago. *"Sh'ma Yisroel, Adonoy Elohanu, Adonoy Echad."* Rudy looked at me surprised. We both knew Fane hadn't set foot inside a synagogue in more than 30 years, since his *bar mitzvah.* I shrugged. "Just in case," I said. "And besides, it couldn't hurt."

The next day there was lots to do. We dressed Fane in his NOBODY KNOWS I'M A FAIRY T-shirt so the undertaker could take him away. We filled out endless forms, got rid of tons of meds, and called hundreds of people, including Fane's father. "Don't you think he'd want to know?" I asked Rudy.

"Whatever," he said with a shrug. And I suppose he was right. Fane's father didn't want to know from his son when he was alive; why should he care he was dead? But I knew Fane would want me to make the call, so I picked up the phone. This time a female voice answered.

"Is Mr. Oppenheimer there?" I asked.

"Who's calling please?"

"It's Missy. I'm a friend of Fane's."

"Yes?"

"He's dead."

"Oh, my God! Harold, Harold!" Fane's stepmother was immediately hysterical. "Harold, come to the phone right now. Harold!"

"What's the matter, Phyllis?" I heard Mr. Oppenheimer say as he picked up the phone. "Who is this?"

"It's Missy. Fane's dead." I have to admit, I did get a little perverse sense of satisfaction at being the one to deliver the news.

"Fane? *Vey iss mir, Gottenyu,* my boy. My son."

Sure, I thought. Now that Fane's dead, Mr. Oppenheimer could once more claim him as his own. "When did he die? Last night? Why did you wait so long to call us? Why didn't you tell me he was so sick?"

Take three guesses, I wanted to say, but even I could not be that cruel. "It happened very fast," I said, even though last night had been the longest 12 hours of my life. "I'll let you know about the funeral."

We didn't really have a funeral for Fane. Rudy waited around until his ashes arrived, and then we walked out to the breakwater and scattered them over the sea. Two weeks later we did have a memorial, and as Fane had hoped, it was *the* social event of the season. The place was packed to the gills with boys: boys in dog collars and leather chaps; boys in tight muscle T-shirts with tattoos strewn across their forearms; boys in faded jeans and baseball caps, dark sunglasses hiding their red-rimmed eyes. It was Fag Hag Heaven, and I played it to the hilt in my silver lamé.

"Did Fane pick out your outfit?" more than one boy asked.

"But of course." I pivoted on my stilettos and walked away so they could admire the way the shoes hit my heels with sensational slaps. The overall mood was strangely festive, like it was all one big party, which it would have been if the guest of honor had graced us with his presence. But he did not, despite his ex-wife's insistence that she could feel his spirit hovering by her side.

When everyone was done *shmoozing* and cruising, the formalities began. Rudy, back from New Jersey for the occasion, played master of ceremonies. He started things off by reading us a letter he had written to Fane, telling him how much he loved him, and by the time he was done there wasn't a dry eye in the house. Then James, who had shaved his head in mourning, took the stage and told us we must not remain silent; rather, it was our responsibility, whenever a gay man died, to make a really loud noise. Then he took a deep breath and let out a wail that made my blood run cold. Fane's ex-wife was next. Though they married as teenagers and were only together for a few years, she said Fane was the only man she had ever really loved.

"Oh, get a life," Rudy murmured. I poked him in the ribs and told him to be quiet. Then it was open season on Fane. His students told us what a wonderful teacher he had been, his colleagues told us what a wonderful scholar he had been, his boyfriends told us what a wonderful lover he had been. Then I stepped up to the podium.

"I have a letter to read," I unfolded a piece of paper, "from Fane's father." There was an audible, collective gasp from Fane's mourners, and then a loud shushing as everyone told everyone else to keep still.

"Dear Missy," I began. "Thank you for telling me about Fane's death and for inviting me to his memorial. Fane and I did not have an easy relationship as you know. We disagreed about many, many things. Still, he was my son, and I did love him in my own way. I am not a bad man, despite what you may think. Perhaps, if anything, I was a bad father. In any event, I want to thank you and all the people who took care of Fane for me. I'm sure it wasn't easy. Fane was not an easy person. But I'm grateful he did not die alone. Sincerely, Mr. Harold E. Oppenheimer (Fane's father)."

"Heavy," someone muttered from the front row.

"What an asshole," someone else mumbled. Then everyone was talking at once, and Rudy had to scream into the microphone that we were serving light refreshments back at Fane's apartment and everyone was invited.

It was strange being back at Fane's house; I hadn't been there since the day after he died. The hospital bed was gone, and Rudy had tagged all the artwork according to the will Fane had left behind. People tried not to seem too excited as they scanned Fane's paintings to see which ones they had inherited, but every once in a while I'd hear an enthusiastic "all right!" burst through the air. There was nothing on the wall with my name on it, but then I had a hunch, and sure enough, there on the mantle was the green ceramic shoe Fane's grandmother had given him that, according to the Post-It on its heel, now belonged to me. I took it home, filled it with candy, and placed it on my kitchen table. Every day I take a few minutes to look at it and remember the good news: Fane no longer has AIDS. And then I pop a piece of chocolate into my mouth: so dark, so hard, so bittersweet.

(for Victor Fane D'Lugin, 1945-1996)

Eggs McMenopause

Insomnia equals insanity. And, believe me, I should know. I haven't slept in two years. Two years. Ever since September 10, 1996, when my period stopped on a dime. Damn. Who knew I was out of eggs? Not me. It's not like I got any kind of warning or anything. One month there I was, bleeding away like a stuck pig, and the next month—bam!—dry as a bone.

So the question is, would I have done anything differently had I known? Thrown myself a party? Saved my last bit of menstrual blood in a jar like Paul Newman's spaghetti sauce? Found some guy to fuck at the Last Chance Motel so I could finally be a mother once and for all? Not that I ever wanted to be a mother, you understand. It's just that once I knew I couldn't be, all of a sudden that's exactly what I wanted to do. Grow big as a house. Give birth. Breast-feed. The whole nine yards. It was ridiculous. Sort of like pining away for a lover after you've broken up with her. You know how it is: You don't want to be with her anymore, *you're* the one who called it quits, you can't even stand the fucking sight of her, but as soon as she has her arm around somebody else's waist, you want her as much as you've ever wanted anyone your whole life. More. And if you make the mistake of telling her that, and if she makes the mistake of running back to you, then—poof!—your desire disappears as finally and completely as my last egg. That's human nature for ya. Go figure. We all want what we don't have until we get it, and then we don't want it anymore.

Like my period. God, when I was a teenager, I was dying to get my period. I was the last kid in my class to get it. All the other girls wore their sanitary napkins like badges. "I can't have gym today, Miss Allbright. I have *my friend,*" they'd say in a stage whisper loud enough for all the other girls to hear. They carried their bodies differently too. Like they had some holy wisdom between their legs that I was just dying to get my hands on. *Please,* I'd pray every night before bed. *Please, I'll do anything. Just let me get my period. Please.* I'd rush to the bathroom every morning, shut my eyes, and listen to the sweet music of my pee hitting the toilet water. Then I'd take a deep breath, wipe, and open my eyes. But every day that pink toilet paper came up with *nada.*

Then one morning I pulled down my pajamas, and before I even sat down on the pot, I saw they were stained with thick, brown blood. I was so surprised, I didn't even know what it was. I thought I was dying. I had no idea how I cut myself down there, since I didn't spend any time down there at all, much less with a sharp instrument. I told my mother, and she slapped me. Twice. Slap, slap, once on each cheek. It's a Jewish custom, though it's also a custom not to tell you it's a custom, so, of course, I thought I had just done one more thing to make my mother mad. After the slaps, she gave me a belt and a sanitary napkin and told me to be careful, I was a woman now, and I'd bleed once a month until I was at least 50, so I'd better watch myself, soon all the boys would be after me.

Well, she was partly right, my mother. I did bleed until I was 50, but the boys were never after me. The girls were after me, or to be more precise, I was after the girls. Girls with their periods, girls without their periods, tall girls, short girls, fat girls, thin girls, I didn't care. I wasn't fussy. I just wasn't happy unless I had some sweet, warm, female thing in my arms. Which I haven't, in case you're wondering, for a long, long time.

It's not that I'm a dog or anything, you understand. It's just that menopause, in case you haven't gone through it yet, doesn't make you feel like the most attractive woman in the world. First of all, you bloat. I looked in the mirror one day and thought, *Damn, who the hell snuck in here when I wasn't looking and injected helium under my skin?* I looked like a balloon from the goddamn Macy's Thanksgiving Day Parade. Second of all, you sweat. Night sweats, day sweats, morning, afternoon, evening sweats. God, I grew hotter than hell and didn't wear a winter coat for two whole years, and New York City in fucking February isn't exactly Miami in July. I couldn't bear the thought of anyone coming near me; in fact, I could hardly stand to be near myself. And on top of all this, I got pimples—pimples!—at my age. I looked like a walking, talking case of Acne Anonymous. And then of course I was so sleep deprived, I could have walked right past Miss America (who happens to be just my type), and I wouldn't have even noticed.

So one night when I couldn't sleep, I started doing the math. I got my period when I was 16, and it stopped when I was 50. That's 34 years, times 12 months a year, equals 408 periods. Four-hundred-and-eight eggs. Could make the world's biggest omelet. Or something.

Call me crazy, but I got obsessed with the number. Four-hundred-and-eight. They say your ovaries are the size of two tiny almonds, so how could they hold 204 eggs apiece? That's a lotta eggs. Being a visual gal, I wanted to see them. I wanted to feel them. So I bought them. I went down to the corner store and bought 34 dozen eggs. A few dozen at a time. I might be crazy all right, but I don't want the whole neighborhood knowing just how loony I am. Luckily, I live in New York, where there's a corner store on every corner. I just worked the neighborhood and bought a few dozen here, a few dozen there....

At first I just stacked the cartons one on top of the other in the living room. Four stacks in the corner: two stacks of eight dozen, two stacks of nine. To tell you the truth, I was a little afraid of them. I had to live with them for a while, you know, get used to them. I mean, to my mind, they represented my unborn children, in a twisted sort of way. I even started naming them. Went right through the alphabet: Annie, Bonnie, Carol, Deliah, Ellen, Francis, Grace. You get the picture. Then I started in with boys' names: Adam, Barry, Carlos, David, Eddie, Frankie, Greg. I had to do it 15 fucking times. Abigail, Betty, Claire, Deborah... Allen, Burt, Craig, Daniel... Amy, Barbara... Angel, Bernie... Pretty sick, huh? That's nothing compared to what I did next.

I unpacked them and started placing them around the

apartment. Now, if you've never been up here, let me tell you, this place ain't exactly the Plaza. It's pretty tiny, just three small rooms, and I haven't redecorated in a while. Since the Ice Age, as a matter of fact. But I'm not complaining. My hovel is perfect for one person. One crazy person and her 408 eggs.

The first place I put them was on the couch. Eight dozen fit there, and another eight fit on the bed. Three dozen covered my kitchen table, and two dozen filled the shower. A dozen fit in the bathroom sink, and another dozen filled the sink in the kitchen. Twenty-three down and 11 to go. I had no choice then but to lay them out on the floor. It looked kind of like an inside-out yellow-brick road. The floor was covered with eggs except for a twisted, windy path that led from the bedroom through the living room, through the kitchen, and out the front door.

When I was finally finished—I have to say it—I felt pretty damn proud. Sure, I had used up my eggs—nothing much to it; women do that all the time—but how many women have actually replaced them? I stood in the narrow path in my apartment, looked around, and felt smug. For about two seconds. And then I started feeling incredibly horny. All those eggs! I mean, have you ever felt an egg, I mean, really felt an egg? They're very sensual, you know. They've got a little weight to them; they're heavy and smooth, not unlike a woman's breast that fits just right in the palm of your hand. I took two eggs off the floor and held one in each paw for a minute, closing my eyes and just bouncing them up and down a little. God, I felt like a cat in heat. No, not a cat, a pussy. I wanted some, and I wanted it *now*.

So what could I do? *Go out, you old fool,* I said to myself. I hadn't been out for about a million years, and the thought of it was more than a little daunting. Had I lost my charm? (Had I ever had it?) There was only one way to find out. Go out. So I did. I got all dressed up in a jacket and tie, did something with my hair, put on my motorcycle boots, and hit the street. I didn't even know if the bar I used to haunt was still there. Part of me prayed it wasn't, and part of me prayed it was. I heard the disco beat half a block a way, and it pulled me inside like a magnet. God, it felt good to be out with the girls.

Now, before you jump all over me and tell me I should be calling them women, let me tell you, these were girls. To my mind, anyway. I wasn't old enough to be their mother, you understand. I was old enough to be their grandmother. Sure, you do the math. Eighteen and 18 is 36, plus 18 more is 54. Which is just a year and a half shy of how old I was. And how shy. I almost turned around and marched out the door the second after I marched in, but traffic was going against me, so I went with the flow and headed straight (so to speak) inside. I mean, what the hell? I had dragged myself out of the house, and there was no one back there waiting for me but the ingredients for about 200 Egg McMuffins. I might as well pretend to enjoy myself.

I headed for the bar and parked it on an empty stool. Asked the bartender for whatever was on tap, leaned back on my elbows, and looked around. Luckily, I didn't have to look far. There were two gals to my right, one more gorgeous than the other. Were they together? It was hard to tell. Both of them were dressed in black from head to toe: black sweaters, black stockings, black skirts, black shoes. So I doubted they were

lovers, because, after all, what can two femmes do together?
But then again, this is a new generation. Femmes go with
femmes, butches go with butches. Hell, I've even heard that
the newest happening thing is for girls to go with boys.
Though what's so new and radical about that is beyond my
imagination.

I pretended I didn't notice the two babes, of course, but I
kept my eye on them and tried to eavesdrop on their conversation. Easier said than done, as the music was really pumping, and, though I hate to admit it, my hearing isn't what it
used to be. I can't believe I'm turning into one of those old
sows who walks into a bar and whines, "Why does the music
have to be so loud? Can't they turn it dow-ow-ow-n?" But like
I've already told you, age does strange things to a person. So
I couldn't really hear, but I could see all right, and let me tell
you, both these broads were drop-dead gorgeous. One of
them had that short, bleached-out-blonde, rhinestone-glass-
es, dog-collar-around-the-neck look. Very East Village, not
exactly my type. The other one, though, I'd lick her boots any
day. She had long black hair down to her waist, and she was
at least six feet tall, even without the five-inch platform shoes.
God, her legs went on forever, and I couldn't stand that they
weren't wrapped around my waist that very minute. But before I could even ask the bartender what she was drinking so
I could send one over with my compliments (a move that
makes them swoon or at least did in the old days), she turned
from her gal pal, tossed all that glorious hair over her shoulder in a huff, and flounced into the crowd.

Now let me tell you, if there's one thing I love even more
than dykes, it's dyke drama. I sidled up to Miss St. Mark's

Place and asked, "Is she your girlfriend?"

"Why don't you ask her?" She pointed to the object of my affection, who had obviously changed her mind and returned to the scene of the crime.

Well, I always was one to follow orders. Pointing to the blonde, I asked the goddess standing before me, "Is she your girlfriend?"

"What did she say when you asked *her?*" Mademoiselle thrust her fists onto her hips and looked at me with blazing eyes.

This was beginning to feel like therapy; every question I asked was being answered with another question. "She said to ask you." I looked the towering Glamazon in the eye and held her gaze as she snorted and shook her head. "C'mon." She held out her hand to my utter delight and amazement. "Let's dance."

She sure didn't have to ask me twice. I slid off that bar stool like a greased pig and let her lead me to the dance floor where I attempted to move these old bones to the music, if you could call it that. All I could hear was some kind of throbbing, pumping techno beat. Perfect for humping, I thought, and as if my girl had a Ph.D. in mind-reading, she pulled me into her and started working away. I hate to admit it, but my knees actually buckled, and I had to hold on for dear life. Luckily there was a lot to hold on to. Like I told you, this girl was beyond tall. Her crotch came up to my hipbone, and her breasts were at eye level. I smelled her sweat and her juice and her perfume and just kept my hip jutted out so she could go to town. "Ooh, baby, you are something else," I murmured and somehow found her nipple in my mouth. Cashmere never tasted so good, let me tell you. A few times I tried to look up at my dancing damsel, but either her eyes were closed, or they were focused in the direction of the bar. Was she using me to make her girlfriend jealous? Did I care? Hey, a revenge fuck was better than a mercy fuck, though to tell you the truth, from this babe-and-a-half I'd have taken either.

When the music changed, we headed back toward the bar, and much to my relief, the Blonde Bombshell was gone. I couldn't tell if Mandy was pissed, relieved, or disappointed. (Once her come was all over my jeans, I figured I had the right to ask her name.) Without a word, she hopped up on that still-warm barstool, drained what was left of her gal pal's drink, and drew me toward her by wrapping those mile-long legs around the base of my butt. I felt her muscles clench as she held me tightly, and I realized I couldn't get away even if I wanted to. Which I didn't, in case you're wondering. I may have gone bananas in other departments, but I wasn't so far gone that I'd look this gift horse in the mouth.

"You live around here, baby?" Mandy whispered, letting her tongue roam the highways and byways of my grateful left ear.

"Just a few blocks away," I panted, and let me tell you, it was a good thing she had me by the butt because my legs were beyond Jell-O.

"Let's go." She released me, and I commanded my skeletal system to get a grip as we made our way out the door. Once outside, I tried to lean her against a lamppost and kiss her a bit, but it was embarrassing for her to have to bend down an entire foot just to get her mouth anywhere near mine. Clearly I had to get this girl on her back as quickly as possible, so we hustled down the street and up the steps to my apartment. I thought of carrying her over the threshold, but when I opened the door, I couldn't believe my eyes. The eggs! I had forgotten all about them. Would she notice? I decided to play it cool, since, after all, what choice did I have?

"Walk this way," I said, bending over like Groucho Marx and waddling down the narrow path to my bed, which was, of course, completely covered with eggs. I thought of whipping away the bedspread, like a magician who pulls a tablecloth out from under plates, glasses, and silverware without disturbing them, but that would have been too dramatic. Besides, it wouldn't have worked.

But Mandy, bless her heart, was foolish with youth, liquid courage, or just a wacky sense of humor. "The yolk's on you," she said reaching for an egg, which she cracked with one hand on the bed frame like a young, beautiful Julia Child. Then she deposited the contents of the shell expertly and neatly on top of my head.

"Allow me," I said, and with cool yolk dripping down the side of my face and neck, I send all eight dozen of those babies flying with one grand, gallant sweep of my arm. As they rolled, cracked, and crashed to the ground, I prayed Mandy wouldn't forsake me and run screaming out the door. But not to worry. I sure know how to pick 'em, if I do say so myself. Mandy just flopped down on the now-clear bed and rolled onto her back, with her hands behind her head and a look that said loud and clear, *OK, I've done my job. Now it's up to you.* God, I love those femmes.

"Over easy," I remarked as I bent down to unbutton her sweater. She wore no bra, and damn if her breasts didn't remind me of two eggs sunny side up. I cracked an egg onto her chest and licked her nipples through the yellow goo. She laughed and opened her legs, which had somehow worked their way out of her skirt. Crotchless panty hose—what will they think of next? Clearly Mandy had been expecting to get some action that night, but being fucked with an organic egg by a butch three times her age probably wasn't exactly what she had in mind.

I moved the lucky egg slowly up one magnificent thigh until it was right up against the path to glory. I pressed it against her and rolled it around and around until the shell was slippery and slick. "You move, it breaks," I said, teasing her clit with the tip of it.

"It breaks, you eat it," she replied, squeezing her legs together and cracking that ova in two.

Well, suffice to say, my cholesterol level skyrocketed that night clear through the fucking roof. I had egg on my face, and I didn't mind one bit. We crunched our way through my entire apartment, and that Mandy wasn't squeamish in the least. I licked egg off her toes, off her nose…. We fucked in every room, and by morning there wasn't an egg left to scramble. Four-hundred-and-eight eggs smashed to smithereens. That's gotta be worthy of the *Guinness Book of World Records*, don't you think? I tell you, I was so spent by the time the sun came up, I didn't know if I was wide awake or dreaming. I shut my baby blues and didn't open them again until that afternoon when I woke up alone in my bed, fresh and clean as a newborn chick. Mandy and the eggs were gone, and so were the bags under my eyes. I blinked a few times wondering if I had imagined the whole episode. Had it all been just part of some deranged menopausal fantasy? I stumbled into the kitchen, where my question was answered by a note I found on the kitchen table: *Thanks for an eggs-citing evening. Love, M.* The note was anchored by one perfectly round, white egg, upon which Mandy had drawn a goofy smiley face with a blue magic marker. And even though eggs were the last thing I wanted, I'd worked up such an appetite from last night's activities, I cracked that sucker in two and fried it up on the spot. And, I tell you, it was the most delicious thing I'd ever eaten in my entire life.

A Femme in the Hand

The first time I saw her, I got weak in the knees, I swear to God. She was a beauty all right, but beautiful doesn't begin to describe her. Try strong. Powerful. Built. I stared at her until my eyeballs ached, and something else ached too: that sweet place between my legs that butches like me don't talk about very much. But that's where I wanted her, and, frankly, the sooner the better. In other words, ladies and gentledykes, in case I'm not making myself perfectly clear, I had it bad.

I guess I've been out of circulation longer than I thought, because for a good 20 minutes, I felt I had no bones in my legs. They just wouldn't budge, even though I kept telling them to move. I mean, as much as I wanted to, I couldn't just stand there all day staring at the vision of loveliness before me. I had to take action. So even though I was scared shitless, I strutted right over to the man standing next to her like I knew what I was doing, cleared my throat, prayed my voice wouldn't crack, and asked, "How much?" The price was fair, so I whipped out my checkbook, scrawled the amount, and in a flick of my Bic, she was mine.

Now, let me tell you something. I know I'm nothing special. Just an average butch. Average height, average weight, average smarts, average looks. But with this baby between my legs, I'd be way above average. I'd be brave. I'd be bold. I'd be bullet-proof. You know what they say, right: clothes make the man? Well, let me tell you what I say: The bike makes the butch.

I swung my leg over my prize and dropped my weight onto the seat. A deep sigh of pure pleasure escaped my lips, and my bones settled inside my skin in a different way than they ever had before. Have you ever felt that all was right with the world, even though you know that babies are crying all over the planet, and we've made a total mess of the environment, and somewhere right that very second some asshole of a man is making a woman do something she doesn't want to do, and you've got job troubles and girlfriend troubles and family troubles, but still, you're amazed at the miracle of your own heart beating inside your chest, and your breath coming in and out of your nostrils without any noticeable effort, and your muscles move a certain way just because you want them to, and hey, you're alive, and the sky is blue, and absolutely nothing else matters? That's how I felt the first time I started up that bike.

My hands were shaking as I inserted the key, but she turned right over, my baby, my darling, my Harley. I still couldn't believe she was mine as I walked her back a few steps to turn her around and point her in the right direction. Then I gave her some gas and picked up my feet, and before you could say *moving violations*, we were out of that tired old parking lot and onto the street.

Now, in case you've never been on a bike—and if you haven't, I feel mighty sorry for you—let me explain why it's so different from riding in a car. It's like the first time I got glasses. I didn't even know the world was blurry as an out-of-focus movie until my mother hauled me in to see old Dr. Norton, who took one look at me and pronounced me blind as a little bat. Not to worry though, my vision was nothing lenses thick as Coke bottles couldn't fix. My mother and I started fighting immediately right in the office over my frames: She wanted me to wear these light-blue, glittery, cat's eye monstrosities, and I, being a baby butch even then, had already picked out a cool pair of square, black frames that made me look like a miniature Clark Kent. Of course, my mother won in the end—after all, she was the one with the checkbook—and I was so pissed I vowed never to let those spectacles within a foot of my face. But when the doctor hooked my new glasses around my eight-year-old ears, the world was so sharp, so bright, so crystal clear, I pushed my butch ego aside and put up with looking like a girly girl (and an ugly one at that) because I just couldn't believe my eyes. It was like I had been transported to another planet. And that's just what riding a bike is like. If you're not Nancy Nearsighted like I am, the only other way I can describe it is through *The Wizard of Oz*. Remember when Dorothy lands in Munchkinland, and all of a sudden the world isn't a drab, dull, black-and-white affair—the world's an amazing, sparkling, dazzling show of Technicolor? That's what life is like on a bike. Everything's in ultra megafocus. That's because there's nothing between you and the world. You're a part of it, and it's a part of you.

See, when you're out on the road, the air unzips to let you

by as you and your bike slice through it, and once in a while a warm pocket of air surprises you, like when you're swimming in a lake and you hit a warm spot of water (which hopefully isn't pee). Smells come and go: the sweet smell of burning leaves in autumn, the even sweeter smell of lilacs and honeysuckle in the spring. If it rains, you get wet; if the sun's out, you get burned. But you don't complain. You're a kid again. Ever hear a kid complain about the weather? Me neither. If it's snowing, a kid makes snow angels. If it's raining, a kid goes stomping in puddles. If it's 90 degrees, a kid heads for the nearest swimming hole. Kids are very Zen; they're right there in the moment, which is how I am on my bike. Whatever comes my way is what I deal with. If there's a fallen tree in the middle of the road, I figure out how to get around it. If there's a scumbag trying to pass me on the right, I figure out how to lose him. If there's a babe on my back seat, I figure out how to give her the best ride of her life. And speaking of babes, I was definitely in the mood to pick one up. It was just about Miller time, so I headed for my favorite hangout, a beer dive called Where the Girls Are. And truer words were never spoken. Especially on a Friday night.

I zoomed into the parking lot and took a space right out front. Separation anxiety hit as soon as I was about two feet away from my bike, but I made myself not look back. *She'll be all right,* I told myself. *And besides, this is my moment, the moment I'd been waiting for my whole life: to walk into a bar with my hair all flattened out on one side and my helmet dangling from its strap off my arm, feeling like the coolest dude in the world.* I swaggered past the dance floor and the pool table and swung my leg over a bar stool the same way I had swung it over my bike a few hours ago, just knowing I was God's gift to women. But that illusion was shattered two seconds later when I ordered a club soda. I mean, how dorky can you get? The bartender, a pretty gal named Fuzzy, raised one perfectly tweezed eyebrow at me, as if to say, *Oh, Jamie, don't tell me you've gone AA on me too?* especially since I usually down a glass of whatever's on tap pretty quickly and immediately snap my fingers for another. But I wasn't taking any chances tonight, not when there was nothing between me and the hard, cold concrete but my reflexes and a four-pound helmet. Pretty funny when you think about it. Many a woman's tried to straighten me out, so to speak, but it took a bike to keep me sober. At least for tonight.

I leaned against the bar and chugged my club like a dyke who had it made. *If that bike isn't a babe magnet,* I told myself, *I'll eat my jockey shorts.* I was sure that by the time I finished my soda and sauntered back outside, there'd be a beautiful broad standing by my Harley, tapping her foot with her hands on her hips, all ready to be my one and only biker chick. Or maybe there'd be a crowd of girls, each one of them sure they deserved the first ride. Maybe there'd even be some pushing and shoving. A cat fight. Wouldn't that be something? Just the thought of it raised me off my bar stool and propelled me back to the parking lot. And believe it or not, there was a crowd of girls standing around my bike, much to my amazement and delight. Better yet, as soon as I got near them, they were all over me. "Hey, man, nice bike. Where'd you get it?" "How much did it set you back?" "What's it cost to fill?" "How big's the engine?"

Christ, was I disappointed. Why, you ask? Because these

are not femme questions, now are they? No, they are not. My
rehearsed, *Ladies, ladies, one at a time, please. Everyone will
get a ride,* stuck in my throat because the mass of females
swarming around my bike wasn't exactly a hen party. It was
just a bunch of jealous butches, one admiring the chrome,
one stroking the leather seat, one fitting her greasy paws
around the handle bars....

"Outta my way," I said, and with a wave of my hand, I
parted the crowd like the Red Sea, claimed what was mine,
and left them all in the dust. Though, the truth is, they left
me in the dust by a mile, because I knew most of those girls,
and I knew they had femmes to go home to. Terry had Susie,
Sal had Rita, Ronnie had Clara, Riki had Buffy. All I had was
me, myself, and I. And even though none of those femmes
were exactly my type, and I loved riding solo, I knew after a
while I'd get tired of feeling the wind at my back. I wanted to
feel a girl at my back, with her arms around my waist and her
legs snuggled up to my thighs, her helmet clinking against
mine every once in a while as she leaned up close to whisper
something in my ear. The girl had to be out there, but the
question was, where?

The problem with this town, though, is it's smaller than
most people's high schools, and I'd already gone through
most of the femmes in this county and the next one over. And
even so, I had yet to find what I was looking for. I wanted a
girl with style. A girl all powdered and puffed who wore lipstick and lace. High heels even. A girl who was no stranger to
hairspray. A girl who smelled like my mama. I know those
kind of girls live in big cities mostly, but I had moved here to
escape the rat race, and if I had done it, wasn't there a chance

my femme counterpart had done so too? You know what they say, right, anything's possible, so I wasn't giving up hope. A friend told me I should put a personal ad in a lesbo paper with a wide circulation, which I thought a fine suggestion. Until I sat down to write it. I never sweated so much over ten little words in my life. Finally, I came up with something I thought sounded clever: "Well-equipped butch with bike looking for high femme to ride." That says it pretty well, don't you think? I thought so too, until the calls starting coming in. One woman actually said, "Do I bring my own pot?"

What, is she planning on moving in already? As I've told you, I'm not the quickest horse in the race, so I'm thinking, *Pot…pot…what can she possibly be talking about here, chicken soup, beef stew?*

"See," she went on, "I didn't know if you wanted me to get stoned first, or wait until you picked me up.…"

Oh, *high* femme. I get it. See what I mean about the dykes around here? "Never mind," I told her. "The bike's in the shop. Maybe some other time."

And that was just the first call. The others aren't even worth mentioning. Except, for what it's worth, let me give you gals out there a few pointers, OK? There are certain things you do not say to a butch about her bike. Number one: "It's nice, but it's not as big as my boyfriend's in college." Number two: "Does it have to be so noisy?" Number three: "Can I drive?" I met some lulus, let me tell you, but they say you have to kiss a lot of frogs before you find your princess. I was getting so desperate, even a frog was beginning to look good to me, but you know, it's always darkest before the light or calmest before the storm or something like that, because just when I was going to bring my extra helmet back to see if I could get a refund (hey, those babies aren't cheap), I got a phone call, and I knew as soon as I heard her voice that this one was different. You've heard of love at first sight, right? Well, this was love at first sound.

"So, you're the butch with the bike?" she said, like she was issuing me a challenge.

"Yep, that's me," I said, in what I hoped was a deep, mature, Marlon Brando kind of voice.

"What color is it?"

"Black with white hub caps and a dash of red. Why?"

"Because," her tone was impatient, like she already thought I was a fool, "I don't want it to clash with my outfit."

"Great," I said, hoping she couldn't hear me grinning like an idiot. "I'll see you on Saturday."

Saturday didn't come a moment too soon. I spent a good part of the morning fussing with my hair (all two inches of it) even though I knew by the time I got to Valerie's house it would be a total, helmet-shaped wreck. I put on my best riding outfit: black leather pants, black leather jacket, black leather boots, black leather gloves. Thank God it was one of those glorious autumn days with just a few wispy clouds in a blue-as-the-sea sky, the air as crisp as the first bite of a perfectly ripened Macintosh apple. Otherwise I'd have sweated to death. Though even if it were 98 degrees outside, I still would have dressed in black leather from head to toe. I could tell from Valerie's voice that she expected it. And I could also tell this was not a woman you'd want to disappoint.

I picked her up at high noon, and I have to say, she looked gorgeous. I'd gotten up extra early to shine up my bike, and

boy did she shine. You know the way the sun glints off the
ocean so it looks like there are hundreds of little diamonds
shimmering up and down with the waves? That's just how
sparkly my bike looked, from chrome to shining chrome.

And Valerie wasn't exactly hard on the eyes either. When I
roared into her driveway, she was standing there wearing
jeans so tight, I wondered how the hell she was going to get
her leg up over the seat of my bike, but hey, that wasn't my
problem. Her T-shirt was even tighter than her Levi's, and
she looked so fine I almost broke my own rule and let her ride
without a jacket, but I wouldn't be able to live with myself if
anything happened to those pretty little arms. She was all in
black like me, except for these sweet little red boots that
damn near broke my heart. Femmes, I swear to God, I'm like
putty in their hands. Make that Silly Putty, because if you
want to know the truth, I was already half in love with Valerie
and totally in lust with her, and she hadn't even opened her
mouth or set foot on the bike yet. But I played it cool. I said
hi, and she said hi, and then the fog I was in lifted slightly,
and I noticed that instead of carrying a pocketbook, she was
clutching an enormous yellow balloon that I hoped to hell she
wasn't going to ask me to tie onto the back of the bike.

"What's with the overgrown lemon?" I asked, handing her
a helmet.

"Oh, P.J. has this rule," she said, rolling her eyes.

"P.J." I stopped dead in my tracks. "Who's P.J.?"

"Oh, did I forget to mention P.J.?" she asked, all innocence.

"Yeah, I guess you did," I answered, already removing my
helmet. A girl like this was bound to have a butch who would

turn me into baba ganoush if I came within two inches of her chick's aura. But who was I more afraid of: P.J., who was nowhere in sight, or Valerie, who was standing there with this are-you-a-butch-or-a-mouse look in her eye that said, *Listen, sister, you promised me a ride, and you damn well better give me one?*

I sighed. "What's P.J.'s rule?" I asked, already tucking my head back inside my helmet.

"P.J. said it was all right for me to go riding with you as long as we keep this between us." She bonked me lightly on the arm with the balloon.

"And how do you figure we're going to manage that?"

Valerie shook her head like she was saying, *You poor butch, you have no imagination,* and unzipped her jacket. She reached down under her T-shirt where the sun don't shine and came back up with a safety pin. "Will you do the honor?" she asked, holding out the balloon and the pin. I popped that sucker while Valerie covered her ears.

"Oh, it broke. Isn't that too bad?" Valerie curled her bottom lip into an adorable pout, looking sad as a little kid at a country fair whose ice cream cone had just dropped to the ground. For a second, anyway. Then she put the safety pin back from whence it came and dangled the bit of deflated rubber in front of me. "Problem solved, sugar. So are we going to spend the whole afternoon standing in the driveway or what?"

"Let's go." I put my helmet back on and started up the bike. I knew Valerie was danger with a capital *D*, but I figured what the hell. I also knew from bike riding that danger and excitement go hand in hand, and I was excited all right. So excited, I could have wrung out my BVDs like a sponge. I practically gushed a geyser when Valerie hopped on behind me and leaned up against my back to put that dead-as-a-doorknob balloon between us and keep it there. "Where should I hold on?" she asked.

I sighed like a butch in paradise and answered with three little words I've been waiting forever and a day to utter: "Anywhere you'd like."

We took off, and let me tell you, P.J. was one hell of a lucky woman because Valerie knew exactly how to ride. She stayed with me the whole time, through every curve, turn, and bump of the road, not letting an inch of air come between her chest and the back of my jacket. You know what it's like riding with a gorgeous chick on the back of your bike? It's like the first time I got contact lenses. I already told you how my world changed 360 degrees when I got my glasses, right? Well, I didn't know things could get any better, until the doc handed me my contacts. I popped those pieces of plastic onto my eyeballs, and the world, which I'd thought looked fine as could be, grew so sharp, it was absolutely breathtaking. I felt like Rip Van Winkle. Isn't he the one who fell asleep for a hundred years? That's how I felt with Valerie on the bike: Something inside me that had been dead to the world had just woken up, and, boy, was it great to say good morning.

We rode for a good hour before my butt began to ache, which of course I couldn't admit, so I asked Valerie if she was ready to take a rest.

"Hell, no," she yelled over the roar of the bike.

"Aren't your legs tired?" I yelled back.

"No," she answered. "I'm used to keeping them spread like this."

Christ almighty, this girl was really something else. I mean, who was taking whom for a ride here? I picked up speed, and off we went, across highways and byways, over hill, over dale, winding our way around beautiful country roads with nothing but that bit of busted balloon between us and not a cloud in the sky. It took every ounce of strength I had not to reach down and squeeze one of Valerie's pretty little hands or reach behind me to stroke one of her sleek, denim-covered thighs. I was in butch heaven and butch hell at the same time, let me tell you, with such a knock-out of a lady a hair's breadth behind me, her hands holding fast to my love handles, her legs pressed up against my quivering thighs. This was more action than I'd had in longer than I'd care to admit, and I was getting mighty worked up, but hey, I'm no homewrecker. There was no way I was going to do anything naughty—unless, of course, Valerie made the first move. And what the hell, maybe Valerie and P.J. were non-monogamous. It was pretty weird that P.J. would let her chick ride off into the sunset with a butch she'd never even met before. What the hell was wrong with her? And even if she didn't give a damn about what I looked like, any butch worth her weight in chain saws would have at least come out to check out the bike.

Well, it looked like I wasn't going to ask, and Valerie wasn't going to tell. It was hard to talk on the bike anyway, and even though I have an intercom system, I don't like to use it. I'm not that much of a talker, especially when I'm on a bike. It's too distracting. I like to just feel when I'm riding, and right then I was feeling pretty fine. So fine, in fact, it didn't even matter what happened between me and Valerie once I took her home and we got off the bike. Just seeing her drop-dead gorgeous face grinning in my rearview mirror was enough for me. Well, almost, anyway. Someday I'd have a femme of my own to ride with, a femme who'd throw her arms around my neck and press her breasts against my back as we rode off into the sunset to live happily ever after, at least for a week or two.

Well, you know what they say, right? All good things must come to an end. The day was fading fast, so I started heading back toward Valerie's place. We'd put in a good couple of hours, and I hoped she'd gotten what she came for. When we pulled up into her driveway, I killed the engine and thanked her for the ride.

"Thank *you*," she said, shaking her head like a horse tossing its mane as she handed me back my helmet. "Why don't you come up for something tasty?" she asked, in a voice that wasn't about to take no for an answer.

"Uh…OK," I said, hanging both helmets onto the bike. I followed her inside and then halfway up the steps, I couldn't help myself. "Um, where's P.J.?" I asked.

"Who knows?" Valerie lifted her hands and shrugged her shoulders. "She could be anywhere."

Anywhere? Like in the bedroom with a shotgun? Even though warning bells loud as sirens were going off in my ears, I kept following Valerie, whose jean-clad ass was pulling me along like a magnet.

She sat me down at her kitchen table and disappeared into the bathroom. I counted silently—one, two, three—and then right on cue, Valerie shrieked like I knew she would, "Oh, my God, my hair!" She came out freshly fluffed a few minutes later and tossed her jacket over the back of a kitchen chair. I

tried not to stare at her breasts, but I was like a deer caught
in the headlights. And Valerie came closer and closer, until
she swung her leg over my lap and plopped herself down, her
face only an inch from mine.

"Want to take me for another ride sometime?" she asked in
a husky voice.

"Uh, sure," I stammered. "How about next Saturday?"

"How about right now?" Valerie leaned even closer and
whispered in my ear.

"Um, I think I'm out of gas," I said weakly.

"We don't have to go very far." Valerie punctuated her sentence with a flick of her tongue against the side of my neck.
"The bedroom's right in there."

I knew I would be a fool to say yes but even a bigger fool
to say no. I knew I should think with my head here, not my
crotch, but they were having one hell of an argument. My
head was saying, *Now, Jamie, don't do anything foolish. You'll
have a femme of your own someday.* And my crotch was saying, *The hell with someday. You know what they say, Jamie:
a femme in the hand is worth two in the...* and as soon as the
word *bush* entered my mind, I knew I was a goner. And so I
was, for I didn't even attempt to protest as Valerie interlaced
her fingers with mine and led me toward her bedroom over
the threshold into Paradise.

Valerie plumped up some pillows and lay back on the bed
as if she had all the time in the world. She smiled at me, and
my heart just turned over because nothing does it to me like
a femme fatale all ripe for the taking. *The hell with P.J.,* I
thought, as I knelt before Valerie and removed her sweet little boots. I took off her socks too and kissed each red-paint-

ed toe. Somehow, tight as they were, Valerie's jeans came off pretty damn quick, as did her T-shirt, black lace bra, and matching bikini underpants. I was practically on fire as I kissed her everywhere—her neck, her breasts, her belly, her thighs, the palms of her hands, the soles of her feet.

I inched my way back up the bed until her head was right next to mine. "I've got a surprise for you," I whispered into her velvety ear.

"I *love* surprises," Valerie whispered back. "Lay it on me, sugar."

Without a word, I took her hand and guided it down between us until it landed on my crotch. "Feel that?" I asked as I unzipped my zipper.

Valerie's eyes widened. "I should have known, you naughty girl," she said, her lips spreading into a grin as her legs spread wide as well. "Well-equipped, indeed."

"Hey, no one can accuse me of false advertising," I said as I rolled on top of her and slid the dildo inside. Valerie gasped a short, sweet, intake of breath, which to me is the most beautiful sound in the world.

We moved slowly at first, getting used to each other, and finding our rhythm, and we were just getting into a groove with our lips and hips locked together and Valerie's fingernails digging ditches down my back when all of a sudden, I felt her stiffen.

"I'm coming," Valerie yelled, turning her head to the side.

"Come on, baby," I said, raising myself up on my elbows to move faster inside her. But Valerie pushed me away.

"I'm coming," she yelled again, clamoring out of bed. "Just a minute, P.J."

"P.J.!" I sat up and tried to get my tool back into my pants, which was easier said than done, because my hands were more than shaking. Even all zipped up, I was in a heap of trouble, as the air was thick with the smell of sex, the bed looked like a hurricane had hit it, and Valerie, for some reason, had gone to the back door in nothing but her birthday suit. I didn't know if I should head for the closet, jump out the window, or dive under the bed, but before I could move a muscle, I heard Valerie's voice, and her words froze me to the spot.

"P.J., where have you been all day? I missed you. C'mon, baby, there's someone in the bedroom I want you to meet."

Oh, my God, was Valerie psycho? Was this a lesbian remake of *Fatal Attraction*? And what the hell was I supposed to say to P.J.? Pleased to meet you? How do you do? Before I could decide, Valerie came back into the bedroom, and the sight of her, naked as the day she was born, undid me all over again. "P.J.'s here," she announced all smiles, like now her day was really complete. "C'mon in, P.J. Don't be shy," Valerie coaxed. She took my hand, and we stood there waiting, Valerie's bare skin rippling in the breeze and me sweating like hell inside my leather jacket, my heart pounding so hard, I was sure my chest would be covered with black and blue marks in the morning. It felt like we stood there for hours, but I'm sure it wasn't more than a minute before P.J. gathered up her courage and strode into the room.

"Isn't she amazing?" Valerie bent down to scoop up the biggest, hairiest, fluffiest black and white cat I'd ever seen. I didn't know whether to kiss Valerie or kill her, I was so relieved. "This is P.J." Valerie extended one of P.J.'s paws for me to shake. P.J. started to purr, and Valerie lowered her head until her ear was next to P.J.'s neck.

"What'd you say, P.J.? Oh, yes, we kept the balloon between us the whole time, didn't we, Jamie?"

"We sure did," I said, relaxing a little and petting P.J.'s head. "So, this is the famous P.J., huh?"

"This is my girl." Valerie scratched the cat under the chin.

"And she's the one who makes the rules around here?"

Valerie looked a little sheepish. "Well, I had to bring the balloon with me, Jamie. I mean, what if you turned out to be a dog?"

"And did I?"

Valerie grinned. "I'd say, sugar, you're more of a wolf."

That made me grin in my boots, let me tell you. We were both standing there rubbing P.J.'s fur, and each time our fingertips touched, my snatch shuddered, and I could tell from her breathing that Valerie's did too.

"So, what does P.J. stand for, anyway?" I asked her.

"Pussy Junior."

I laughed. "Is there a Pussy Senior?"

Valerie gave me a look that was already becoming dear to me and batted her big, brown eyes. "Does a femme wear mascara?"

I took that to mean yes. "So, when do I get to meet her?"

"You already have." Valerie reached for my hand again and led me back to the bed. "And I think it's high time you two got better acquainted."

"Sounds good to me," I said, but before I could lay Valerie down, P.J. leapt onto the bed, turned around in a circle three times, and plopped down right in the center of the sheets. "I wasn't talking about you," Valerie said, picking up her pet. "Why don't you go into the kitchen for a while?" She shooed the cat out, and before she shut the bedroom door, I had already unzipped my zipper. We hit the bed flying and resumed right where we had left off, and believe me, it wasn't long before all three of us, Valerie, P.J., and I, were yowling to beat the band.

Girls Will Be Girls

*E*veryone keeps asking me how could I do it, how could I do it, but that's the wrong question. The right question is, How could I not do it? I had to do it. Nicki was so handsome, so charming, so sure—no, cocksure, no, cuntsure—of herself, and if that isn't a word, in her case it damn well should be....

✛ ✛ ✛

Look, I still say I didn't do anything wrong. It's not like I forced her or anything. Didi was a willing participant, more than willing. And I didn't know she was Gwen's girlfriend. I thought she was a client, like me. And by the time I found out, it was way too late to go back....

✛ ✛ ✛

I'd like to fucking kill them both. Put their heads in twin vices and then turn the grip until the metal plates squeeze their faces so tightly their eyeballs pop out and roll down the floor *like four glass marbles. If I weren't a therapist, I'd be scaring myself, but luckily I know the difference between appropriate feelings—being so angry you want to kill someone—and inappropriate actions—picking up a knife or a shotgun or a vial of poison and actually doing the deed....*

❖   ❖   ❖

"Honey? I have to go." Gwen called up the steps to Didi, who was probably still in the bathroom. These days she was always in the bathroom when Gwen left for work. Gwen put her hand on the banister and her foot on the first step and called again. "Didi?"

"Mgwfh." Didi appeared at the top of the stairs in a torn terry cloth robe, her mouth full of toothpaste, her long, black hair all tucked up under a shower cap. Was it only a year or two ago that Didi used to get up before Gwen so she could serve her breakfast in bed, wearing nothing but a short, black something-or-other from Victoria's Secret catalog? Those sure were the good old days, weren't they? Or were they? It had all been so long ago, Gwen wasn't sure whether they had actually happened or if she'd made them up.

"See you later." Gwen gave a half-hearted wave and let her hand drop to her side. She waited another minute, hoping Didi would reemerge from the bathroom and fly down the steps to give her a big hug and a tasty smack on the lips, but the only thing she heard running was water in the sink, so she turned and left for the office.

❖   ❖   ❖

Didi spit a gob of toothpaste into the sink with much more force than necessary. Of course, she'd stayed in the bathroom to avoid Gwen. I'll be damned if I'll give her a good-bye kiss in the morning when she hasn't given me a real good night kiss in weeks. Weeks! Didi unscrewed a jar of Noxema and plastered her face with white goop. When was the last time they'd had sex? She tried to remember. It was March, almost spring when a young girl's fancy turns to…yeah, right. Well, they must have had sex on Valentine's Day. They weren't that far gone, were they? That would be over a month ago. Jesus Christ, I'm only 38 years old, Didi thought. I deserve better than this. She stepped into the shower and turned the head so the water rained down onto her skin in hard little bullets. What the fuck was she going to do? She had tried everything: coming on strong (that made Gwen feel pressured), coming on not so strong (that made Gwen feel guilty), not coming on at all so Gwen would have a chance to initiate (that made Gwen feel obligated).

Didi sighed as she soaped up. They'd talked about it a million times, and it always came down to the same thing. Didi always wanted more, and Gwen was too easily satisfied. According to Gwen, Didi was stuck in some Hollywood fantasy and couldn't accept that life wasn't like the movies. Real people sometimes were too tired to have sex. Or too preoccupied. Or just weren't in the mood. Real people had jobs, bills to pay, menstrual cramps. And besides, they usually managed to get down every weekend or so, so what was the problem?

The problem, according to Didi, was that they had turned into a lesbian version of her parents. Sex once a week (if she was lucky) usually on Saturday night, usually in the exact same way (a few kisses; a little tongue action on the right breast, then the left; two fingers circling her clit counterclockwise; turn on the TV for the eleven o'clock news). Well, Didi had had it with that. She started refusing Gwen's Saturday night advances on principle, even if she was in the mood. It was all so predictable, so habitual, so *boring*. And Gwen, hurt by Didi's rebuff, just gave up. Gwen wasn't too worried, though. She knew sex waxed and waned in most relationships, and theirs was no exception. It would come around again.

"It doesn't just come around," Didi informed her. "You have to make it happen."

"Just let go," Gwen had replied. "Don't try to force and control everything. One day, when you least expect it—"

"You'll fall in love," Didi had finished Gwen's sentence for her. "Hopefully, with me."

✤　　✤　　✤

Gwen unlocked the door to her office and stepped inside. Instantly she felt calmed and soothed, even though she hadn't been aware that her body was filled with tension. She hoped her clients had a similar experience when they walked through the door, but she knew most of them didn't. When a client walked into a therapy session, she might feel sad, angry, anxious, vulnerable, distraught, terrified, or a myriad of other emotions, but seldom did she feel calm. On the other hand, Gwen loved being in this "room of her own," with the beige walls and ecru carpet. It had taken her months to scour every department store in Connecticut to pick out just the right furniture: the flowered couch that was elegant yet comfortable, with plenty of throw pillows in maroon, green, and brown; the tan bamboo end tables with matching tissue box holders that were not too subtle yet not too obvious; the cream-colored leather recliner in which she always sat; the cherry desk and file cabinets that hid behind a bamboo screen; the seascapes on the wall; the stained-glass tropical fish in the window. Gwen inhaled deeply, trying to gulp down a few breaths of tranquility before the day, with its inevitable surprises, began. Anything could happen in a therapy session. That was what Gwen found so exciting about the work. And so scary. And so satisfying. Gwen had to be ready for anything. And she was.

Of course, Didi threw this in her face. "How come you can be so spontaneous at work when you can't be that way at home?" she'd asked more times than Gwen would care to remember. Didi hadn't said anything this morning, but she didn't have to. The three vertical lines smack dab in the middle of her forehead—her "mad as hell" lines—were as prominent as the nose on her face. They'd been there all night too—or at least until Gwen had fallen asleep. How can Didi sleep with a furrowed brow? Gwen had wondered, watching her as she'd waited for her own eyelids to droop. Maybe she hadn't really been sleeping, but if Didi were faking, Gwen certainly didn't want to know about it. Any conversation they had would just be a continuation of the two-hour fight they'd just been through, and Gwen couldn't take any more of that.

The evening had started out peacefully enough. Gwen had gotten home a little after nine, and Didi hadn't picked her usual why-do-you-have-to-work-so-late fight. ("Why do you have to work so late, Gwen?" "Because that's when most people see their therapists, Didi." "No, Gwen, that's when most people see their girlfriends.") No, in fact, Didi had dinner on the table: homemade curried squash soup, baked halibut, a salad of baby greens, and a chilled bottle of wine. How the hell was I supposed to know that Didi served the entire dinner with no panties on under her skirt? Gwen wondered, her own forehead beginning to furrow. When Didi pointed this out to her, Gwen didn't feel she had any right to be annoyed.

"Why didn't you just tell me you were seducing me over supper?" she'd asked Didi, trying to keep the exasperation out of her voice.

"I shouldn't have to *tell* you," Didi snapped. "You should just be able to *tell.*" And the evening had gone downhill from there, with Didi getting that bitter, sarcastic tone to her voice. "You never even think about sex, Gwen. It never even occurs to you that I just might have something in mind besides coconut cream pie for dessert."

"I thought you were just doing something nice for me," Gwen snapped back. "I didn't know there were expectations involved. I didn't know I had to put out afterward. Christ, Didi, sometimes you're just like a man."

"*I'm* like a man? A *man?*" As soon as Gwen said it, she knew it was a huge mistake, but she couldn't snatch the word in mid air and stuff it back in her mouth, much as she wanted to. No, Didi was off and running. "How would you even know what a man is like, Gwen? You've never even been with a man." Somehow, just by shifting her tone of voice, Didi could take something Gwen was incredibly proud of and turn it into something that made her feel ashamed. "At least men think about sex more than once in a blue moon. At least with men, sex is fun, not something to process about. No wonder so many dykes go straight." A direct blow below the belt, since Gwen's last lover had done exactly that. And once Didi got this nasty, the evening was way beyond salvaging. Gwen and Didi had screamed at each other for a good two hours and then gotten into bed back to back, as far away from each other as possible. Only in her sleep did Didi turn toward Gwen, and the sight of her face, slack and vulnerable, despite the creases in her brow, melted the ice around Gwen's heart. *Why do we have to fight so much?* she'd asked Didi silently. *Can't we just be nice to each other?*

Gwen sighed and shook her head, trying to clear it of her personal problems to make room for her professional ones. Let's see. She flipped through her calendar and automatically reached to the top of her head for her reading glasses, which were usually perched there. Damn, she thought. I left my reading glasses on the night stand. And I think I have an appointment with the eye doctor today too. Yep. Gwen squinted and held her calendar as far away from her face as the length of her arms would allow. She had a new client, Nicki, coming in at ten, and then an eye doctor appointment at eleven-fifteen. It was nine-fifty now. She had just enough time to call Didi at home and see if she'd bring her glasses up to the office at eleven. She really didn't want to talk to Didi at the moment, but she didn't have a choice. There was no way she could make it all the way home and back after her client, and the eye doctor would charge her if she canceled with such little notice. Gwen almost laughed. She could practically hear a Greek chorus of clients chanting, "Now you know what it feels like," as more than one had complained about her 48-hour cancellation policy. Oh, well. What goes around comes around, Gwen thought as she picked up the phone.

✣   ✣   ✣

Didi was flat on her back with one hand pinching her left nipple and the other deep inside herself when the phone rang. She had no intention of getting it, especially when she heard Gwen's voice emitting from the answering machine. "Honey, are you there? I need to ask you to come downtown for me."

"I'll come for you all right," Didi said, pinching herself even harder. Her body responded appropriately. There was nothing like righteous anger to put Didi in the mood. She let her fingers do the walking until her orgasm exploded, sending satisfying ripples all the way up to the flush on her cheekbones and down to her arched little toes. She stretched with satisfaction and then curled on her side to rest for a minute, before getting up and walking into the kitchen. Feeling lazy, she punched star 69, even though it cost a few cents extra, and let AT&T redial Gwen's office number.

"What?" she asked, after Gwen had said hello.

"I forgot my reading glasses, and I have an appointment with the eye doctor this morning," Gwen said.

Immediately Didi's head was filled with disdain: How could you be so stupid? You never check your appointment book before you leave the house. What's wrong with you? But she decided to restrain herself and not be mean to Gwen. She couldn't be nice exactly, as that would communicate the wrong message to Gwen, namely that everything was all right, which it wasn't. But she supposed she didn't have to be nasty.

"Let me guess—you want me to bring them down for you." Didi paused. "What's it worth to you?"

Everything has a price, doesn't it, Gwen thought, but she knew enough not to say so. "How about I take you out to lunch?" she said instead. "I'll probably be done by noon, and then I don't have anyone until two o'clock."

In the old days, Didi would have said something suggestive, something like, "Why don't we just come back home for a quick bite?" or "Let's just eat in, if you know what I mean." But the old days were long gone, so she just said, "I have lunch plans," even though she didn't. "What time should I bring them by?"

"My client will be gone by ten-fifty," (and hopefully won't give me grief about her 50-minute hour, thought Gwen) "so if you could get here right after that, I'd still have time to get across town."

"OK, Gwennie, see you later." Didi hung up the phone and, still in a postorgasmic haze, drifted back to the bedroom to get dressed.

Nicki was running late, but she didn't give a shit. It was her hour—no, 50 minutes, the shrink had been really clear about that—so who cared if she used her time circling through town looking for a parking space? *You should have left the house earlier, you always wait 'til the last minute, would it kill you to be on time for once in your life?* "Oh, shut the fuck up," Nicki said to the voice in her head, which belonged to her ex-lover. Or was it her mother? Well, I guess the shrink will help me figure that out. Nicki slammed on the brakes as a car pulled in front of her, and then she parked front end in to save herself a precious minute. She sprinted the three blocks to the shrink's office, ran up the steps, and knocked at the door. Instantly it opened, and a short, slim, athletic-looking woman with green eyes, red hair, and a million freckles on her face extended her hand. Her fingers were covered with freckles too. "I'm Gwen," she said.

"I'm late," Nicki said back.

Gwen smiled. "Pleased to meet you, Late. Why don't you come in?" Gwen stepped back to let Nicki inside, flipped over her DO NOT DISTURB sign, and then motioned toward the couch as she took her usual seat on the recliner. Nicki dropped onto the sofa and spread her long legs out in front of her. What should she say? Shouldn't the shrink begin, warm her up a little, make her feel at home? Or were they just going to sit there and stare at each other for however much of her 50 minutes was left?

"So, Nicki," Gwen leaned forward slightly in her chair, "why don't you tell me what you want out of therapy and how you think I can help you."

Why don't you come in? *Why* don't you tell me...Nicki wondered *why* all of Gwen's sentences started with the word *why*. *Why* don't you just say something? Nicki asked herself. Christ, this is costing you a dollar a minute, don't be such a goddamn idiot. Gwen waited, and Nicki stared at her feet. Then she looked around at the walls, taking in the ocean motif, Gwen's diplomas, the few hanging plants. Finally she spoke. "*Why* don't you tell me *why* you don't have a clock in here?"

Gwen ignored the hostility and pointed to a small, silver square on the table at her elbow. "I do have a clock."

"But only you can see it."

"Does that bother you?" Gwen asked.

"It doesn't *bother* me," Nicki said. "I just don't think it's fair."

All's fair in love and therapy, Gwen thought, keeping her face neutral and then rearranging her muscles so that she looked kind. "If you'd like to keep an eye on the time, you're welcome to wear a watch when you come here. Or you can ask me how much time you have left."

"How much time do I have left?"

Gwen did the math. "Thirty-nine minutes."

"That's a minute a year," Nicki said.

"You're 39?" Gwen asked, to keep the ball rolling.

"Yeah. I bet you thought I was older, didn't you? It's the hair." Nicki ran her hands through her salt-and-pepper brush cut. "I never thought I'd go gray before I turned 40."

"When will you be 40?"

"In October. October 30th."

"And are you having any feelings about your 40th birthday?"

Feelings, yeah, right. That's what therapy was all about, wasn't it? Feelings. Nicki sighed. "How old are you, Doc?"

Gwen smiled at the nickname. It was given with more than a grain of sarcasm, but nevertheless, it was a good sign. "I'm 43."

"Older and wiser," muttered Nicki. "Look, Doc, I don't really think I need therapy. Other people think I need it."

"Which other people?"

"My ex-lover Marnie, for one."

"Why does she think you need therapy?"

"Because we broke up, and she thinks I'm fucked up. Why else?"

"And why did you break up?" Gwen fixed Nicki with her eyes so she would stay engaged.

"I started feeling trapped, you know what I mean? Like I couldn't breathe or something. Marnie was always asking me these questions like 'What time are you coming over?' 'When will I see you this weekend?'" Nicki's voice grew shrill. "'What are you thinking, Nicki? What are you thinking, Nicki?' Christ, I hate that. Can't a person keep a thought or two to herself?"

"Sounds reasonable to me." Gwen nodded her head to offer support. When Nicki didn't go on, Gwen prodded her. "So, what did you do? Did you tell Marnie you needed more space? Did you tell her you wanted to break up?"

"None of the above." Nicki sat up a bit straighter on the couch. "I had an affair."

"You had an affair." Gwen reflected Nicki's words back to her, keeping any hint of judgment out of her voice. "And then what happened?"

Nicki shrugged and tried in vain to tame the grin that was popping out all over her face. "You know, the usual."

Gwen shook her head slightly to indicate that no, she didn't know, so Nicki would explain. "Marnie screamed and cried and threw things, and then we had the best sex of our lives, and I promised I'd break off the affair, but, of course, I didn't. So we had a few more scenes, and then Marnie kicked me out."

"So now are you seeing the woman you had an affair with?"

"Hell, no." Nicki wasn't even trying to hide her smile now. "As soon as Marnie and I broke up, Shawna started acting just like a wife. 'What should we do this weekend?' 'When are we moving in together?'" Nicki's voice was high and whiny again. "Please. A wife is the last thing I want."

"What do you want?" Gwen asked gently.

"I want what everybody wants," Nicki said. "I want to fuck whoever I want to fuck whenever I want to fuck them, with no strings attached."

Gwen was reminded of a poster she and Didi had once seen in an art gallery. A buxom redhead, her hair half a shade lighter than Gwen's, was pictured with a balloon caption coming out of her mouth that read, *I want to be faithful, but I want to amuse myself like a whore.*

"And you think that's what everybody wants?" Gwen asked.

"Isn't it?" Nicki asked back

"Is it?" Gwen threw the ball once more into Nicki's court.

"What do you think?" Nicki persisted.

"I think," Gwen glanced at the clock to her left, "that our time is up."

✤   ✤   ✤

Didi found a parking space three blocks from Gwen's office and sauntered up the street, looking in the windows of the various shops she passed. "Oh, those are cute," she said aloud, pausing to stare at a pair of open-toed, red suede pumps. "That's nice." She studied a blue silk dress that would surely bring out the color of her eyes. I could use a new dress, Didi thought as she made her way up the street. Or a new

something. She yanked open the door of Gwen's office building, climbed the steps, and waited outside Gwen's door in
case she was still with her client. Didi was a little early as
usual—a habit she couldn't break no matter how hard she
tried—and Gwen's DO NOT DISTURB sign, which they had
stolen from a weekend getaway at a Holiday Inn years ago,
was still on the door.

Didi paced the short hallway once, twice, three times, and
just as she was about to pivot on her heel, the door to
Gwen's office opened and a woman stepped into the hallway. Didi knew therapy etiquette demanded she keep her
eyes down and pretend not to notice her, but this woman
was meant to be noticed. She was butch for one thing. How
butch? Well, if Didi didn't know that Gwen only saw female
clients, she'd have sworn she was a man. She had short, sil-
very black hair that made her look very distinguished and a
sleek, elegant profile. Didi met her eyes and smiled; the
woman smiled back and lifted both palms to the ceiling, like
she was apologizing for something. For making Didi wait
outside? For being in therapy? Didi wasn't sure, but one
thing was certain: The woman was hot. She was tall, with
broad shoulders, muscles-rippling-in-the-wind arms, and
Martina-size hands. Hands a woman like Didi could sit in.
Ooh, is she my type or what? Didi asked herself as the
woman ran down the steps. Didi's type was a woman who
everybody thought was ugly growing up because she was too
mannish. A woman who refused to put on a dress and, when
forced to, looked as out of place as Didi did in a jacket and
tie. A woman who got called "Sir" in restaurants. A woman
who caused scenes in ladies' rooms. A woman who made

your mother faint. That's the kind of woman Didi liked.

Of course, that's not the kind of woman I married, Didi reminded herself as she waited for Gwen, who was undoubtedly taking some notes and checking her answering machine. Gwen was a jock, just this side of butch. A soft butch, really. A roll-over butch. Not the kind of butch who slings you over her shoulder and carries you off to bed where she has her way with you, like it or not. No, from the beginning, Gwen had been a perfect gentleman, the type of butch who asks you if you're in the mood, and if you are, what can she do to please you? Didi couldn't have asked for a more considerate lover. No, what she wanted was a less considerate lover. A lover who didn't care if it was dinner time and she hadn't eaten lunch, so couldn't they eat first and fuck later? A lover who didn't care if her teeth were brushed first or if she was going to rip Didi's dress or ruin her brand-new manicure. A woman like the butch who had just left the building, no doubt to go home to some lucky girl for a little afternoon delight. Sigh. Didi threw herself back against the wall, pressed her knuckles up to her mouth, and bit down hard in an exaggerated swoon. What a woman. She was probably in therapy to talk about what a pain it was to have so many girls after her all the time. Or maybe her girlfriend didn't appreciate her. Maybe she was thinking of leaving her. God, if I had someone like that to come home to every night, she wouldn't want for anything, Didi thought, just as Gwen opened the door.

"Hi, baby." Gwen put her arm across Didi's shoulder and steered her inside. "Did you bring my glasses?"

"Glasses? Oh, right." Didi shook her head as if she were shaking off a dream. A wet dream. God, that woman. Didi wanted to ask Gwen her name, but she knew she couldn't. She sat down on the couch, and just knowing that her rear end was touching the very fabric that had grazed the bottom of the butch's jeans only moments before was enough to make her wet. Didi squeezed her thighs together and rummaged through her pocketbook. "Here you go."

"Thanks, sweetie. Sorry if I messed up your day off. You sure you can't have lunch with me?"

Didi looked at Gwen as if she barely remembered who she was. "I can't today. Sorry." She stood up and gave Gwen a hug. "I'm sorry about last night, Gwennie." Her apology was motivated by guilt, not remorse, but Gwen didn't have to know that.

"Me too." Gwen pushed Didi back so she could look her in the eye. "Let's start over, OK? Why don't we have a quiet night together, just the two of us?"

"A quiet night together" was Gwen's euphemism for sex, and Didi knew she should be pleased, but she wasn't. Why don't we have sex right here right now? she wanted to scream. But she knew Gwen would never even consider having a quickie in her office. She'd say it was *inappropriate*—her favorite word. Gwen was looking Didi in the eye, and she knew she needed to say something, but she had nothing to say.

"You better go." Didi gave Gwen a chaste kiss on the lips and pulled away.

"I'll be home at six-thirty, OK?" Gwen said, sounding to herself like Nicki's ex-lover. Did Didi feel trapped? Unable to breathe?

"OK, honey." Didi softened, motivated by guilt again. "See you later."

"Want me to drive you to your car? I'm parked out front."

"No, that's OK," Didi said, "I kind of feel like walking."
They left Gwen's office together, and Didi ran down the steps
as Gwen trailed behind, removing her DO NOT DISTURB sign
and locking the door.

✜   ✜   ✜

Nicki leaned against the hood of her car, smoking a cigarette and thinking about Didi. She'd only caught a glimpse of
her in the hallway, but one look told her everything she needed to know. Didi was in therapy with the Doc either because
she was single and miserable about it or because she was
trapped in a lousy relationship. She had that I-haven't-been-
laid-in-months look: a certain tightness around the mouth, a
certain sadness about the eyes. And what beautiful eyes she
had: an amazing blue, the same blue as the sky in the
seascape hanging in Gwen's office, right next to the window.
Nicki had a weakness for women with blue eyes and black
hair. Not to mention big tits. And Didi was built all right.
Maybe she was single. Hell, maybe she was straight, but that
had never stopped Nicki before. That woman doesn't need
therapy, Nicki thought. All she needs is a good fuck, and I'm
just the one to give it to her. *What are you thinking, Nicki?
What are you thinking, Nicki? Christ, if Marnie could hear
now what I was thinking....*

Nicki threw her cigarette into the gutter and stubbed it out
with her boot. She was just about to get into her car when she
looked up and saw a woman walking up the street. A woman
with long black hair, and even though she was wearing sun-

glasses, Nicki would bet her life that underneath them was a pair of beautiful, sky-blue eyes. She pretended to fumble with the lock on her door as the woman approached the maroon Saturn in front of Nicki's car. The maroon Saturn with the rainbow bumper sticker on the fender. All right, Nicki thought, almost punching the air. This is my lucky day. She watched Didi rummage through her shoulder bag for her keys and then chastised herself: *Don't just stand here like a moron, Nick. Do something before she gets away.*

"Uh, don't I know you?" Nicki called in Didi's direction.

Didi looked up and almost gasped. Oh, my God, it's her, she thought, so flustered she actually dropped her keys.

"Allow me," Nicki said, putting one hand behind her back and the other against her stomach so she could bow down like a knight in shining armor. She picked up Didi's keys and extended them with a flourish.

"Thank you, kind sir," Didi lifted the keys from Nicki's hands—those hands!—and felt herself blush.

"You're welcome, m'lady." Nicki straightened up, admiring Didi's blush and thinking, thank God she's not politically correct. "So, wasn't that you I saw outside Gwen Kessler's office?"

"That was me, all right." Somehow Didi found her voice.

"Is your time up already?" Nicki wasn't wearing a watch, but she knew it couldn't even be eleven-thirty yet. "Unless you only get a 30-minute hour."

Didi laughed. "Sometimes I leave early," she said, playing along, "when I can't take it anymore."

"I know what you mean." Nicki nodded. "So, how long have you been seeing the Doc?"

"Oh, about five and a half years." At least that much was true.

"Really?" Nicki was truly surprised. "You don't look that fucked up."

Didi laughed again. "Thank you...I think." She took off her sunglasses and looked into Nicki's eyes, which were a deep, beautiful brown. "How long have you been seeing her?"

"Oh, I just started." For some reason, Nicki didn't want to let on that she'd just had her first session.

"Really?" Didi raised her eyebrows. "You don't look that well-adjusted."

"Tit for tat," Nicki said, glancing down at Didi's chest for just the briefest of seconds before looking her in the eye again. "Hey, you want to grab a cup of coffee or something?"

Oh, my God, Didi thought, what am I going to do? "I can't," she said, wishing she was the kind of girl who could. "Maybe some other time."

Nicki saw Didi's hesitation but didn't push it. "Hey, no problem. I'll see you next week."

"Next week?" Didi's stomach fluttered.

"Yeah, next Monday, outside the Doc's office. We'll be like ships passing in the night."

"Oh, right, I guess so. See you next week then." Didi put her sunglasses back on and was just about to unlock her car door when Nicki reached for her hand and brought it up to her lips.

"Next week, don't forget. Same bat time, same bat channel." Nicki held onto Didi's hand for a second too long—or a lifetime too short—before letting go. I'll never wash this hand again, Didi thought as she got into her car. Nicki got into her truck and started the engine as Didi did the same. Nicki waited for Didi to pull out first and licked her lips as she watched her drive away.

✧   ✧   ✧

Gwen came back to the office at quarter-to-two and checked her messages. She was hoping for a kind word from Didi, but no such luck. What the hell was her problem? Gwen scoffed as she reset her answering machine. I promised her a quiet evening together, and she knows damn well what that means, so what more does she want? Gwen ran her thumb and forefinger across her eyebrows as she checked her afternoon schedule. She had the Bulimic coming in at two, the Incest Survivor at three, the Pothead at four, and the Mid-life Crisis at five. Gwen knew she shouldn't think of her clients as merely labels—and, of course, she knew they were much more than that—but it was just a little game she played with herself. And how would she label Nicki? It was too early to tell what her real issues were, but fear of intimacy was definitely at the top of the list. She had pretty classic symptoms: feeling trapped by everyday domesticities, having an affair to create distance in a relationship. Maybe I should label Nicki "the Gigolo," Gwen thought with a wry smile. Nicki wasn't the type to stay unattached for long, that was for sure. Gwen wouldn't be surprised if Nicki took up with someone before their very next session. Well, whatever. She was sure she'd hear all the gory details sooner or later.

✤   ✤   ✤

Didi spent the rest of the day running errands and thinking about Nicki. At the grocery store she squeezed avocados
and imagined Nicki smearing guacamole all over her thighs.
At the video store she returned the Barbara Stanwyck film
she and Gwen hadn't had time to watch and imagined checking out something sexy to see with Nicki, maybe something
silly and campy like *Showgirls* or something intense and erot-
ic like *Henry & June*. At the stationery store she bought a box
of envelopes and then browsed through the racy greeting
cards, imagining herself sending a dirty card to Nicki. I could
tape it to Gwen's office door next Monday, Didi thought, looking at a card picturing a blond woman in a leopard print bikini with impossibly fat-free thighs. I don't even know her
name, though. I'd have to address it, "To the beautiful brown-
eyed butch who has a ten o'clock appointment." Didi in-
dulged herself in the scene: Nicki would bound up the stairs
to Gwen's office, put her hand on Gwen's doorknob, and stop
mid turn as she noticed the card. She'd know who it was from
even before she opened it, and a huge smile would break
across her face. Before she even finished reading it, she would
have turned from Gwen's office and run down the steps, eager
to call Didi, who of course had written her phone number at
the bottom of the card, above the place where she had kissed
it, leaving a luscious lipstick impression of her mouth, along
with a million *X*'s and *O*'s....
Of course, that's not really what would happen, Didi
thought, putting the card back on the rack. In reality—stone-
cold, boring, old reality—Gwen would get to her office long

before Nicki and take down the card. Would she even give it to her? She'd have to, wouldn't she? Wasn't it a federal offense to tamper with someone else's mail?

Didi drove home and sorted through the clean clothes waiting for her in the laundry basket. As she put away her white cotton bikini briefs, her hands reached into her underwear drawer for her black lace panties. Gwen had given them to her ages ago when they'd first gotten together. Should I put them on tonight? Didi asked herself. Give the girl a thrill? Do I even feel like having a "quiet night together"? No, Didi said to herself. What I really feel like having is a noisy night together—a night full of shrieks and gasps and screams and shudders and moans. With that incredibly handsome butch. Didi's hands reached back further to pull out the black crotchless panties she had bought herself months ago but never worn. She was saving them for a special occasion, but none had as yet presented itself. Would an affair with the butch be special enough? "Oh, yes," Didi said out loud, holding the silk panties up to her face and rubbing the smooth material against her cheek.

"You better get a grip, kiddo." Didi put away her underwear and went into the kitchen to start supper and make herself some tea. But try as she might, Didi couldn't distract herself. Everything reminded her of sex: the banana in the fruit bowl, shaped so much like the dildo Gwen refused to even try; the campy refrigerator magnet that pictured the cover of a pulp fiction novel called *Wanton Women* (at first Gwen didn't get it and thought the magnet said *Won Ton Women*); even the kitchen floor where Didi and Gwen had had sex a few times, back in the beginning when they couldn't keep their hands off each other.

In the beginning, in the beginning...Didi poured herself some peppermint tea and began to chop some onions. "In the beginning, there was the Word and the Word was Sex," she said to the cutting board. In the beginning, she and Gwen had spent their lunch hours mauling each other, they had taken an old woolen blanket to the movies to lay across their laps, they had arrived at every pot luck, party, and political rally freshly fucked for all the world to see.

When had it happened? Didi asked herself as she took out some carrots and celery and continued to chop. When did getting a good night's sleep become more important that getting a good night's fuck? It was around our two-year anniversary, Didi reminded herself. Right around the time we decided to move in together. Right around the time I almost had an affair with Tracy, the pitcher on Gwen's softball team.

Didi was no dummy; she had read all the psychology books (Gwen had a huge stack of them piled next to her side of the bed), and she knew that the moment a couple took one giant step toward greater intimacy—whether that be moving in together, getting married, or having a baby—one of them was bound to get scared and develop a crush or, better yet, have an affair. And Tracy, like the ten o'clock butch, was just Didi's type: tall, dark, and handsome. So shy, she could hardly look at Didi, and when she did, the merest hint of a smile from Didi would make her blush and turn away. Tracy was the kind of girl Didi knew she could wrap around her finger in the wink of an eye. A girl who would turn herself inside out to please her. Tracy was a baby butch whose new identity fit her a little too tightly. She needed to prove herself, and Didi knew if she gave her the high sign, she'd be at her beck and call in a heartbeat. So she did.

It was the week Gwen was visiting her mother in Minneapolis, so Didi had set the scene: helpless femme all alone with car trouble after a game on a rainy night. Didi had gone to watch the game, which had broken up early because of the weather, and then waited until everyone was gone before making her move. She had parked her car next to Tracy's and stood in the parking lot waiting, getting wetter and wetter by the minute until Tracy finished goofing around with her teammates and then made her way over to her car. By then Didi, who hadn't worn a bra on purpose, had been thoroughly soaked and looked, in her own opinion, much like Bo Derek in the movie *10* when she emerges from the ocean in that sopping wet T-shirt.

"Hey, Didi, what's up?" Tracy had asked her, waving from the driver's side of her car.

"I'm out of gas," Didi replied breathlessly, her voice a flawless rendition of Betty Boop's.

"I'll take you home." Tracy gallantly unlocked the passenger side of her car and held the door open as Didi got in.

"I'm drenched," Didi shivered and clicked her teeth together in a staccato chatter. "Can't you warm me up a bit?"

"I'll turn on the heat." Tracy blasted some air, and Didi shook herself harder. "That's just making me colder. It's this sopping wet shirt," she said, whipping it over her head. "I hope I'm not catching hypothermia."

"Here, put this on."

Leave it to jocks, Didi thought, to always have an extra sweatshirt handy. She ignored the navy blue pullover. "Tracy, don't you know body heat is the best way to warm a girl up?" Didi asked, snuggling up to Tracy, who really had no choice but to put her arms around her.

"How about a little kiss?" Didi closed her eyes and puckered her lips.

"Uh, what about Gwen?" Tracy asked, her voice stuck somewhere down in her throat.

"Gwen who?" Didi answered and leaned forward for a kiss that did not disappoint her. When they were both breathing heavily, Didi pulled back and placed Tracy's hands on her breasts. "Don't you play second base?" she murmured, grasping Tracy's wrists and moving her hands around in slow, small circles. Tracy groaned and bent her head to Didi's nipple. "C'mon, baby." Didi licked Tracy's ear. "I know you want to score, don't you? Don't you want a home run?" It was all very romantic with the rain beating down on the roof, thunder rumbling in the distance, and the car windows steaming up, not to mention the delicious forbiddenness of it all. But just as Didi leaned back and placed Tracy's hands between her thighs, Tracy stiffened and pulled away.

"What's the matter, baby?" The words came out all jagged and bumpy, as did Didi's breath.

"It's nine o'clock," Tracy said, her voice full of panic and regret. "I have to call my girlfriend."

"Your girlfriend?" Didi was furious, though of course she had no right to be. "I didn't know you had a girlfriend."

"Well, we just started going out last May and then in September she left to go to grad school."

"Where's she going to school?"

"In Tennessee."

"Tennessee? She left *you* to go to school in *Tennessee?*" Didi sounded incredulous. "That's the most ridiculous thing I've ever heard. What kind of girlfriend would leave a handsome butch like you a thousand miles behind?"

"Well, she'd already been accepted when we started dating."

"So? What's more important: your career," Didi lifted one palm to the ceiling, "or your girlfriend?" She lifted her other palm so that her hands looked like the scales of justice and then tipped them in the girlfriend's favor. Tracy didn't say anything, so Didi went on. "When was the last time you saw this alleged girlfriend?"

"Christmas vacation. We don't have a lot of money."

"Oh, Tracy, that was five months ago. That's a long time for a girl like you to go without getting any. You poor, poor thing." Didi made herself sound totally sympathetic. "You deserve so much better than that," Didi purred. "You deserve someone who can pay attention to you and give you what you need, not someone a thousand miles away. Someone who's right here," she pressed Tracy's hands against her breasts again, "and here." She took Tracy's left hand and put it on her right thigh. "And here." She put Tracy's right hand up against her soaking wet crotch.

Tracy started giving herself up to the moment and then chickened out. "I can't. Sorry," she mumbled, taking her hand away and starting the engine.

"I can't believe a fucking phone call to your so-called girlfriend is more important than fucking me." Didi grabbed her T-shirt and leapt out of the car. She had never been so goddamn humiliated in her entire life. The girlfriend could have waited a half an hour, for God's sake. I mean, you would never see that happen in a movie, now would you? No, of course not. Though Gwen would be quick to point out that that was the difference between the movies and real life—except, of course, that Didi had never told Gwen about that little scene with Tracy in the car. She had just driven home (empty gas tank—yeah, right) and gone at it with her vibrator, yet again.

Didi put the vegetable casserole in the oven and looked at the clock. She could use a session with her vibrator now, but there wouldn't be enough time before Gwen got home. Something is really, really wrong, Didi thought, if I'd rather play with my vibrator than play with my girlfriend. She poured the rest of her lukewarm tea down her throat and went into the living room to wait for Gwen.

✤   ✤   ✤

On the way home from work, Gwen stopped to pick up some flowers for Didi. She looked at all the ready-made bouquets—the various arrangements of daisies, irises, carnations, and tulips—and decided to go all out and buy a dozen roses. That'll show her I'm sorry, Gwen thought, even though she wasn't sure exactly what it was she was supposed to be sorry for.

"Do you want a card?" The salesclerk wrapped the flowers in lavender tissue paper and pointed with her elbow as she took Gwen's money.

"Yeah, thanks." Gwen picked out a card and started to write. "Dear Didi," was the easy part. But what should she say after that? "I'm sorry" was risky, since it might remind Didi too much of their fight. Gwen could just hear Didi say, "*What are you sorry for, Gwen?*" and that would only lead to trouble, because whatever Gwen answered wouldn't be right. "Let's start over," could easily backfire too. "We're always starting over, Gwen," Didi would say. "Just how many times do you think we have left?" Gwen took her change and pondered the card for a minute. Well, she thought, when in doubt, go for the old standby: "I love you." Gwen knew it lacked originality, but it would simply have to do.

Gwen lay the roses carefully on the passenger seat and drove home. She pulled into the driveway and fussed with the flowers for a minute before opening the front door. "Didi, I'm home," she called, dropping her keys on the little table in the hallway where they always put the mail. Gwen started sifting through bills and circulars, calling again, "Didi?" When there was still no answer, Gwen dropped what she was doing and sniffed the air like a dog. She smelled a combination of vegetable-almond casserole, coconut spice incense, and strawberry candles. Not only that, Marvin Gaye's "Sexual Healing" was playing on the stereo.

Gwen smiled and put down the mail. This was more like it. Maybe they'd have a nice evening after all. Thank God I bought the flowers, Gwen thought as she started to climb the steps. "Di-di," Gwen called her name in a sing-song voice. "Are you in here?" She nudged open the bedroom door to find Didi, stretched out on the bed in a black lace teddy, bathed in soft candlelight.

"Hi, lover," she held out her arms. "I've been waiting for you."

"Shut your eyes," Gwen said. "I brought you a surprise."

Didi sat up and did what she was told, and Gwen came into the room. "Here," she said, laying the flowers in Didi's arms.

Didi opened her eyes. "A dozen roses?" She buried her nose in the petals, inhaling deeply. "Oh, Gwennie, you shouldn't have."

"Why not? Nothing but the best for my girl." Gwen sat down on the edge of the bed and patted Didi's knee. "Read your card," she said, reaching past Didi to snap on a light.

"Don't." Didi stopped her. "I'll read it later," she said, laying the flowers beside her.

"Let me put those in some water for you." Gwen got up and took the flowers.

"Can't they wait?" Didi lay back down again. "C'mere," she said, opening her arms.

"It'll only take a minute," Gwen said, heading for the door. "I'll be right back."

"They can wait, Gwen," Didi said, her voice getting just the tiniest bit sharp. "But I can't."

"Aren't you being a little overdramatic?" Gwen asked. "You don't want your roses to dry out, do you?"

Fuck the roses, I don't want my cunt to dry out, Didi thought, feeling the lines in her forehead start to crease. "C'mon Gwennie, be a little spontaneous for once in your life. Be here now," she said, patting the bed.

"I spontaneously spent 35 bucks on these flowers, Didi. Let me at least run downstairs and put them in the refrigerator."

"Oh, all right." Didi instantly regretted the harshness of her voice. "But hurry back, lover," she said, trying to smooth things over.

Gwen left the room and headed for the kitchen. She moved things around a bit to make room for the roses in the refrigerator and ignored the loud growl that emitted from her stomach. If I take 30 seconds to eat something, she'll kill me, Gwen thought, studying the shelves for the briefest moment before she shut the refrigerator door and climbed back up the stairs. "I'm here now," she said, standing at the edge of the bed.

"Come here," Didi said, reaching up for Gwen. "I have a surprise for you too."

"Oh, yeah?" Gwen lay down beside Didi and took her in her arms. "What is it?"

"If I told you, it wouldn't be a surprise, would it?" Didi leaned back so Gwen could kiss the corner of her neck. "You'll know in a minute."

Gwen proceeded with more than a bit of trepidation. The last time Didi had surprised her, she'd placed a strawberry halfway up her vagina for Gwen's tongue to find. Then of course she'd gotten mad when Gwen wouldn't eat it. "That's disgusting," Gwen had said, yet another mistake on the score-board of her sexual fuck-ups.

Gwen kissed Didi on the lips and snuck her hands up under her teddy, grazing her breasts with her palms softly at first and then more insistently as Didi grew aroused. Didi pulled Gwen's shirt out of her trousers and ran her fingernails lightly up and down her freckled back. Gwen began to relax. "This is nice, Didi," she said, lifting up the black lace cover-ing Didi's breasts. Didi moaned as Gwen's tongue found a nipple. After a few minutes she arched her back, her signal to Gwen that she was ready to go further. Gwen, keeping her mouth where it was, reached down, and began to pull at Didi's underwear.

"No, keep them on," Didi whispered, her mouth close to Gwen's ear.

"Why?" Gwen stopped what she was doing to ask.

"You'll see," Didi said. She took Gwen's hand and placed it over her crotch, which was exposed.

"What?" Gwen sat up and took a look. "What do you have on, Didi?"

"They're cut outs," Didi leaned up on her elbows. "Do you like them?"

"They're weird." Gwen fingered the silk. "What's the point of them?"

"Duh. They're supposed to be sexy." Didi threw herself back on the pillow, exasperated. "Don't you think they're sexy?"

"I think *you're* sexy," Gwen said, putting her mouth back on Didi's breast. She kissed her round belly, licked her tender naval, and then let her tongue roam the perimeters of Didi's new underwear. Didi moaned and groaned, but all the while, the word *weird* echoed through her mind like an annoying itch just out of reach. And then—she couldn't help it—right at her moment of climax, she let herself imagine it was Nicki between her legs, not Gwen. Didi was sure Nicki would never utter the word "weird" upon coming across a pair of crotchless panties. No, Nicki would probably say "wow" or "cool" or maybe even "far out," if anyone even said that anymore.

Gwen wiped her mouth on Didi's thigh and came up to kiss her. "I love you, Didi," Gwen said, looking into her eyes.

"I love you too," Didi said back, and she did. But if I love her, why am I thinking about someone else while we're doing it? Didi rested in Gwen's arms for a minute and then let her hands roam the familiar landscape of Gwen's taut, muscular body: her small firm breasts, her flat-as-a-pancake belly, her coppery pubic hair. This is fine, Didi told herself, listening to Gwen's breathing quicken. This is nice. This is enough. But deep in her heart, she knew it wasn't.

✦   ✦   ✦

Nicki looked at the clock at her bedside: quarter-to-eleven. What a ridiculously early time to go to sleep. Nicki wasn't tired; she just had nothing to do. It had been a long, long time since Nicki had gone to bed alone for so many nights in a row, and frankly, she was getting more than a little tired of it. I could call Marnie, she thought, see if she wants me to come over. Or if not, we could at least have a little phone sex. Nicki picked up the cordless phone but just as quickly put it down again, remembering what Marnie had said last time she'd called.

"I mean it, Nicki," Marnie said in a tone of voice Nicki had never heard before. "I'm not taking you back this time. I'm too good to be cheated on. I deserve your undivided attention."

"I know you do, honey. And I'm going to give it to you this time. I promise."

"Nicki." Marnie said her name like something distasteful, a rotten apple, an unexpected worm. "You ever hear this story about a woman walking down the street who falls into a hole?

It takes her three days to climb out of the hole, but she does it. The next day, she walks down the same street, falls into the same hole, and it takes her two days to climb out of it. The next day, she walks down the same street, falls into the same hole, and it takes her one day to climb out of it."

"Not the sharpest knife in the drawer," Nicki said, but Marnie went on.

"The next day," she continued, "the woman walks down the same street, trips over the hole but catches herself before she falls into it. The next day, she walks down the same street, but she walks around the hole. And the next day," Marnie paused for dramatic effect, "the woman walks down a different street."

"And what is the point of this story?" Nicki asked.

"The point is, Nicki, you are the hole. And I am walking down a different street."

"Christ, where'd you hear that, Marnie? One of your stupid 12-step meetings?"

"They are not stupid, Nicki." Nicki could practically hear Marnie's lips curling into a frown. "For your information, I heard it in therapy, which is where I think you should be, if you want to know the truth."

"Therapy? I don't need therapy."

"No? You don't think your little habit of cheating on me every time we start to get close is a problem?"

It's a problem for you, Marnie, Nicki had wanted to say. *It's not a problem for me.* But she had held her tongue.

"I'm not getting back together with you until you've done some work on yourself, Nicki. This is really hard for me, you know." Marnie's voice cracked with a sob. "I love you, you moron. You know I do. But I can't take this anymore."

"Baby, c'mon. Just let me come over. I'll make it all right."
Nicki couldn't stand to hear Marnie cry.

"No. No way. I don't want to see you or speak to you until
you've gone to therapy. Or something. And straightened yourself out."

Nicki had been all ready to make some kind of crack about
how she'd rather die than "straighten" herself out, but she
knew Marnie was in no mood for jokes.

"I'm hanging up now, Nicki," Marnie said, really crying now.

"Wait, Marnie—"

But true to her word, Marnie had hung up the phone.

Shit. Nicki knew she couldn't call Marnie, knew that one
therapy session wouldn't appease her just yet. She could call
Cynthia, who Nicki knew had a huge crush on her. She'd
danced with Cynthia ("Call me Cyn—wink wink") a few times
and even made out with her once in a parking lot. But Cynthia was too annoying with those big Kewpie doll eyes and
that squeaky Melanie Griffith voice. Then there was always
Shawna, but Nicki didn't even like Shawna very much. See,
that was just it. None of her little affairs had ever meant a
thing to Nicki. Why couldn't Marnie understand that? She
just had to sow her oats once in a while. Was that such a
crime? You know, like a guy going to a strip joint or a hook-
er. Straight women seemed to understand. You know, boys
will be boys and all that. Why couldn't Marnie just shrug her
shoulders, shake her head, and say with a little smile, "Oh,
well, girls will be girls"?

Well, forget Marnie. Who Nicki really wanted to call right

now was the Woman of the Dropped Keys, the woman she
had met outside Gwen's office. What's she doing right now?
Nicki wondered. Getting her brains fucked out by some lucky
woman, no doubt. Well, who knows? Maybe something good
will come out of therapy. Maybe next week I'll hang around
again, wait for her to come out of Gwen's office, not take no
for an answer this time when I ask her out for coffee. Nicki
lay back on her pillow, shut her eyes, and let visions of Didi
dance through her head as she tried to fall asleep.

"I met someone I like, Doc, someone I really, really like."
Nicki had shown up on time this week, which pleased Gwen,
who took her punctuality to mean she was eager to start her
session rather than as an indicator of the truth: Nicki was
eager for her session to be over and done with so she could
catch a glimpse of Didi again.

Gwen leaned forward to express interest. "What do you like
about her?"

"Everything!" Nicki leaned forward too and then threw
herself back against the couch. "She's got the most gorgeous eyes for one thing. They're this incredible shade of
blue that makes you want to dive right into them, you know
what I mean?"

Gwen smiled. Nicki's excitement was practically conta-
gious. And besides, she knew exactly what she meant, for her
own lover's eyes were blue too. Of course, they were en-
hanced by tinted contact lenses, but nevertheless, they were
beautiful just the same.

"Can you talk about yourself in the first person?" Gwen asked. "Can you say, 'They're so blue they make *me* want to dive right into them'?"

"Why?" Nicki was annoyed that Gwen was changing the subject, reminding her this wasn't one of her butch buddies she was describing her newest love interest to, this was therapy.

"It just makes things more personal, brings things closer to home," Gwen said. "Trust me, OK?"

"Sure, Doc," Nicki said. Nothing could ruin her good mood this morning. It was ten-fourteen (she'd worn a watch today), which meant there were only 36 minutes to go before she got to see her black-haired beauty.

"So, what else do you like about her?" Gwen tried to get Nicki back on track.

Her tits, Nicki wanted to say, but she didn't know if she could be that frank with the Doc just yet. "Her style," Nicki said, looking off into the distance as if she could see Didi. "I like the way she walks, I like the way she talks."

"Does she have a name?" Gwen asked.

"I'm sure she does, but I don't know it yet." Nicki wanted to say, *You know her name, Doc, and a lot of other stuff about her too,* but something told her that having a crush on one of Gwen's other clients was a strict no-no, so she kept her mouth shut.

"You don't know her name," Gwen repeated, nodding her head thoughtfully. "Why don't you tell me how you met this woman?"

Nicki was only too happy to keep talking about Didi. "It was one day last week, when I was getting into my car. I spotted her coming up the street because, Doc, this is a woman you can't help but notice."

"*I* can't help but notice," Gwen said.

"Yeah, you would notice her too," Nicki agreed.

"No, Nicki, I want you to say 'I' when you're talking about yourself, remember? 'This is a woman *I* can't help but notice.'"

"Yeah, yeah, yeah. This is a woman I can't help but notice." Nicki felt like she was back in English class all over again. "Anyway, her car was parked right in front of my truck, and she dropped her keys when she was unlocking her car door. So I picked them up, and we talked for a minute, and I asked her out for coffee, but she said no, and then she drove away."

Gwen's eyebrows rose. "That's it?"

"That's it." Nicki nodded, pleased with herself.

"And she's someone you like. Someone you really, really like." Gwen was careful to repeat Nicki's words exactly as she had said them.

"Yep, I like her all right," Nicki couldn't agree with Gwen more.

"And what happens next? Are you going to see her again?"

"Oh, definitely. Abso-fucking-lutely." Nicki nodded vigorously.

"How can you be so sure?" Gwen was more than a little curious.

"Some things you just know, Doc. You just feel 'em right here." Nicki made a fist and punched herself lightly in the stomach. "Instincts, you know? Gut feelings. I have a feeling about this girl. I know our paths are going to cross again."

"And when they do?"

"Baby, watch out!" Nicki smacked her fist into her other hand.

"Nicki, didn't you tell me you asked her out for coffee, and she said no?" Gwen asked. Nicki nodded. "So, what makes you so sure things will be different next time you meet?" Gwen tried to see if she could make a dent in Nicki's overconfidence.

"Well, first of all Doc, you never push a woman the first time you ask her out."

"*I* never push—"

"*I* never push a girl the first time," Nicki corrected herself. "And second of all, now that I know she likes me, all systems are go to really pour on the charm."

"I'm confused," Gwen said. "How do you know that she likes you? You asked her out, and she said no."

"Doc, it's not what she said, it's how she said it." Nicki spoke slowly and patiently, as if she were explaining a simple math problem to a very young child. "First of all, she was blushing the whole time she was talking to me. Second of all, I could tell she wanted to say yes, but she couldn't. And third of all…"

"Third of all?" Gwen leaned forward again.

"Third of all, you just—I mean, I just know women. And this one is ripe for the picking."

Gwen decided to ignore Nicki's macho leanings. "And how are you going to turn on the charm?" she asked.

"Oh, that's simple, Doc. I could write a book on that one."

"Show me." Gwen pointed to a stuffed animal, a giraffe, standing in the corner. "Pretend that's her. What would you say to her?"

"You're kidding, right?" Nicki looked at Gwen, at the giraffe, and back at Gwen again.

"No, I want to see you pour on the charm. I want to see how you communicate to a woman that you're really interested in her." God knows I could use the pointers, Gwen thought. "Trust me," she added, sensing Nicki's nervousness. "Just give it a try."

"Oh, OK." Nicki stood up. "Let me get myself together here." She whipped a comb out of her back pocket and ran it through her close-cropped hair. Then she tucked her shirt into her jeans and shook out each pants leg. "OK," Nicki said, "first of all, you start with your walk." Gwen decided to let Nicki speak about herself in second person rather than interrupt. "You stand real tall, see, like this. Gives you an air of confidence, a sense of purpose." Nicki strode right over to the giraffe. "Hi, how are you? Nice to see you again." Nicki pantomimed lifting one of the giraffe's hoofs and giving it a kiss. "You're looking lovely today," she said, and then turned to Gwen. "You act very direct, Doc. None of this playing hard-to-get stuff. That's for femmes. You want her to know from the beginning you're in charge. Got it?" Gwen, who truly was fascinated, nodded.

"Now your voice. You lower it just a tiny bit. Nothing obvious but just enough to give it a little sexy edge. You know, like they do on the radio." Nicki turned back to the giraffe and cleared her throat. "How about a stroll in the park, m'lady?" Nicki extended her elbow, presumably so the giraffe could take hold of it. "See, Doc," Nicki sat back down on the couch. "If you play your cards right, there's nothing to it."

"And what if she says no?" Gwen asked, tilting her head to one side.

"No?" Nicki looked puzzled, like the thought of a second refusal had never even crossed her mind. "Unacceptable, Doc. *I* never take no for an answer."

✤　✤　✤

Didi was a wreck. A total, total wreck. It was ten-thirty, and she had to leave the house in exactly eight minutes or she'd miss her, and she certainly didn't want to do that. As soon as Gwen had left the house, Didi had thrown open her closet door and tried on practically every outfit she owned, for she wanted just the right look: incredibly sexy but in an off-hand-ed way, like she hadn't planned her ensemble on purpose; she just always looked drop-dead gorgeous in whatever old thing she happened to throw on. All week Didi had thought about Nicki. Twice she had even dreamed about her. And one morning she'd woken up right before the alarm went off, her vagina opening and closing in sweet little throbs. Didi had lain absolutely still, marveling at the sensation, not wanting to wake Gwen up and share it with her. No, this is mine, Didi thought, her hand traveling down between her legs to feel her wetness. I haven't had a sex dream in years. She knew she should nip this thing in the bud, knew she was asking for trouble, knew she shouldn't do what she was about to do, and yet knew she was going to do it anyway.

This is my life, she said to her reflection as she brushed her hair in the mirror. Not Gwen's life. Mine. This has nothing to do with her. This has to do with me. I deserve this. I need this.

Couldn't you pick someone else? Didi's reflection asked her back. Someone who lives far away, like in upper Mongolia maybe? Or at least someone who isn't one of Gwen's clients?

Didi brushed her hair furiously, sending her split ends flying. "I can't help it if the most beautiful butch on the planet happens to have Gwen as her therapist," she said out loud, rifling through her makeup bag. "It's all Gwen's fault anyway," she reminded herself as she untwisted the cap of her navy blue mascara. "If she would only try a little harder in the sex department, I wouldn't have to go looking somewhere else." Didi knew Gwen would say, "But honey, we just had sex last week, and it was fine, so what's the big deal?" Gwen just didn't get it. Sure they'd had sex last Monday night, but it was like that had filled their quota, so Gwen was out of the hot seat for a week and a half or more. Didi, on the other hand, was hot to trot the minute they were finished, but she knew better than to ask Gwen for another go-around that very night. Gwen was hungry, Gwen was tired, Gwen had some reading to do for one of her clients....

Didi had thought about sex every waking minute since last Monday: in the car, whenever a love song came on; on the street, whenever she walked by a couple (Is their sex life better than mine? Didi wondered); and at work, whenever anyone, male or female, plopped themselves down into Dr. Carlton's chair and opened wide. Is he a good kisser? Didi had wondered, holding the suction while Dr. Carlton filled a cavity. Does she give good head? Twice that week, Didi had been so far away in a daydream, she had forgotten to ask a patient to rinse out her mouth, and both patients had reached up to tap her on the arm, practically drowning in their own saliva. And on Tuesday, the day after she had met The Butch (Didi had started thinking of her that way, with capital letters), she had let a patient walk out of the office with a bloody bib still clipped around her neck, not exactly a welcome sight to the people nervously reading back issues of *Entertainment Weekly* in the waiting room. Didi kept waiting for the doctor or one of the other dental assistants to ask the obvious question—"Are you in love?"—but since everyone knew she and Gwen were an old married couple, no one did. Which was probably just as well, Didi thought as she blotted her lipstick. No use getting anyone's suspicions up before anything even happens.

And what makes you think something is going to happen? Didi asked herself as she grabbed her car keys out of the mail basket. Oh, something's going to happen all right, Didi told her reflection as she gave herself a final once-over in the mirror in the hallway. I can feel it in my bones. "And other places too," she said, squeezing all the muscles in her crotch together, once, twice, three times for good measure, before flying out the door.

✛　　✛　　✛

"We only have a few minutes left," Gwen glanced at the clock and then back at Nicki. "May I make a suggestion?"

"Go for it, Doc." Nicki was feeling fine, extremely fine. According to her watch, she only had five minutes to go until the bell rang, and she was free to pace the hallway, waiting for her fair lady to show. Nicki had it all figured out: She'd say hi before her therapy session and then wait downstairs until it was over. Then she'd take her out for coffee—no, better yet, she'd take her out to lunch. To some fancy restaurant where they had heavy silverware and cloth napkins and candles on the table even in the middle of the afternoon. Maybe they'd split a bottle of wine. And a sexy appetizer. Oysters on the half shell maybe or some gooey dip thing they'd dunk crisp vegetables into, their fingers brushing one another's every time they reached for a bite. Maybe she'll start playing footsies with me under the table, Nicki thought, already feeling the heat. Maybe I'll do her right there in the restaurant, under the tablecloth....

"Earth to Nicki, Earth to Nicki..." Gwen held both hands up to her mouth like a megaphone. "Come in, Nicki."

"Sorry, Doc." She actually looked sheepish.

"Where did you go?" Gwen knew the question could lead Nicki off into a tangent, and they really only had a minute or so left, but this was the first time she had seen a flicker of emotion cross Nicki's face, and it could be important.

"Oh, I was just in La La Land, Doc. You know, thinking about my girl." She focused her eyes on Gwen. "So, what's your suggestion?"

"It's more of a question than a suggestion," Gwen said, reminding them both she was not being paid to give advice. "You just ended two relationships, right? One with Marnie and one with Shawna." Gwen said their names slowly and deliberately so the women would be real to Nicki, not just notches on her belt. "So, I want you to ask yourself why you're in such a hurry to get involved again."

Nicki looked at Gwen blankly as she went on. "Is this woman—who you really don't know at all, Nicki—is she really that special, or is she just there, someone for you to fill the void with, the empty space, someone to distract you from thinking about other things? What would it be like for you to spend some time without a lover? What are you afraid of?"

"Oh, she's special all right—" Nicki answered a bit too quickly and too defensively, even to her own ears.

"Ssh, ssh, ssh." Gwen held up one finger to her lips. "I don't want an answer, Nicki. I just want you to think about it. And anyway…"

Nicki finished Gwen's sentence for her. "I know, I know. Our time is up."

✢   ✢   ✢

Nicki closed the door of Gwen's office behind her, a big grin already sprouting on her face. But the hallway she stepped into was empty. Hmm, that's strange, Nicki thought, leaning her back against the wall to wait. I wouldn't have pegged her for a girl with a punctuality problem. Femmes like that are usually the early birds, the ones who don't like to be kept waiting. Maybe she's as ambivalent as I am about being in therapy. Or maybe she's sick. Nah. She'll show. Nicki clasped her hands behind her back and tapped the heel of her right boot against her left toe. She was dying for a cigarette, but she could wait. She stood in the hallway for another few minutes, until Gwen popped her head out of her office.

"Nicki?" Clearly Gwen was surprised to see her there. "Did you forget something?"

Think fast, Nick. "Uh, I was just looking for the bathroom."

"Oh, I'm sorry. I forgot to tell you. It's on the third floor.

Up the stairs and take a right."

"Thanks, Doc. See you next week." Nicki, having no choice, turned and started up the steps.

Gwen headed downstairs to put a few quarters in her two-hour meter. It was a beautiful morning, and the sun felt good on her face and arms. Maybe I'll go get the paper and a cup of coffee, she thought, glancing at her watch. Ten-fifty-five. Her eleven o'clock appointment, a mother-daughter team she'd nicknamed "The Dynamic Duo," had called to say they'd be ten minutes late, so Gwen had just enough time for a stroll around the block. Usually she stayed cooped up in her office all day, since the real world took her out of "therapy head," and she really needed to focus. But sometimes she really need-ed to stretch her legs too. And this was one of the first warm days of spring, after a particularly awful winter (though Con-necticut winters were nothing compared to what she'd been through growing up in Minnesota). And besides, Gwen wanted to give Nicki enough time to leave the building without the awkwardness of bumping into her again. She was definitely a strange one, that Nicki. Strange in an interesting way, though. Gwen was sure there was a wounded little girl deep beneath that Don Juan facade. And she hoped Nicki would stick around long enough for Gwen to make her acquaintance.

Didi pulled into a parking spot on the corner of Eighth

Street and Main and killed the engine. She felt her heart racing in her chest, and she hadn't even gotten out of the car yet.

"Are you sure you want to do this?" Didi said as she pulled the rearview mirror toward her to check her makeup and look herself in the eye one last time.

"Look, I'm just having coffee with the woman. Coffee." Didi wiped a tiny smudge of lipstick off her front tooth and an imaginary speck of dust off the shoulder of her dress. "There's nothing wrong with coffee. Coffee is only coffee." Didi pushed the mirror back into place and shut her mouth. She couldn't stand to hear that phony tone that always crept into her voice whenever she was lying. Even to herself.

✢   ✢   ✢

Nicki came out of the bathroom, went down the steps, and paused on the second floor. Had she missed her? She leaned her ear against Gwen's door, but it was impossible to tell if anyone was in her office. Damn these soundproof walls. Nicki pulled herself away from the door and sighed. I guess I'll come back at ten-to-twelve when her session is over. Hopefully, she won't decide to cut out early again.

And what if Gwen sees you? What are you going to tell her? That you're still looking for the bathroom? Nicki shrugged her shoulders as she headed down the steps for the street. I'll think of something, she told herself. Like maybe I had some therapeutic insight I just had to share with her that minute. Or whatever. Meanwhile, I've got 40 minutes to kill. Think I'll get myself a cup of coffee.

❖   ❖   ❖

Gwen walked down to Tenth Street and stopped at the corner. Did she have time to go one more block? If she skipped getting the paper, which she probably wouldn't have time to read anyway, she could walk a little more. And the fresh air, even full of carbon monoxide as it was, did feel good. *Oh, go on, Gwennie, be spontaneous for once in your life.* Gwen smiled at the sound of Didi's voice in her head and continued down the block.

❖   ❖   ❖

Didi got out of the car and slung her pocketbook over her shoulder. God, what a glorious day. Maybe she and The Butch could take a romantic stroll through the park. Yeah, right. Didi looked down at what she was wearing. A turquoise summer dress with a white cardigan draped over her shoulders and two-inch sling-back heels. She wasn't exactly dressed for walking. She was dressed for fucking, especially since she was wearing her good white, silk panties and matching lace bra under her outfit. Didi had considered going all out and wearing a garter belt and stockings or even her crotchless underwear, but she'd decided to hold off on those until next time. "Next time? You don't even know if there's going to be a this time," Didi reminded herself as she hurried toward Gwen's office over on Eleventh.

Nicki ducked into Mug Shots and ordered a cup of joe. The walls of the café were covered with snapshots of Connecticut celebrities drinking coffee out of the enormous mugs the joint was famous for—hence the name—and Nicki settled into a booth that boasted photos of Paul Newman and Katherine Hepburn. Just as she took her first sip of caffeine, Nicki remembered she'd only put two quarters in her meter and was probably at that very moment getting a parking ticket. Damn, which was worse—getting a ticket or wasting an entire cup of Colombian Gold? Nicki added more cream to her coffee to cool it off so she could quickly gulp it down.

Gwen walked an extra block all the way down to Ninth Street. So much for my cup of coffee, she thought, turning to walk back uptown. Hopefully, the Dynamic Duo hadn't arrived early. The last thing she needed was those two—disgruntled even on a good day—waiting outside her office, tapping their feet and checking their identical watches. Gwen still had five minutes to spare, but she broke into a light jog anyway, just in case.

Didi stopped just short of Tenth Street, smiling at a sight for sore eyes. Nicki's truck. She'd only seen it once, but still, she'd recognize it anywhere. Maybe I'll just wait right here, she thought, running her hands along the shiny black hood. She went around to the passenger side and saw Nicki's meter had run out. Silly girl, Didi thought, rummaging through her purse for a quarter. She noticed the door of the truck was unlocked, and before she could think about it, hopped right in. Who in the world is this brave new girl? Didi wondered. She hoped she wouldn't have to wait too long to find out.

Nicki finished her coffee and slapped two dollars onto the table. She had just enough time to feed the meter and get back to Gwen's office before her dream girl's appointment was over. She hurried up the street with her head down, almost bumping into an exceedingly tall woman, who was being trailed by a younger, equally tall woman who had to be her daughter.

"Whoops. Sorry, ma'am," Nicki said to the older woman. "Excuse me." She tipped an imaginary hat to the daughter. The two women glared at Nicki and then at each other before they continued on. Why don't you take the pickles out of your asses and smile a little? Nicki wanted to shout after them, but she kept her mouth shut and hurried on.

Gwen went straight over to her answering machine and rewound the tape. She wasn't sure exactly why she felt so compelled to listen to her messages after each and every client, but she knew if she didn't, the blinking light on her desk would totally distract her for the entire session. And just when was the last time something life-changing and earth-shattering had come in over the wires? Gwen couldn't remember, but still, one never knew. Gwen had just enough time to hear that the pictures she'd brought in last week to be developed were ready, before there was a knock at her door. She reset her machine, sat down in her chair, and called out to her clients, "Come in," like she'd been sitting there all morning, just waiting for them to arrive.

✧   ✧   ✧

Didi wasn't wearing a watch, but the clock on Nicki's dashboard told her it was eleven-sixteen. Where was she? If her session had ended at ten-fifty (and Didi knew Gwen never, ever, *ever* let her clients go over), she would have had more than enough time to get back to her truck by now. Unless she was going somewhere else after therapy. Like to work. Didi wondered what kind of work The Butch did. Definitely something with her hands. Oh, those hands. Didi pictured them in her mind and squeezed her thighs together. She hoped Nicki wasn't meeting another girl for lunch. She hoped Nicki had been thinking about her all week and was chomping at the bit to see her again. What had she said again? Same bat time, same bat channel?

"Oh my God," Didi said aloud. "She probably waited for me right outside Gwen's office and now she thinks I'm not showing up. Oh, I am such an idiot." Didi grabbed her pocketbook and fumbled for the handle on the door.

✧   ✧   ✧

By shading her eyes from the sun with her hand and squinting, Nicki could see from half a block away that she still had time on her meter, for the little red flag that pops up when the time runs out was nowhere to be found. How bizarre, Nicki thought. I'm sure I only put two quarters in. Unless some stranger performed a random act of kindness and senseless beauty. Nicki was just about to turn and head back for Gwen's office when the door to her truck opened. "What the hell?" Nicki's heart started thumping as first one leg—and a shapely one at that—and then another poured itself out of the side of her truck. Speaking of senseless beauty…well, I'll be, Nicki thought, her lips curving into a smile. I sure picked myself a live one. Hot damn. She straightened up so she stood tall in her boots and cleared her throat as she headed directly for her truck.

✣   ✣   ✣

"Hi."

"Greetings, m'lady." Nicki took Didi's hand and gave a little bow before kissing the tips of her knuckles. Didi felt her toes curl inside her shoes and her insides turn to jelly. She couldn't believe she was standing on the street, smack in the middle of downtown—in broad daylight yet—holding hands with a perfect stranger. And boy was she perfect. Nicki was wearing a crisp white shirt that had been ironed within an inch of its life and faded jeans that had a big worn spot halfway up her right thigh. Didi tried not to stare at the bit of flesh she saw peeking out from behind the thin threads of denim, but it was all she could do to keep herself from bending in half to put her tongue right there.

"So, how do you like my truck?" Nicki asked, petting the side of the cab like an old, beloved cat.

"Oh, I hope you don't mind. I had to straighten out my stockings, so I just hopped right in."

"Let me see." Nicki turned Didi around and saw what Didi already knew: She wasn't wearing stockings at all. "Looks pretty good to me. Say," she spun Didi around by the shoulders and almost kissed her on the spot, "how come you're not in therapy?"

"I changed my time slot," Didi looked boldly into Nicki's eyes, "so I could spend some time with you."

"Oh, yeah?" Nicki's whole face lit up.

"Yeah." Didi couldn't remember the last time she felt this happy. She bathed herself in the light of Nicki's smile as if she were soaking up the sun. "So," she said, "I was hoping your offer for a cup of coffee was still on."

"Right this way, m'lady," Nicki offered her arm and turned in the direction of Mug Shots.

"Uh…" Didi's eyes darted up the street. She knew Gwen hardly ever left the office—in fact, she usually brought her lunch so she wouldn't have to go out—but once in a while she had been known to take a walk or run an errand between clients. And what if someone had canceled? Surely Gwen would take advantage of such a gorgeous day and spend some time out in the sun. Shit, Didi thought. I'm already getting paranoid, and I haven't even done anything wrong…yet.

"I have an idea," she said, placing her hand on Nicki's arm and ignoring the heat singeing her fingertips from the touch. "It's such a beautiful day. Why don't we go for a ride?"

Why don't we just fuck in the truck? Nicki thought, but said instead, "Sounds good to me," before opening the door with another gallant flourish and helping Didi inside. Didi buckled her seat belt and straightened her skirt—hitching it up a few inches to show off her thigh—as Nicki got behind the wheel.

"We're off," Nicki said, just as they passed Didi's car.

I should have parked in a garage, Didi thought, and then gave a little shrug of her shoulder. A parking ticket's a small price to pay for love. Love? She almost laughed out loud. How can I be in love? she asked herself. I don't even know The Butch's name yet.

Nicki drove north, heading out of town onto a quiet, country road. Soon buildings were replaced by trees, and the noise of horns and sirens faded away as wind and birdsong filled the air.

"This sure is a pretty road," Didi said, staring out the window.

"We should have brought a picnic." Nicki scolded herself for not thinking ahead. We could have done it right here, she thought, but I don't even have a blanket in the car.

"We can stop for something if you want." Didi felt luxurious, as if she and The Butch had all the time in the world. "Are you hungry?"

Nicki glanced from the road to Didi's face for a split second. "I could eat *something*," she said with a wicked grin.

"I bet you could," Didi said, squeezing Nicki's hand, which had found its way across the front seat to nestle against the side of her leg.

They drove in silence a little while longer, Nicki's hand

resting on Didi's lap and Didi's hand resting on Nicki's fore-arm. She traced the blue veins rippling through Nicki's mus-cles and almost came right then and there. I am going to die, she thought, grasping Nicki's hand and holding on for dear life. Nicki looked over and gave Didi a smile, a beautiful smile, full of openness and kindness and appreciation and longing. She turned back to the wheel and pulled off onto a dirt road.

"Where are we?" Didi asked, as Nicki turned off the engine.

"Right here," Nicki said, gathering Didi in her arms.

"Wait a minute." Didi undid her seat belt so she could move closer.

"I can't. I can't wait one second longer," Nicki said and kissed Didi long and hard on the lips. Didi opened her mouth to welcome Nicki's kiss. She was so strong, yet so tender. Didi felt as if she were melting, dissolving, disintegrating right there in Nicki's arms. Surely she would fall apart at the seams if Nicki let go of her. *Oh, hold me forever,* she breathed silent-ly as Nicki kissed her neck, her throat, her shoulders, the lace at the top of her dress.

"You are gorgeous." Nicki raised her head to look deep into Didi's eyes. "Those blue eyes, this black hair…" Nicki took a handful of Didi's hair and rubbed her face with it. "This luscious body." She pressed Didi tightly to her chest and ran her hands over her back, stopping to caress the top of Didi's trembling ass.

I love you, Didi thought, her eyes shut and her head arched back. *Take me. I'm yours. Please.* She took long, deep breaths as Nicki covered her arms with little kisses and then slowly sucked each of her fingers and tongued the center of her palm.

"You're delicious," Nicki said, gathering Didi up again. "Give me those lips." She devoured Didi's mouth like a woman who hadn't kissed anyone in days, weeks, years, and then licked her face all over like an overgrown, happy puppy.

Rip my dress apart, Didi wanted to scream. *Bite my breasts off.* But words eluded her; all she could do was pant and moan.

Nicki's fingers were itching to get underneath all that fabric. Her hands were dying to feel those ample breasts, that soft, sweet belly, the wondrous valley that lay between those dreamy, creamy thighs. But she pulled away from Didi, ran her fingers quickly through her cropped hair, and turned on the ignition.

Didi's heart raced even quicker than before, a feat she couldn't believe was humanly possible. "Is something wrong?" she asked, lifting her hips off the seat to pull down her skirt.

"Yes," Nicki said, looking over her shoulder to back out the truck. "Something is very, very wrong."

"What?" Didi didn't even try to hide the panic in her voice.

"What's wrong is," Nicki ran one finger up the length of Didi's leg before removing her hand to shift into first, "an old beat-up pickup is no place for a beautiful woman like you to be fooling around in. You deserve the works: flowers, candles, wine, a big brass bed...."

"And?" Didi's voice filled with hope as Nicki squeezed her knee.

"And," Nicki smiled that warm, sexy smile, "I am taking you home."

✢   ✢   ✢

After the Dynamic Duo left her office, Gwen called Didi, but she wasn't home. She's probably in her studio, Gwen thought. Isn't that where she said she was going today? Didi belonged to an artist's collective that rented out space in an old mill building on the river out at the edge of town. Didi wasn't really a serious artist—she was more of a dabbler—but she had made some nice things that hung on the walls of their home and Gwen's office. For a while Didi had worked with clay, then stained glass, and then watercolors. Her newest passion was making collages, and frankly Gwen didn't think these "pieces," as Didi called them, were anything a four-year-old couldn't do, but of course she never said as much. Didi was still trying to "find herself" as an artist; she told Gwen, she was still "experimenting." Gwen considered calling Didi at the studio, but the phone was down the hall, and Didi didn't like to be disturbed. Coming to the phone meant she had to get up from her easel, wash her hands, lose her concentration....

Maybe I'll take another quick walk around the block, Gwen thought. She always scheduled herself a half-hour break in the afternoon. She did have some phone calls to return and some articles to read in the tall stack of professional journals forever growing on her desk. I can just take those home, she thought, glancing at the teetering pile. And the phone calls can wait an hour. Gwen felt restless today, though she didn't know why. She had a nagging urge to hear Didi's voice, but clearly Didi wasn't available. It's probably the weather, Gwen thought, grabbing her backpack and heading for the door. It's not natural for a human being to be cooped up inside on a fabulous day like this, not counting five-minute meter runs every two hours. And I never did get that cup of coffee.

Gwen locked her office door and jogged down the stairs.

"Hi."

"Hey, how are you?" Gwen nodded to Carrie, another therapist who rented an office in the building. "Gorgeous day, huh?"

"Yeah, I hate to come back inside. But gotta pay the rent, right?"

"Right." Gwen held the door open as Carrie stepped inside and Gwen stepped out. She walked down Main Street, crossing to the sunny side of the street and heading for Tarts, her favorite bakery. Just her luck, the treat she could never resist—chocolate chip cookies laced with pecans *and* macadamia nuts—had just come out of the oven. Gwen bought two, even though she had promised Didi she would make an effort to cut down on sweets. What else could Gwen do to get through the day: smoke a joint, have a drink? A treat every now and then was a healthy thing, a sign she was giving herself something she enjoyed, something she deserved. "Are you sure it isn't a self-destructive thing?" Didi had asked, reminding Gwen she did have high cholesterol and not only that, both her parents and her grandmother had adult-onset diabetes. Gwen hated when Didi threw therapy talk in her face. "I'll know when I'm being self-destructive," she had said.

"Like Melanie?" Didi asked, referring to a lesbian therapist in town who everybody knew had a more than slight drinking problem.

"I'm sure she's working on it," Gwen replied, though she wasn't sure at all. What could the woman do, go to AA meetings, where she was sure to bump into half her clients? "Anyway, she's a very good therapist."

"How can she be a good therapist if she can't even solve her own problems?" Didi's voice carried a sneer.

"Didn't you ever hear the expression, 'Do as I say, not as I do'?" Gwen asked. "You know, like a doctor who smokes or a nurse who's on drugs, or…"

"A dentist who never gets her teeth cleaned." Didi finished Gwen's sentence and dropped the subject, but Gwen knew what had been unsaid: *How good a therapist can you be, Gwen, if your own relationship is so fucked up?*

Gwen didn't want to be thinking about her and Didi's problems, but unfortunately, they had this ugly habit of just popping into her head whenever they felt like it. She and Didi had had a good time a week ago, and that seemed to satisfy Didi. Gwen hadn't initiated sex over the weekend because Didi had made it pretty clear she didn't want to be Saturday night once-a-weekers. Maybe they could fool around tonight. But would Didi get mad that now Monday nights were becoming a habit? Gwen wished she could be more spontaneous, but frankly, she didn't know anyone who was. Not her friends (not that they talked about their sex lives much), not her clients (and Gwen knew way more than she wanted to know about most of their intimate habits), not anyone who had been together for more than five or six years. In fact, most of the women who came into Gwen's office complained that they hardly ever had sex—once a month or even less often—so Didi should consider herself damn lucky. All those books and articles about how to improve your sex life were such bullshit. Since everyone seemed to be having the same problem—not enough sex—then maybe the problem had more to do with people's unrealistic expectations than with what was actually going on in their bedrooms. It was like the whole world being on a diet. There were a million diet books out there, but there was nothing wrong with women's bodies. The problem was in their minds, which had bought the message that they were too fat, that they had a problem because they didn't wear a size zero, that they didn't look like hipless teenage boys. What a world, Gwen thought, shaking her head.

She turned to head back to her office when something caught her eye: the sun glinting off a maroon car. A Saturn. What was Didi's car doing downtown in the middle of the day? Plus, her meter had almost run out. Gwen fished in her backpack for some quarters, put two in the meter, and then had an idea. She pulled out a notebook and pen and wrote Didi a love note, saying the kinds of things Didi had begged her to say so many times. She tucked the note under Didi's windshield wiper, and then, whistling a little tune, turned and walked away.

✧   ✧   ✧

"Here we are, m'lady." Nicki pulled into the parking lot of a brick apartment building and shined her smile on Didi. "May I have the pleasure of showing you inside?"

"The pleasure is all mine," Didi said, relieved Nicki lived nowhere near her and Gwen. She'd had a fleeting moment of panic on the way over, a wave of fright that Nicki lived next door to them or halfway down the street. You're being ridiculous, Didi told herself over and over as the truck raced down the highway. You would have noticed her if she lived within a 20-mile radius of the neighborhood. Don't be insane.

But Didi did feel more than slightly crazy for going home with a woman whose name she didn't even know. But she couldn't ask her now. They were way beyond introductions. And besides, how could she ask someone whose fingertips had grazed her nipples (they had stopped once more and groped each other like teenagers) to tell her her name? And not knowing The Butch's identity just added to the delicious mystery of it all. It was like they were under a magic spell that Didi was in no hurry to have broken with mundane conversation about what their names were, what their jobs were, where they had grown up, where they had gone to school....

Nicki took Didi by the hand and led her into the hallway and up the stairs. How much of a pit was the place today? Had she even made the bed? Was there any food in the house? Not that they'd be spending any time in the kitchen. No siree. They were going directly to the bedroom, do not pass go, do not collect $200. Nicki pushed the door open and gestured for Didi to go inside. Didi stood in the middle of the living room for a minute, unsure of what to do.

"Do you want something to drink?" Nicki asked, to be polite.

"No." Didi dropped her bag onto Nicki's couch. "I want you," she said, holding out her arms.

"Ditto," said Nicki, diving right into them.

✤   ✤   ✤

Gwen nodded her head thoughtfully as The Woman Who Loved Too Much went on and on about why she had just gone back to her rotten, no-good, worthless, son-of-a-bitch, lying, cheating husband. Yeah, yeah, yeah, just dump the bum, Gwen thought, glancing to the right for a second, to take in the unblinking red light on her answering machine. Why hadn't Didi called? Surely she would have gotten back to her car and read the note by now. And surely it had pleased her. Was she too involved in whatever silly art project she was working on to pick up the goddamn phone?

"What do you think I should do?"

"No, the question is, what do *you* think you should do?" Gwen turned her attention back to her client, giving an old standby answer to an old standby question.

✣   ✣   ✣

"Let's go into the bedroom, darlin'," Nicki said, ungluing her lips from Didi's and coming up for air.

"Good idea." Didi propped herself up on her elbows and adjusted her dress, which was all bunched up underneath her. The backs of her thighs burned a little (though not un-pleasantly) from rubbing against Nicki's carpet, which was full of cigarette ashes and crumbs. Where were the candles, the flowers, the wine she had been promised? Nicki reached out a hand to help Didi to her feet, and as if she had read her mind, pointed to the bedroom. "You go in there, m'la-dy, and make yourself comfortable. I'm going to hunt up a candle or two."

"OK." Didi stepped through the doorway and looked

around. The first thing she noticed was the bed, of course, a queen-size four-poster affair made of smooth walnut (not brass, as promised), with an arched, elegant headboard. Didi wondered if Nicki had built the bed with her own two hands, as surely it was an extension of herself: handsome, dark, and very smooth. The bed was sloppily made, with a navy blue quilt thrown haphazardly across it and two pillows in mismatched cases bunched up on the side nearest the wall. At least it doesn't look like anyone else slept here last night, Didi thought, reaching to pull the covers back. She stopped herself as a framed poster hanging over the bed caught her attention. It was a photo of a woman, a redhead, with enormous breasts popping out of the top of her dress, like a heroine on the cover of a romance novel. She was staring straight out at the camera with a pleading look in her eye, and a caption looming over her head read, *I want to be faithful, but I want to amuse myself like a whore.*

"I don't believe it." Didi kneeled on the bed to get closer to the poster. She and Gwen had seen this exact same print years ago in an art gallery, and it had triggered one of their famous fights. Didi loved the print. She thought it was funny, campy, true, and marvelous; in fact, she had wanted to buy it and hang it over their bed, just as Nicki had done. But Gwen thought it was totally idiotic. "You want to amuse yourself like a whore, Didi?" she'd asked once they were safely back in the car, for Gwen would never fight in public. God forbid one of her precious little clients ever saw her being less than perfect; God forbid they saw she was only human. Who knew what would happen to their precious little psyches; it could set them back for years.

"Didi, Didi, Didi," Gwen shook her head. "Don't you know love lies here," she pointed to the space between Didi's ribcage where her heart beat in anger, "not here?" Gwen indicated the space between Didi's legs, safely zipped inside her jeans. "The day you learn the difference between love and lust, Didi, is the day you grow up."

Didi's response had been to sing "I Won't Grow Up" at the top of her lungs with as much defiance and gusto as Mary Martin had poured into the number when she played Peter Pan so many years ago. Gwen just shook her head again and started up the car.

"You like the poster?" Nicki gestured to it with the lit candle she was holding, before placing it on top of her dresser between an overflowing ashtray and a half-empty coffee cup.

"I love it." Didi stole one last look at the naughty redhead before turning away.

"Yeah, that just about sums it up," Nicki said, closing the curtains to darken the room. She knelt down on the bed next to Didi and reached back to unzip her dress. "Whoops, I forgot something." She kissed the tip of Didi's nose. "Don't go away."

"Hurry back, lover," Didi reached out her arms as if to hug the empty space where Nicki had just been and then dropped them to her sides, horrified. Hadn't she said those exact same words a week ago to Gwen? Gwen, Gwen, Gwen, get out of my head. Didi raised her fingertips up to her temples and squeezed, as if she could willfully push her girlfriend out of the hard drive of her mind. Just for a few hours. Just for the rest of the afternoon. This is my time, Didi thought, fiercely. Mine, Gwen. Mine, mine, mine.

✣   ✣   ✣

Gwen pressed her fingers to her temples and rotated them around in little circles at the side of her head. Not a headache. Not today. Not with four more clients to go. Gwen flipped her calendar back to February and looked for the little "p" indicating the first day of her last period. Yep, just as she had suspected, exactly 28 days ago. Oh, great, Gwen thought. I should start bleeding right after supper. Didi will love that. Gwen could set a clock to her cycle; she bled every 28 days, and she always got a headache about five hours before the blood began. Then the stomachache started, then the backache, then the cramps, then finally the blood. So much for a romantic evening, Gwen thought, as she glanced at the notes she had taken last week on her next client. Now, if anything, the note she had left on Didi's car would be a false promise, just one more round of ammo for Didi to pull out in their next fight. Like it's my fault I'm getting my period today, Gwen thought, already defending herself. Like I can really control my cycle.

You bleed every 28 days, Didi would say to her. *You knew you were going to start today. You left that note just to taunt me.*

Do you have to be so goddamn literal? Gwen would scream back. *Can't you take a rain check? We've got the rest of our lives.*

The rest of our lives…Did Gwen really want to spend the rest of her life fighting with Didi? She opened the top drawer of her desk for the little bottle of Advil she kept there. There was only one pill left, and it definitely took two to do the trick.

Shit, Gwen thought, knowing there was no time to run to the drugstore before her four o'clock came in. Shit, shit shit.

✣   ✣   ✣

Nicki strode over to her telephone, unplugged it, and turned down the volume of her answering machine. Wouldn't it be just my luck, Nicki thought, if Marnie called this afternoon? Marnie hadn't called in weeks, since she'd hung up on her, but still, she'd always had this uncanny sense of timing and seemed to know the exact moment Nicki started fooling around. Not that it mattered now, as she and Marnie were officially broken up, but still, Nicki would go running back to her in a minute if she'd just stop being so stubborn and give her another chance.

If you still want to be with Marnie, why are you getting involved with someone else so quickly? Nicki could hear Gwen's voice in her head as clearly as if she were right there in the room, sitting on her beat-up, living room couch. *Why don't you spend some time without a lover?* Gwen continued. *What are you so afraid of?*

"Life's too short, Doc," Nicki said aloud. She shook her head rapidly, trying to clear it of Gwen's voice like a dog shaking off water. Another thought popped into her mind: She remembered taking Marnie out to dinner once, to a fancy restaurant she really couldn't afford. It had been her birthday or their anniversary or something like that. There had been a quote from something called the Talmud written on the wall right above their table: "When a man faces his maker, he will have to account for those God-given pleasures of life which he failed to enjoy."

"How about when a woman meets her maker?" Nicki had asked stroking Marnie's thigh. "Or, like the bumper sticker says," she let her hand go higher and higher up her lover's leg, "why postpone joy?"

❖   ❖   ❖

Gwen's head throbbed, ached, pounded, threatening to split in two. She remembered seeing a cartoon once, where a man had opened his head, like a box with a hinged lid, and poured coffee directly inside. That's what Gwen wanted to do right now, pop the top of her head off and remove her brain, just for a little while, just until the pressure went away. Maybe she could ask her next client if she had any Advil in her purse. But then she'd probably think Gwen wasn't feeling well enough to listen to her properly. No, she just had to hold on, through three more clients. Luckily they'd all been with her for over a year, and none of them were particularly challenging.

"I can do it, I can do it, I can do it." Gwen gave herself a pep talk, like the train in *The Little Engine That Could.* Only a couple of hours left before she could do what she yearned to do: go home, crawl into bed, and lay flat on her back, absolutely still.

❖   ❖   ❖

Didi lay on top of Nicki's bed, flat on her back, absolutely still. Where would The Butch touch her next? She was completely naked, and Nicki knelt above her, teasing her skin with a soft black feather. Didi wanted her to get down to business already, she wanted to feel her fingers, her mouth, her tongue, but at the same time, she'd be content if this ticklish torture lasted forever. When was the last time anyone had paid attention to her so absolutely and exquisitely? Had anyone really ever?

"Roll over, baby," Nicki whispered close to her ear. Didi did as she was told—she would have jumped out the window if Nicki had asked—and felt the feather travel down her back from the nape of her neck to the top of her bikini line. And then she felt something else—a hand? No, a tongue—right at the small of her back an inch above the crack of her ass. Didi gripped the edge of the mattress as Nicki, still licking her back, reached between her legs and pushed a finger inside.

"Somebody's ready," Nicki said, reaching up with her other hand to grab one of Didi's breasts. "Tell me, sweet thing, does m'lady like to play with toys?"

"Oh, yes," Didi breathed, focusing on the sensations Nicki's touch was pulling out of her body. And then—she couldn't help it—with a gasp and a moan and a shudder, she came in trembling waves on top of Nicki's hand.

"Oh, my God." Didi's words came out in soft, little pants. "I'm sorry." She felt like a total idiot, like a guy who couldn't hold an erection or suffered from premature ejaculation.

"Sorry?" Nicki lowered her head toward Didi's to look her in the eye. "What are you sorry for?"

"I came too soon." Didi thought she might cry. Had she ruined everything? But Nicki only looked at her with an expression of puzzlement on her face.

"You can never come too soon," she said, stroking Didi's

back with the flat of her hand. "And anyway, I'm sure there's a lot more where that came from."

Didi smiled, rolled onto her side, and opened her arms. "Go get your toys," she said, so happy she could faint, "and let's find out."

✛   ✛   ✛

Nicki sighed the sigh of someone who knew she had just completed a job well done. Didi rested in her arms, practically purring as Nicki absently stroked her cheek. Nicki felt lazy; her mind meandered from here to there, as if she were floating on her back in the ocean, rocking from wave to wave. There was nothing she liked better than holding a girl, who wanted for absolutely nothing, at least for the moment. And this girl, at least for the moment, was utterly, utterly spent. What would it be like, Nicki wondered, to really go for it this time, to try and be faithful, to be somebody's one and only? Why not give it a try with this one? They sure didn't come much hotter. She could try it as an experiment, no fooling around for…let's say a year. Now hold on a minute, let's not be too hasty here, Nicki said to herself. Let's say six months. That would take us up to…she ticked off the months on her fingers: April, May, June, July, August, September. Wouldn't that be something, to be with only one girl through the entire summer? That means no screwing around at Michigan or any of the other women's music festivals. It would be hard, but maybe she could do it. Maybe Sleeping Beauty here would even come with me, Nicki thought, giving Didi a little squeeze. Then we could have a little repeat performance of

this afternoon's activities in the woods, a mattress of pine needles underneath us, and nothing above our heads but the
starry, starry sky....

"Honey, you sleeping?" Nicki tickled Didi's cheek with a
lock of her hair.

"Ummm." Didi snuggled closer against Nicki's body and
then sat up with a start. "Oh, my God, what time is it?"

Nicki reached for the clock on her night stand with a lazy
arm. "Ten to seven. Why, what's the matter, got a date?"

"Uh, sort of. I mean, not a *date* date or anything. I just have
to be somewhere at eight-thirty."

"Oh, that's too bad." Nicki hoped she sounded convincing.
Part of her was sorry to see the babe go, and yet part of her
was relieved too, as she wasn't that anxious for Didi to spend
the night. Once that happened, the next thing you knew she'd
want to leave a toothbrush in the bathroom, then she'd ask
Nicki to keep a box of her favorite cereal in the kitchen cup-
board, and then before she turned around, it would be good-
bye freedom and hello moving truck.

"You want to take a shower with me?" Nicki asked, tracing
the slope of Didi's nose with the tip of her finger.

"Uh-uh." Didi caught Nicki's finger and sucked it into
her mouth, licking it round and round for a minute, before
expelling it with a pop. "I want to smell you on me all the
way home."

"Good idea." Nicki smiled, and Didi felt her blood quick-
en. She could never say something like that to Gwen. Gwen!
Oh, God, Gwen. Didi pushed her out of her mind. She wasn't
ready to deal with reality yet.

"Think we could find my dress?" Didi hitched herself up

on one elbow and peered over the side of the bed. Nicki gathered up Didi's clothes as she rose on shaky legs. "Whoa," she said, steadying herself on the side of Nicki's dresser. She felt all woozy and giggly, like Geena Davis when Brad Pitt got through with her in *Thelma & Louise.* "I don't know if I can make it."

"Sure you can." Nicki, in just her boxer shorts, came over to give Didi a hand. "Lean on me," she said, putting an arm around Didi's waist and then inching her hand up to give Didi's left nipple a few strokes and a pinch.

"Oh, you're a big help," Didi laughed and slapped at Nicki's fingers as they both tumbled back down on the bed.

✣　　✣　　✣

Gwen was so glad to get home, she didn't even notice Didi's car wasn't parked in its usual spot in the driveway. She made a beeline for the bathroom and slid open the door of the medicine cabinet. Thank God the pills she needed were there, because no way did she have the strength to get back into the car and drive to the drugstore. Gwen took the aspirin bottle into the kitchen to get some water and hit the playback button as she passed the answering machine.

"Hi, Gwen." Didi's voice was breathless, like she was in some kind of hurry. There was probably another artist panting down her neck waiting to use the phone. There usually was. Gwen had urged Didi more than once to put a private phone in her studio, and she had looked into it, but there was some problem with running an extra line into the building or something.

"Listen, I'm going to be home late, so go ahead and eat without me if you want, OK? I'm working on a project, and it's going really, really well." Gwen heard Didi pause, then yell to someone in the background, "Hold your horses, I'll be off in half a sec." Then she spoke back into the phone. "I'll be home soon. Love you," and then she hung up the phone.

Gwen pressed the rewind button, took her aspirin, and climbed into bed. She was disappointed Didi wasn't home, but then she scolded herself. "Don't look a gift horse in the mouth," she murmured, getting under the blankets. What she needed more than anything right now was peace and quiet, and if Didi had been home, what would be the chances of that?

✤   ✤   ✤

Nicki double-parked beside Didi's car, shut off her truck, and took Didi in her arms. God, it felt good to hold someone close again. She was surprised at the intensity of her feelings; she really didn't want to let the woman go. "When will I see you again, sweetheart?" Nicki whispered into Didi's hair. "Soon, I hope?"

Didi nestled into Nicki's embrace, soaking up her own contentment while she tried to come up with an answer. One transgression was possibly forgivable: It was a slip-up, a mistake. She could always say she had just gotten caught up in the moment, and carried away. It was merely a crime of passion. But a repeat performance…that took thinking and planning and scheming. That was a deliberate decision. It's like the difference between involuntary manslaughter and first-degree murder, Didi thought. And if I don't stop now, Gwen will probably kill me when she finds out. But on the other hand, if I never see Nicki again, I'll probably end up killing myself.

"You're not falling asleep, honey, are you?" Nicki pushed Didi's hair behind her ear and kissed her velvety lobe. "Does m'lady have a phone number?"

"Why don't you give me yours?" Didi pushed herself off Nicki's chest and searched her purse for a pen. "I'll call you."

Something's up, Nicki thought, writing her name and phone number on the slip of paper Didi offered. Having been on Didi's side of the fence, Nicki knew she must have a girl-friend. Why else would she refuse to give up her phone number? Wouldn't you know it, Nicki thought, adding a P.S. under her name. I always thought going out with someone who had a girlfriend would be perfect, a guaranteed buffer from getting too involved. But now that the tables are turned, I don't like this one bit. I'm the one who should have a girl on the side, not *be* a girl on the side.

She handed Didi the paper and pen and drew her in for a long, good-night kiss. Didi melted into Nicki's arms and then pulled away. "We better stop," she said, placing both her hands on Nicki's shoulders and pushing her back, "before we get arrested."

"You'll call me?" Nicki asked as Didi got out of the car. Christ, I sound like a goddamn femme, she thought, more than a little disgusted with herself.

Didi waved the piece of paper she held tightly in her hand. "Of course I will," she consulted the note, "Nicki."

The sound of Didi's voice wrapping itself around her name for the first time brought a huge smile to Nicki's face. "All right then. Drive safe. Hey," she called, "are you going to tell Gwen about this?"

"Gwen?" Hearing Gwen's name fly out of Nicki's mouth was so unexpected and bizarre that Didi couldn't comprehend it for a minute. It was unfathomable, like seeing her mother at a Lesbian Avengers meeting.

"Yeah, Gwen...you know, our therapist." When Didi still didn't say anything, Nicki went on. "She might not like it—two of her clients going out with each other."

Are we going out with each other? Didi wondered but didn't ask. Instead, she said, "It'll just be our little secret then."

"Fine with me." Nicki kissed her fingertips and waved good-bye to Didi. "Hey," she said again, pointing to Didi's windshield, "you got a parking ticket."

"Oh, shit." Didi looked at her car and then shrugged. "Never mind. It was worth it." She blew Nicki a kiss and watched her drive away.

✤   ✤   ✤

Didi reached under her windshield wiper for not one but two parking tickets. Gwen will kill me if she sees these, she thought, getting into her car. Then she burst out laughing. "These are the least of my problems," Didi said aloud, placing the tickets on the seat beside her. "Oh, God, what have I done?" Didi sat motionless behind the wheel for a few minutes, listening to herself breathe. She wished she could sit there forever where it was nice and safe, a cocoon, a womb, a haven from the rest of the world. Didi clicked on the overhead light to study the note still in her hand. She traced the

letters with her index finger: "Nicki—555-3277. Call me!"
Underneath was a scrawled P.S. "I'm not washing my hands
until I see you again, so you better call me soon, you sweet
thing, you."

Didi brought the note up to her lips and kissed it. She felt
drugged, delirious, drunk on love. *You mean lust,* Gwen's
voice chastised her loud and clear. When lust ends, real love
can begin.

When lust ends, take me to the bridge and throw me into
the Connecticut River, Didi thought, turning on her car. She
picked up the parking tickets beside her to access the damage. The first one was for $15. Not too bad. The second
one…the second one wasn't a parking ticket at all. It was a
note written on yellow legal paper. From Gwen.

Dear Didi:

*I've been thinking about you all morning long, and I can't
wait until this day is over so we can shut off all the lights and
just get into bed. I want to kiss you and hold you and make
you come with my fingers and tongue deep inside you. You are
the most beautiful, gorgeous, sexy woman alive, and I'm glad
you're mine.*

Love,
Gwen

Oh, my God. Didi stared at the note, speechless. Gwen had
never, ever written her a love letter like this in all the years
they had been together. Why now? Didi looked up at the ceiling and beyond, where God—if there was a God—was looking
down upon her. "Why me, why now?" she asked, in a poor

imitation of Nancy Kerrigan on the day the skater had gotten whacked in the shin. Didi felt like she had just gotten whacked too, whacked right where she lived, right in her heart.

She drove home slowly, wondering what she could possibly say to Gwen. Dear, sweet, darling, loyal, unsuspecting Gwen, who had undoubtedly bought Didi's story of spending all day at her studio working on a project. It would never even cross Gwen's mind that Didi was somewhere else, doing something she shouldn't be doing. And how would she to explain her outfit? Didi had planned to arrive back at the house long before Gwen got home from work, with plenty of time to shower and change her clothes. And never mind her outfit. How was she going to explain the huge hickey on the underside of her breast? Nicki's kisses had felt so wonderful, Didi had almost lost her senses and let her place a huge bruise on the side of her neck. But she'd stopped her just in time. "I do have to go to work tomorrow," she'd said, glad for the ready excuse.

"They won't see this at work," Nicki's response was just to go lower, "unless you're a stripper." And with that she'd sucked greedily on Didi's tender skin. Didi didn't have the heart to stop Nicki at that moment by telling her she had a girlfriend. But she probably knows anyway, since I didn't give her my phone number, Didi thought. I mean, the woman's not an idiot. Didi was grateful Nicki hadn't pushed it. "Maybe *she* has a girlfriend," Didi said to her reflection in the rearview mirror. The thought filled her with despair.

"What am I going to do?" she asked herself. Break up with Gwen to take a chance on Nicki? *Nicki, Nicki, Nicki.* Didi's heart screamed out the woman's name with every beat. She had never felt so happy, so filled, so alive. Gwen would say lust like this could never last. Just look at them: They had been pretty hot and heavy in the beginning too. So if Didi stayed with Nicki for five years, would they turn into old, married farts like her and Gwen? It was hard to imagine. And yes, she and Gwen had been hot, but not like this. Didi felt her swollen lip with the tip of her finger. I suppose I could always tell Gwen the truth, she thought, pulling into the driveway. She'll know the minute I walk in the door anyway. Unless she's blind as a bat.

Gwen awoke in darkness and peered toward the clock. What time was it? Did she care? Her headache was subsiding, but her lower back ached, and the cramps were definitely kicking in. If labor is anything like this, Gwen thought, not for the first time, I'm sure glad I never had a baby. Maybe I should get up and look for the hot water bottle. Or eat something. And where was Didi? Why wasn't she home?

Gwen rolled onto her back and stuck a finger down her underpants. No blood yet. Bleed, bleed, bleed, Gwen told her body, for once she started, her cramps went away pretty quickly. Gwen had read somewhere, in some hippie, groovy, get-to-know-your-body book, that having sex could speed a woman's cycle; the contractions from an orgasm could bring down the blood. Well, as long as my fingers are down there anyway…Gwen began to move her hands in a way she knew gave her pleasure. I wish Didi were here, she thought, opening her legs a little wider. But then again, this was nice too; Gwen rarely—if ever—did something merely to please herself.

✤   ✤   ✤

"Gwen?" Didi ran into the house in a panic and then made herself calm down and take a few deep breaths. God, I look a fright, Didi thought, catching a glimpse of herself in the hallway mirror. She'd already concocted her story: She was dressed like this because she had taken her slides to a gallery that afternoon, and then she'd gone out for dinner with Sandy, the woman in her building who made those amazon warriors out of feathers, beads, and clay, the ones Gwen sort of hated and sort of liked. And then she was so excited about her latest painting, she just had to work on it a little more before she came home, and Gwen knew—didn't she?—how Didi lost all track of time when she was completely absorbed in a project....

Didi glanced through the mail as she stalled for time, gathering courage to face Gwen, who was surely waiting for her in their bedroom upstairs. God, why do I have to justify myself? Didi thought, the welcome feeling of anger quickly replacing the uncomfortable feeling of guilt. Nicki didn't ask me who I was calling when I told her I had to use her phone. Nicki didn't ask me why I wouldn't give her my number....

Well, Nicki is just perfect, isn't she? Didi could hear Gwen ask. Why don't you just run away with her and ride off into the sunset and live happily ever after?

Because, Didi said to Gwen silently, if we got married and moved in together, we'd probably just wind up like me and

you. I'm not an idiot. I saw *Bridges Of Madison County*.
Though it was hard for Didi to imagine she and Nicki stuck
in a rut, she had already noticed a few habits of hers that
would definitely get on her nerves. Nicki's lack of cleanliness,
for one thing. Didi had been more than slightly repulsed at
the sight of a crotch curl lodged in the soap dish on the edge
of Nicki's bathroom sink. She would never leave something
that disgusting lying around, and neither would Gwen. But
was that any reason to stay together—compatible cleaning
habits? Then again, was amazing sexual chemistry enough to
base a relationship on? After all, Gwen—the Gwen in her
head—was right: Didi didn't know a thing about Nicki, not
even her last name. And if she had so easily fallen into bed
with Didi, what made her think she could trust Nicki would-
n't turn around and do the same with somebody else? No,
Nicki didn't strike Didi as wife material. Maybe staying married to Gwen and seeing Nicki on the side was the perfect answer. But the truth of the matter was, Didi was so worn out
from the conversations spinning around and around inside
her head, she couldn't even remember the question.

✣   ✣   ✣

"Didi, is that you?"

"Who else would it be, lover?" Didi sat down on the edge
of the bed and stroked the back of Gwen's head. Even
through the darkness, her hair shone like a bright, new
copper penny. "Are you sleeping, Gwennie? It's not even
ten o'clock."

"I know. I had my period headache."

Thank God, Didi thought to herself. Aloud she said, "Oh, you poor thing. You want me to make you some tea?"

"In a minute." Gwen rolled over and sat up halfway. "Where have you been?"

"The studio. Didn't you get my message?"

"Yeah. I saw your car downtown."

"Oh, I know. I ran out of turpentine, so I had to go in and pick some up."

"Turpentine?"

"Yeah, you know, for my oil painting."

"Oil painting? I thought you were still doing collages."

"Gwen, I told you I had started working with oils weeks ago. Don't you remember?" Of course you don't remember, Didi thought to herself. What's so important about Didi's little art hobby? But if a client had started a new art form, Didi was sure Gwen would have remembered. More than remembered. She'd probably congratulate her on using her creativity to express herself. Didi on the other hand...

"I guess so." Gwen knew she didn't sound very convincing. "It's just this headache. You know I can't think clearly when I'm like this."

Yeah, right, Didi almost said, but she didn't want to push it. If they started fighting now, who knew what would fly out of her mouth? She decided to change the subject. "Thanks for your note, Gwen."

The note! Gwen had forgotten all about it. "Didi, don't be mad. I meant what I said. I really did. I really wanted to...It's just you know what I'm like when I get my period. If you want, we can..."

"Shh. I'm not mad. Why would I be mad?"

Because you always get mad at things like this, Gwen thought, peering at Didi through the semidarkness.

Didi continued stroking Gwen's hair. "Why don't you just lie here and relax? I'm going to change my clothes and make us some tea, OK?"

"OK." Gwen collapsed back against the pillows. Didi was being so nice, for a change. Usually, she didn't care if Gwen had a headache, a stomachache, malaria, or walking pneumonia. If they had planned on having sex, they would have sex, damn it, whether one of them was at death's door or not. Maybe Didi was finally growing up, Gwen thought, as she shut her eyes. "Honey," she called to Didi, who had stepped into their walk-in closet, "I'm sure I'll feel better tomorrow night, and then we can..."

"Shh." Didi stepped into the room half naked. "Don't worry about it, Gwen. I loved your note. You just rest now. We have the rest of our lives to have sex." And so the lying begins, Didi thought, remembering her friend Angela saying the same thing to her one afternoon when she had been visiting with her two-year-old. Nina had wanted grapefruit juice because Didi was drinking some, but grapefruit juice was too acidic for her two-year-old tummy. Angela had poured some apple juice into a cup and said to Nina, "Here, drink this, sweetheart. It's the same juice." Nina looked suspicious for half a second, but then took the juice, greedily gulped it down, and asked for more. "And so the lying begins," Angela said, winking at Didi, and pouring her daughter another glass of juice. Didi was surprised Nina hadn't caught on; after all, apple juice and grapefruit juice looked, smelled, and tasted totally different from one another.

I guess people really do believe what they want to believe, she thought, tossing her dress into their dry-cleaning bag. She put her hands through the sleeves of her bathrobe and then wrapped both ends of the terry cloth belt tightly around her waist, as if they were Nicki's arms. "Nicki, Nicki, Nicki," Didi whispered into the darkness. Then she stepped into her slippers and crept down to the kitchen to start the tea.

✣   ✣   ✣

"What's up, Nicki?"

"Hey, how you doing, Frances?" Nicki threw an apron over her head, grabbed a knife, and started slicing up the onions that Frances had laid out for her. "What's for lunch, Boss?"

"Quiche Lorraine, turkey meatloaf, penne with portabello mushrooms. You know, the usual." Frances looked up from her recipe card and gestured with her wooden spoon. "What's that about?"

"What?"

"That shit-eating grin on your face. You look like you won the goddamn lottery last night."

"I did, in a manner of speaking." Nicki let the smile she was trying in vain to keep undercover stretch itself out even further. "I'm in love, Boss, L-O-V-E love."

Frances groaned and shook her head. "Christ, not again, Nicki. Don't tell me you're back together with Marnie?"

"Marnie who?" Nicki scraped onion slices off her wooden cutting board into a round, metal bowl.

"OK, not Marnie." Frances poked some mushrooms she was grilling with the edge of a spatula. "What was that other one's name, Sheryl, Sheila...."

"Shawna. It's not her either."

"Who is it then?"

"Her name is..." Nicki paused for a minute. She really did-n't want to tell Frances the woman had gotten away without giving Nicki her name. Or her phone number. But she didn't want to lie to her, either. "Believe it or not, Frances, she never told me her name. Her mouth was too busy doing other things."

"You don't even know her name?" Frances broke some eggs into a bowl. "Where the hell'd you meet her?"

Whoops. Nicki certainly didn't want Frances to know she was in therapy. "You know," she said. "Around."

"Around, huh? You sure do get *around*, Nicki." Frances shook her head as she searched for her eggbeater. "I don't know how you do it."

"You know how I do it, Boss. I've told you a million times."

"I know, I know. Stand up straight, be direct, talk in a deep voice." Frances cleared her throat. "So how long do you think this one's going to last, Romeo?" she asked in her best imita-tion of James Earl Jones harking Bell Atlantic. "A month? A week? Or just a one-night stand?"

"Frances, you cut me to the quick. Ugh." Nicki held the knife to her belly with both fists and pretended to commit hari-kari. "This one's different, I'm telling you. This one's for real."

"Yeah, yeah, yeah. As real as these." She tossed Nicki a box of vegetarian bacon bits. "Hey, do me a favor. Give those to Jenny to throw on the salad bar."

"All right, all right, but listen, I mean it this time, Frances. You'll see."

"You know who you are, Nicki? You're the dyke who cried wolf. How am I supposed to believe you after all these years? You've gone through more women than Wilt Chamberlain."

"I wish."

Frances snorted. "See what I mean?"

"Hey, variety is the spice of life." Nicki tossed Frances the nutmeg she needed for the quiche. "Ah, Frances, you're just jealous." She lifted a huge bowl of potatoes waiting to be peeled and brought them over to the sink.

"Jealous?" Frances snorted again. "I'm not jealous, Nicki. And in case you haven't noticed, I believe in the Paul Newman approach to marriage."

"Which is?"

"You never heard what he said? 'Why go out for hamburger when you can have steak at home every night?'"

Nicki chuckled. "I like that," she said, but then all of a sudden she stopped laughing. If her new chick had a girlfriend, and Nicki was fairly sure she did, did that make the girlfriend steak and Nicki merely hamburger?

To call or not to call, that was the question repeating itself like a broken record over and over in Didi's mind. She'd picked up the phone a hundred times since Monday: at home when Gwen was in the bathroom or downstairs on her exercise bike; at work in-between patients; on the street while she was running around doing errands at the post office, the bookstore, the bank, the copy shop. Just do it, Didi told herself, quoting the Nike slogan and picking up the receiver. Just say no, she told herself two seconds later, as if Nicki were a drug.

Didi knew what she had done was awful. Wonderful too, but awful just the same. What if the situation had been reversed? What if Gwen had cheated on her? I'd fucking kill her, Didi thought, staring into a cup of coffee, which was all she could manage to order for lunch. It wasn't like Didi to drink real coffee in the middle of the day, but then again, it wasn't like her to hop in the sack with a complete stranger in the middle of the day either. And besides, if Gwen ever had an affair, after being so stingy with her in the sex department, Didi would have every right to blow her cork. Gwen, on the other hand, could hardly blame Didi; after all, it was no secret that her needs hadn't been met for a long, long time. Still, Didi knew she had violated Gwen's trust. But what was she supposed to do? Say to Nicki, "Wait a minute. Before you put your tongue back in my mouth, I have to call my girlfriend-my girlfriend, who, by the way, happens to be your therapist"?

Didi signaled to her waitress for a refill. She picked up the warm coffee cup, held it to her forehead, and pressed hard. What a mess she was in. Not only had she lied to Gwen, but she had also lied to Nicki. Should she tell Nicki that Gwen was her girlfriend, not her therapist? Would it damage the sacred therapeutic relationship, which Gwen considered holier than the Goddess herself? And what would Nicki think? Would she be really pissed off that they were starting out their relationship based on a terrible lie? Is that what you're doing, Didi asked herself, starting a relationship? If that is what you're doing, then you better call the woman.

Even though she knew Nicki's number by heart, Didi

opened her lipstick case and took Nicki's note out of it. Just the sight of Nicki's handwriting made her smile. *You sweet thing, you...* She remembered Nicki calling her that, and other things too: sweet thing, beautiful lady, honey thighs, rose-in-bloom. Didi felt a blush creep up her cheeks as a deep and soulful sigh escaped from her lips. I can't see her again, Didi told herself. I've got to deal with Gwen. Either break up with her so I can be with Nicki or work things out. One or the other. You can't have your cake and eat it too.

Why not? Didi wondered, as right on cue a waitress walked by with an enormous piece of chocolate cheesecake for the couple sitting in the window seat across from Didi's booth. Why can't I have my cake and eat it too?

I wish I had someone to talk to about this, Didi thought, cupping her hands around her mug. But who? No one at work, that was for sure. And no one at the studio. They all knew Gwen, and that would put them in an awful position. Besides, could they be trusted? Didi didn't have that many close friends in the area. Acquaintances, yes, but no one she could really confide in, no one who wasn't also a friend of Gwen's. Theirs was such a small community, and Gwen had lived in town a lot longer than Didi. Gwen knew everyone, from softball, from her years at the food co-op, from just being around.

Who Didi really wanted to talk to about all this was Gwen. *God, Gwen, you won't believe this,* she could just hear herself saying. *I can come five times in one afternoon. Isn't that amazing?*

That's nice, dear, Gwen would say. *Can you pass the salt?* God, sometimes Gwen was just like Didi's parents:

I graduated third in my class, Mom.
Good, good.
I got into a juried art show, Dad.
Good, good.
I started using oils, Gwen, and I'm really excited about it.
Good, good.

Didi was sure she had told Gwen she had switched mediums, and she was just as sure it had gone in one ear and out the other. Nicki would pay attention, Didi thought. *I just know Nicki would think everything I do is important.*

"Anything else? Another refill?" Didi's waitress was back.

"No, thanks." Didi put a few ones on the table, feeling bad she had sat there for almost an hour and ordered only coffee. She took the singles back and replaced them with a five. *There,* Didi thought, pushing herself up from her seat. *At least that's one less thing I have to feel guilty about.*

✢   ✢   ✢

Gwen bled until Friday, which really ticked her off. *Don't tell me I'm going to be one of these women who hit menopause and start bleeding for weeks at a time,* she thought, stopping at the drugstore on Wednesday for yet more tampons. She was especially annoyed because she wanted to make good on her promise to Didi—the promise she had written on her note—and a whole week had gone by without her being able to do so. If they didn't have sex this weekend, that would be a full two weeks, and Didi would surely start in on her, which was the last thing she needed. *Why the hell does Didi have to keep score anyway?* Gwen wondered. *She didn't* think it mattered how often they had sex; what was important was how much they both enjoyed themselves when they did have it. Sometimes Gwen thought Didi only wanted to make love so she could keep up with some imaginary standard she set for them—once a week, twice a week—whatever the current statistic was for lesbian couples, according to the newest survey in *Girlfriends* magazine.

Tonight was definitely going to be the night. It was Friday, and if they had sex tonight, Gwen was pretty much assured a hassle-free weekend. Didi had said she was going to spend a little time after work at her studio, and that was fine with Gwen. It was perfect, in fact; it gave her time to prepare. Gwen's plan was to give Didi the perfect romantic evening, and not because it was her birthday or their anniversary or Valentine's Day. Just because. Because she loved her.

Did Gwen love Didi? Of course she did. Most of the time. But Didi had been so distant lately. So distracted. Like last night she had offered to brush Didi's hair, something she hadn't done for a long time. Didi loved having her hair brushed, her "crowning glory," which was so black it was almost blue and so straight, Didi often joked about it: "I'm not straight, but my hair is." But Didi hadn't been interested last night. "Thanks, Gwen, but I'm not in the mood," she'd said, with this absent look on her face. When Gwen had questioned her about it, she'd said, "I'm just thinking about my painting, Gwen. You know how obsessed I get." Sure, it was all right for Didi to obsess over a piece of artwork, but it wasn't OK for Gwen to obsess over a client. At least a client was real, a person who needed some help, not a piece of paper with colors splashed all over it.

Now, now, now, Gwen chastised herself. She knew she should be more supportive of Didi's artwork. And she would be if she could understand it or at least see the point of it. When Didi had been doing pottery, at least the objects she'd made were functional as well as pretty. And when she was doing stained glass, at least she'd been making things Gwen could recognize: a waterfall, a rainbow, a tree. But this abstract stuff…

Gwen remembered a card they had once seen in a bookshop that had a photo of a little kid cooking on it. He was making spaghetti, and there were spatters of tomato sauce all over the place: on the stove, the counter, the kid's face and apron, the walls.… The caption underneath the photo read, "The young Jackson Pollack." Gwen had thought it was very funny; Didi did not. Didi was always trying to drag Gwen to art galleries, and sometimes Gwen went, but it was hard for her to hide her boredom—just as it was nearly impossible for Didi to muster up (or even pretend to muster up) some enthusiasm at a sporting event. "Just come to a WNBA game with me," Gwen had pleaded. "It's women's basketball. I'm sure you'll like it."

"What's there to like?" Didi replied. "A bunch of girls trying to shove a ball into a basket? Please. I'd rather go to the movies."

It was true they didn't have that much in common, but Gwen didn't think that was so important in a relationship. She could always find another jock to go to a game with, and Didi could always get another artist from her building to accompany her to a museum. The important thing was what was in their hearts.

Gwen set the table with candles, flowers, and champagne and checked on the scallops-in-wine casserole browning in the broiler. She had already lit long sticks of incense in the bedroom and put a present on Didi's pillow: a beautifully wrapped box with a silk bra and panties set inside. At first Gwen had been doing all this for Didi's sake—to get her off her back by getting her *on* her back—but as she ran around the house making sure everything was perfect, she began to feel more than a teeny bit excited. A night of getting down and dirty was long overdue, and it would definitely improve things between them. Didi's right, Gwen thought, I really should make more of an effort. I have been taking her for granted lately. I do get wrapped up in my work. Well, who says you can't teach an old dog new tricks? Starting right now, I'm going to pay more attention to my girl. Gwen nodded her head firmly. She only hoped she wasn't a day late and a dollar short.

Wouldn't Sandy ever go home? Usually the building was empty on Friday nights, which is why Didi had gone there straight after work. She didn't want to make her phone call from the street, and she certainly couldn't make it from home. Gwen had told her she had a surprise for her, and Didi knew it had something to do with sex, for surely her period was over by now. Just what I need, more sex, Didi thought. She had actually been sore for a few days after her romp with Nicki, and she'd been sorry when the feeling went away. As long as her body ached, she knew their encounter had been real. Now she wasn't so sure.

Friday night was probably a good time to call Nicki. More than likely she'd be out, and Didi was hoping to get her answering machine. If Nicki answered, Didi wasn't sure she'd be able to resist her. The way she was feeling right now, she could easily be persuaded to jump in her car, drive right over, and even spend the night. Of course, she had no idea how to find Nicki's place, but a minor detail like that had no place in her fantasy.

Didi grabbed a sketchbook and magic marker and started scribbling what she'd say if she got an answering machine. "Hi, Nicki. It's Didi," she wrote, and then stopped. You can't tell her your name, you idiot, Didi reminded herself. What if she tells Gwen? Yes, they had said they wouldn't tell Gwen (of course, Didi wouldn't), but could she really trust Nicki? After all, wasn't the point of therapy to tell your therapist absolutely everything? So maybe her goose was already cooked or would be come Monday. Didi crossed out the sentence and started over. "Hi, Nicki. It's me," she wrote. That was better. Surely she would know who "me" was—unless the tape on her answering machine was full of such messages from girls Nicki had ravished that week.

"Nicki, I really had a good time the other day," Didi wrote, "but I can't see you again. I'm married." Didi hesitated, than added the words, "to your therapist," then crossed them out again. How could she ever tell Nicki that? She ripped the page out of her book, crumpled it up, and threw it toward the trash. It missed.

"Hi, Nicki. It's me," Didi wrote again on a fresh piece of paper. Then she stopped and chewed on the end of her marker. Why couldn't she just be spontaneous? Isn't that what she was always nagging Gwen about? Just pick up the phone, Didi. Say whatever pops into your head.

"Being spontaneous is what got me into this mess in the first place," Didi reminded herself out loud. But was she sorry? Not a bit.

"Hi, Nicki. Want to marry me?" Didi wrote the word *yes* underneath the sentence, then drew a heart with the words *Nicki and Didi* inside it. Just as she was adding *forever* at the bottom, Sandy knocked on the door frame, making Didi jump ten feet in the air.

"Did I scare you? Sorry." Sandy took a tentative step into the room as Didi shut her sketchbook with a *whap*. "I just wanted to let you know I was leaving, and I think you're the last one left in the building."

"Thanks." Didi raised her arms over her head and stretched, as if she were awfully tired. "I was just closing up too. I'm not going to stay much longer."

"Do you want me to wait for you?"

"No, that's OK. Have a great weekend." Didi had to literally sit on her hands to keep from shoving the woman out the door.

"OK, you too." Sandy went back into her own studio to gather up her things, and Didi practically held her breath until she heard Sandy close, lock, and check her door. She waited until her footsteps faded down the hallway and out the front door, and then she gave her an extra few minutes to get into her car and drive out of the parking lot. Sandy was just the type to turn back around, run up the stairs singing "Forgot something," and let herself back into her studio again.

When a good ten minutes had gone by, Didi took a deep breath and went into the hallway to pick up the phone.

✛   ✛   ✛

Nicki rushed home from the restaurant as she had every day that week, practically pouncing on her answering machine, as if it were to blame for not recording the message she longed to hear. What was the deal here? Nicki knew the woman had had a good time—no one could fake shrieks like that—so why wouldn't she want to see her again? Unless it was the girlfriend thing. But if having a girlfriend hadn't stopped her the first time, why would it stop her the second time or the third time or the fourth or the fifth or the sixth? Maybe she was out of town or something. But still, how hard could it be to pick up the phone and make a lousy call? God, I sound just like my mother, Nicki thought, when she caught me sneaking into the house at three in the morning from a party, or just like Marnie, when I was late coming over from somewhere I never should have been in the first place. Funny how all Nicki's girlfriends wound up reminding her of her mother sooner or later. Well, this new one wouldn't. She was different. Didn't much seem like the nagging type.

But what if she wasn't the phoning type either? Nicki cracked herself a beer, lit a cigarette, and put her feet up on the coffee table. Christ, will you look at me? She shook her head. All alone waiting by the phone on a Friday night. Just like a girl. Usually it was the other way around. Usually it was Nicki who kept the girls waiting, it was Nicki who called the shots, it was Nicki who was the love-'em-and-leave-'em type.

Nicki bent over to unlace her boots. The shoe was on the other foot, and it was more than a little tight.

Where was Didi? The casserole was going to burn if Gwen kept it in the oven much longer. And if she took it out, it would get all dry. Didi hadn't said an exact time, but Gwen thought for sure she'd be home by now. She's probably all wrapped up in that art project of hers, Gwen thought, shaking her head. She was trying to change her attitude and be more supportive—even admiring—of Didi's commitment to something that would never get her anywhere. No, that didn't sound exactly right, but still she was trying.

"I'm going to call her," Gwen said, removing her oven mitts. Art project or no art project, it was Friday night, the weekend—their weekend—and Gwen was ready to start it. She dialed the number, and a busy signal rattled against her ear. Christ, those artists. What if this were an emergency? And who's to say it wasn't?

A wave of heat, like a hot flash, coursed through Didi's body as soon as she heard Nicki's voice on the answering machine. She waited for the beep and then spoke quickly. "Hi, Nicki. It's me," Didi said, her heart pounding. "Listen, I had a wonderful time the other day," Didi looked at her script, "but—"

"But what?" Nicki's voice broke in.

"But," Didi faltered. "What are you doing, screening your calls?"

"You betcha." Nicki had really been in the john, but Didi was too much of a lady to be told that. "I didn't want to speak to anyone but you."

"Is that so?" Didi's mouth broke into a wide smile, despite her resolve. "Nicki?"

"Yes, sweet girl?"

Shit. She wasn't going to make this easy, was she? "Nicki," Didi took a deep breath. "I don't think I can see you again."

"What?" It's not that Nicki hadn't been expecting this—after all, it had been five days, and Didi hadn't called—but still, hearing the words was like a punch to the gut. "You can't mean that, darlin'. Didn't you have a good time with me?"

Good time was an understatement. She'd had a great time, a fabulous time, the time of her life. But still… "Nicki, I wish I didn't have to tell you this, but I have a girlfriend."

"I know, honey."

"You do?" Shit, was she on to her?

"Sure. I knew it the minute you wouldn't give me your phone number."

"Yeah, well…" Didi didn't know what to say. *I still want to be friends* was more than pathetic. It wasn't even true. She didn't want to be Nicki's friend at all. She wanted to be her lover.

"Hey, I understand." Nicki leaned forward on the couch and reached for her pack of cigarettes. "But you know, it's awfully cruel to break up with someone over the phone. Can't I just see you once more? Just for coffee?"

Coffee. Yeah, right. It was supposed to be just coffee the

first time. Years from now, Didi thought, coffee will be our own private joke. We'll probably be saying, "Want to have coffee?" instead of "Want to fuck?" in front of our grandchildren.

"C'mon, baby doll, you're killing me." Nicki's voice traveled over the phone wires through Didi's ear directly into her heart. "Have coffee with me on Monday. Just coffee, I promise."

"Cross your heart?"

"Cross my heart," Nicki said, crossing her heart with crossed fingers.

"I don't know...." Didi knew the minute she saw Nicki she'd be a goner.

"C'mon, lover girl, don't you trust me?"

"Of course I trust you. I don't trust myself."

Bingo. There was the sentence that was music to Nicki's ears.

"Hi, Gwennie. Sorry I'm so late." Didi hung her jacket in the hall closet and came into the kitchen. "Oh, this is beautiful," she said, admiring the white tablecloth, the pink roses, the red candles.

It was beautiful an hour ago, Gwen thought, but she kept it to herself. "Where were you?" she asked, setting a casserole dish on the table.

"My studio." At least Didi wasn't lying this time. "That smells delicious. What is it?"

"Scallops." Gwen lifted the lid off the dish with a flourish.

"Scallops?" Didi looked at Gwen, puzzled. "You don't even like scallops."

"They're OK." Gwen crossed the room in search of a serving spoon. "And anyway, they're your favorite dish. Once in a while I can do something special for my girl."

Hmm. Strange, Didi thought, as she sat down at the table. Was Gwen getting suspicious? She hadn't made a special meal like this for her in ages. "When did you have time to do all this?" she asked, as Gwen opened the champagne.

"This afternoon. It didn't take that long." Gwen poured champagne into two glasses and then raised hers. "To us," she said, clinking Didi's rim.

"To us," Didi said, looking down as she took a sip. I feel awful, she thought, as she lowered her champagne glass and lifted her fork. She's trying so hard, and I'm such a shit. Didi took a bite of her food. "Gwen, it's fabulous," she said, grateful she could utter another sentence that wasn't a lie. "So, what's the occasion?"

Gwen looked up from her plate. "No occasion. I just wanted to do something special tonight." She gave a little wink. "If you know what I mean."

Didi pretended to be very interested in her food. "This is so good, Gwen. I was practically starving." She shoved a few mouthfuls in quickly and then washed them down with a big swallow of champagne. What the hell, maybe getting drunk would help the situation. "What's for dessert?"

"You're for dessert." Gwen took one more bite and then laid her fork down with an air of finality. "Let's go into the bedroom," she said in a deep voice.

Didi looked up from her plate. "Do you have a frog in your

throat, Gwennie? You sound funny."

"No, I'm fine." Gwen coughed into her hand a few times. So much for the Clark Gable routine.

"I'll do the dishes," Didi got up from the table and started clearing. "You did all this cooking. It's only fair."

"Oh, leave the dishes, Didi. C'mon. Don't you want to see what your surprise is?"

"But they'll get all crusty." Didi caught herself saying what Gwen usually said, as Gwen held herself back from spouting Didi's words, *Oh, for God's sake, can't you be spontaneous for once in your life?*

"I'll do the dishes later." Gwen strode over to Didi and held out her hand.

"Gwen, what's wrong with your back?"

"My back? Nothing. Why?"

"I don't know. You're standing funny. Like you're all stiff."

Strike two for Nicki's how-to-seduce-women tricks. Luckily Gwen didn't know any more of them, since three strikes would make her out. "C'mon, baby. I've been waiting all day for you." Gwen held out her hand, and Didi took it, for after all, what choice did she have? She let Gwen lead her up the steps into their bedroom, where a gift box wrapped in bright red paper lay waiting on her pillow. Didi looked at Gwen, who just smiled and gestured for her to open it. Didi sat down and pulled at the ribbon. A month ago or even a week ago, this would have thrilled her, but now that she'd been with Nicki... Forget Nicki, Didi told herself. Be here now. With Gwen. Your girlfriend. The woman you married. The woman you swore you'd be faithful to. Didi and Gwen hadn't had a real commitment ceremony, but they talked about it every once in a while, and they had exchanged rings one year on vacation in Provincetown. They weren't gold bands, and they didn't even wear them on the right finger (Gwen had picked out a pinkie ring with a labyris etched into it, and Didi had chosen a snake with a ruby eye she wore around her index finger). But still, neither of them had ever given a girlfriend a ring before. That meant something. Or at least it used to.

Didi opened the box and pushed back sheets of cream colored tissue paper. "Gwen, this is beautiful." She oohed and ahhed over the black silk garments inside.

"They'll be even more beautiful once you put them on." Gwen dimmed the light and turned on the stereo. "Why don't you change, and I'll be back in a minute?"

Oh, God, I can't do this, Didi thought, putting the lingerie back in its box. "Gwen?"

"What, honey?"

"Gwen, I...I can't."

"What?" Gwen came back into the room.

"I'm just...I just feel like cuddling tonight. Would that be OK with you?" Didi did want to cuddle with Gwen. She wanted her to hold her and stroke her and reassure her everything was all right, even though it wasn't.

"Are you sick?" Gwen felt Didi's forehead.

"Um, a little. My head hurts. I think it's the fumes from the oil paint. You know, another woman in my building had to give them up because she was getting headaches, and I might have to also."

"Why don't you lay down, and I'll give you a back rub? You can have your surprise another night."

"My surprise? Didn't you give me my surprise?" Didi gestured toward the box on the bed.

"That's not all of it," Gwen opened the top drawer of her night table and got out some massage oil.

"What's the rest of it?" Didi was curious, despite herself. She lay down on her belly and lifted up her shirt.

"Do you really want to know, or do you want to wait?" Gwen rubbed the oil on Didi's back and started lightly kneading her shoulders.

"I really want to know." Didi mumbled into her pillow.

"Stay right there," Gwen hopped off the bed and was back in a minute. "Remember this?"

Didi lifted herself up on one elbow to see what Gwen was extending out to her: a leather harness held together with three silver rings. "What are you doing with that?"

"I'm going to use it. Isn't that what you want?"

Oh, God, now Gwen was going to use the strap-on? Now, after Didi had begged her for years to just give it a try? They'd had so many fights about it—"Harnesses are for horses," Gwen had said—that Didi had just given up. Gwen thought dildos were gross, she'd said so many, many times. "If you want that, Didi, why don't you just do it with a man?"

"Just because a woman likes penetration doesn't mean she's straight," Didi had explained with exaggerated patience, as if she were an instructor in Remedial Lesbianism 101. But Gwen had always disagreed. Until today.

"I'm really sorry, Gwennie," Didi said and then, to her own amazement, burst into tears.

❖   ❖   ❖

"Why don't you tell me about your childhood, Nicki?" Gwen stared at her client with an I'd-like-to-get-to-know-you look.

"Forget all that, Doc." Nicki rearranged her lanky frame on the couch, and let her promise to Didi fly out the window. "I've got news."

"All right. What's your news?"

"Remember that girl I told you about, the one I met a few weeks ago?"

Gwen nodded. "The one who wouldn't have coffee with you."

Nicki looked at Gwen like she was more than a few cards short of a full deck. "We're way beyond coffee, Doc. We spent the entire afternoon in the sack last week, and let me tell you, this girl can do it like there's no tomorrow. We did it in bed, on the floor, on the kitchen table…Oh, man." Nicki licked her lips as if she were savoring something wonderful. "I tell you, Doc, I think I'm in love."

"Really?" Gwen wasn't surprised in the least, but she tried to make her voice convey otherwise. "How did all this happen?"

"Well," Nicki let out a long breath. "We went for a ride in my truck, and one thing led to another…"

"Whoa, Nellie." Gwen pantomimed reigning in a horse. "Nicki, did you ever see the famous *Seinfeld* yadda-yadda-yadda episode? You're skipping over some major details here. Just how did one thing lead to another?"

"Well," Nicki said again. "I pulled off the side of the road and just kissed her. A slick trick, Doc. You let a girl know…"

"*I* let a girl know…"

"Right, right, right. I let her know I couldn't even wait to get back to the house, I just had to kiss her right then and there."

"And then?"

"Then she was just putty in my arms." Nicki grinned, obviously pleased with herself.

"I guess congratulations are in order." Gwen smiled too. "What's her name?"

"Her name?"

"Yes, her name."

"Why do you want to know her name?"

Gwen tried to appear noncommittal. "It would make it easier to talk about her, that's all." When Nicki didn't say anything, Gwen pushed. "Is there some reason you don't want me to know her name?"

"Uh…yeah." Nicki looked down at her boots and then looked up. "You see, she has a girlfriend."

"She has a girlfriend." Gwen repeated Nicki's sentence and let it hang in the air between them for a second or two. "Did she tell you she had a girlfriend?"

"Not at first. At first she wouldn't give me her phone number, so I guessed that was why. And then she didn't call me for a few days, so I figured she was wrestling with her conscience."

"And then?"

"Then she called and told me she couldn't see me anymore."

"And how did you feel about that?"

"I knew she didn't mean it. I asked her if she'd just meet me for coffee, and she said yes. In fact, I'm meeting her this afternoon."

"And are you really just going to have coffee with her?"

"Doc, what do you think?" Nicki raised one eyebrow at Gwen.

"I think…" Gwen paused. "I think a lot of things, Nicki, but I want to know what you think."

"You think I'm a horrible person, don't you, Doc?" Nicki shook her head. "Whenever anyone cheats on her girlfriend, the other woman gets all the blame. Listen, Doc, *I* didn't promise to be faithful to her girlfriend, whoever she is; *she* promised to be faithful to her. And I'm sure she would be if she was getting some at home. Which she obviously isn't. So if anyone's the bad guy here, it's her."

"Which her?" Gwen was a bit confused. "I need some names here, Nicki, if I'm going to follow all this."

Nicki couldn't bring herself to tell Gwen she didn't know the love of her life's name, so she said nothing.

"It's a matter of trust, Nicki, that's all. It says to me that you don't trust me yet, and I'm curious about that. You know, don't you, that everything you say in here is confidential?"

"But what if you know her?" Nicki asked. "How do I know I can trust you? I pour my heart out, and all you do is sit there in that chair and nod your head."

Ah, now we're getting somewhere, Gwen thought. Aloud she said, "Are you angry with me, Nicki?"

"No." Nicki's voice exploded. "It's just that I'm telling you the most intimate details of my sex life here, and I know nothing about you."

"What do you want to know?" Gwen asked.

"Tell me something about your sex life," Nicki said, "and then we'll be even."

"That isn't appropriate, Nicki. And I don't think it would be helpful to your therapeutic process." Gwen kept her face neutral as she spoke the words. What could she possibly tell Nicki? That her girlfriend, who was usually so hot to trot, had avoided her all weekend, even though she'd bucked herself up to try some things she swore she'd never do? "Did you think about what we talked about last week, Nicki? That maybe you get involved with women so quickly because you're afraid of being alone?"

"Yeah, I thought about it," Nicki said, even though she hadn't. "But Doc, what if this girl is really the one? How could I let her get away?"

"Nicki, you spent one afternoon in the sack with her. A lifetime relationship is based on a lot more than that. And besides, unavailability is the ultimate aphrodisiac."

"Meaning?"

"Meaning, if this woman weren't involved with someone else—in other words, if she were truly available—my guess is you'd feel a lot differently about her."

"You're wrong, Doc."

"Maybe. I guess time will tell. And speaking of time…"

The two women said it in unison: "Our time is just about up."

✤ ✤ ✤

A skirt or slacks? The black top or the blue one? Plain white panties or something a little more exciting? Didi stood in front of her bureau, stark naked, trying to figure out what to put on. We're just having coffee, she reminded herself, so what difference does it make which bra I wear? Still, a girl likes to feel sexy, even if it's just for herself. Didi had read that in *Elle* or *Vogue* or one of the other magazines in Dr. Carlton's office, and it was as good an excuse as any to put on her favorite beige satin camisole. And anyway, she thought, I could always say I was wearing it for Gwen.

Poor Gwen. Didi couldn't help feeling sorry for her. She'd tried to initiate sex three times over the weekend, and Didi just couldn't respond. She really wanted to—if only because slacking off in the sex department was a sure sign someone was having an affair (she'd read that just last month in *Cosmo*)—but she just couldn't get it up, so to speak. And the more understanding Gwen had been about it, the more turned off Didi had become. Why don't you just get mad? she'd wanted to scream. How can you believe these stupid excuses? A headache—now that was a classic. Being tired. Oh, please. Nicki would never buy any of it, Didi was sure of that. But she really had to deal with Gwen first, before she and Nicki got too involved. It wasn't right. Surely Nicki would understand that. Would she wait for her? It wasn't fair to expect as much, but still, she could always hope. And if Nicki didn't...well, maybe it wasn't meant to be. But if it wasn't meant to be, why had they bumped into each other that fateful Monday, only a few short weeks ago? Didi hardly ever went up to Gwen's office. No, the gods had put a gift right into Didi's hands, and maybe she was being ungrateful for not accepting it. Obviously it was fate. Or was Didi just bullshitting herself?

Didi combed her hair, threw on a dab of lipstick, and ran out the door, humming that old Mamas and Papas hit, "Monday, Monday." She was meeting Nicki at eleven-fifteen at

Mae's Diner, a seedy 24-hour joint at the edge of town. Nicki had wanted to meet at Mug Shots, but that was way too close to Gwen's office. "My girlfriend works in that neighborhood," Didi had said, and Nicki understood immediately. It was such a relief to be able to tell Nicki the truth (or at least part of the truth), and so nerve-racking to have to lie her face off to Gwen. She was really going to be in hot water one of these days when Gwen asked to see this oil painting she was supposedly so obsessed with. Gwen thought Didi was spending the day in the studio, and she would head over there, just as soon as she was through with Nicki. And she was through with Nicki, really she was.

Then why are you meeting her for coffee? a little voice inside Didi's head asked her. "Who the hell are you, Jiminy Cricket?" Didi asked aloud as she started the car. She wanted to get to the diner first, before Nicki did, and already be seated in a booth. A booth near the window. That way she would have the advantage. She could watch Nicki's tall frame walk through the parking lot and see those powerful hands pull open the diner's door. She could watch her dark eyes search the booths for a sign of Didi and see her face light up (hopefully) as soon as she caught sight of her.... "You are really asking for it, girl," Didi met her own eyes in the rearview mirror. But Nicki had said, and Didi agreed, that it was cruel to break up with someone over the phone. But what was there to break up? A one-night—make that one-day—stand?

Didi pulled into the parking lot of the diner and shut off her car. There was no truck in sight, and a thought suddenly occurred to her. What if Nicki had decided not to show up? What if she had set her up, so she'd have the last laugh? No, she wouldn't be that cruel, would she? She didn't have a mean bone in her body. Or did she? Didi hated to admit it, but the fact of the matter was, she didn't know Nicki at all.

✤   ✤   ✤

As soon as Nicki left the office, Gwen checked her answering machine. Unbelievable. The Dynamic Duo had canceled again. Those two were forever calling at the last minute to say they were going to be late or they weren't going to show at all. Clearly, money wasn't an issue—the mother always sent the check promptly—so it had to be something else. A power struggle, no doubt. The mother was much more interested in getting their "heads shrunk," as she put it, than the daughter, who'd barely said two words the entire session last week. *Honey*, Gwen wanted to tell her, *do you know how many women would shed tears of joy if their mothers would come to therapy with them? Sure it's hard, and your mother is a piece of work, but at least she's trying.* But of course Gwen couldn't say that. No, she was going to have to read them the riot act about how important consistency was in the therapeutic process and how they had to make more of an effort and blah, blah, blah…. On the other hand, why did Gwen care? After all, it was nice to be paid $95 to just sit on her ass for an hour. But then again, it wasn't right to take advantage of people like that.

What should Gwen do until her twelve o'clock? She didn't know what she wanted to do, but she did know what she didn't want to do: She didn't want to think about Didi and what was happening in their relationship. It was all so classic, such an open and shut textbook case—hadn't she counseled a mil-

lion lesbian couples in this same situation?—that Gwen wanted to scream. What was going on was this: Didi had been the
"yes person" in their relationship for so long, the person who
always wanted sex, that now that Gwen was also becoming a
yes person, Didi had to become the "no person," the person
who didn't want to have sex, to balance things out. They had
switched roles as automatically and easily as if Gwen had put
on a pair of Didi's high heels, and Didi had put on Gwen's
soccer cleats. It was ridiculous, it was ludicrous, it was frus-
trating, but it was real; Gwen had seen it more than a thousand times. There was always a "yes person" and a "no person" in a relationship, for if there were two "yes people," the
couple would never do anything but have sex (which sounded great in theory but didn't work too well in practice, not in
long-term relationships anyway). And if there were two "no
people" in a relationship, the couple would never have sex.
The object for a couple in treatment was to try to get past the
positions, which each person took on rather early in the
game, and just be real with each other. To undo the polariza-
tion that so often occurred and strike a balance. Gwen and
Didi's pendulum had swung so far to one side, it was inevitable that it had to swing to the other side before it came
to rest comfortably in the middle. Gwen knew all this, but still
she couldn't help feeling hurt at Didi's rejections all weekend.
And she couldn't talk to Didi about any of this, because Didi
would just tell her to stop "therapizing" her. *I'm not one of
your fucking clients*, Didi would be sure to say. *I'm your fucking girlfriend*. Though nonfucking girlfriend was more like it.
For the past couple of days anyway.

　　She'll come around, Gwen told herself, I just have to be patient. But still, as a way of reassuring herself, Gwen decided to spend the free hour she had reading up on sexual dynamics in lesbian relationships. What the hell. Even though she considered herself an expert on the subject, she'd be the first to admit she still had a lot to learn.

Nicki hopped into her truck and started driving toward the outskirts of town, where her dream girl was surely waiting. Did she look all right? She was wearing a black T-shirt and tight jeans—her James Dean look—and she'd just gotten a fresh haircut on Saturday. Nicki knew she looked good; if asked, *irresistible* would be the word she'd use to describe herself. Still, if the Blue-Eyed Beauty felt guilty enough about cheating on her girlfriend, all the good looks in the world would get Nicki exactly nowhere.

And speaking of guilt, the teeniest, tiniest, twinge of it began to eat away at Nicki as she drove. Sure, she had promised not to tell Gwen about the affair but only because they didn't want the Doc to know that two of her clients had gotten all hot and heavy with each other. And since Nicki didn't even know her girl's name, there was no way Gwen could figure it out. Unless... Nicki stopped at a red light and rested her forearms on the steering wheel. Unless Lover Girl was doing the same thing: telling Gwen about the new woman in her life without using Nicki's name. If so, Gwen would surely put two and two together. But who cared, really? Was it a crime to go out with another one of Gwen's clients? It's not like she was going out with her girlfriend or anything. Nicki didn't even know if Gwen had a girlfriend. It wasn't "appropriate" for her to know. Nicki wondered what kind of girl Gwen would go out with. Probably another jock like herself. Someone who would get up early on Saturday mornings to go jogging or in-line skating, or bike riding or some other activity that was equally athletic and horrifying.

The light turned green, and Nicki drove on. Oh, forget Gwen, she told herself. Think about your girl. Suppose she had confessed all in therapy. What would she say? Nicki could just hear her voice: *I met the strongest, sweetest, handsomest, sexiest, butchest woman on the planet.* Yeah, that sounded pretty good. It was true, after all. If it weren't, why would Didi's car be right there in the parking lot? Nicki pulled next to the Saturn and gave it three taps for good luck before opening the door to the diner and going inside.

"Hi, Handsome." The word slipped out of Didi's mouth before she could stop it.

"Hi, Gorgeous." Nicki took Didi's hand and kissed it. "God, it's been a long week." She slid into the booth across from Didi, not letting go of her hand.

Didi stared at their interlaced fingers for a minute, not daring to look up into Nicki's eyes. The truck stop was safe—no one she knew would dare enter such a smoke-filled, greasy spoon establishment—so she wasn't worried about being spotted. Still, she knew she should let go of Nicki's hand. But she couldn't, not with Nicki cradling Didi's hand between both her own, stroking it, soothing it, comforting it quietly as if it were a frightened pet.

"So, what's this about not being able to see me again?" Nicki cut right to the chase, before they even had a chance to order.

"Well, I have this girlfriend," Didi started to explain but then stopped as their waitress approached.

"What'll it be?"

"Just coffee," Didi said, somewhat embarrassed that Nicki still had her by the fingertips. What would the waitress think? Oh, fuck it, why should she care?

"Ditto," Nicki said. The waitress left and came right back with two steaming cups.

"Let me know if you need anything else," she said, walking off in a huff.

"Now where were we, sugar?" Nicki released Didi's hand and tapped a sugar packet against her palm. She dumped it into her coffee, added some cream, and stirred. "Mind if I smoke?"

Didi did mind but shook her head no anyway. See, she said to herself. I could never really be with her. She smokes. Didi couldn't stand cigarette smoke, and she wondered if Nicki would give up the habit if she asked her to, the way Gwen had given up her beloved cat Stella because Didi was allergic to her. And Gwen had absolutely adored Stella. She'd had her since she was a kitten—picked her out of the litter because not only was her fur the same orangy-red color as Gwen's hair, but they also had the same green eyes—and they'd been best buddies ever since. Stella wasn't too big of a problem at first—Gwen and Didi just spent most of their time at Didi's apartment—but she became a huge issue the minute they moved in together. Didi felt bad about it, and they'd tried everything: using air filters, vacuuming every other day, keeping Stella out of the bedroom even though she cried all night. But still, Didi's eyes were perpetually swollen, and she couldn't go more than half an hour in the house without having a sneezing fit. Finally, Gwen sat her down one day and said, "Listen, I've been thinking. It's either you or Stella."

"And?" Didi still remembered how hard her heart had pounded.

"It's you, silly." Gwen looked at Didi in amazement, like how could she possibly think there was any other option? "My mother will take her, and that way I'll still get to see her a few times a year."

"Oh, Gwen." Didi threw her arms around her and held her while she cried, that day, and the day they put Stella on a plane to Minneapolis. Gwen said it was no big deal, but Didi knew it was. Would Nicki do something like that for her? She wondered.

"So, sweet cheeks, what are you thinking?" It was the first time Nicki had ever asked a girl that question.

"Nothing," Didi lied. "Listen, Nicki, you're really terrific, and I know you'll make some lucky girl very happy someday. And I wish it could be me." Nicki put her cigarette down and took Didi's hand again. Didi held on tight. "I just have to sort things out with my girlfriend first, you know? It's not right for me to do this to her."

"What about you?" Nicki asked. "Is it right for you to do this to you? And to me?"

"No," Didi whispered. "It isn't right at all. I'm so confused."

"Poor you." Nicki held Didi's hand for a minute and sat completely still, staring at the gold, ruby-eyed snake ring winding around Didi's index finger. Then she started stroking Didi's skin, lightly tickling her palm, her wrist, her forearm, completely oblivious—or seeming oblivious—to the effect her touch was having on her. "Honey pie," she said, as if Didi were capable of having a normal conversation when she was practically oozing off her seat. "You have to do what's best for you. I know how hard it is to carry on an affair, believe me. I've done it myself, but those days are over. In fact, when I met you, I swore I was going to turn over a new leaf."

"Really?" Didi breathed the word.

Nicki nodded. "That's what's so ironic about all this. I decided I was really going to be good this time. That you deserved that. And I deserved it too. I want to know what it's like to be true blue to someone, to be their one and only. But," she shrugged, "I guess it wasn't meant to be." Nicki sighed, took a puff from her cigarette, and stared off into space for a minute. "But if it wasn't meant to be," she turned back to Didi and looked her straight in the eye, "then why did we meet? I thought it was fate."

"I did too. I was just thinking that on the way over." Didi couldn't believe what Nicki was saying. Was it fate? Should she take a chance? Throw caution to the wind? Throw Gwen to the dogs?

"Fate can be cruel." Nicki waxed on, feeling philosophical and more than a little melodramatic. "Why didn't we meet when we were both single? I guess for me this is payback time." Marnie would sure get a kick out of this, Nicki thought, smiling ruefully. Not to mention about 200 other girls. "We're star-crossed lovers, just like Romeo and Juliet." Nicki decided to pour it on thick.

"You read Shakespeare?" Didi practically squealed.

Nicki nodded. It was only half a lie after all. Marnie had dragged her off to see the movie with Leonardo DiCaprio, but Didi didn't have to know that. "Now, no one's going to do anything foolish like kill themselves, are they?" Nicki raised one eyebrow at Didi. She shook her head no. "Yep, I guess it's time for old St. Nick to be alone for a while," Nicki went on, feeling sorrier and sorrier for herself. "It won't be so bad. TV dinners, beef stew out of a can, Spam sandwiches…"

Didi made a face. "That sounds horrible."

Nicki shrugged. "It won't be forever. I'm sure I'll find someone eventually. But I doubt she'll be as beautiful and sexy and sweet as you." Nicki looked at Didi again, so caught up in the tragedy of the moment, that two fat tears actually formed in the corners of her eyes.

Didi stared hard across the table, as her eyes misted over too. Oh, what the fuck, she thought. I've already crossed the line, so what's one more afternoon? "Let's get out of here," she said, squeezing Nicki's hand and raising it to her lips to give her knuckles a kiss. Didi had planned on sticking to her guns—really she had—but she'd never expected all this to happen. And besides, call her a pushover, but Didi never could stand to see a grown butch cry.

✢   ✢   ✢

It was different this time. Just as intense but sweeter somehow. Like they both knew it couldn't last forever, so every precious moment counted. What was it that Didi had read: The key to happiness was to live each day as if it were your first? Or was it to live each day as if it were your last? Either way, the thought that she might never see Nicki again filled her with a longing and a passion and a fierceness she had no idea was inside her. She bit Nicki's biceps, she licked her callused palm, she sucked her lips greedily until they were swollen twice their size. And she gave herself up completely, letting Nicki put two, three, four fingers completely inside her, all the while making such raw, wild, savage noises that she was afraid Nicki's neighbors would call the police, thinking some weird ritualistic animal slaughter was taking place inside Apartment 44G. Nicki coaxed everything out of Didi and then some, telling her over and over how beautiful she was, how special, she had never met anyone like her before, and she was sure she never would again.

"Shh. Don't talk. Just hold me," Didi said when they were both spent, as was the better part of the afternoon. And this time, when Didi staggered to her feet and began to get dressed, Nicki decided, even though she didn't want to, to simply let her go.

Though she hated to admit it, Gwen was growing awfully tired of listening to other people's problems. *Just don't eat it,* she wanted to yell at the Bulimic. *Just get over yourself,* she wanted to scream at the Mid-life Crisis. What Gwen really wanted to do was go home, put her feet up, and watch a good college basketball game, even though she knew that would piss Didi off. Or maybe she felt like doing it *because* it would piss Didi off. Gwen wanted to ignore Didi; after all, she was only human, and her response to being hurt was to hurt Didi back. But that was the beauty of being a therapist: Gwen could psych herself out by analyzing her own behavior. The average person would act as if she were saying to her lover, *Fine. You don't want to have sex? Then I don't want to have sex either,* in hopes that a little reverse psychology would work and that by going back to being the "no person," her lover would become the "yes person" again. Sure, that sounded OK in theory, but Gwen knew that attitude would only result in the two of them going right back to their same old pattern and getting stuck there all over again. No, what she had to do, whether she wanted to or not, was use a little reverse reverse psychology. Gwen had to keep pursuing Didi; she had to charm her and woo her, as if they were just starting to date. Kill her with kindness, so to speak. Gwen remembered an anti–Viet Nam War demonstration she had seen on the news years ago, when protesting hippies had placed daisies inside the barrels of soldiers' guns. When someone expected a confrontation, and you came at them with kindness, it usually knocked the wind right out of their sails. And since Gwen was expecting Didi to pick a fight that evening, as they'd now gone a full two weeks without any action in the bedroom department, she had to be prepared.

Maybe I'll take her out to dinner, Gwen thought, glancing over her calendar. I'll be done with clients by seven-thirty, and we could use a romantic evening on the town. And besides, Didi was a lot less likely to pick a fight out in public than she was inside the privacy of their own home. Gwen made an eight-thirty reservation at their favorite Indian restaurant and then called Didi at home. There was no answer, but Gwen had expected that; she was undoubtedly at the studio, working on her masterpiece. I'll just pick her up at eight, she thought. As a surprise. Oh, that won't work. She'll be all grungy and full of paint. I guess I'll have to go home first, pick up a change of clothes for her, and then go to the studio. Maybe I'll pick up some flowers too. Make it a special night neither one of us will ever forget.

"So is this really good-bye? I'm really never going to see you again?" Nicki couldn't believe Didi would just take off like this, not after the afternoon they'd just had. The sex had been unbelievable, outrageous, fucking transformational. Nicki felt like a giant, a king, a god who could do absolutely anything. The feeling was intoxicating, and she was in no hurry to let it go. No, at the moment, Nicki was in no hurry to do anything at all. In fact, she was so content she felt as if she could stay like this forever: lying naked on her side, her head propped up on one elbow, practically hypnotized by Didi's arm as it moved up and down, up and down, slowly brushing out her long, black, shiny, luxurious hair.

"Never say never." Didi turned to look at Nicki and then turned quickly away, as the sight of her lying there, all lean and muscle, practically undid her all over again.

"I have a present for you." Nicki sat up lazily and opened the top dresser of her night stand. "Remember this?" She rummaged around and then reached over to tickle Didi's cheek with a feather.

"Of course." Just the lightest touch of the feather on her face reminded Didi of how it had felt last week (was it only last week?) when Nicki had used the feather to tease her belly, her back, her... Don't go there, Didi brought herself up short. Or you'll never get your butt out of this apartment again.

"I could never touch anyone else with it after being with you." Nicki placed the feather carefully in Didi's hand, as if it were something rare and precious, which it was. Her very first lover had given it to her, an older femme who had certainly shown her a trick or two. "Just a little something to remember me by."

"Oh, Nicki, do you really think I could ever forget you?" Didi let out a deep sigh. She wished she had something to give Nicki, but what? Jewelry was out of the question. Both her snake ring with the ruby eye and the locket around her neck had been presents from Gwen. Giving Nicki her underwear was way too tacky. And what was in her purse? Half a packet of Lifesavers, a stray bobby pin or two, matches, stamps, pens, an old lipstick, her address book. "I wish I had something to give you,"

"You've already given me more than I deserve." Oh, I am so incredibly smooth, Nicki said to herself. She pulled a pair of jeans up her long legs and threw on a T-shirt. "C'mon. If you really have to go, I'll walk you to your car."

Didi stopped in front of the Saturn and hesitated before opening the door. Was this really it? At least now she knew how to get to Nicki's house, if she ever wanted to come back. No, scratch that. It wasn't a question of wanting to come back; of course, she *wanted to*. But would she ever have the courage to? Because she swore next time she saw Nicki, it would be as a single woman. But did she really want to break up with Gwen?

"Bye, lover." Nicki enfolded Didi in her arms and held her tightly against her chest for a minute. Then she gave her one last long smooch before letting her get into her car and slowly drive away.

✛   ✛   ✛

Gwen slid into a parking space, killed the engine, and checked herself out in the rearview mirror before getting out of the car. She had decided to change her clothes too, as long as she was stopping home to pick up an outfit for Didi. She'd put on tan pants, a black jacket, and a light green shirt that Didi said brought out the color of her eyes. For Didi, she'd chosen a blue silk dress still in its dry-cleaning bag along with a white sweater in case the restaurant was chilly and a pair of black shoes. Romeo's got nothing on me, Gwen thought, checking out her image once more before going around to the passenger side to get the roses she'd brought, along with Didi's outfit. She went into the building and climbed the steps to Didi's studio. Maybe she'll show me her painting, Gwen thought as the heels of her boots made loud clicking noises down the old wooden hallway. And whatever I think, I'm going to tell her I love it. That it's the best thing she's ever done. That her work is really coming along.

Gwen turned the corner and saw to her surprise that Didi's door was closed. And not only closed but locked. That was strange. Gwen would have thought Didi would want to work with the door open because of the fumes from the oil paint. She knew Didi was shy about letting the other artists in the building see her work, but still, what was more important, your ego or your health? She knocked on the door, but there was no answer. Maybe Didi had run out for a cup of coffee? Gwen walked to the end of the hall and looked out the window, but Didi's car wasn't in the parking lot. She walked back to Didi's studio, and even though she knew she wasn't in there, knocked again.

"Hi, Gwen. You looking for Didi?" Sandy appeared in the doorway of her own studio. "I haven't seen her today."

"You haven't?"

"Nope. I mean, I only got here a little while ago myself. You probably just missed her. Do you have a date?" Sandy looked at the flowers, the dress, Gwen's freshly pressed jacket.

"Um, sort of."

"Lucky girl. Hey, are you in a hurry?"

"Um, sort of," Gwen said again. "Why?"

"I wanted to move some shelves, and I can't do it myself. It'll only take a second, and you won't get dirty, I promise. Didi and I tried to do it last week, but she wasn't strong enough. Would you mind?"

Yes, Gwen thought, but she didn't want to offend Sandy. After all, she was Didi's neighbor, and you never knew when you might need a good neighbor.

Sandy saw Gwen hesitate. "Listen, you can take your jacket off, and I'll give you a smock. It'll only take us ten minutes, I promise. Please?"

"All right." Gwen glanced at her watch. If she left in ten

minutes, they could still make it. And the restaurant was closer to home than it was to here anyway. Should she call Didi
and tell her to put on something pretty? Nah, that would just
ruin the surprise. Gwen carefully took her jacket off and
reached for the smock Sandy offered. Just her luck to run into
a damsel in distress.

✣   ✣   ✣

Didi was glad Gwen wasn't home yet. She was probably just
finishing up with her last client or catching up on her paper-
work. Or maybe she's mad at me, Didi thought, because of
this weekend. Maybe she's not in a great big hurry to get
home and see me, and really, who could blame her? Didi
stepped out of her clothes and into the shower. She wished
she could wash the smell of smoke out of her hair without
washing the smell of sex off her body. She wished she could
keep seeing Nicki without breaking up with Gwen. Or she
wished she could keep seeing Nicki and not break up with
Gwen until she was sure Nicki would be as good a girlfriend
as she was a lover. You know, like how would Nicki be if Didi
ever got sick? Two years ago, when Didi broke her ankle,
Gwen was an absolute angel. It was so ironic—Gwen was the
jock, the one who was always running, bike riding, playing
rugby and softball, while Didi's idea of exercise was lifting the
remote to see if any *Mad About You* reruns were on. Yet it was
Didi who had slipped and fallen on the ice that winter and
wound up with her leg in a cast. Gwen had done all the cooking, the shopping, the cleaning plus made runs to the video
store and the art supply shop (Didi had been into charcoal

sketches at the time) and never said one word about it. And
there were a million other things Gwen did too. Like the time
Didi casually mentioned that the Ninth Street Bakery in the
East Village made the best seven-layer cake imaginable, and
Gwen had driven all the way to New York that weekend, two
and a half hours there and two and a half hours back, just to
surprise Didi with a thick, gooey slice. And then there was the
whole money thing. Would Nicki agree to spend part of their
budget on studio space for Didi, when her artwork didn't
bring in a dime and in fact cost them a pretty penny every
month, what with the paints, the brushes, and all the other
supplies? Of course, Gwen made twice as much money as
Didi, but she was more than generous with it and never fussed
about her girlfriend's less than adequate paycheck. Gwen's
career was everything to her, but Didi didn't have a career.
She had a job; her art was her life. And even though she knew
Gwen thought the studio was more than a little indulgent, she
still wrote out the check month after month after month.

As Didi worked a puddle of apricot shampoo through her
hair, a whole montage of images swept across her mind: Gwen
waiting at the top of some mountain she'd insisted they climb,
not angry that Didi had taken so long but excited to share the
view; Gwen picking her up after work one day and whisking
her off to the city for a mystery date (they'd eaten a delicious
dinner at Rubyfruit's and then seen *Phantom of the Opera);*
Gwen playing gin rummy with Didi's father, even though she
hated cards; Gwen braving the dance floor even though she
was terrified to dance. Didi knew she was being more than a
bit sentimental; in fact, she could practically hear Barbra
Streisand singing "The Way We Were" on the sound track of

her mind. Still, corny as it was, the feelings were real. Gwen was so good to her, and she was such a shit. "I don't deserve her," Didi said aloud as she rinsed the lather out of her hair.

Gwen heard Didi say something, but she couldn't make out the words. She'd heard the shower running and decided the hell with dinner. She'd just get undressed, sneak into the bathroom, and jump Didi in the shower. Catch her by surprise. Not give her a chance to say no. Granted, they were getting a little old for vertical sex, but sometimes you just had to take a chance. Gwen squared her shoulders, took a deep breath, and pulled the curtain back.

Nicki went back upstairs and threw herself down on her bed. God, what a day. She was exhausted and exhilarated. Wasted and wired. Should she go out and get something to eat? Nah, that would take too much effort. And besides, she could never go downtown looking like this. She'd have to take a shower. And who wanted to wash away the delicious smell of sex clinging to every pore of her body? Nicki hugged a pillow to her chest and inhaled deeply. She smelled sex all right—this was the very pillow that had spent the last several hours under m'lady's hips—but she smelled something else too. Some kind of shampoo or perfume. It smelled sweet and flowery and very, very feminine. Almost fruity. What was it—oranges, pears? Whatever it was, Nicki wished she could drink it. Or take a bite of it. She grabbed the pillow with her teeth and shook her head back and forth, growling, like a puppy with a new rope toy. She felt frisky all right. Like she didn't know what to do with herself.

"You've got to calm down, Nickeroo, and try to get some sleep. You have to go to work tomorrow, remember?" Nicki smoothed the pillow down next to her, and as she reached over it to grab her cigarettes from the night stand, something caught her eye. What was that on the pillow? One long, lone, black, shiny hair. So, the Femme Fatale had left her a present after all. Nicki picked up the hair and stretched it out to its limit. "Christ, this thing must be over two feet long," she said, extending her arms wide. Not only was Didi's hair long, but it was also strong. Nicki stretched it as far as it would go and then pulled on it, but the hair held tight. If a girl's hair was that strong, what did that say about her heartstrings? Nicki wound the hair around her index finger, then unwound it, then wrapped it round and round again. Would she call? She had to. Nicki would never admit it, but her nerves felt frayed and taut, as taut as the long black hair she once again held out in front of her, one end in her left hand, the other in her right, the whole damn thing stretched but holding way beyond its breaking point.

✤   ✤   ✤

"That's it, baby. Just relax. I've got you. I won't let you fall." Gwen leaned back against the shower tiles, cradling Didi in her arms and supporting her against her torso as her hands traveled over Didi's breasts, her belly, her vulva, her thighs, her silky pubic hair. Didi let her head fall back against the place where Gwen's neck met her shoulder, amazed her body still had the strength to respond, and grateful that Gwen had caught her in the shower, where it was impossible for her tell the difference between the tears and the tap water running down her cheeks.

✢   ✢   ✢

"Bye, honey. Have a great day." Gwen kissed Didi on the lips and left the house whistling. Funny how she felt all her problems were over, and Didi felt all her problems were just beginning. As soon as Didi heard Gwen's car pull out of the drive way, she called the office and told them she wouldn't be in. "I'm feeling a little under the weather," she said, which wasn't that far from the truth. Didi was sick of lying—to Gwen, to Nicki, now to the office, and most of all to herself. Who was she kidding, thinking she was the kind of person who could remain in her relationship and fool around on the side? It had been fine while she and Gwen weren't having sex. But after last night, she knew she couldn't keep this up. Having sex with two girls on the same day, less than an hour and a half apart, was way too much for her. She had to either tell Gwen they were through or give Nicki up. How would she decide?

There must be someone I can talk to about all this, Didi thought, as she went back to bed. But who? Maybe I should see a therapist. "Yeah, right," she said aloud. Every therapist in town knew Gwen and consequently knew Didi. Gwen would kill Didi if she confided their problems to one of her colleagues. Maybe there was a hotline she could call. Dial 1-800-I-had-an-affair. Maybe they could all go on *Jerry Springer*. Didi could see herself and Nicki sitting on stage with identifying words underneath them: "I slept with my therapist's girlfriend." "I slept with my girlfriend's client." Then they'd bring Gwen out, and she and Nicki would get into a knock-down, drag-out, screaming, hair-pulling cat fight. Wouldn't middle America just love that?

Didi dragged herself out of bed, pulled on a robe, and poured some coffee into her favorite cup, a white porcelain mug with the words "Queen for a Day" etched on its side in gold lettering. Her old college housemate Douglas had sent it to her when he first moved out to San Francisco a year and a half ago. That's who I can call, Didi thought. Douglas. They hadn't spoken in a while—in fact, Didi only remembered talking to him twice since he'd moved to the West Coast—but theirs was the kind of friendship that could be picked up at the drop of a hat like no time had passed. They'd seen each other through countless girlfriends and boyfriends (well, countless in Douglas's case anyway) all through their 20s and early 30s as well as career moves, family troubles, and identity crises. Yes, Douglas was perfect. He'd tell her what to do. It was only a little past seven in the morning on the West Coast, but this was an emergency. Douglas would understand. Didi hoped Douglas, not Tony, would pick up the phone, and he did, right on the first ring.

"Yeah?" Douglas's voice was thick with sleep.

"Hi, Dougie. It's me." Didi was one of the very few people still allowed to call Douglas that.

"Didi? You OK? What time is it?"

"Ten-fifteen my time, seven-fifteen out there. Listen, I'm sorry I woke you up, but this is an emergency. Dougie," Didi took a deep breath, "I had an affair."

"What?" All of a sudden Douglas was wide awake.

✛   ✛   ✛

Nicki cruised into the restaurant 15 minutes late. "Sorry, Frances," she mumbled, lifting her apron off its hook.

"Where the hell you been?" Frances asked, though she wasn't really mad. "There's a pile of apples over there with your name on it." She pointed with her rolling pin. "Hop to it, soldier. Chop, chop."

"Yes, Boss." Nicki rolled up her sleeves and got right to work.

"So, rough night last night?" Frances asked once Nicki had made some headway on the fruit.

"No."

"No? What happened to the dame from last week?"

"Nothing happened to her," Nicki said, her tone nonchalant.

"If nothing happened to her," Frances looked up from the pie crust she was rolling out, "then why didn't you spend the night with her?"

"Because, if you must know," Nicki squeezed some lemon juice over the apple slices so they wouldn't turn brown, "I spent the afternoon with her."

"A little afternoon delight? Oh, to be young again." Frances let out an exaggerated sigh. "So, are you still in L-O-V-E love, Nicki?"

Nicki nodded casually. She would never tell Frances that not only was she in love, but she also had one of Didi's hairs all wrapped up in a tissue tucked away in her back pocket. She'd heard only that morning about some rich guy who was spending $5 million to have his dog cloned so that when the mutt died, he'd have another one just like him. Nicki thought that was a great idea. Maybe she could clone the babe—not that she had $500, let alone $5 million. But you had to admit, it was the perfect solution. Then there'd be two of her dream girl: one for the girlfriend, whoever she was, and one for herself.

✢   ✢   ✢

Gwen had left the house a bit early, leaving enough time to run an errand. A very important errand. She wanted to follow up on last night's success by sending flowers to Didi at her office. The way to a femme's heart was definitely flowers, and nothing impressed a girl more than sending them to her at work, where all the other dental assistants, not to mention the hygienists, the receptionist, even the dentist herself, would turn green with envy. "Is it your birthday?" they'd be sure to ask.

"No," Didi would say. "She sent them just because."

Just because, Gwen wrote on the card. *Just because I love you.* There. Who knows? Maybe she'd get lucky again tonight. Gwen couldn't remember the last time she and Didi had had sex two nights in a row. Maybe she'd jump her tonight after work. Maybe they'd do it every single night this week. And next week too. All of a sudden Gwen was feeling her oats. And wouldn't Didi be happy about that.

✢   ✢   ✢

"Diana Dana Samuelson, what in the world are you talking about? Wait, hang on a second, I'm going into the other room." Didi half listened to Douglas explaining to Tony that no, no one had died, as she pondered her choice of words: *I had an affair*, as opposed to *I'm having an affair*. Was her fling with Nicki already over? Had she already decided?

"So, tell me. I'm all ears," Douglas was back on the wire.

"God, where to begin?"

"It's always best to start at the beginning." Douglas did a snippy imitation of the Glinda, the Good Witch of the North from *The Wizard of Oz*. "I want to hear everything, Didi, and I mean *everything*. Starting with the $64,000 question: Does Gwen know?"

"Of course not. What do you think I am, nuts?"

"I don't know, darling, you tell me. Where did you meet this girl?" Douglas paused. "We are talking about a girl here, aren't we?"

"Of course. Douglas!" Didi was appalled. "All right, are you sitting down?"

"Yes."

Didi decided to go with the philosophy, worst things first. "Dougie, she's one of Gwennie's clients."

"What!" Douglas's voice rose in horror, tinged with a bit of delight. "You're boinking one of her clients?"

"Shh. I don't want Tony to hear."

"Don't worry, precious. That boy could sleep through an earthquake, and as a matter of fact, last week he did. Didi, did I hear you correctly? She's one of Gwen's clients?"

"Yeah, I know. I'm a real *shmuck*."

"Skip the self-hatred and just give me the facts."

"OK." Didi recounted her sordid story, starting from the very beginning and bringing Douglas up to yesterday's activities.

"What do you think I should do?" she moaned. "I'm such a wreck I couldn't even go to work today."

"That's the first smart thing you've done. And the second smart thing you did was call your fairy godmother."

Didi smiled. "Do you have a magic wand?"

"I have a wand all right. Is it magic? You'll have to ask Tony." Douglas paused. "Not that he's seen it recently."

"What do you mean? Are you boys having trouble in the boudoir?"

"Yes. We bought these new taupe curtains that looked great in the store, but they don't match the bedspread, and we threw out the receipt."

"Douglas." Didi was less than interested in his interior decorating problems. "C'mon. I just spilled the beans. Now it's your turn."

"Let's just say this, dearheart. You remember that old commercial, 'You don't have to be Jewish to love Levy's rye'?" Even though he couldn't see her, Didi nodded. "Well, you don't have to be a dyke to have lesbian bed death, either."

"You're kidding." Didi was truly shocked. "I thought you boys went at it all the time."

"Stereotyping." Douglas sang the word. "And don't all you lesbos have crewcuts and sensible shoes and clothes all covered with dog hair?"

"No, seriously, Dougie. Are you and Tony having problems?" The boys had been together even longer than Didi and Gwen had, and Didi couldn't imagine what would tear them apart.

"I'm not talking about years here, Didi. Tony and I just haven't done the evil deed in a few weeks. Oh, all right, maybe a month. You know how it is, with our schedules. I work days, he works nights, weekends there's a lot to do around the house…"

"But don't you think those are just excuses?" Didi poured herself a fresh mug of coffee. "I mean, shouldn't you be making time for each other?"

"Sure, we should be, and I'm sure we will soon. But you know, Didi, sometimes it's good to take a little break. We've been having sex with each other for almost seven years now. Sometimes its nice to take a breather and then reconnect again."

"Really?"

"Yeah. It's like…hey, what's your favorite food?"

Didi thought for a minute. "Key lime pie."

"OK, so let's say you had key lime pie morning, noon, and night, every day for two years. Don't you think you'd get sick of it?"

"No."

"Hey, work with me here, Didi, would you? I'm trying to make a point. My point is, too much of a good thing can be wonderful, as Mae West has said, but it can also be not so wonderful. If you didn't have key lime pie for a month or two months or six months, God forbid, and then all of a sudden you had it again, you'd be amazed that it was about a million times better than you even remembered. And believe me, it wouldn't be another six months before you ate it again."

"Yeah, well, what about this?" Didi wasn't buying Douglas's metaphor so easily. "Let's say your favorite food was key lime pie, and then all of a sudden you went to the store and there was some strawberry rhubarb on the shelf. You'd never tried it before, so you took some home. And it was absolutely delicious, the best thing you ever had, a thousand times better than key lime pie. Shouldn't you keep on eating it?"

"Trust me, dollface, pie is pie. Strawberry rhubarb, Boston cream, lemon meringue…they all start to taste the same sooner or later."

"I doubt it."

"You doubt *my* words of wisdom?" Douglas feigned shock.

"Cool your jewels, Douglas, and just forget the pies. Listen, let me ask you this: Don't you and Tony fool around during dry spells?"

"You mean with other boys?"

"I sure don't mean with other girls."

"Didi, you are way behind the times. Tony and I are monogamous at the moment. We have been for a while now."

"Really? I thought all you boys…"

"Tut, tut, tut," Douglas scolded her again. "Now enough about me and Tony, princess. Let's talk about you. What are you going to do here?"

"I don't know."

"Well, what do you want?"

"I don't know that either."

"All right, here's a question. If I really did have a magic wand, and I could grant you one wish, what would it be?"

That was easy. "I'd want you to meld Gwen and Nicki together, so I could stay with Gwen, but have great sex with her, like I do with Nicki."

"That can be arranged, Didi."

"How?"

"How? Silly question, silly girl. That's up to you."

"What do you mean, that's up to me?"

"I mean," Douglas spoke with exaggerated patience, as if he were addressing a child, "*you* have to bring some intense sexual energy back to your relationship, Didi. Gwen doesn't have a chance here, what with you running around with this Vicki—"

"Nicki."

"Vicki, Nicki, Dicky, whatever. It's Gwen you should be thinking about, Didi. Like when you first swooned over this big, bad butch outside Gwen's office, you should have just brought that energy home and jumped Gwen the minute she walked in the door. That's why Tony and I decided to be monogamous. Our sexual energy was all over the place, and there was none left to give to each other at home."

"Leave it to me," Didi moaned, "to call the only fag on the planet who's anti-nonmonogamy."

"I'm not anti-nonmonogamy, Didi," Douglas said. "In fact, I'm sure at some point Tony and I will open up our relationship again."

"Oh, so then you're anti-monogamy?"

"No, Didi. I'm not really anti-anything. Oh, except maybe one thing."

"What?"

"I'm definitely anti-dishonesty."

"Ouch."

"Exactly. Hey, if you want to do it with girls, boys, cows, sheep, chickens, whatever, just do it inside, and don't scare the horses. As long as you're not breaking any understanding that's there between you and Gwen. And I believe, unless I've already hit male menopause and my memory is shot, that you and Gwen are an exclusive item."

"You're right." Didi hung her head, disappointed that Douglas wasn't automatically taking her side. He was too good a friend to do that. Unfortunately.

"And what about this Nicki character?" Douglas asked. "You think she's so perfect? You think she doesn't look like shit in the morning? You think she doesn't have blood stains on her underwear?"

"Gross!" Didi pretended to gag on her coffee. "Douglas, how do you know about things like that?"

"Sisters. Sisters." Douglas started singing the duet Rosemary Clooney and Vera Ellen had made famous in *White Christmas*, a movie he and Didi had watched together many times. "I had four of them, remember? Anyway, pumpkin, I bet you could name three things right off the bat that would drive you crazy if you moved in with this fantasy creature." When Didi didn't respond, Douglas prodded her.

"C'mon, muffin. Three things."

"All right, all right." Didi hated the way Douglas was bursting her bubble. "Number one: She smokes."

"Ooh, good one."

"Number two: Her place is a pit."

"Excellent."

"And number three…" Didi didn't want to say this one aloud.

"Number three? C'mon, peanut, Mommy's waiting."

"I'm not sure, but I think she has a lot of trouble in the staying-faithful department."

"And you think you could change that?" Douglas snorted.

"Well, she said she was turning over a new leaf with me." The sentence sounded pitiful, even to Didi's ears.

"Yeah, right. Her and President Clinton. Now you listen to me, munchkin." Uh-oh, here it comes, Didi thought. Lecture time. "Gwen is a wonderful person, and she treats you like a queen. Well, not like this queen," Didi imagined Douglas pointing to his chest with his pinkie held at a dainty angle, "but you know what I mean. You'd be a fool to lose her, so just pull yourself together."

"Do you think I should tell her?" Didi whispered, as if Gwen were there in the room.

"Well…" Douglas paused. "Honesty is the best policy—"

"But, Dougie, she'll kill me!"

"—but you don't have to tell her right away." Douglas continued as if he hadn't been interrupted. "I'd wait a good ten, 20, 50 years. You know, one day you'll be sitting in the old dyke nursing home, and you'll say, 'Honey, remember that client, Nicki you had?' And Gwen will say, 'Nicki who?' and you'll tell her and you'll both laugh about the whole thing."

"You think so?"

"Sure, baby. Remember, timing is everything. So for now, this will our little secret. We'll simply refer to it as your research project. OK, petunia?"

"Dougie, you're the best. Thanks for saving my ass."

"Hey, it's not the first time," Douglas reminded her. "And I doubt it'll be the last."

✤   ✤   ✤

"Honey, I'm home," Gwen called in an exaggerated tone, like some TV husband on a sitcom from the 1950s. "Didi?" Gwen walked into the kitchen and then yelled up the stairs. "Didi? Are you up there?"

"Yes," Didi called softly. "Come upstairs."

Gwen hung her jacket in the hall closet and then trotted up the steps. "Are you in bed, Didi?" she asked, even though her eyes told her the obvious. "Are you sick?"

"I don't feel good," Didi said in a little girl voice.

"What's the matter, honey?" Gwen sat on the edge of the bed and felt Didi's forehead. "I don't think you have a fever. Does your stomach hurt?" Didi nodded. "Why didn't you call me at the office? I would have picked up some soup or something. Did you leave work early?"

"I didn't go in at all."

"You didn't?" This wasn't like Didi. "Oh, then you didn't get my flowers."

"Flowers?"

"Yeah, I sent you roses at work."

"You did? Why?"

"Why?" Gwen looked at Didi and tapped her on the nose. "You silly goose. Does there have to be a reason other than you're the best girl in the world?"

Oh, shit, Didi thought, as again she burst into tears.

Nicki didn't get upset until Friday night, but then when it hit her, it hit her hard. The chick hadn't called, wasn't calling, and wasn't going to call. And there was nothing she could do about it. She didn't know her name, her number, her address, nothing. Nicki had gotten it into her head somehow that since Didi had called last Friday night, she'd call this Friday night too. But she didn't. And the louder the silence in Nicki's apartment grew, the more convinced she became that Didi was meant to be her one and only girl.

She waited in her apartment as long as she could on Saturday morning, just in case the phone decided to ring, but as she'd already been late to work twice that week, she couldn't push it. She got to work exactly on time and started slicing carrot rounds without even saying good morning to Frances.

"Why so glum, chum?" Frances broke the silence after they'd worked together side by side without a word for half an hour.

Nicki replied with a mere shrug of her shoulders.

"Girl trouble?" Frances asked with a knowing look. "Don't tell me it's over, Nicki. I thought this one was different. I thought she was the love of your life. I thought she…"

"Frances, I wouldn't bust my chops if I were you," Nicki was in no mood to be teased this morning, "especially right now when I'm holding a knife."

❖   ❖   ❖

Didi managed to get through the weekend without thinking about Nicki too much; in fact, it had been one of the nicest weekends she and Gwen had had for a really long time. Friday night they ate at their favorite Indian restaurant, and Saturday morning they woke up early to go out to breakfast and then cruise the neighborhood for tag sales. In the afternoon they lay down for a nap but wound up not getting a wink of sleep. Didi was puzzled over Gwen's new amorous leanings—she'd read somewhere that having an affair was a sure cure-all for a stagnant relationship, but she'd never really believed it. And how could that possibly be true, especially when it was Gwen's behavior that had changed, and Gwen didn't even know about the affair. Or did she? No, Didi thought as she rested in Gwen's arms. If Gwen knew anything, Didi would be sure to hear about it.

They stayed in Saturday night, ordering Chinese food and renting a video. Then on Sunday, Gwen wanted to go hiking, and Didi surprised her by offering to go along. It's not that she was so keen on fresh air and exercise; she just didn't want to be alone with the telephone. But now it was Monday, and Gwen was at work. And soon Nicki would be at her office. And soon after that, Nicki would be waiting to see if Didi would show up to meet her. And she wasn't going to. She was going to her studio for real this time, even though the last thing she felt like doing was painting. What she really felt like doing was bawling her head off, tearing her hair out, rending her clothing, something, anything, to express her grief. It's not that Didi doubted her decision—she'd even said as much to Douglas who'd called her three times that week ("Just checking in on my favorite slut")—it was just hard to let Nicki go. Douglas, who dabbled in Buddhism every once in a while, told her she *had* to let go, and that other good things would come her way as soon as she made an empty space available to them. And she knew he was right. And the sex with Gwen had been good that weekend. More than good. Terrific. But not earth-shattering. Not like it had been with Nicki.

"But you are married to Gwen," Didi reminded herself as she got dressed. "Good, sweet, adorable, dependable, loyal, trustworthy Gwen." Didi knew she had to get out of the house, but she knew if she went to her studio she'd wind up staring at a blank canvas for the better part of the day. I think I'll go to the mall, she said to herself, gathering up her jacket, her wallet, her keys. There's nothing like shopping to lift a girl's spirits. I deserve a reward for all this. And maybe I'll get something nice for Gwennie. A present. She deserves something special today too. Just because.

✛   ✛   ✛

"So, let me ask you a question, Doc."

Nicki's energy was different today. There was a slowness, a seriousness, almost a heaviness about her that wasn't there before. Gwen was pleased; usually it took four or five sessions for a new client to really take to therapy, and frankly, she hadn't been sure Nicki would stick around that long.

"OK, shoot." Gwen leaned forward, resting her elbows on her knees to show Nicki she had her undivided attention.

"Uh…does anyone ever flunk out of therapy?"

"Flunk out?" Gwen studied Nicki's eyes, which were serious. She wondered if Nicki had dropped out of college. Or maybe even high school. "No, Nicki," she said. "No one ever flunks out."

"Does anyone ever get kicked out?" she asked.

"No," Gwen said, "though I suppose there's always a first time." She wasn't exactly sure why she had added that, and she wondered what big confession Nicki was working up to.

Had something happened with the woman Nicki had just started seeing? Had she cheated on her already? No, that wasn't it. Nicki would be proud of herself if she were seeing two new women at once. Unless…Gwen had a startling thought. What if Nicki had slept with a man? She waited for Nicki to say something, the silence growing between them.

"So, everything I say in here is confidential, right?" Nicki asked. "Even the fact that I come here?"

"Absolutely, Nicki." Now Gwen was sure Nicki's impending confession had something to do with a man. Either she'd slept with one, or—here was a thought—maybe she was thinking of becoming one. She was definitely the butchest woman Gwen had ever had in treatment, and she wouldn't be surprised if she were struggling with her gender identity. Gwen had often wondered how she would handle that situation, since she had a woman-only practice. But when did a female-to-male transsexual actually become a man? The day she started identifying as one? The day she started taking hormones? The day she had the operation? It would be cruel to desert a client at any stage of the process. And besides, it was not only cruel, it was against professional regulations.

As if Nicki were reading Gwen's mind, she asked another question. "Doc, are there any official rules around here?"

"There are a few." Gwen nodded her head. "For example, if I thought you were going to hurt yourself or somebody else, I would have to report that. Or if I suspected there was some kind of abuse—child abuse, domestic violence, elder abuse—going on in your home, I would have to report that too."

"But you'd never tell anyone I was in therapy, would you, Doc?"

"No, Nicki."

"And you'd never tell me who any of your other clients were, would you?"

"No, Nicki." Gwen repeated herself using the exact same tone of voice.

Nicki let out a deep sigh and stared at her hands for a long minute. "Let me ask you this, Doc. Suppose I was going to hurt myself, and you were the only one who could stop me, but you refused to. Wouldn't that mean I got to report you?"

"What are you getting at here, Nicki?"

"See," Nicki looked up, and Gwen was surprised at the degree of pain etched on her face. "You know the girl I've been seeing?" Gwen nodded. "She's decided she can't see me anymore; she's going to work things out with her girlfriend. And I don't even know her name or her number, and I really want to call her."

"Does she really want you to call her?"

"How can I find out? It's not fair," Nicki's voice held more than a touch of anger. "You have to tell me who she is."

"And how can I do that, Nicki?"

"She's one of your clients, Doc." At that, Gwen's eyebrows rose. "See, I met her here, in the hallway, the first time I came to see you. I was going out, and she was coming in. Then she changed her appointment so we could spend time together. You have to help me out here, Doc, or I really am going to hurt myself."

Gwen tried to gauge Nicki's seriousness. She knew she was just trying to get information from her, but there was always a chance she was desperate enough to make some feeble attempt to injure herself. Not that she would ever give out another client's name, but still, she wondered who Nicki was talking about.

"I'm sure you know who she is, Doc. First of all, she's absolutely gorgeous. She's very, very femme, with long black hair and big blue eyes. She's like, I don't know, five-foot-five maybe, and really built...."

Gwen kept her eyes blank, as her mind wandered over her client list.

"Listen, Doc, think back to the first time I came here. It was exactly four weeks ago. I left at ten-to-eleven, and she was just coming in for her eleven o'clock appointment. But she left early, because I saw her out at her car, a maroon Saturn, with a rainbow bumper sticker on it. I've been meeting her on Mondays since. Let's see, what else can I tell you?" Nicki closed her eyes for a minute, as Didi's image rose in her mind. "I know. She wears this really unusual gold ring on her finger that looks like a snake, with a ruby eye..."

"Didi?" The word popped out of her mouth before Gwen could stop it. "You slept with Didi?"

"Her name is Didi?" Nicki was delighted. "I thought you couldn't give out another client's name." She couldn't help but gloat.

"Didi isn't my client, you asshole," Gwen snarled, half rising out of her seat. "She's my girlfriend."

"Your girlfriend?" Nicki's voice cracked.

"Yes, my girlfriend." Gwen shouted as she pointed a shaky finger at the door. "Goddamn it, Nicki, you slept with my girlfriend. Now get your ass off that couch and out of this fucking office."

✢   ✢   ✢

After Nicki left, Gwen began to shake. I'm in shock, she said to herself. It can't be true. I can't believe I just kicked a client out of my office. My supervisor's just going to love this. She got herself a drink of water and then flipped open her appointment book. A month ago, a month ago…yep, there was Nicki's name all right, written in green to signify she was a new client. And then, right after that, Gwen had had an eye doctor's appointment at eleven-fifteen. Oh, God. Gwen sank onto her desk chair. So it was true. She thought back to that day, and suddenly it all became crystal clear. She had forgotten her glasses that morning and called Didi to bring them to her office. And then what? A month ago, a month ago…think, Gwen, think. The day was a blur to her, but Nicki said she and Didi had met every Monday. That was Didi's day off. Had they gone to their house? Had they done it in their bed? Had they met just last Monday, when Gwen had come home and found Didi in the shower?

I am going to fucking kill her, Gwen thought, folding her arms on her desk and resting her head on them. She shut her eyes as if she could shut out the horrible news she had just heard. *One of my clients, Didi,* Gwen's mind railed. *You had to pick one of my fucking clients.* Fucking clients, that was the truth. That woman would fuck anything on two legs and maybe even three.

Gwen kept her head down on top of her arms and took some deep breaths. It was ten-forty-five; she had 15 minutes to go until her next appointment, and wouldn't you know it, today of all days, the Dynamic Duo hadn't canceled. Shit.

❖   ❖   ❖

Didi found the cutest summer jumpsuit (blue, of course) at
Neiman Marcus and treated herself to a new pair of shoes and
a pocketbook as well. Then she went into the bookstore and
bought Gwen a beautiful hardcover book on women in sports
along with a card that said "I'm mad" on the cover and
"about you" inside. She bought Gwen a box of her favorite
candies too: milk chocolate-covered hazelnuts, along with a
chocolate bar shaped like a football. All this shopping gives a
girl an appetite, Didi thought, deciding to treat herself to a
nice brunch instead of just grabbing something at the food
court. She briefly considered the payphone outside the
restaurant but walked right by it, knowing Nicki wasn't home
anyway. She was probably just getting out of therapy. Didi
wondered what she had talked about with Gwen. Had she
mentioned her? Nah. I bet she's on to another woman already. Yeah, that was probably it. When she hadn't heard
from Didi on Friday night, she'd just gone out to a bar and
picked up some other lucky girl. Oh, well. Didi let just the
slightest wave of sadness wash over her before she shooed
Nicki out of her mind. Thank God for Douglas, she thought,
as her hostess showed her to her booth. He was absolutely
right: You get out of a relationship exactly what you put into
it. And from now on Didi planned on putting everything she
had into her relationship with Gwen, so the two of them
would live happily ever after.

✛   ✛   ✛

Nicki lingered outside Gwen's office until eleven-fifteen,
just in case Didi (Didi!) had changed her mind, but no such

luck. Then she waited by her truck, which she had parked on the same street as she had the day Didi had climbed out of it, sure that if she wanted to meet up, that's where Didi would go. Would she show? How could she not? Nicki paced back and forth, smoking a cigarette and thinking about what had just happened. Was Didi really Gwen's girlfriend? How could that be? She couldn't imagine the two of them together. First of all, Gwen was shorter than Didi. Second of all, Nicki and Didi were a much better match. But the Doc wouldn't lie to her. No, it was Didi who had lied. Imagine that.

Nicki threw her butt on the ground and stubbed it out with her boot. If Didi rounded the corner now, she didn't know if she would kiss her, shake her, scream at her, or confess to her that the jig was up, and Gwen knew the truth. But she couldn't even do that much, because Didi hadn't had the common courtesy to give her her phone number. *Warning, warning,* Nicki tried to communicate telepathically to Didi. *Your ass is grass, Didi. Warning, warning.* Nicki had little faith that Didi would pick up her psychic signals, but she tried to relay them anyway. She knew what Didi was in for; after all, she'd been in that position many, many times, and as of yet, it had never been pretty. Oh, well, Nicki thought, climbing into her truck. I tried to warn her. That's what the bitch gets for lying to me.

❖   ❖   ❖

"Come on in," Gwen called out, lowering herself into her professional chair. The door opened, and the Dynamic Duo entered, the mother leading the way as usual, the daughter sulking behind. They sat down on the couch, not looking at

Gwen, both of them waiting for the other one to begin. Gwen didn't know who she wanted to smack first, the daughter for being so sullen or the mother for being so smug. As the silent power struggle between the two intensified, Gwen surpressed a sigh. I'm not in the mood to deal with them today, she thought, let alone the rest of my clients. She went over her upcoming appointments—her day was unusually full—and heard Didi's voice echo in her mind: *You care about your clients much more than you care about me.*

What about you? Gwen's own voice screamed at Didi inside her head. *You care about my clients more than you care about me too—at least one of my clients.* Gwen shook her head slightly to try and clear it, but instead she cleared her throat.

"I'm sorry," She was just as surprised to hear the sound of her own voice as her clients were. "I'm sorry," she repeated, "but I just learned about a family emergency, and I'm going to have to cancel our session today." My supervisor is going to have a field day with me next week, Gwen thought, as she waited a minute to let her words sink in. "You won't have to pay for today, of course," she reassured the mother, "and I'll see you next week at our usual time."

"C'mon, Sara." The mother rose in a huff, her tone of voice implying they would be just as happy to take their business elsewhere, as she headed for the door.

"I'm sorry about your bad news," Sara said, reluctantly following her mother. Gwen almost said, *Sara, why don't you stay?* out of pity for her, but, of course, she didn't. She just closed the door behind them and picked up the phone to call the remaining appointments of the day. And then, even though she could probably lose her license for it, she opened the top drawer of her desk and reached for her phone list of colleagues in the area. It's not revenge, Gwen told herself as she dialed the first number. It's my moral responsibility and civic duty to warn them all about a sexual predator who might be on the lookout for a new therapist: a walking, talking homewrecker by the name of Nicki Flynn.

✤ ✤ ✤

Didi held her packages high as trophies as she made her way through the parking lot back to her car. Even though it was only two o'clock, and she could get in a good couple of hours of work before Gwen got home, she decided to skip the studio today. No, today was a special day: She had resisted temptation and made a new commitment to Gwen. And to herself. That called for a celebration. What Didi was going to do was drop all her packages off at home and then head for the supermarket to buy the ingredients for a special dinner for Gwen. Gwen wouldn't know what they were celebrating of course, but Gwen didn't have to. If she asked, Didi would say she'd made a special dinner "just because." In fact, maybe they'd institute a new tradition: "just because dinners" once a month to show how much they loved each other. This month it was Didi's turn; next month it would be Gwen's.

Chicken tetrazzini or Steak Diane? Didi flipped through the recipe file in her mind as she turned their corner and pulled into the driveway. She was so preoccupied with planning her menu that she didn't even notice the shiny, silver vehicle parked outside their house until she went to the back of the Saturn to retrieve her purchases from the trunk. I hope nothing's wrong, Didi thought as she headed for the door. What in the world was Gwen's car doing home in the middle of the day?

✛   ✛   ✛

Who could she tell? Marnie? Surely she could tell Marnie she'd gotten kicked out of therapy. Marnie wouldn't laugh at her, would she? She'd probably say, *What'd you do, Nicki, screw your therapist?* And Nicki would have to say, *No, not exactly...* Marnie would probably think it was funny, Nicki thought, but she was wrong.

"Oh, Nicki, you're impossible," she said when Nicki told her what was going on. "How could you sleep with your therapist's girlfriend?"

"I didn't *know* she was my therapist's girlfriend," Nicki tried to defend herself.

"Yeah, right. And the first time you took me out, I didn't know that wasn't a banana in your pocket."

Nicki smiled. A sexual reference was a damn good sign. "Does that mean you want me to come over tonight, babe?"

"I want you—" Nicki could tell Marnie was weakening.

"Come on, lover, I'll bring some champagne, some candles...just like old times."

"Nick..." Marnie uttered her ex-lover's name like it was the saddest syllable in the world. "I wish I could just say yes, but I can't. Not until you get some help."

"But I went to therapy, babe. What more do you want?"

"How many times did you go, Nicki?"

Did today's session count? She couldn't very well say

three and a half. "Four times."

"Four sessions? Nicki, some people stay in therapy for years."

"I can't afford to go for years, Marnie."

"You can't afford not to, Nicki." Marnie paused. "Sorry, that was mean."

"Damn right it was."

"All right, I'm sorry. Listen, Nick, I'll make you a deal. You find yourself a therapist, and go for ten sessions, and then we'll get together and talk. OK?"

"OK, OK." Nicki hung up the phone, lit a cigarette, and reluctantly reached for the yellow pages.

✤   ✤   ✤

"Why don't you tell me why you're here?"

Gwen winced, wondering if that's what she sounded like to her new clients. She had called dozens of colleagues, asking about out-of-town therapists (pretending she needed a referral for a client of course), and the name Joyce Daniels had come up many times, always with glowing reports. She has to be superconfident, Gwen thought, if she's seeing patients in her own home. Even with a separate room and entrance, I would never do that. No, Gwen liked to keep her boundaries sharp: her personal life over here, her professional life over there, and never the twain shall meet. But speaking of trespassed boundaries... Gwen glanced over at Didi, who was sitting next to her on the couch, staring down at her hands as if they were the two most fascinating objects on the planet. Let her speak first, Gwen thought, turning away in disgust. She's the reason we're here in the first place. If she hadn't… Gwen couldn't bear to finish the sentence, even silently to herself. She couldn't even look at Didi without thinking about her and Nicki kissing, her and Nicki touching, her and Nicki…

How could I have been such a goddamn idiot? Gwen wondered for the millionth time since Nicki's last therapy appointment. First Didi won't let me anywhere near her, and then she turns into this total sex kitten—both sure signs of having an affair—and all the while my client, *my client*, is describing this hot new chick she's madly in love with. And the whole time, Didi is telling me she's working on her painting, she's going to be late coming home from the studio. The studio, the studio, the studio. From now on, little Miss Picasso can pay for her goddamn studio all by herself. I'm not putting one penny more into her goddamn alibi. I feel so stupid, Gwen thought, leaning her elbow on the arm of the couch and dropping her head in her hand. I feel so angry, so devastated, so…so…*betrayed*. And the worst part was Gwen had counseled so many lesbian couples in this exact same situation. *Sure, it's a breach of trust*, Gwen remembered telling them, *but it's not the end of the world.* If you both choose to, you can work through it. Many couples who've weathered such a storm have wound up being even closer and more intimate than before. *Crisis means danger plus opportunity*, Gwen would say, quoting a poster she had seen downtown in a New Age bookstore. *Try to think of this as a blessing in disguise*, she'd add, *a time to learn about forgiveness. A time for healing. A time for spiritual growth.* Yeah, right.

Didi didn't want to say anything, afraid she would cry if she opened her mouth, and she hated even the thought of crying in front of a complete stranger. Who the hell was Joyce Daniels? She didn't even know if the woman was a lesbian or not. Gwen had to pick the therapist, of course, because it couldn't be someone who knew her professionally, so they'd had to drive over an hour, all the way into Massachusetts. What a pain in the ass. At least Joyce hadn't sounded too bad on the phone. She'd insisted upon having a few words with Didi after Gwen was through talking to her, and she'd made some good suggestions too. "You might consider coming here in separate cars," Joyce had said. "Couples therapy can be very intense, and I don't want you continuing to process on the drive home. My experience has been that it's best for couples to take some space from each other after the session." And before the session too. Didi had no desire to spend over an hour in the car with Gwen not saying even one lousy word to her. Oh, she'd had plenty to say the day she confronted her all right, but she'd barely uttered a complete sentence to her since.

Didi continued to stare down at her hands as that afternoon played like a movie in her mind. She'd walked into the house all happy and excited with her packages from the mall. "You all right?" she'd called out to Gwen, who was sitting at the kitchen table with her head in her hand just as she was right now.

"Did you do it in our bed, Didi?" Gwen spoke so softly and so calmly at first that Didi didn't even know what she was talking about.

"Did you do it in our bed?" Gwen asked again, her voice starting to rise. "Answer me, goddamn it. Did you and Nicki do it in our bed?"

"No," Didi answered, and with that one tiny word, she'd sealed her fate. Instead of saying, *I don't know what you're talking about, Gwen,* or *Did we do what in our bed, Gwen?* or *What are you nuts, Gwen?* or even *Nicki who?* Didi had told the truth, and nothing had been the same since.

"Where'd you do it then, huh, Didi? On the couch, on the floor, on the goddamn kitchen table?" Gwen banged her hand down so hard that the salt and pepper shakers jumped.

As if it mattered so much where they had done it. As if that was the most important thing.

"Just tell me this, Didi." Gwen hissed out the words through clenched teeth. "Did you fuck one of my clients in this house? Did you? Did you?"

Didi stared at Gwen, whose face was the color of an over-ripe tomato, thinking, "No wonder they say redheads shouldn't wear red." A giggle started working its way up her throat, but fortunately she was able to push it back down.

"I'm going to ask you one more time, Didi, and I want to know the truth. Did Nicki ever set foot in this house?"

"No."

"What godawful lies did you tell her about me, huh, Didi? Just how much does one of my clients know about my personal life?"

Oh, that's what she's so concerned about. And once Didi realized that, the desire to surpress being cruel went straight out the window. "For your information, Gwen, your name never even came up. Nicki and I had more important things to talk about. Not that we did that much talking…"

"Fuck you, Didi," Gwen had screamed at the top of her lungs. "Fuck you."

"No, fuck you," Didi had screamed back. "All you care about is what this means to you professionally. You don't even care about us, Gwennie. You don't even care about *me.*" Then, of course, Didi had burst into tears and said she was sorry—I'm sorry, I'm sorry, I'm sorry—she must have said it a thousand times. But it was no use. Gwen wouldn't give her the time of day.

I said I was sorry, Didi thought, glancing across the couch at her girlfriend. What more do you want from me, Gwennie? Blood?

Joyce Daniels studied the couple seated before her, trying to discern some information from their energy and body language. Gwen Kessler and Didi Samuelson. What was there between them? Plenty of anger—it was so intense, Joyce was surprised her couch wasn't smoldering—but there were other things too. Love, certainly, and sorrow, and even a bit of compassion. And something else Joyce could barely put her finger on. Oh, yes, there it was. Sexual tension, so thin you could slice it with a feather.

✣   ✣   ✣

Nicki was running late again, but she didn't care. Let the shrink wait. It was her money. Christ, this one was even more expensive than the last one. Who makes 75 bucks an hour? But the bitch wouldn't budge, and it didn't seem like she had any other options. It must be open season on the loony bin, Nicki thought, as she sped down the highway. I can't believe I'm driving all the way to Massachusetts for a goddamn therapy appointment. But try as she might, she'd had no luck finding one lousy therapist in the entire state of Connecticut who would take her. Nicki had called and left identical messages on at least 35 answering machines: "Hi, this is Nicki Flynn, and I'm looking for a therapist. My number is 555-3277. Please call me back." Half the shrinks hadn't even returned her call, and all the ones who had told her they weren't taking on any new clients. No room at the inn, sorry. Over and over and over. Only one therapist had been kind enough to even give her a referral. Christ, Nicki thought, Marnie better take me back after all this. Or at least chip in and help me pay for gas.

OK, exit seven, right at the end of the ramp, go three blocks down, take a left on Monroe Street and a right on Clyde. Fourth house on the left, park out front, go in the side door. Nicki pulled up to the curb, killed the engine, and then inhaled with a sharp gasp. There, right in front of her car, was a Saturn. And not just any Saturn. A maroon Saturn. With a rainbow bumper sticker on it. Could it be? Nicki got out of her truck and approached the car for a closer inspection. "Well, I'll be damned," she said, noticing a very familiar-looking black feather hanging from Didi's rearview mirror. Nicki didn't believe in fate, despite what she'd said about it to Didi, but this was just too weird. Now she and Didi *were* seeing the same therapist, with back-to-back appointments. Life doesn't imitate art, Nicki thought ruefully. Life imitates lies.

The windows of Didi's car were open, so Nicki reached inside and touched the feather. Should she take it? What would Didi think if she came out of Joyce Daniels's office and the feather was gone? Would she know Nicki had made off with it? Maybe she should leave her a note. No, wait. Nicki had a better idea. She walked around to the passenger side of Didi's car, opened the door, and lowered her long frame onto the seat. Slid it away from the dash to make room for her legs. Tilted it back at a comfortable angle. Might as well get cozy, Nicki thought as she lit up a cigarette and glanced at her watch: three-forty-seven. If this shrink gave out 50-minute hours like Gwen did, it wouldn't be long. No, any minute now Didi would waltz right out that door. And Nicki could hardly wait to see the expression on her face, because if there was one thing Nicki loved, it was a big, fat, when-you-least-expect-it, hit-'em-right-between-the-eyes surprise.

Glossary of Yiddish and Hebrew Words

Hebrew words are denoted with (H). Yiddish spellings are not "official," as the only correct way to spell a Yiddish word is with Hebrew letters. Instead, the words are transliterated according to the author's ear. Likewise, the usage of Yiddish words may vary according to where one is from. Lastly, many Yiddish words have adopted English suffixes (i.e., shvizting), as Jews who came to America learned to speak English and sprinkled this new foreign language with words from the mameh-loshen *(mother tongue), which really do lose something in the translation.*

babka: special kind of cake that's very light, often made with sugar and cinnamon

bima (H): platform in front of the synagogue from which the Torah is read

bubbe: grandmother

challah: beautiful braided bread eaten on Shabbos and holidays

chutzpa: nerve

dayenu: it would have been enough for us

eppes: for some inexplicable reason

faygeleh: little bird (slang for gay man)

feh: ugh

girlchik: affectionate term for girl

Gottenyu: Oh, my God

goy: person who isn't Jewish

Haggadah (H): narrative read aloud at the Passover seder that tells the story of the exodus of the Jews from Egypt

hock: to bother

kugel: noodle pudding

maideleh, maidl: young girl

mameleh: endearment (literally, "little mother")

matzo: unleavened bread

matzo ball: dumpling made of matzo meal, eggs, oil, and salt, usually served in chicken soup

menorah (H): eight-branched candelabrum used on Chanukah

meshugeh: crazy

meshugeneh: crazy person

mitzvah (H): blessing

nosh: snack

nu: so, well

nudnik: pest

oy: expression of surprise, sorrow, fear, pain, excitement, etc.

Pesach (H): Passover, the eight-day holiday commemorating the exodus of the Jews from Egypt

pupik: navel

Rosh Hashanah (H): Jewish New Year

seder (H): the Passover meal (literally, "order")

Shabbos: the Jewish Sabbath

shah: hush, keep still

shayneh: beautiful

shayneh maideleh: beautiful girl

shiksa: girl or woman who isn't Jewish (not complimentary)

shlep: to drag or carry

shlock, shlocky: junk, junky, something that is cheaply made

shmaltz: excessive sentimentality (literally, "rendered chicken fat")

shmocktails: not a Yiddish word per se; when *sh* is put in front of a word, it mocks and dismisses that word ("cocktails, shmocktails")

shmooze, shmoozing: to talk, socialize, "make the rounds," etc.

shmuck: jerk, unlikeable person

shul: synagogue

shvitz, shvitzing: sweat, sweating

Sh'ma Yisroel, Adonoy Elohanu, Adonoy Echad (H): the most common Hebrew prayer. Many Jews try to die with this prayer on their lips. (literal translation: Hear, O Israel, the Lord our God, the Lord is One)

simcha: great pleasure or happiness

takeh: really

tateleh: endearment (literally, "little father")

tochter: daughter

tuchus: buttocks

utz: to nag, move along

vey iss mir: woe is me

Vildeh Chayah: wild beast

Yom Kippur (H): Day of Atonement

zaftig: plump, juicy

About the Author

MARY VAZQUEZ

Lesléa Newman is an award-winning author and editor whose 28 books include *Out of the Closet and Nothing to Wear*, *The Femme Mystique*, *The Little Butch Book*, *A Letter to Harvey Milk*, *Still Life With Buddy*, *Pillow Talk: Lesbian Stories Between the Covers*, and *Heather Has Two Mommies*. Her literary awards include creative writing fellowships from the Massachusetts Artists Foundation and the National Endowment for the Arts, Second Place Finalist in the Raymond Carver Short Story Competition, and a Pushcart Prize nomination. In addition, five of her books have been Lambda Literary Award finalists. She divides her time between Massachusetts and New York. Visit her Web site at http://www.lesleanewman.com